ROWAN SPEEDWELL

Published by
Dreamspinner Press
5032 Capital Circle SW
Ste 2, PMB# 279
Tallahassee, FL 32305-7886
USA
http://www.dreamspinnerpress.com/

This is a work of fiction. Names, characters, places, and incidents either are the product of the author's imagination or are used fictitiously, and any resemblance to actual persons, living or dead, business establishments, events, or locales is entirely coincidental.

Love, Like Water
Copyright © 2013 by Rowan Speedwell

Cover Art by AngstyG, www.angstyg.com
Cover Photograph: TomCoolPix
Cover Model: Nicko Morales

Cover content is being used for illustrative purposes only and any person depicted on the cover is a model.

All rights reserved. No part of this book may be reproduced or transmitted in any form or by any means, electronic or mechanical, including photocopying, recording, or by any information storage and retrieval system without the written permission of the Publisher, except where permitted by law. To request permission and all other inquiries, contact Dreamspinner Press, 5032 Capital Circle SW, Ste 2, PMB# 279, Tallahassee, FL 32305-7886, USA.
http://www.dreamspinnerpress.com/

ISBN: 978-1-62380-786-3
Digital ISBN: 978-1-62380-787-0

Printed in the United States of America
First Edition
July 2013

For Vicki Childs, for all the conversations starting with "So, write anything lately?" and ending with "Keep writing!" A half century isn't long enough to be friends with you.

Muchas gracias to Manuel Elizondo for his insights into Puerto Rican culture and life in Humboldt Park; to Lynda Fitzgerald, beta reader extraordinaire; and to J.P. Barnaby, best critique partner ever. And to Vic and Lin, who wouldn't rest until they got me into the saddle.

No podria haberlo hecho sin su ayuda.

Love, Like Water

Prologue

IT WAS always the same dream. The warehouse, reeking of cigarette smoke, diesel fuel, and desperation; the slow yellow flash of the lights rotating on the idling forklift, reflecting off the oily floor; the slosh of water against the riverside dock; the sharp, angry voices of the men around him.

And the woman—barely a woman, more a girl, her tight T-shirt stretched over the rounded belly she had her hands clasped on. Four, maybe five months pregnant, just starting to show. She was on her knees in front of the angriest of the men. "Little bitch!" He smacked her with the butt of the pistol; she went sprawling, her long dark hair spilling around her bloodied face, blending with the swirls of black oil on the floor. "How much did you take?"

"Not much, 'Chete," she whined, and tried to get up. He kicked her in the thigh and sent her down again. "Just a little, a few bucks—*para el niño...*"

"Bullshit *el niño*," Machete Montenegro said, and kicked her again.

"Boss," Joshua—*José*—said quietly.

"Shut up, *pendejo*. Lina, how much?"

"Two grand," she admitted, weeping openly now. "Just two grand. For the baby...."

"Fuck the baby. It wasn't for the baby or you'd be long gone. Where is it?"

"Adelicio has it," Lina admitted. "I gave it to Adelicio."

"Fuck," 'Chete said. He looked over at where José and the rest of his men stood. "I'm done with her. Finish it."

"Boss...."

"*Do it.*"

JOSHUA sat up in bed, sweat soaking his T-shirt and pouring down his neck at the remembered sound of the gunshot. God damn it—it had been four months, and he was still fucking dreaming about it. It wasn't as if 'Chete hadn't ordered people killed before. It wasn't as if he hadn't killed people himself, for that matter. But it was always men before—rival gang members, traitors, whoever 'Chete or the other bosses said. Never a woman.

Never a pregnant woman. He ran his fingers over the fuzz of his growing-out hair, longing for a cigarette, longing for a drink. Longing for the heroin that once buzzed in his blood and kept him solid in the hell that had been his life for so long.

"You all right?" The tinny voice came from the speaker by the door. They'd taken to monitoring his room at night after the last couple of nightmares had left him broken and hysterical. They weren't his jailers, he reminded himself. They were trying to help.

The problem was he didn't know if there was anything left of him to help.

MORNING came eventually, and with it, the weekly visit from his mother. He hated the way she looked: far older than should be accounted for by the three years of his exile, as he thought of it. She'd shrunk in on herself, the tall slender beauty curved as if bracing for a

Love, Like Water

blow, the sleek dark hair streaked with silver. He knew she'd visited him in the early days he didn't remember, and thought maybe that was the reason she watched him with such fearful eyes, though he was always careful to move slowly and speak gently to her. Their conversation was of simple things—his sister's new boyfriend, his mother's business concerns, his uncle's ranch—small, casual tidbits of news, without emotional resonance. Once or twice in the last few weeks, she'd tentatively mentioned the trial, but only in passing, as if it was something that didn't quite matter. It didn't, really. His part in that was done. It wasn't as if he'd have to go to court—the evidence the Feds had was more than enough to put them all away.

But when the trial was done, so was he. There was nothing after the trial. It was as if the world had ended, leaving only a long, empty, blank space. He couldn't imagine anything after that.

This morning his mother was wearing a spring jacket in a primrose yellow that made her dark hair glow. She'd had her hair colored so that the gray didn't show, and she'd had her nails done. It looked so pretty he couldn't help but smile, despite his weariness. "You look nice," he said.

"Thanks, sweetheart." She reached up and kissed his cheek, running her hand over his fuzz of hair, just as he had during the night. "It's growing out. That's nice. I didn't like the shaved head. Made you look mean."

"That was the whole point," he said gently. He knew what she meant—it made him look skeletal, with his sunken cheeks and hollow eyes. He'd put on some weight since he'd been here, but it wasn't more than a handful of pounds. He had no appetite. He only really wanted the drug. He only really wanted to forget. "So what's the occasion?"

"I talked to your Uncle Tucker last night."

He smiled politely and held the wooden guest chair for her, then sat across from her on the edge of the narrow bed. "How is Uncle Tuck?"

"Oh, he's good. He's making noises about getting old, but he always does that." She fidgeted a moment, then said, "The lawyers came to see me. And Mr. Robinson."

All the pleasure of seeing her drained away. "He's not supposed to see you," he said tightly. "He's supposed to leave you alone."

"It's all right, Joshua," she assured him. "He wanted to let me know—to let *you* know—that the hearing is over. Your part of it is done. This nightmare is over. The evidence they have is more than enough to put those bastards away forever, and the grand jury agreed. They aren't being granted bail. Now it's just the trial, and that won't happen for years yet."

He stared at her, at the new happiness in her eyes, the relief, and felt only the same emptiness. "That's nice."

"Nice? It's wonderful. As soon as you can leave here, you can start over...."

"Ma."

She stopped. He spread his hands wide—those long-fingered hands, still broad across, though the tendons were sharp against the thin skin: the hands of a junkie. The hands of a killer. "I got nowhere to go."

"Mr. Robinson said...."

"Mr. Robinson can go to hell." There was no vitriol in the words—they were just words. "Do you think I have a snowball's chance in hell out there? Yeah, they got Montenegro. But the cartel's still in business. They'll come for me, once they know I'm out. The minute I hit the street they'll realize I was the one that sold out Montenegro, and I'm dead."

"They won't look for you. They think you're in prison here in Cincinnati. Mr. Robinson said you and they were very careful not to involve us. They don't even know your real name, so we're not in any danger of reprisals. You can leave, and be safe."

He cocked his head, looked at her, the words making no sense at all to him. "What?"

Love, Like Water

"That's what I wanted to tell you. When Mr. Robinson said it was all over, and you were free to go, I called your uncle. He's been wanting you to come to the ranch, to stay there and maybe take over someday, if you like it. Those terrible men won't find you there. You can have your old life back. You can be my Joshua again, and leave all this behind. Cathy and the kids can come see you on vacations—they don't even remember you anymore." She smoothed her hand over his cheek. "I hardly remember you anymore. I want my Joshua back."

He stared at her bright dark eyes and thought, *Your Joshua is dead, lady.*

Chapter 1

ELI leaned on the fence and watched the kid working with the sorrel mare. She was feeling the cooler weather September was bringing, and she frisked delightedly around the patient boy. It was good to see her lively. He remembered when she first came here, her coat dull and shaggy, scarred from abuse and neglect, her tail tangled and droopy and her eyes sunken and hopeless. Now her tail flew like a red silk flag, the upswept conformation hinting at Arabian blood, her dark liquid eyes bright, her coat clean and well-brushed and healthy, though there were still white streaks where the scars had been. She was one of the lucky ones; too many of the rescue animals that came here lived such a short time before the years of neglect and damage took their toll. When she'd arrived, he'd judged her to be about twenty, at least, and was shocked when the vet said she was no more than five. Now, she looked it. "Jesse," he called softly in his calmest voice, not wanting to startle either the mare or the boy, "see if you can get her to take the bridle. She took it yesterday—I want her to get used to wearing it."

"Sir," Jesse acknowledged with a faint nod, his voice low and calm, just as Eli had taught him. He moved slowly toward where the bridle was draped on the fence, never letting his attention stray from the mare. When he picked up the bridle, it jingled softly, and the mare bounced, not so much startled as seeing it as a new game. God, she was so young—she and Jesse would make a good pair once the boy had finished training. The Pueblo didn't have a tradition of horsemanship,

Love, Like Water

but Jesse—a member of the Isleta Pueblo near Albuquerque—hadn't let that stop him. He was a natural, only fifteen and already one of Eli's most promising students.

Jesse began speaking to the mare, very softly. The mare stopped bouncing, flicking her ears forward in interest. He didn't move but let the horse come to him, and she did, shifting in tiny steps, pretending not to move forward even as she let the boy's musical voice and nonsense words—or maybe they were Tiwa, Eli didn't know the difference—lure her to him. When she finally stood snuffling Jesse's hair, the boy raised his hands slowly and let her sniff and lip the bridle before easing the bit into her mouth. He held it there a moment, then slowly slipped the leather straps over her head, letting her accept it at each stage, until the bit was settled in the gap behind her teeth. The only thing Jesse had to do was fasten the chin strap. He murmured to her softly as he scratched beneath her chin on his way to the buckle, and when he'd fastened it, scratched her cheek beside the leather and steel. "Beautiful girl," he said, loud enough for Eli to hear it. "Beautiful, beautiful girl."

She bobbed her head as if in agreement, then bounced away, the moment broken. They watched her carefully, but she didn't seem to mind the bridle—didn't try to scrape it off against the fence as some of them did, with damage to both the horse and the bridle. "Good," Eli told Jesse, who came and leaned against the fence beside where Eli stood. "You're coming on."

"She's a sweetheart," Jesse said.

"Yep. I think you're a good pair—I'm going to see if Tucker'll be willing to assign her to you once you're done. Give you some time to get used to each other's quirks before the next NFS mustang roundup." The Triple C, Tucker Chastain's ranch, was one of the contractors for the National Forestry Service, which managed the mustang herds on federal land. "You can't ride in the roundup 'til you're sixteen, but if I recollect, you'll have just hit that mark by next spring. In the meantime, though, you're gonna have to take on a few more projects like Sallee, here."

"I'm up for it," Jesse said.

"I know you are, *chico*." Eli tilted his hat back and scratched his forehead. "Okay, give her another twenty minutes with the bridle, and then I want you to introduce her to neck reins. Loop 'em up so they don't dangle, but lay 'em across her withers so she gets used to the feel of them."

"Yessir," Jesse said.

"Eli!"

Eli shot the kid a grin. "Gotta go—Big Boss is callin'." Jesse gave him a matching grin, then turned his attention back to the mare. Eli straightened his hat, then turned and headed for the barn where Tucker waited. "Boss."

"Eli. Kid's looking good."

"Yeah, he's a natural."

"Seems to have an affinity for that animal."

"Yessir. Sallee and him are a good match, personality-wise. She'd make a good mount for him—he's about outgrown Charlie. He's ready for something a little more lively, more a challenge to him."

"Yeah." Tucker indicated the bench beside the barn door. It was in the shade, and Eli settled down on it gratefully. Chastain dropped down beside him, stretched out his long legs, and folded his arms across his chest. They sat that way in silence a moment; Eli didn't have anything to say, and Tucker, he knew, took his time about saying what he did.

Finally Tucker shifted and said, "What do you think about the men we have on the payroll?"

Eli frowned. "Good men. Can't say I've had a problem with any of them in general. Couple of them a bit mouthy, but since we got rid of that drunk, Leon, I think they're a good bunch. Why? Thinking of laying someone off?" He didn't like the idea, but Chastain was the owner, and he knew what the financial situation was better than Eli would.

"No. Bringing someone on, actually."

Love, Like Water

The frown deepened, and Eli sat thinking. He might not know the finances, but as foreman, he sure knew the workload, and it didn't warrant an extra hand. Unless Chastain was planning on bringing on more work. "You taking on more animals?"

"Not anytime soon. Not 'til the bank and I decide what's gonna happen with the additional acreage. But that'll be months yet."

"Then we probably ain't got work for another hand. Not so's it'd be worth what we'd have to pay him."

"He's not a hand, exactly." Tucker blew out a breath. "My nephew's coming out. I need the help with the business, and I'm thinking of training him up to run the place after I retire."

"You're not thinking of retiring yet," Eli said. He knew that for a fact—Tucker loved the ranch, loved the work, and was only in his late fifties. Far too young to think about retirement.

"No. But I'm spending more and more time on managing the business end, and less and less time training horses. Josh is a smart guy, a city guy, and I figure he'll know what to do about websites and Facebook and Twitter and all that shit."

"I thought he was some big shot FBI agent," Eli said idly.

"He was. I don't know the facts, but I know this last assignment of his went bad somehow, and he quit. He's been in the hospital a while, and Hannah wants him out of the city and someplace he can take his time recovering."

"He get shot or something?"

"Hell if I know. You know those Feds—they don't tell you nothing you don't need to know."

The only Feds Eli knew were the guys at the NFS and the ones at the Bureau of Indian Affairs, and they were all pretty decent fellas, so he didn't say anything. He just nodded and stared out across the paddock.

"So I figured we'd kill two birds with one stone. Josh can come out here and get his health back, and I can teach him about ranching while he's doing it. Working in the office probably won't hurt, either."

"I don't think I've met him," Eli mused. "I know your niece and her kids—they were out a couple summers ago—but he ain't been out here so's I remember."

"Not since he was a kid. They used to come out every summer. Hannah's been living back East since college." He didn't say anything more. Eli knew that there wasn't a Mr. Hannah, and Josh and Cathy had their mother's last name (though Cathy was married and divorced, from what Tucker had told him), but he didn't know anything more than that. Wasn't his business anyway.

"So why d'ja ask about the men? You think they won't be happy with a Fed living among 'em?"

"Him being a Fed ain't the issue. I was thinking more about him being my nephew, and him not knowing nothing about ranch life and all. Could be a lot of resentment and such."

Eli shook his head. "I don't think that'll be a problem. As long as he ain't an asshole, I think he'll be fine. Can he at least ride?"

"Hell if I know," Chastain said again. "He did as a kid."

"Then he'll probably be fine. There'll be some jockeyin', the same way there is whenever we take on a new hand, but it'll all shake down okay. As long as he ain't a prissy bitch or an asshole, and seeing as how he was an FBI agent, I kinda doubt he's a prissy bitch."

"He better not be an asshole," Chastain said. "I don't need the trouble, and I'd really like to know that I'm leaving the ranch in good hands. Of course, I can't make that decision until I get to know him, right?"

"You sick or something? Talking about retiring, and leaving the ranch in good hands.... Jesus, Tuck, you're making me nervous."

"Nah, I'm fine. I'm just.... Shit, Eli, I'm turning fifty-nine next birthday. In another year I'll be sixty. Out here, sixty is damn old."

"Yeah, it is," Eli said, then grinned as Tucker elbowed him.

"Says the guy who's half my age."

Love, Like Water

"No, I'd be half your age if you were sixty-six. Jesus, old man, no wonder you need help with the business end of the ranch, if you can't even figure right."

"Hey, I may be old, but I can still fire you."

"No, you can't, 'cause you can't find nobody else that'll put up with your cranky ass."

They grinned at each other a moment, then Tucker shook his head. "So. Josh'll be staying in the house, so you don't need to find space for him in the bunkhouse. You're just lucky I ain't putting him in your place."

"That's the foreman's cottage," Eli pointed out. "I'm the foreman. That's non-negotiable."

"I'm still the boss."

"Yeah, and you live in the boss's house. You gonna make your FBI nephew who ain't been on a ranch in dunno-many years the foreman?"

Tucker shuddered. "Oh, hell no. Okay. You're safe. Anyway, Hannah didn't know when he'd be coming out—she needed to talk to him yet and arrange things. I'll let you know as soon as I do. There's not much you need to do, at any rate. Just your job."

"And I do that anyway. But thanks for the heads up. You want me to pass the word among the *vaqueros*?"

"Sure. Might as well keep them in the loop." Chastain sighed. "I suppose there'll be all kinds of speculation about my health after this."

Eli grinned. "You bet your ass, old man. Better make sure you git out here and show 'em you're still alive, or they'll be taking bets on your life expectancy."

"Smartass." Tucker got up, kicked him lightly in the boot, and sauntered off back towards the house.

Chapter 2

THE flight from Chicago had coincided with a meeting of ranchers in Colorado Springs, so his uncle wasn't able to pick Joshua up at the airport as he'd originally planned. He'd offered to send his foreman into Albuquerque to pick him up, but Joshua didn't want to take the man from his work for the four-hour round trip. Instead, he'd found a Greyhound bus route that would take him to Miller, the town closest to the ranch, and his uncle would have someone pick him up there.

It was fine with Joshua; the long ride on the bus gave him a chance to mentally adjust to being away from the city streets that had been the borders of his life for the last three years, and to see the country he would be living in for the foreseeable future. The high desert was an interesting mix of dry, sere vegetation, a lot of pointless little shrubs scattered like lint balls on the blanket of yellow dust, and rare larger plants and even trees along riverbanks. The occasional dark distant splotch of forestland showed black against the sunlit flanks of mountains. There were hours and miles between sight of people or even other cars. Joshua, used to the constant barrage of visual input from the crowded streets he'd just left, found the empty road and the equally empty vistas wonderfully restful.

The others on the bus didn't bother him, either. There seemed to be a high percentage of Native Americans and Hispanics, tired-looking mothers with restless children and a few working men in denim shirts and ball caps with the logos of earthmoving machinery and crop

Love, Like Water

companies. Some of them glanced questioningly at the black denim jacket hiding his stick-thin arms, but the air conditioning was turned up high, and he was always cold these days.

Most of the passengers got off at dusty, isolated stops along the highway, and a few had gotten on along the way, but the bus was more than half empty when it pulled up to a stop just outside a dusty little town. "Miller," the driver called back to him, and Joshua got up, pulled his backpack off the overhead rack, and climbed down the steps and out into the hot, dry air. It felt good after the chill of the bus. The driver had gotten off first, opened the luggage storage bin, and pulled out the duffel with Joshua's tags. Joshua gave him a ten-dollar tip and shouldered the duffel, looking around wearily as he did for the ride his uncle had promised him. The only person waiting there was a real live cowboy lounging on the dropped tailgate of a huge, battered pickup truck, his head against one side of the truck bed, his gray hat tipped over his eyes. Despite the heat, he had on a long-sleeved shirt, sleeves all the way down, beat-up gloves on his hands, and boots over jeans so dusty it was hard to tell where the boots ended and the jeans began. He apparently was used to the heat—he looked cool and relaxed. Joshua regarded him a moment, then started toward the truck.

ONLY one guy got off the bus at the Miller bus stop. Eli eyed him from beneath the brim of his old Resistol and thought, "Can't be him." He knew his expectations were based on the portrayals of FBI agents on TV and in the movies, and it wasn't likely that Tuck's nephew would be wearing a black suit and tie over a standard white shirt, but he'd still sort of expected it. But this guy—no. No way was he the government sort.

Well, he was in black, anyway—black jeans, black T-shirt, black denim jacket despite the heat (Eli was used to it. He figured a guy from back East wouldn't be, but he seemed to be wrong). His buzz-cut hair was black too. His skin was the sort of washed-out yellowish color Mexicans got when they were sick, but his features weren't Mexican.

Hispanic, yeah, but something further east—Puerto Rican or Cuban, maybe.

And he was *skinny*. Not just lanky, not just lean, but skinny, sick skinny. Guy his size should weigh maybe 180, but Eli judged him to be down around 130. His wrists were gaunt where they stuck out from the sleeves of the denim jacket, like sticks, the hint of ribs visible through the T-shirt under the open jacket. As he walked toward the truck, he shambled like an old man, but his upper body was held tight and stiff, like he was braced for a blow. He walked like the human version of the abused animals the Triple C got sometimes, like a horse beaten too long for no reason at all.

And then Eli met the guy's dead eyes, and thought, shaken, *If I saw a horse with those eyes, I'd shoot it myself.*

"Triple C?" the guy said.

Eli swung his legs down off the tailgate and offered a gloved hand. "Elian Kelly," he said. "Call me Eli."

The guy's handshake was firm, but with no real strength behind it. "Joshua Chastain. My uncle said you're the ranch foreman?"

"Yep." Eli took the duffel and tossed it into the truck bed, closed the tailgate, then gestured at the passenger side door. "Hop in. We're about forty minutes from town—should be home for supper. Sorry about the long ride from the airport. Tuck really wanted to pick you up there himself, but the meeting in Colorado's about some government contracts, and he needed to be there. He handles all the business stuff. I just handle the ranch."

"It's all right," the man said. He buckled himself in with hands that shook. Cursing under his breath, he wrapped his arms around the backpack in his lap and focused on the road ahead.

Eli turned the truck on and looked over at him. "You okay?" he asked quietly. "Tuck said you were in the hospital—not recovered yet?"

"No." The guy stared forward expressionlessly.

"Well, the Triple C's a good place to recuperate," Eli said cheerfully. "Fresh air, plenty of exercise, and we've got a helluva good cook. Tuck's always complaining that he's putting on weight. I just tell him to get out and work more with the stock. We could always use the help. You ride?"

"Used to."

"It's like riding a bicycle. God knows with all the horses we've got, we can find a good match for you."

Joshua nodded. Eli waited for him to comment, then realized he wasn't going to. Shit. This was going to be a long drive.

"I don't know how much you remember of the Triple C," he said, in an effort to get a conversation going. "Tuck said you were a kid the last time you were here."

"Yes."

"Right. Well. What do you know about it?"

"Nothing. It's a horse ranch. I didn't think people still did that."

"Well, we do. Not saying it's easy keeping your head above water, especially in this economy, but your uncle Tuck has a really good reputation in the community for his training techniques. Especially with problem horses. He trains people as much as he trains horses—we've usually got a handful of students on site at any time. We're in between right now—there are a couple coming in a couple of weeks."

Silence.

Eli went on doggedly, "We get horses from private owners to train. We also take rescues from the ASPCA and rehabilitate them. And we participate in the mustang culls the government runs to manage the wild horse population."

"You break them for the government?"

Eli winced. "We don't 'break' horses. We tame them and train them and whatdayacallit, socialize them. Then they get sold to people and organizations who work with them. Don't let Tuck hear you call it 'breaking' them—too many people do, and then it's up to him to fix 'em."

"Doesn't sound like there's much money in it. Sounds like a social service."

"Well, not in that part, no. But Tuck also trains performance horses. Rodeo, mostly, barrel-racing, cutters, that sort of thing. Some movie stock. Sales of that pretty much finance the other stuff. And the private training. The ranch is really more like a training facility than a working horse ranch."

JOSHUA sat and listened to the guy talk, finding a whisper of interest he wouldn't have thought still existed in his blackened soul. The guy had a soft, easy voice, restful and slow, like he was smiling inside. It made Joshua feel like he was in a completely different universe, one where people actually cared about what happened. Rescued animals? Fixing broken horses? The guy made Uncle Tucker sound like the Saint Francis some of the mamás in the bodegas talked about. Nobody was like that. Joshua was willing to bet even the saint had spin doctors working full time for him. He wondered what it was he was going to find at the ranch, and how this soft-spoken, laconic man fit in as foreman.

He barely remembered Uncle Tucker—just as a big guy in a big hat who always smelled like horses. Joshua's grandfather had still been in charge of the ranch then. Joshua must have been about eleven the last time he'd been here, so that would be about sixteen years ago, since his grandfather had died when he was still in junior high. There hadn't been a lot of money to travel by that point; his mother had gone back to the ranch for the funeral alone, and when she'd come back, she didn't talk about the ranch for a long time. It wasn't hard to figure out that she and Uncle Tucker had had a fight of some kind. But apparently the war was now over, with his mother and Tucker reconnecting sometime during the three years Joshua had been on assignment. That was good. She needed some man she could depend on. God knew she couldn't depend on *him*.

Love, Like Water

At a break in the monologue, as the driver made a tight turn down an unmarked road, Joshua asked, "Why did he send you?"

"Say what?"

"Why did he send you? You're the foreman, and it's a big ranch—why not send some other less important person to pick me up?" He wasn't sure what made him ask. Maybe the easy voice made him feel interested himself. It just seemed peculiar to Joshua.

"Well, you're Tuck's nephew."

"So?"

"So, you're his nephew. Wouldn't be right sending some joe to pick you up, like you were a stranger or something."

"I am a stranger," Joshua pointed out. "He hasn't seen me in sixteen years."

"Don't matter. You're family. Wouldn't be polite. The men know this. Tuck sends one of them to pick you up, means you're not important. Start you off on the wrong foot."

Joshua considered this in silence as they drove. Status. Honor. He understood that. It was important on the street, too. Maybe more important than anything else. Except greed.

There were fences along this stretch, and once a fading sign, with a J tilted on its side. Kelly noticed his glance and said, "The Rocking J. Went into foreclosure a couple of years ago when the owner died. No kids, nobody worth leaving it to. Shook Tuck up, I think. He started talking to his sister—your mama—more, then. Guess he was already thinking about bringing you out here, but thought you were pretty much set with the FBI." He pronounced it as three separate letters, F-B-I, instead of running it together the way Easterners did, *efbeye*. "Tuck's negotiating with the bank to see if he can pick up some of the acreage, but thinks the price is too high. There's water, though, and that matters. He'll probably get it, if he wants it. Usually does. Can talk a squirrel outta its nuts." They drove a few minutes, then Kelly said, "Shame about the ranch, though. Hate to see it go. Getting fewer and fewer of the old ranches left—too hard to make it out here. Suppose someone might buy up the rest of it, turn it into a dude ranch or something—that wouldn't be too bad. We bought some of the stock for the Triple C. I think they auctioned the rest to put towards the balance of the mortgage."

"There's a mortgage?"

"The Triple C? No. Had one a few years back, but Tuck sold a bunch of stock to a movie ranch near Cupertino and was able to pay it off. Tuck don't like being indebted."

Neither do I, Joshua thought, *but see where that's got me.* He shrugged and turned back to the window, tightening his arms around the backpack. He was getting tired—it was a three-hour flight from Chicago, prefaced by two hours at the airport and followed by a four-hour bus ride, and now this. The sun was starting to lower—already the truck's shadow on the passenger side was lengthening. Tired, but not sleepy; his nerves buzzed anxiously and he felt sick. Stressed about the traveling, stressed having to make conversation with a stranger, stressed with moving to a completely different part of the country and a different way of life. Tiredness and stress were bad; they fed the hunger and the weakness. He wanted the drug—he always wanted the drug, but when he was tired and stressed he wanted it more.

A part of his brain was taking in and processing what the driver was saying, the way it always did. It would store it and let him access it when he needed to. This strange quirk of his brain was part of what made him so good at undercover operations; he never needed to take notes that might be found, or make phone calls that might be overheard, or upload data that might be hacked. Everything he saw, everything he heard was his own uploaded data, even if he wasn't paying attention to whatever it was that was going on, even if he was in a situation that required his attention while things went on in the background. He could carry on a conversation, deal with bosses and dealers and junkies and whores in his José persona, and Joshua's brain would be noticing and noting everything. Even when he was strung out, high, or barely conscious, he kept collecting data.

The problem with that was that he never forgot anything.

"You know?"

Love, Like Water

Joshua tracked back, found the comment, "Can't tell Tuck anything," and responded, "Yeah." That was sufficient. The driver went on talking. Joshua went on not listening.

But the guy's voice was nice, low and easy and soft, a gentle voice, a kind voice. The kind of voice that might lure animals into trusting it. Too bad Joshua wasn't an animal, and any trust had been burned out of him long ago. But the voice was nice.

"... here."

Joshua opened his eyes just as they turned under a wooden arch similar to the one they'd passed with the tilted J, but this one was freshly painted and new-looking. The three C's of the Triple C—for Joshua's grandfather Charles and *his* parents, Claude and Catherine— were picked out in deep green paint on a tan background, the letters turned so that the open ends faced each other and made a sort of Celtic knot design. There was a wire gate beneath it, but it was open to let them drive under the arch and down the drive to the house, bumping over the wooden bridge that crossed one of the creeks that watered the ranch.

It was smaller than Joshua remembered but still big enough: a two-story adobe style with an arched front entrance leading into an open-air courtyard with a tiled patio and central fountain, and nestled in a grove of ancient cottonwoods, the green coolness a welcome relief from the endless high desert he'd been traveling through all day. It had been a showplace of sorts at one time, Joshua remembered from stories his mother had told, but he could see through the arch that the fountain was dry. The creek was running though, the water clear and sparkling, so it wasn't from drought.

Where the drive branched to circle around the front of the house, Kelly kept the truck to the right and headed for the back. There, the house had a wide wooden porch overlooking a dusty yard, a paved side lot with a handful of cars and pickups parked, and the paddocks and corrals surrounding the stables and barns. There was quite a lot of activity going on, even this late in the evening. A pair of cowboys on Appaloosas were corralling a small herd of dusty horses while a third hung on the open gate, waving the horses in with his hat, and another couple of guys were unloading bales of hay from a flatbed and carrying them into a pole barn. At the stables, a young boy was leading a rangy bluish-gray horse in through the wide doorway; he stopped as the truck came to a halt a few yards away and tipped his hat at them.

"That's Jesse," the foreman said as he put the truck in park. "He's the youngest of our trainees and a natural. His mother's our cook, so he's lived here most of his life. You have any questions and Tuck or I ain't around, go to Jesse." He got out of the truck and Joshua followed suit.

The foreman picked up Joshua's duffel and slung it over his shoulder, waiting for Joshua to get out of the truck. He didn't seem impatient, though a faint frown crossed his face when Joshua lost his balance a moment and had to lean on the truck. He said nothing, however, just waited until Joshua was stable again, then led the way into the house. "Tuck said he fixed up the downstairs guest suite for you for now, since you're still on the mend. Later if you like, you and him can decide where you want to be—there's a half a dozen rooms upstairs nobody's usin'."

The back entrance led into the kitchen, where a plump little woman was bustling between stove and center island, getting supper ready, Joshua supposed. She looked up when they came in and grinned widely. "Señor Joshua!"

"Sarafina?" He blinked. How did she get so *small*? In his memory, she was a giantess, wielding her wooden spoon like Little John did his quarterstaff.

"*Sí*! You think I'd go away? No, I'm here forever, I think. Come, sit down, eat. You are much, much too thin!" Now her round face creased in distress as she took in the full glory of Joshua's heroin-junkie gauntness. "You have been sick!" she accused.

Well, that was one way of putting it. "Yeah," he said.

"Tucker said that, but this...." She tsked sternly. "We'll fix this."

Joshua gave her a faint smile and sat down at the table in the chair she directed him to. He set the backpack on the floor beside him and

Love, Like Water

looked up at the foreman, who was grinning in amusement. "I take it you two are old friends?" he said.

"I remember her," Joshua said.

"Yeah, I get that. Well, you just sit there and get some chow down you. I'll drop this in your room—it's the second door on the right down the hall."

"You tell those *vaqueros* that dinner will be ready in a half an hour," Sarafina instructed Eli. "Give me a little while to get some food down Joshua and get him tucked in. He's tired. He won't want to be bothered his first night home."

"Yes, boss," Eli said. She flapped her apron at him and he went out of the kitchen, chuckling.

"Eli's a good boy," Sarafina said as she set a plate in front of him, then dished out some enchiladas from the ceramic dish she'd been keeping warm in the oven. "Eat those, and I'll have a salad for you. And bread."

He stared down at the food, feeling faintly nauseated, but he picked up the fork and took a bite. It had a different flavor from the stuff he'd eaten in Chicago, but he couldn't say how, not anymore. His sensitivity to tastes was as dead as the rest of him. "It's good," he said, and choked down another bite. "You don't have to go to any effort," he said. "This is good. I'm too tired to eat much, anyway."

He could feel her eyes burning into the back of his head as he ate a couple more bites, making sure they were from the same enchilada so that she could salvage the rest. When he finished one, he set the fork down. "Thank you," he said, and bent to pick up the backpack.

"Joshua...."

"Thank you, Sarafina. Really, I'm just tired." He gave her what he hoped was a reassuring smile, then got up and went in search of his bedroom.

It was right where Eli Kelly had said it would be; he recognized the duffel on the foot of the bed on top of the pieced quilt. Joshua closed the door, then went to the bed and took it off to set it on the flagstone floor next to the rug. The backpack was set next to it, and Joshua sat on the edge of the bed.

The room was an improvement over the one he'd had at the rehab center. The walls were white, but the quilt and rug and Navaho-inspired drapes were brightly colored, and the warm sandstone floor was a deep honey that glowed in the fading light. And the mattress was firm. That was good. Joshua wrapped his arms around himself and lay down on his side, still in his coat. As he drifted to sleep, he heard the thump of doors and the sound of voices, but they didn't impact him, and he paid them no attention.

S<small>ARAFINA</small> had waited until after the rest of the men had left the kitchen to talk to Eli. He knew she wanted to give him an earful, so he took his time over his coffee. Once they were alone, the men off for evening chores or the bunkhouse, and Jesse up in his room doing homework, Sarafina poured herself a cup of coffee and sat down at the big table across from him. "So," she said, "did Tucker tell you what is wrong with Joshua?"

"Said he was hurt on assignment with the FBI. Hurt bad enough to quit."

"That is not 'hurt'." She pointed indignantly in the direction of the spare bedroom. "*That* is *sick*. He's a sick man, Eli. Traveling all day and all he eats is one little enchilada?"

"Maybe he ate on the plane," Eli said, but even he knew that was hedging, and deserved the scornful look she gave him.

"He did not, nor on the bus, nor in your car. He looks as though he hasn't eaten for *days*. Tucker will not be happy when he gets home tomorrow morning."

"Well, I ain't terribly happy right now," Eli said. "I agree with you, sweetheart. There's something seriously wrong with that boy."

Love, Like Water

Chapter 3

THE meeting had been a good five-hour drive from home, and normally Tucker would have stayed over at the hotel afterward. But when the group of his friends had finished dinner and drinks at the local cattlemen's club, it was two in the morning, he was wide awake, and the text message from Elian Kelly—*Josh here. Sarafina worried @ him*—had made him anxious enough that he bade his friends good-bye, got into his truck, and headed back down the road toward home.

He knew some of what his nephew had gone through—at least as much as Hannah knew, which wasn't a terrible lot. He'd listened to her cry with worry during the last couple of years of Josh's assignment, when she couldn't get in touch with her son, and again a few months ago when he'd come back, and Hannah had found him so terribly changed. Drugs were involved, which worried Tucker, but Hannah had insisted that it wasn't Josh's fault, that he'd been forced into it by circumstances, and that he was doing his best to break away from it. That had been part of the reason Hannah had wanted him to take Josh, to get him away from the drugs. The other part was that apparently Josh was still in danger from some of the people he'd put away—or their compatriots—though Hannah had assured him she and Cathy and the kids were perfectly safe. They and the ranch weren't even on the bad guys' radar, which was some comfort.

But Hannah had said that Josh had gone through some kind of chemical detox and that he was on the mend. It was just the psychological effects of the addiction that he needed to deal with, and the ranch would be just the place to do that. He could learn a new job and build a new life, far away from the stresses of the city, and hopefully put everything else firmly in the past.

So Tuck had been expecting someone who was ready to make a change in his life, but Eli's text—*Sarafina worried @ him*—made him think twice. Sarafina was a wise woman.

The sun was just coming up as he drove into the ranch yard and parked the Silverado beside the house. Inside, Sarafina was already at work, kneading dough for the hands' breakfast. She looked up at him as he entered, her face surprised. "Home already?"

"Didn't stay over," he said. "I'll catch a nap this afternoon. How is everything?"

"Normal. Elian is in charge, so of course everything is normal."

"I mean about Josh."

She didn't answer right away, but kept kneading the dough. Finally, she stopped, set the ball in a bowl and covered it with a dishcloth, then said, "He has very bad dreams."

"Oh?"

"Yes. They wake him. They wake *me*, and I'm upstairs. When I come down, he is awake and tells me he's fine. But he is not fine, Tucker. He is very not fine."

"Is he still asleep?"

She shrugged. "He's still in his room. He ate one enchilada last night, Tucker. *One*."

He said seriously, "Then he is sick, Sarafina." It was true. Sarafina's enchiladas were nectar of the gods. Anyone who could turn them down—or worse yet, eat only *one*—was sickening for something.

"I told you that." She put the bowl in the oven, then went to the big refrigerator. "You go see him, Tuck."

Calling him "Tuck" meant she was dead serious. He nodded, and went down the hall to the bedroom he'd chosen for Josh.

Love, Like Water

When he opened the door, he almost backed out and went to ask Sara who the hell was in his house, because that *couldn't* be Josh. Josh was only twenty-seven or twenty-eight. The photo Hannah had sent him on Josh's graduation from the FBI Academy was of a tall, grinning young man, broad-shouldered and strong. Not this shattered wreck of a scarecrow, dressed in black, with black fuzz on his head, deep gouges where his cheeks should be, and a knife blade of a nose. Appalled, Tucker stepped into the room and stood looking down in dismay at his nephew.

Josh opened his eyes and, faster than Tuck could have believed a wreck of a man like that could move, was off the other side of the bed, a knife in one hand and an expression of rage and fear on his gaunt face. Tuck flung his hands up in a gesture of surrender and said, "Josh?"

The man stared at him a moment, then the adrenaline or whatever had fueled his response drained out of him. He dropped his hands, tossed the knife onto the bedspread, and said dully, "Hello, Uncle Tucker."

"Sorry to startle you," Tuck said quietly, moving slowly to sit on the edge of the bed and retrieve the knife. It looked like one of Sarafina's steak knives. He must have picked it up in the kitchen last night, or sometime after Sarafina had gone to bed. Tuck put the knife on the nightstand. "Sit down, son, before you fall down."

Josh sat gingerly on the other side of the bed. "No. I'm sorry. I... I don't react well to things."

"Understandable. Your mother said you've had a rough time of it."

His nephew shook his head. "I'm sorry. I don't...." He stopped and folded his arms, his hands cupping his elbows. "I appreciate your letting me come here."

"You're family. This is your home from here on out, if you want it to be."

Josh raised his head and met Tuck's eyes. "Don't make promises," he said expressionlessly. "You don't know all the facts yet."

Moving slowly, the way he would with the wildest mustang fresh off the range, Tuck rose and went around to Josh's side of the bed. He reached out and took one sleeve of Josh's jacket in finger and thumb, and tugged gently until Josh's arm slid out. He did the same with the other, then tossed the jacket onto the chair in the corner.

Josh immediately put his arms back in the same folded position, but Tuck wasn't done. He put his hand—still so slowly, so gently—on Josh's wrist, and pulled the arm out. As he'd expected, the skin on the inside of the elbow was riddled with needle marks.

"Heroin?"

Josh nodded and closed his eyes.

"Hannah said there was an issue with drugs, but she didn't say what," Tuck said, trying to keep his voice steady. "She said you went through some kind of detox and rehab?"

"Yes. I'm clean." Josh was silent a moment, then said bitterly, "As clean as a heroin addict gets."

"Well," Tuck said mildly, "not much chance you'll be able to make a connection out here. Nearest ranch is fifteen miles west, and Miller's the closest town. Had some trouble a few years ago when some dumb kids set up a meth lab, but they blew it and themselves to kingdom come. Might find some marijuana around, and down on the rez you might find some peyote, but the shamans are real particular who gets to that. So, I'd say you're stuck."

"Thanks," Josh said. He looked down at his arm. Tuck released him, then said, "Sarafina said you had a rough night. Don't feel obliged to get up—you look like you could use the rest, and she can bring you breakfast here. You got pajamas in that duffel there? Can't imagine denim's all that comfortable to sleep in."

Josh shook his head. "She doesn't have to go to any trouble."

"She'd do it anyway, even if I didn't ask her. You're family."

"You said that."

"And I'm gonna keep saying it, until you believe it. Look, Josh, your mama told me everything she knew, which I'm betting ain't anywhere near everything. You tell me what you're comfortable telling

Love, Like Water

me, and not a stitch more. Soon's you're feeling better, you come work with me in the office, and when you're up to it, you can help out with the stock. Can always use an extra pair of hands. Fact is, I've been needing someone to help me with the business end of this for a while. I'm not interested in all that society network stuff, and websites and blob posts."

"Blog posts," Joshua said. He looked up and met Tuck's eyes again, and Tuck couldn't help but feel that he'd made some little breakthrough. At least the boy's lips were twitching, as if trying to smile.

"Blog posts. Whatever the hell they are. And handling the government paperwork for the NFS roundups is always a pain in the patootie."

"Your foreman told me some of that stuff. You contract with the federal government?"

"Yeah, the National Forestry Service. They manage the wild horse herds around here. Sometimes the BLM—Bureau of Land Management—does, but there's been kind of an outcry about them using helicopters to herd the mustangs, and that surely does mess with their heads. Lot harder to train an animal for the saddle that's scared to death of loud noises. So the NFS took over a good portion of that end of it. We round 'em up on horseback—less traumatic that way."

Joshua nodded.

"But that's all stuff you'll hear about later." Tucker picked up the duffel and dropped it on the bed beside Josh. "Get out your jams and crawl into bed for a while."

Josh nodded again, and opened the duffel. Tucker stood a moment, watching him, then went quietly out of the room, closing the door behind him.

In the kitchen, Sarafina was waiting with an enormous mug of coffee. Eli was sitting at the table, a twin to the mug in front of him. His hands were cupped around it, and he was staring down into the black liquid. "How much did you hear?" Tucker asked bluntly.

Eli's eyes were sober. "Enough."

"Then you know he's clean."

"He's detoxed or whatever they call it," Eli corrected. "Maybe he's clean and maybe he's not. He'll bear watching, family or no."

Tucker let out a long, heavy sigh, and sat down across from Eli. Sarafina set the mug on the table and went back to the granite counter, where she started cutting out rolls. "Yeah. He's got a strong will—always has—so if anyone can beat this thing, he can. But you're right. He'll bear watching, if only for his own safety."

"You sure you want to take this on?"

"He's family." Tucker sipped the coffee. Hot as sin and twice as smooth; he thought maybe Sarafina added something to it, chicory or something. "I'm giving him the benefit of the doubt. Besides, not much he can get into out here. And I don't think any of the hands would be inclined to risk a good job by acting as a connection or whatever they call it."

"True enough. Still, time will tell." Eli shook his head. "I hate waste."

"Yeah, me too."

Jesse came barreling into the kitchen at a dead run. "I'm late!" he yelped. His mother handed him the brown paper bag with his lunch and a burrito wrapped in a paper towel, and he fled out the door on his way to the end of the drive where the school bus would pick him up. "We'll have to watch out for Jesse," Tucker said.

"Joshua will not hurt Jesse," Sarafina said firmly. "Joshua won't hurt anyone. He needs to be protected, not suspected."

"I hope you're right, Sara." Tucker drank more coffee.

Sarafina put two laden plates in front of the men, and they both wordlessly dove into the piled eggs and sausage.

Love, Like Water

Chapter 4

WHEN Josh woke again, the light had changed, to a deeper light that he thought might signify afternoon. He'd slept better than he had last night—he didn't remember any dreams, and Uncle Tucker had been right; the sweats he wore as pajamas were a lot more comfortable than the jeans.

The closet doors were open and he could see that some of his clothing had been hung up there. His duffel was on the floor of the closet, and his backpack set on the desk chair in the corner. A bottle of water was on the nightstand. He shifted to his side and reached for it, cracking the seal and drinking about half of it before stopping. Despite the unfamiliarity of his surroundings—his eleven-year-old self hadn't been one for remembering much about the inside of the house, but he thought he could probably walk through the barns blindfolded—he was starting to relax, for the first time in… years. Years, for certain. Certainly before the day in his superior's office when he was asked to volunteer for a dangerous mission, one they wouldn't normally give to such a green agent, but one he was so uniquely suited for—to go undercover with the gangs on the West Side of Chicago, to infiltrate the biggest gang and find evidence of their connection to the cartel that ran drugs into the city. His father had been Puerto Rican, and a long-ago member of a local gang that had been absorbed by one of the newer ones. He hadn't married Joshua's mother; he'd been killed in a drive-by shooting a month or two before the twins were born. But his parents had fallen in love with Joshua and Catherine, and tolerated their mother, so he'd had something resembling a family.

Hannah had finished school with their help, gotten a decent job, and moved out of the neighborhood while the twins were still little, but they'd stayed connected with their Rosales grandparents—almost better than they had with Hannah's parents, the Chastains, who lived so far away. He spent as much time running around the streets of his grandparents' neighborhood as he did his own; in fact, most of his childhood friends had been from his father's old stomping grounds. But his grandparents had died when he was in high school, and Hannah hadn't liked his being down there so much when the gangs were so prevalent. Instead, they'd moved to Cincinnati when Joshua and Cathy were fifteen.

So when the assignment came up, and the Bureau needed a young, streetwise Hispanic kid, Joshua was the natural choice. He knew the culture, he spoke the language, and he looked the part. He'd been eager to take on the assignment, and his superiors had already made note of his almost-photographic memory.

He'd been perfect.

He shoved aside the sheet he'd used for a blanket—it was warm in the room, especially in sweats—and sat up on the edge of the bed, his head in his hands. He'd hated Uncle Tucker seeing the scars on his arms; it was almost as if as long as he could keep those hidden, no one would know. But that was ridiculous, of course. All anyone had to do was look at him to know he was trash. At least his hair was growing out some, and hiding the gang tattoo he had on his shaven head. He was never going to shave his head again—that tattoo at least would stay hidden forever.

His stomach growled and he blinked in surprise, then remembered that, aside from the one enchilada he'd barely choked down last evening, he hadn't eaten in twenty-four hours. His not eating was nerves, mostly—his appetite was gradually coming back, but stress had a tendency to kill it again.

Sarafina must have been a mind reader—or else the rumbling had been loud enough to hear in the kitchen—because she appeared a

Love, Like Water

moment later with a tray. "Good morning, Joshua!" she sang. "I have breakfast for you!"

"Thanks," he said, and started to get up.

"No, no. You stay put." With one foot, she shoved the empty little desk—the kind of thing a kid might have in his room—over next to the bed and set the tray on it. "Tucker says you rest, you rest. I have eggs and toast and sausage and tea."

"Coffee...," Joshua began, but she shook her head.

"Not yet. Tea. When you have eaten, then coffee. Your belly will not be ready for coffee without anything in it." She clucked disapprovingly. "Especially not after being empty so long. We're going to get you healthy again so you can take care of Tucker and the ranch. That's your job. My job is to get you there."

The smells coming from the tray were heavenly and Joshua felt hungrier than he had in months. Years.

"Then when you're done eating, you'll take a shower, and then sit out on the porch and get some fresh air. Tomorrow you can start working with Tucker." She finished setting out the dishes on the desk, then tucked the tray under one arm and regarded him thoughtfully. "You need a lot of food, but not all at once, so there's not a lot here. If you are still hungry in an hour, tell me, and I'll fix you more. That is how it works with the horses. We feed them small amounts often or else they get the colic, and that is a sad, sad thing."

"I promise not to get colic," Joshua said soberly. She gave him a brilliant smile.

"Of course you won't." Her voice was confident. "We know how to take care of neglected animals around here." With a wave, she left him alone to eat.

Which he did, slowly and thoughtfully, a bite here, a bite there, until the dishes were empty.

ELI had been riding fences most of the day, checking to make sure the stretch that bordered the abandoned Rocking J spread was in decent shape, now that there wasn't the maintenance partnership the two ranches had always had. The fences, wire and wood, were susceptible to all kinds of weather and nature-related damage, and there'd been an unseasonal thunderstorm that had come through a day or two ago. He'd found two places where the fence posts had pulled loose, leaving the wire on the ground, and fixed them. Fortunately, the ranch hadn't had any stock out to pasture at this end of the ranch, or there would have been lost animals and possible hoof damage from the fallen wire. The lost stock they would have retrieved sooner or later, but damage to the delicate frog of a horse's hoof could lead to serious infections if left untended.

Fortunately, it wasn't more than just a matter of digging a new hole for the posts and reattaching the wire, tools for which he carried with him. By the time he turned his mount back toward the ranch house, it was coming up on suppertime, but the whole length of the fence had been inspected.

The sun was starting to drop behind the mountains by then, and he and the horse cast a long gangly shadow that looked kind of like the drawings he'd seen of Don Quixote on his skinny nag. He'd always liked the story—it was sad, but it was true in a lot of ways; dreams mattered, and dreams were easily broken. He'd had dreams, once, of making a name for himself in the rodeo, of someday maybe going to college and becoming a vet, or of owning his own ranch, but those dreams broke easy, too, when his dad died. Then it was quitting school to go to work full time, to see that his ma was taken care of, and that Jake and Samantha had a chance at their own dreams. That was okay, though. Ma was happy up in Portland with her new husband (new, hell, they'd been married for ten years now), Jake was doing something in business in Cheyenne (he'd tried to explain what he did to Eli, but Eli kept falling asleep), and Samantha....

Well, he supposed Samantha was doing okay. She was doing what she loved, and hadn't asked him for a dime since she hooked up with the rock band she played guitar with—and the band's piano player. They didn't make much money, but she seemed happy. So that was good.

Love, Like Water

But sometimes he missed them. Missed the cold clear air of Wyoming, and the broad grasslands, and the deep snows of winter. Missed home and hearth and the companionship of people who knew him, who loved him. And though he'd found his place here at the Triple C, sometimes he just missed the *belonging*.

Not that it was all beer and skittles (whatever the hell skittles were, aside from the candy, and he was pretty sure those wouldn't go too well with beer). His dad sometimes drank too much, and sometimes he and Ma would fight in low, quiet tones they thought the kids couldn't hear. But everyone's folks did that, and he didn't know a single grownup male who didn't drink occasionally. It didn't mean they weren't happy. It didn't mean they weren't loved. He never doubted that.

He did doubt his dad would have been happy about his being gay. So that, he kept quiet. Dad probably wouldn't have thrown him out, or beat him, or any of the horrible shit he'd heard from other gay guys, but it would have been hard for him to deal with. It didn't matter—by the time Eli was sure he was really gay, Dad was gone. He never did tell Ma.

Eli had had a few years in the rodeo, earning a few extra bucks in prize money on occasion, but mostly just beating the shit out of his body. When he started to feel old and stiff getting up in the mornings, he quit. He'd been twenty-five.

Just about the age Tuck's nephew had been, from what Tuck said, when he took on the assignment that had messed him up.

He rode along the main road back to the house, since he was there already, and stopped to pick up the mail Henry'd stuffed into the box. Not a lot: a few bills, some flyers, and the Miller Post-Dispatch, the town's eight-page newspaper, which was mostly advertisements and the odd birth or death notice. To his surprise, though, the front page had a picture of the ranch and a short piece about Tucker's nephew, "a noted FBI profiler." He snorted. Got it wrong again. At least they didn't have a picture of the guy—there was nothing notable about him the state he was in.

Joshua was sitting on the porch in one of the rockers when he rode up. He tipped his hat to him in a casual salute before riding into the stable where he stripped the mare down and gave her a good brushing before turning her loose in the paddock. When he came out, Tuck was sitting beside his nephew. Eli pulled off his gloves and slapped them on the side of his thigh to dislodge the dust. "Evenin', Tuck. Josh. Glad to see you're both looking rested." Eli sent Tuck a mock-indignant glance. "While the rest of us were out riding fence and ya know, working."

"Privilege of being the boss. How's the fence?"

"Fixed. Couple places we'll need to replace rotten posts, but they'll hold another couple of weeks, likely. Long as we get 'em replaced before winter. 'Course, if you end up buying that parcel, we'll just have to move it, anyway."

"It's likely I'll buy at least a few hundred acres. I think I can get them down another couple thousand. I'd like to expand the training facilities, maybe add more cattle, since it's decent grazing land with the creeks watering it. And we'll be picking up more stock after all. A couple of the ranchers up north are getting out of the wild horse business, so there'll be more coming our way."

"How come?"

Tuck shrugged. "More money in cattle, and that's their primary business. The money the government pays for the trapping isn't great, and they're not in the business of training, so they just have to ship the animals somewhere else anyway. So we're working out a deal to take over some of the land they cover. They'll lend us some men for the initial roundup and to move 'em, but we'll take the responsibility."

"Can we manage?"

"Well enough, especially if Joshua picks up the bookkeeping end of it and I can get back out in the field." Tuck added, "Rodney says the bay mare's pregnant. I'm thinking the proud papa's that stallion that came in with the bunch we culled in June. I knew we oughta gelded him quicker."

Love, Like Water

"Woulda had to catch him quicker. He was slicker'n snot, that boy."

"Sad but true."

"What happened to him?" Josh asked.

Eli was surprised; he hadn't thought the man was paying any attention to the conversation. "Once he was gelded, he calmed down considerable. Nice horse. Barrel racer bought him last month. Gonna train him over the winter and put him on the rodeo circuit next spring. He'll be good at that—quick as lightning and agile as a snake. Mustangs make good rodeo horses, once they're socialized." Eli leaned on the porch railing. "So what else did Rodney say?"

"Who's Rodney?" Joshua frowned. "Did I meet him at lunch?"

"No, he's the vet. Was here this morning when you were asleep." Tuck turned back to Eli. "Clean bill of health for the stock he saw today—he'll be back next week to look at the rest."

"Good." Eli nodded. "Oh, by the way, I stopped for the mail." He pulled the wad of papers out of his back pocket. "We made the front page."

"What?" Tuck took the mail from him and opened the newspaper. "Profiler? Heh. Joshua, you know you're a noted FBI profiler?"

Joshua raised an eyebrow. He did look better, some, Eli thought—he was still gaunt, that wouldn't change overnight, but some of the shadows had vanished from beneath his eyes, and while those still weren't anywhere near human, they at least weren't *quite* as dead. They at least looked like they had a soul behind him. Probably due to Sarafina's feeding him.

God, Eli thought, *he's gonna be nice looking when he gets some meat on his bones and some life in his face.* He shook himself mentally.

"Profiler?" the guy said. "Well, better that than the truth."

"What's the truth?"

Joshua looked at him. "Failure, mostly."

"Failure? That's bullshit, boy!" Tucker rarely got that incensed, and Elian didn't remember the last time he'd flown off the handle like that. It was so unlike the soft-spoken horse trainer he knew that he recoiled in surprise. "Your mama told me they were able to put that whole damn gang behind bars and you never even had to testify because the information you got them was so solid. So don't you go saying you're anything like a failure around where I can hear it, you understand?"

Glancing at Joshua, Eli noted that the man's head had gone back, his nostrils flared, and his eyes had gone flat and dead like they had been the first time he'd seen him. Just like a mustang fresh off the range might look, faced with a stranger with a rope—defiant, frightened, wary. "Tuck," he said quietly.

His boss stopped, blinked, took a good hard look at Joshua, and deflated. "Shit," he said softly. "Sorry, Josh." He put out his hand, slowly, carefully.

Joshua looked at it, at him, and dropped his head forward, letting out a long sigh. When he raised his head, his eyes were tired. "It's okay," he said wearily. "It's just your truth. But you gotta remember something, Uncle Tucker. The end almost never justifies the means." With that, he got up and shambled back into the house.

"Fuck," Tucker said. Eli was surprised. Tucker almost never swore like that.

"You okay?"

"I'll live. Damn it. I blew that one, didn't I?"

"He ain't gonna be easy, Tuck." Eli took the couple of steps up to the porch and hiked himself up onto the railing. "He's smart and he's tough, and he's pretty damn bruised. You just gotta hope he's got heart underneath all that bruising. He kinda reminds me of one of the horses we get from the ASPCA—maybe he'll respond to the same kinda treatment."

"He's a man, not a horse."

Eli shrugged. "Both animals, in the long run. You're a smart man, boss. You'll figure him out."

Love, Like Water

"It would help if I knew what happened to him. What drove him to the drugs. I mean, shit, Eli, the boy I knew couldn't 'a done that. Something must have changed him drastic."

"Mebbe. Whatever it was, he's dealing with it now, and that's what matters."

"True enough." Tucker sighed, then said, "Another thing—speaking of Animal Cruelty...."

"Shit, we got another one?"

"One? Hell, we've got five. Outta Kansas. Trailer's coming in Saturday. Three mares, two geldings. Old man died on his farm and nobody knew about it for weeks." Tucker shook his head. "My worst nightmare. At any rate, they had to euthanize a couple of them but they think these might make it. Rod's gonna be back out Saturday morning to meet the trailer."

"I'll have the guys get the small barn ready. Let's keep them together for now, 'til they adjust."

"That's what I was thinkin'."

Eli said slowly, "I had another thought...."

"What's that?"

"Most of what they're gonna need for the first few weeks is just tendin'. Nothing complicated. Socialization, mebbe. Someone to watch their feed so they don't overeat, make sure they get water, aren't pushed around by any of the other horses. Make sure they don't get sick, or if they're injured, that the wounds don't fester. A babysitter."

As one, they turned and looked at the house. "You think he can handle it?"

"Yeah, I think it might bring him out of himself, y'know? Give him something else to think about. I'd wait 'til we see what they look like, though—if there's any chance one won't make it, we might want to rethink that. No sense him getting attached to an animal that doesn't have a chance of making it—or having him *not* getting attached, if he thinks it won't."

37

"Yeah, I can see that." Tucker leaned back and stared at the porch roof. His eyes narrowed as he thought. Eli watched him and waited. Finally, without changing his regard, Tuck said, "Let's put Ricky with him to assist. He's interested in eventually going to vet school, and this'll give him some practice with managing animals." Ricky was one of Jesse's friends and worked for them part time. "He can help out in the afternoons, give Joshua a break, and do some of the heavy lifting Joshua can't manage yet."

"He's supposed to be here tomorrow afternoon. I can talk to him then."

"Introduce him to Joshua, but don't say anything about the project to him. I want to make sure Joshua can handle it before I give it to him." Tucker looked worried. Eli could understand why. "I want him to work in the office, but his health is so poor I'd rather him be in better condition before I set him to a desk job. Yeah, I know that's counter… whatever it is they're calling it these days, we used to just say ornery—"

"Counterintuitive," Eli supplied.

"Yeah, that. But he needs fresh air and to get some strength before I stick him in the office."

"Can't say as I'd argue with that. Fresh air, plenty of rest, and Sarafina's cooking'll make a new man outta him."

"Hope you're right, son," Tucker said. "Hope you're right."

Love, Like Water

Chapter 5

THE days settled into a slow rhythm that somehow, through its very simplicity, started to ease some of the pain. The nightmares were still bad, still waking him several times a night, but Joshua found it easier to fall back to sleep afterwards than he ever had. He slept with his window open, and the scent of dust and desert plants and Sarafina's herb garden worked better than any of the sleeping pills they'd given him in the hospital. And the sounds: the wind, the rustle in the trees, the distant howl of a coyote or wolf—were there even any wolves left in the wild? And in the morning, the cackle of hens, the crow of a rooster, Sarafina rattling pans in the kitchen, and finally, the unmistakable noise of the hands coming in to eat.

There were a handful of employees who lived on the ranch, but most of them lived between there and Miller. Despite being the high desert, there were a surprising number of small ranches and farmsteads along the stretch of road to Miller, watered by a branch of the same Rio Galiano that kept the ranch alive. Eli had taken the time to introduce him to most of them, but Joshua had just filed the names away for future reference. They all seemed to have jobs that kept them busy; the ranch bustled from dawn 'til dusk. The ones Joshua saw the most of were Eli and Jesse, Sarafina's son, who were always around. The others didn't seem to have anything to do with Joshua.

He always waited until the last of them had gone before venturing out of his room. He'd stayed on the first floor—being down the hall away from the kitchen and having his own bathroom gave him a feeling of privacy he hadn't had in a long time. It helped that, after that first day, neither his uncle nor his housekeeper came in without invitation.

Even when Sarafina wanted to dust or do laundry, she always asked his permission first. He was quick to grant it, just as he was quick to come out when the last of the hands had finished breakfast, so that he could eat and let Sarafina clean up without dragging out her morning. It was bad enough she had to fuss over him like that—he'd never had anyone wait on him like she did, and it made him uncomfortable. Just not as uncomfortable as eating with those strangers would. Sometimes he offered to help, but she always shooed him out onto the porch or into the cavernous living room.

Tucker hadn't seemed eager to let him help either, with the ranch or with the bookkeeping. He was blunter about it than Sarafina was, telling Joshua point blank that he didn't want him stuck in the office until he was in better health. He did promise to have something for him to do by the weekend, and in the meantime, he told Joshua, he'd have to entertain himself with reading or watching movies streamed from Tucker's Netflix account.

He'd tried the movies, but his attention span was nonexistent, and he ended up shutting them off more often than not. He did manage to get all the way through *Brokeback Mountain*, but it was such a sad ending that he went back to bed and stared at the ceiling for hours, and couldn't bring himself to watch anything at all after that. The books in the house were mostly about ranching, and he supposed he ought to try reading some of them, if he was going to stay here, but when he tried, the words swam in front of his eyes and he'd given up in frustration.

A book on the native flora and fauna of New Mexico caught his eye. It was mostly pictures, with short descriptions beneath each photograph. That he could manage, especially since when he got tired, he could just close the book and pick it up again when he woke up from his nap. He didn't have to think or remember or analyze; all he had to do was take in the information and store it for later. The ranching books all seemed to work from a supposition that the reader already knew

Love, Like Water

something about ranching, so the text didn't make sense to him, but the picture book was easy.

That was what he was reduced to: easy.

He'd never taken life easy. He'd graduated college by twenty, gone straight through the police academy and into a job with the Cincinnati PD, and when his lieutenant recommended him for the FBI, he'd not only gotten into the academy there, but ended up one of the youngest field agents in the Bureau's history. His weird memory had helped, but so had his will and his brains. He wasn't used to easy. He didn't *want* easy. But his body was fighting him all the way. Not only with the weakness, the weariness. But even though he'd gone through rehab, even though the doctors and therapists had told him the need for the heroin was all psychological at this point, he still felt the need for it. Sometimes he felt like he was quivering under the skin, his muscles and tendons twitching uncontrollably like a horse trying to dislodge a fly. Sometimes his nerves buzzed all over until he thought he'd go insane from the sensation. And other times he just hurt, like an old man with arthritis.

He knew his uncle was just watching out for him, that he meant to be kind. That he really did want Joshua to rest. Joshua wished he had the energy to argue with Tucker, to *make* him put Joshua to work, but it was far too difficult. And if even *asking* to work was too much effort, maybe Tucker was right to keep Joshua resting.

But it wasn't restful. It was *frustrating.*

He'd taken to sitting on the porch in the shade most of the day, on the cushioned bench just outside the kitchen door. From there he could watch the ranch, but not interfere or get in the way, and if he closed his eyes and dozed, no one seemed to notice or comment on it. If he wasn't sleeping, he was watching, analyzing the way the ranch worked, the way the people interacted with each other, the way they reacted to Uncle Tucker, the way they responded to the foreman. Tucker was active, working with the horses in the big main corral, striding in and out of the various ranch buildings, or leading out a group of cowboys only to return hours later herding what seemed like dozens of horses.

Eli, too, was everywhere at once, but where Tucker was in charge, larger than life, Eli was quieter, appearing instantly when called for, always there, always aware, but unobtrusive. Just steady and reliable. Joshua noticed too, that when one of the men needed something, or had a question, it was to Eli that they went. It was a good pairing, Tucker and Eli—Tucker was the leader, Eli the efficient second-in-command.

Tucker always made time to check on Joshua, to make sure he was comfortable and resting, and that he didn't need anything. But it was Eli who would stop in passing, lean up against the bottom of the stair rail, and *talk* to Joshua, explaining what they were doing in the corral, where the men were going on their horses, what was being delivered, where the newest batch of horses were coming from. He'd watch Joshua with those patient eyes, as if calculating how much he could take in at a time, and seemed to know just when it was too much. Then he'd smile that slow smile, touch the brim of his hat, and walk away.

Joshua still felt like an outsider, but less of an unwelcome one.

He was sitting outside on the porch one morning, the picture book in his lap and his eyes closed against the relentless high desert sun, when he heard the sound of engines, louder than the ranch's trucks and equipment, and with a strange timbre. He opened his eyes to see a big old Cadillac pulling into the yard, followed by an enormous horse trailer. The Caddy's door opened and a man got out. He was dressed like any of the hands here, but he had a doctor's bag in one hand. The trailer pulled up on the other side of him, and as the driver got out of the cab, several of the hands, Tucker, and Elian Kelly came out of one of the barns. The trailer driver shook Tucker's hand, then Eli's, and then the three of them and the guy Joshua assumed was the vet walked to the back of the trailer, unhitched the ramp that served as the back door, and eased it down to the ground.

As he watched, Eli ducked into the trailer, and a minute later the back end of a horse appeared, shuffling down the low slope of the ramp to the ground. Joshua stared in disbelief. The horse was barely a hide over bones, the ribs sharp against the skin, the hipbones flared. A

Love, Like Water

skeleton of horse, like something out of the creepy fairy tales his *abuela* used to tell him. The horse's head drooped, and it moved slowly, passively, hopelessly.

The man with the bag—the vet?—inspected the horse carefully, then he said something to Tucker, who nodded and signaled for one of the hands to come over. He put the lead rope of the hackamore the horse wore into the man's hand and said something to him. The hand nodded and led the horse away, moving slowly, keeping pace with the animal's speed.

They repeated this four more times, each of the horses just as gaunt, just as hopeless as the first. But when one of the hands came up to take the last one's lead, the horse gave a little bounce, throwing its head back as if it were trying to rear, but without the energy to do so. The man startled and stepped back, but Tucker and Eli didn't move. Eli put his hand gently on the horse's withers and the beast quieted, but refused to budge.

Then the trailer driver said something, and climbed into the trailer, returning a moment later with something in his arms. The horse bent his head to the pale gray bundle; the driver handed it to the hand waiting to take the horse, and the horse followed meekly after.

Tucker stayed by the other two men, but Eli crossed the yard to lean on his accustomed place at the foot of the stairs to the porch, against the stair rail. "What was that about?" Joshua asked.

Eli chuckled. "Turns out the horse made friends with one of the cats from the farm they came from. Cat managed okay after the owner died—there ain't never a shortage of mice around a farm. Fortunately, it was mostly tame. Barn cats aren't usually, so it might have been a house cat that was lucky enough to be outside when the old man went. But the horse wouldn't leave without it. Animal welfare's usually pretty careful with the animals they rescue, and in a case like this, they'll just take both animals along."

"It's nice, I guess, that the horse has a friend. Seems to have a little more spirit than the others."

"Yeah," Eli said softly. "Sometimes friends give you strength you don't know you have."

"I wouldn't know." Joshua watched his uncle shake hands with the trailer driver, watched the trailer roll along the turnaround behind the near paddock and head back down the drive toward the road, watched his uncle and the vet as they turned and walked into the barn, heads together as they talked. He purposely didn't look at Eli; he knew the man would be watching *him* with those bright, patient eyes. He didn't know why—there was nothing judgmental, nothing pejorative about the look. It was more like he was waiting, but waiting for what? For Joshua to jump up and run around, waving his arms insanely as he went over that final edge? For Joshua to suddenly start talking like everyone else around here, easily, as if words were their friends and they didn't have anything to hide? He didn't know what Elian Kelly wanted, he just knew that the patient watchfulness made him nervous, made him curious, made him crazy.

Made him want to walk over to where he stood, put his head on his shoulder, and wait for those patient arms to come around him, pat him gently, and tell him everything was going to be okay.

He shook himself mentally and said, "So what are you going to do with those horses? They look ready for the glue factory."

"Not here," Eli said, still in that soft, easy voice. "We're gonna try and get them better. Doc'll give 'em vitamin shots. We'll put them on a special diet, watch them, take care of them, try to get them back to being horses again instead of animated skellingtons."

"What then?"

"Then it depends. We find homes for some of them. Some of them stay here. That sorrel mare Jesse's playing with in the far corral? That's Sallee. She looked just as bad as any of these when she got here a few months back."

Joshua studied the horse. It was on a lunge line, with Jesse, Sarafina's boy, in the center of the paddock. The mare was cantering steadily around the boy at the end of the lunge line. "He's teaching her voice commands," Eli said. "Most Western stock learn both voice

Love, Like Water

commands and neck-reining. Using the reins is fine unless your hands are full, so most working horses need to be able to follow voice orders too. The saddles we use aren't like them fancy English types, where the horse can feel your butt and thighs telling 'em what to do, so we gotta be able to talk to our mounts. Otherwise you might find yourself hauling on a three-hunnert pound calf and your horse not cooperating 'cause he don't understand what you're doing and you got no way of telling him."

He was looking out at the pair in the far corral, so Joshua took a moment to sneak a peek at him. It was still early in the day, so he hadn't acquired the patina of dusty sweat he usually had by evening—though he'd always shown up at supper washed and wearing a fresh shirt, his curly sun-streaked hair still damp from his shower. He seemed to take pride in himself, earthy and practical as he was. Joshua thought of days wearing the same filthy jeans, the same sweat-stained T-shirt, not caring if he was clean, not caring if his teeth were brushed or his hair washed. Not caring. He tried harder now, because he didn't want to disappoint Uncle Tuck, but it wasn't because *he* cared. Elian Kelly cared. Not only about his job, and the horses, but about himself. Joshua wondered what it would be like to take pride in oneself again. He'd done it before, but that was long ago.

Sometimes friends give you strength you don't know you have.

Did Elian Kelly think of himself as Joshua's friend? Joshua had had friends, once—again, long ago. College friends, friends at the Academy, friends among the other young agents in the Cincinnati field office before he'd transferred to Chicago for his exciting new assignment. He supposed to his college and Academy friends, he'd dropped off the face of the earth; the field agents might know what happened to him, but it was more likely they were told his assignment was successful as the FBI measured success and that he'd resigned immediately afterward. Maybe some of his college friends had tried to get in touch with him, but his mother and Cathy had been kept in the dark as to his whereabouts for his own safety during his assignment, and now.... Now there was no point. He was in New Mexico, and likely to stay here, and besides, his friends from college wouldn't know him. Hell, *he* didn't even know him.

But he was getting to know Elian Kelly, and he was starting to like him. The thought worried him, for some reason. It was as if every time the man looked at him, he saw a different Joshua, one that Joshua wished really existed. He wanted to be the Joshua Eli saw, but he was afraid he wasn't. And someday Eli would see the real Joshua, and that would be the end of any hope for friendship… if friendship was what it was.

Tucker came out of the barn with the vet and they climbed up to the porch, the vet settling in one of the rockers and Tucker sitting on the porch rail the way Eli had the other night. "So," he said, but it wasn't as a preamble to anything else, just a comment.

Eli said, "I don't reckon you've met Joshua, Rodney. Tuck's nephew."

"I figgered as much," the vet said. He stuck his hand out for Joshua to shake. "Rodney Lathrop, local vet."

"Joshua Chastain, local nephew," Joshua said seriously. The vet grinned and they shook. "So what's all that about? Are those horses even gonna make it?"

"Oh, yeah, they should. They were the lucky ones—they were out in a corral, and while they suffered some exposure, there was a trough to catch rainwater for drinking, and they at least weren't up to their ankles in filthy wet straw. They had to put down two horses that were in stalls in the barn—hoof rot. These babies aren't much but starved."

A thought occurred to Joshua. "You need to pen the cat."

Three pairs of startled eyes met his. "Say what?" the vet asked.

"I read that cats have a kind of homing device in their heads? That when you hear about cats traveling thousands of miles back to a house their family moved from, it's because the cat still thinks it's home. That you gotta keep a cat shut up for a couple of days until the homing thing in their head resets to recognize that the new place is home."

Love, Like Water

"Hmm," the vet said. "Makes sense."

"You like cats, Joshua?" Tucker asked with interest.

"Yeah, they're okay." He'd liked them once. He supposed maybe he someday might again.

"We've got an old kennel we can probably fix up for it," Eli mused. "Keep it in the stall with the horse, and it should be fine. Just need to find something to use for a litter box. Sand we got plenty of."

"Get it set up and Joshua can take over the cat," Tucker said. "That'll be in line with the rest of his job."

"The bookkeeping?" Joshua was puzzled.

"Nope. Tending our new guests."

"I don't understand."

"Well, not much to begin with. Ricky'll take care of that—he's the red-haired kid you seen around with Jesse. But I thought mebbe you'd like to take on a little light work. Monitoring their health, making sure they're getting enough sun and exercise...."

"I don't know anything about that." Joshua felt his throat tightening. "I don't know how to take care of anyone... anything. I...." His throat closed in panic.

Eli said quietly, "It's okay, son. You and Tucker can talk about it later, right, Tuck?"

Josh saw the two of them exchange a glance, and he felt stupid and helpless. Then Uncle Tucker said, "Sure, Josh. Didn't mean to spring it on you. And it ain't like it'd be solely on you or anything. We'll talk after supper."

Joshua nodded. He stood up, closing the picture book, and said, his voice thick as tar, "Okay. Later," and fled to his bedroom.

The last thing he heard as he let the screen door close behind him was his uncle's heartfelt "*Shit*."

47

Chapter 6

IT WAS cooler in the barn, shaded from the sun, with all the hot air far above under the roof panels. The smells.... Joshua closed his eyes a moment, taking in the dusty scent of hay, the tang of saddle oil, the mustiness of old wood, and, of course, the pungent stench of horse, despite the fact that the barn was cleaner than most specimens. When he opened his eyes, the kid Ricky, all long bones and elbows, stood on his shovel, grinning. There was a laden wheelbarrow behind him. "Kinda overpowering if you ain't used to it," he said.

Joshua regarded him a moment. He'd met the kid the other afternoon; he was a friend of Jesse's who had a part-time job at the ranch. The lanky, jug-eared redhead was the physical opposite of the compact, darkly lovely boy, but according to Sarafina, the two had been best friends since kindergarten. "I was just thinking," Joshua said slowly, "that it reminds me of when I was a kid here."

Ricky scratched his head. "You were a kid here?"

"A long time ago." Joshua nodded at him and went past on his way to the stall with the cat kennel in it.

The gelding who'd adopted the cat had turned out to be a pretty bay under the layers of mud and shed hair, and despite the bones that stuck out beneath the reddish brown coat. The two boys had worked all morning currying the new arrivals—not just for cosmetic reasons, but so the vet could inspect them for any lingering wounds or infections. The bay stood now with its head down against the side of the wire

Love, Like Water

kennel they'd found and cleaned up for the cat, who was curled up so that the horse's breath ruffled the long, matted fur. Despite the wire between them, they seemed content. So Joshua just stood for a while, leaning on the big stall—Tucker had called it a "loose box"—and watching the two of them.

After a bit though, the horse raised its head and looked at Joshua, snorting softly. "Sorry, fella," he murmured, "but I haven't got anything for you...."

"Sure you do," Ricky said in an undertone. Joshua glanced over his shoulder and saw Ricky holding out a bucket. Joshua took the bucket. Inside were oats, some pieces of carrots and apples, cut up small, and a few handfuls of grass. "Tuck told me to make up some of this, to get them used to us, but they're pretty friendly. Not like some of the ones we get here that are afraid of their own shadows. These guys are just hungry."

Indeed, the gelding was moving slowly, carefully in their direction, his attention on the bucket. Joshua took a handful of the mixture and held out his hand, palm flat, the offering open. After a moment, the horse came up and snuffled up the treat, his wet, fuzzy lips moving delicately over Joshua's skin. Joshua had thought that maybe it would be rougher, too eager to eat, but the gelding was a gentleman. "Do we know their names?"

"Nope," Ricky said. "I think Tuck might have a list, but I ain't seen it." He set the shovel to the side and trundled the full wheelbarrow out, leaving Joshua with his equine friend.

"YOU seen Josh?"

Tucker finished taking the bridle off Mary Sue, scratched her cheek, and hung up the bridle on the nail next to her stall before answering. "He went into the small barn right after lunch. Ain't seen him since. Ricky's been in and out of there, though. Maybe he seen him."

"Ricky left for home about quarter hour ago."

"Well, then, if you're concerned, best you go check out the small barn." Tucker gave Eli a long glance. "Taking him under your wing, Eli?"

Eli felt himself flush. "He's your nephew, you should be doing it."

"Thought I was." Tucker leaned back against the wall and folded his arms. "But I'm kind of thinking you like the boy. You spend enough time chatting him up."

"He's not a boy," Eli pointed out. "He's pretty close to my age. And I do like him."

Tucker studied him with wise eyes. "I expect you do. He'll be a good-looking man when he fills out some—always was a handsome boy."

"Jesus, Tuck, I shoulda never come out to you." Eli kicked the bale of hay next to Mary Sue's stall. "What are you, some kinda matchmaker? First Jack Castellano, now Joshua. Couldn't you have been an ordinary homophobe and canned my pink fairy ass?"

"So are you attracted to him?"

"It's not… I don't…. Damn it, Tucker! It ain't like that. Okay. I like him. More'n that, I feel for him. He's lost and kinda lonely, and it breaks my heart to see him like that. Make of that whatever you want." Eli rubbed his head in distraction. "But I ain't *thinking* about that right now. Jesus. He's got way too much to deal with."

"Well, I been reading, and they say that men think about sex every eight seconds, and gay men every five…."

"Holy fucking shit, Tuck!" Then he caught Tucker's grin and shook his head. "Asshole."

Tucker's grin faded. "Seriously, though, son, I don't like to see you setting yourself up for a fall, Elian. Even if Josh is queer, which I ain't never heard nothing about, he's got a lot of baggage he's carrying around with him. The little Hannah was able to tell me was that he was pretty deep undercover with some Latino or Hispanic or whatever they call themselves these days, gang, and you know those guys *sweat* macho. Now, I don't know anything about your gay dar"—he pronounced it as two separate words—"but I'm thinking he couldn'ta been gay in that kinda crowd. Which tells me, if he *is* queer, then he hid it so well I'm kinda wondering if he even knows it anymore."

Eli kicked the bale of hay again, then sat down on it with a thump. "Since when you got delusions of being a shrink? Most men your age and your place in life wouldn't tolerate me, let alone their own kin, being gay. Let alone act like it's okay."

Tucker snorted. "Come on, Eli, I ain't a dick like that and you know it. Never thumped a Bible in my life, and I could give a shit who you're screwing when you head off to Albuquerque for the weekend. But you can't stop me from being concerned about you—you ain't just my foreman, you're my friend too, and the son I never had."

"I thought Jesse was the son you never had."

"He's my younger son. Man's entitled to more than one son, ain't he? For that matter, Josh is my son too, now that he's here. So if you thought about getting with him I'd have to think of it kinda like incest." He grinned and ducked Eli's mock blow. "Seriously, though, I don't give a rat's ass what you're inta, but Josh is fragile, son."

"Well, shit," Eli said, "and here I was just about to go find him and bend him over a hay bale. Jesus H. Roosevelt Christ, Tucker, *I* know he's fragile! I may be gay, but I ain't *stupid*. And I wasn't thinking of him that way at all." *Liar*, his internal critic smirked. *Yeah*, he thought back at it, *but not now. Not 'til he's well. And if he turns out to be gay, too. Which, as Tucker says, ain't likely.* "I just am worried about the boy, is all. There's a lot more going on with him than just recovering from some addiction or other. And shouldn't he have some kind of counseling or something? And not just you, *Doctor* Chastain. I read that recovering addicts need to have regular counseling."

"Hell if I know. I know he was in some kinda program for a few months."

"And he still looks like shit," Eli pointed out. "So much for the program. Yeah, maybe it got him clean, but he ain't gonna stay clean if he don't have some kind of help."

"So help him," Tuck snapped. "I haven't got a clue what to do for the boy. You're closer to his age. Mebbe he'll listen to you."

Eli shook his head. "I dunno, Tuck. I don't know how to handle people—all I know is horses."

"Then treat him like a goddamned horse." Tuck threw up his hands. "If you can convince him to see a shrink in Albuquerque, then I'll find him a goddamned shrink. If he don't want to, can't do much to change his mind. He's a man grown—and a damn strong one to come through what he's been through, little as I know about it. Can't force him." His voice lowered, and he shook his head. "I'm worried, Elian. If you can help him, talk to him...."

"'Take him under my wing'?"

Tucker snorted. "That's right, throw an old man's words back in his face. Yeah. You do that. See if it works. Hell, at this point, he probably needs a friend more than anything else."

"I've got no objections to being his friend, if he wants me to," Elian said slowly. "I just ain't sure he wants one right now."

"Yeah, well, a horse fresh off the range don't exactly want to be friends with you either, but you know they're happier once they are," Tuck pointed out.

"Can't argue with that." Eli stood up from the hay bale he'd been sitting on and slapped his Resistol against his thigh and butt to dislodge the straw that stuck there. "Guess I'll be in the small barn if you're looking for me."

Tucker grunted in response and picked up Mary Sue's currycomb.

Dismissed. Eli grinned and headed outside, to cross the yard to the small barn. It was an older building than the big stables and pole barns that housed the rest of the stock and the farm equipment. The lower half was quarried stone; the upper, weathered gray timber. From what he figured, it was probably the first of the barns built on the ranch,

Love, Like Water

the one that was built with the house back in the 1920s. This barn was strictly working class. If it had ever had paint, it had faded to a featureless gray, but for all that, it had its own sort of dignity. And it was built like a brick shithouse, solid as a rock.

The doors were open, but inside it was shaded and, despite the diffused sunlight that streaked through the open doors in the loft, about twenty degrees cooler than outside. And quiet: Eli could hear the mumbling sound of mourning doves in the eaves and the steady crunch of five neglected horses eating. Four of them were in plain stalls, but he walked down the aisle to the fifth, placed in a loose box big enough for the oversized kennel crate they'd fixed up for the cat. Leaning on the top of the door, he looked in.

Josh was there, sitting in the hay against the stall wall where the kennel was, his long legs stretched out in front of him, his fingers curled into the wire of the crate. The cat lay against the side of the crate, his head under Josh's still fingers. The bay nosed at the hay under Josh's legs, but Josh didn't move.

Eli watched him sleep. The tight lines of strain had eased from his face, leaving it softer and him looking younger than he had before, closer to his twenty-eight years. His face looked thin, rather than gaunt. A few days of rest, fresh air, and Sarafina's cooking had taken the sickly yellow cast out of his skin, though it would be a while before he gained back the missing weight. But that was all right—it would happen, and right now, it was probably more important that Josh start to feel comfortable where he was.

He couldn't think of him as "Joshua," though Tuck had said he preferred it—it was pretty clear, even to someone as unsophisticated as himself, that insisting on his full name was just Josh putting up another barrier. That calling him "Josh" might lead to things like, oh, conversation. Shared jokes. The occasional smile. And maybe something horrible like friendship. Not for the first time, Eli wondered what exactly had been done to this poor damaged creature to make him so wary.

Horses were easy. If they'd been beaten, they showed scars, they shied away from the touch of a hand or the sight of a crop. He'd even known one that went berserk when they tried to sweep the stable. Those cues were easy to read. The problems weren't easy to fix, but once they had an idea of what they were dealing with, they knew what they had to do. People, now? People were funny. They were smart, and peculiar. So knowing what would set someone off wasn't easy to pinpoint.

Take his old man, God rest his soul, because someone had to. He was usually pretty levelheaded, unless something triggered one of his rare drunks. He hadn't been a mean drunk, but Eli hated it when he drank anyway. And he never could figure out what the triggers were. Maybe if he had, the old man would be alive today, instead of getting smeared across five hundred yards of Wyoming highway in the dead of winter.

The horse nudged the crate and the cat woke up, stretching. The movement pushed Joshua's hand against the wire, and Joshua woke up. Eli watched it, watched the way he blinked in the stray sunbeam that had settled on his face, watched how he looked up at the grazing horse and smiled.

God, that smile—slow, a little uncertain as if he'd forgotten how to do it. It put a dimple in one cheek that Eli suspected would still be there when he got the weight back, and showed teeth even and white against the tan of his skin. Eli had thought that the boy might be passable-looking once he was recovered, but that smile made him realize that face was made to break hearts. He thought maybe his might be the first....

He must have moved or made a sound, because Josh's head whipped around to stare at him, the smile vanished and all the tension flared back in his body. He could have wept to see it return. "Just me," he said quietly. "Checking to see if you got et. Horses'll eat meat if they're hungry enough."

Joshua's eyes widened. "They will?"

Eli laughed. "Nah, I'm fooling with you. Sara says you don't sleep so good—didja have a nice nap?"

"Pretty good," Josh said distantly. He turned to look at the cat, which was standing up and doing that cat stretching thing with the arched back.

Love, Like Water

"How's the cat doing?"

Joshua shrugged. "Bored and hates being in the cage."

"Lucky you didn't get bit. Cats are poisonous. Friend of mine nearly lost his arm from a cat bite."

That startled a laugh out of Joshua. "They aren't poisonous. They just have a lot of bacteria in their mouths. Some cats more than others. This one, given the way he's been living, probably more." He reached in and scratched the cat's head. "But you're not a biter, are you?"

"Good thing for you. So what do you think of Rory?"

"Rory?"

"The horse." Eli gestured at the horse—an easy, nonthreatening wave of his fingers so the horse wouldn't startle. It looked up in interest. "That's his name. Tuck says it's an old Gaelic name meaning 'red'. Though he could tell me it's an old Gaelic name for hockey puck and I'd believe him."

"No, that would be ''nerfalon'," Joshua said soberly.

"Would it?"

"No." Again, that slow smile, this time directed at Eli. He felt his knees go weak. "It's payback for the man-eating horse comment."

"Smartass." It was the only comment Eli could come up with; he thought maybe Joshua's smile had fried his brain.

Slowly, carefully, he unhooked the latch to the box and came in. Rory raised his head and snuffled his shirt. Eli fed him a handful of mix from the bucket hanging outside the stall. Joshua sat in his corner and watched them.

When Rory was finished, Eli shoved his big head gently away. "You ate it all, you stupid horse," he said in a soothing voice. In the same voice, he said to Joshua, "You can tell they were treated pretty well before the old man died. They each have their own tack, and it's good quality. Turns out the old man had a son killed in Afghanistan that used to work the farm with him. I expect he just kinda lost the will to live after that."

Joshua said nothing, just listened.

"The folks that shipped 'em here sent the tack along too. Needs some oiling—looks like it hasn't been used for a while. But once these guys are a bit better, they'll be happy to have their own gear again." He glanced at Joshua, who was gazing at his knees, which he'd drawn up and wrapped his arms around. "Play your cards right, and I reckon Tucker might give you this boy all for your own. Once he's fleshed out, he'll be about the right size...."

"No."

Eli raised an eyebrow, but didn't answer. He just waited.

"I don't want a horse." He'd drawn his knees in tighter; he was so thin the bones seemed to go straight up and down. "I'm not going to have a horse. I don't want it. I don't want this cat, either."

"Nobody offered you the cat," Eli pointed out gently.

"Well, if they did, I don't want it." Joshua dragged in a long slow breath, then let it out again. "I'm here to work, that's all. Uncle Tucker needs my help, I'll give it to him. I don't want anything else."

Eli left off petting the horse and took the three steps to stand in front of Joshua. "If people want to give you things, son, you take 'em and say 'thank you'. That's the way people do it."

"There's always a cost," Joshua replied shakily. "There's always a snake in the woodpile. Nothing's free. Tanstaafl."

That sounded German to Eli. He frowned and scratched the back of his neck. "Sorry, I don't know that word. I know *mach schnell* and *glasnost* and that's about the extent of my German."

The laugh that broke from Joshua this time was light and brittle. "It's not German—and neither is *glasnost*—that's Russian. 'Tanstaafl' is the acronym for 'there ain't no such thing as a free lunch'."

Eli thought about it. Yeah, guess it was. "Well, maybe not. But there's ways and ways of paying up, son."

"I'm not your son."

Love, Like Water

"Nope." He reached his gloved hand down. "Come on. It's nearabouts supper time and you need to wash up after spending your afternoon sleeping with that beast."

"Which, the cat or the horse?"

"Take your pick." Eli waited.

Finally, Joshua reached up and put his hand in Eli's. Careful not to squeeze the bones too hard, Eli hauled him to his feet.

His legs must have been asleep, because he staggered a little; he put his free hand out to touch Eli's shoulder for balance. They stood close a moment, one of Joshua's hands in Eli's, the other burning a patch on his shoulder, as if they were about to dance.

Joshua went very still. Startled, Eli met his eyes. They went dark and hooded a moment, and Joshua's breath was warm and sweet on Eli's cheek. Then the black lashes went down, shy as any girl's, but he didn't draw away.

Curling his fingers around Joshua's, Eli said raggedly, "Josh...."

The boy started as if he were just waking up, took a step back, jerked his hand loose from Eli's, and bolted. Eli spent a moment calming the horse, then went in search of Joshua.

Chapter 7

JOSHUA forced himself to keep to a brisk walk crossing the yard to the house, instead of running like he wanted to. Thank God Uncle Tucker wasn't around; if it were near suppertime as Elian had said, he was probably inside getting washed up. The rest of the hands, too—the yard was deserted, and that was good. Good.

He slipped into the house and skated past Sarafina, who was busy with something on the stove. Once in his room, he crossed to the bathroom, locked the door, and turned on the shower. Setting it as hot as he could possibly stand, he stripped off his clothes and got in, crumpling to the floor and caving in on himself, shaking. God. God. This was not good. This was so not good. He'd nearly blown it, nearly lost control. Nearly opened wounds he'd never be able to bear.

But Eli had been so gentle, so calm. So kind. It had seemed natural to reach out to touch him, to let the foreman balance him, to reach out for his steadiness and steel. To let someone else take point, for just a moment. To rely on someone else. To rely on *Eli*. Joshua dragged in a broken breath.

And for that one terrifyingly wonderful moment, to *see* Eli. To let Eli see *him*.

Oh, God.... But that was no prayer—he'd stopped believing in God a long time ago. He wished he still believed. Wished there was some higher power he could pray to. Then he wouldn't feel this need to lean on anyone else. It had been bad enough, in the rehab center,

Love, Like Water

knowing he depended on those people for his sanity, and they were professionals, paid for their service, the best the Bureau could afford. He wouldn't dare ask anyone else to help him, especially not someone like Eli, who had a job, who had a life, who didn't need a parasite like Joshua Chastain dragging him down.

He'd looked so startled when Joshua had touched him—of course he had. Men didn't grab hold of men the way Joshua had. Even though no skin had made contact—Eli had had on his battered gloves, and Joshua had only caught at the man's shirt-covered shoulder—Joshua had felt the sharp sting of attraction. To a cowboy, no less. To his uncle's ranch foreman. The only thing that could have been worse would have been if Joshua had been attracted to 'Chete Montenegro. He let out a short, hysterical bark of laughter. A ranch was every bit as macho an environment as the People or the Folks or any of the gangs that made up those two West Side nations. He was sure they had ways of dealing with interlopers every bit as brutal as the "violations" he'd witnessed and participated in and suffered in the gang.

He had no place here. He couldn't stay.

Dragging in a breath in a sob, he turned his face up to the scalding water. He had nothing. He had nowhere to go. He'd spent three years somewhere he didn't belong; he couldn't bear another moment of that feeling.

He thought of the long bus ride from Albuquerque. Thought about the long drive from the little hick town where the bus had dropped him.

Thought about the empty desert stretching out as far as the eye could see.

Thought about the desert inside him, equally empty. Emptier.

The water went cold and he dragged himself out of the tub. Sitting on the edge, he rubbed his face dry with a sodden towel—apparently the steam from the shower had made everything wet. It certainly had steamed up the mirror, but that was okay. The one thing Joshua didn't want to look at was himself.

"Did you find Joshua?" Tucker asked as Eli came into the kitchen.

"Did, but he took off. Thought he came in the house."

"I ain't seen him. Sara? Josh been through here?"

"I don't know. I've been fixing dinner," she said. "I did not hear him, but he is very quiet. Check his room."

Tuck nodded and went down the hall. Josh's door was open, but the bathroom's was closed and he could hear the shower running. He returned to the kitchen and said, "Guess he's there taking a shower. Why'd he bolt?"

"Hell if I know," Eli said, shrugging. "He was sitting in the straw in the loose box sleepin'. He woke up, we talked, I pulled him to his feet and he bolted. And before you ask, no, I didn't put any gay moves on him."

"Wasn't gonna ask," Tuck said mildly. "Boy's got his own way of thinkin'."

"Maybe you need to talk to him. Find out what's wrong. I didn't do nothin'."

"I believe you. I'll talk to him after supper." He was about to say more, but the door banged open and several of the hands came in, talking about the movie they were going to watch in the bunkhouse that night, so he left it at that.

Josh didn't come in for supper, but there was nothing unusual about that—having all the guys around seemed to bother him. After the rest of them cleared out, Sarafina made up a tray and handed it to Tucker with a Look; he nodded and carried it down the hall to Josh's room.

The door was closed. He knocked lightly with his free hand, and at Josh's subdued "come in," he pushed the door open and brought the tray in.

His nephew was sitting on the side of the bed, his elbows on his knees and his hands dangling between. Tucker set the tray on the desk. "Sarafina made chicken tonight. It'd be a crime for you to miss it."

Love, Like Water

"Thanks," Joshua said but made no move to get up and take it.

"Y'oughta eat."

"Yeah. Thanks."

Tucker sighed and dropped down onto the bed beside Josh. "You want to talk about it?"

"About what?"

"About whatever got you so upset? Did Eli say something to rile you? 'Cause he probably didn't mean it. He's a good guy, Eli. He don't mean nothin'."

"He didn't say anything."

"Did he do anything?"

That got a response. Joshua looked up at him, his expression blank. "Do what?"

"I don't know!" Tucker threw his hands up. "But he musta done something for you to get all riled with him!"

"I'm not riled with him. It's nothing, Uncle Tuck. It's just.... I'm just tired." Joshua's head dropped lower as he went back to staring at the floor. "I'll be okay. I'm just tired."

Tucker put a hand on his shoulder and said gently, "Well, that's why you're here, to get your strength back. Eat your supper, and go to bed early. Things'll look better when the sun rises—allus does."

Joshua nodded. Tucker gave his shoulder a squeeze and then went back to the kitchen. Eli and Sarafina were waiting. "He says he's just tired. Guess we just leave him be. Maybe in the morning we can start him supervising the feeding in the small barn, get him used to being out there and working."

Eli looked troubled, but he nodded. "I wish I knew what shook him up like that."

"Who knows." Tucker rubbed his hair with both hands. "I reckon there'll be plenty of times we can't figure out what he's thinking. Might as well get used to it."

THE same dream, the same riverside warehouse, the same stink of oil and fear. This time, however, Joshua didn't wake at the sound of the shot. The coppery stench of blood filled his nose as he gazed down at the dead girl, watching the blood, dark as oil, creep in tendrils across the stained concrete.

"That is done," 'Chete said, but the tone of his voice was distinctly less than approving. "Though, José, I think you maybe question me?"

"No, boss," Joshua said steadily, not taking his eyes off the dead girl. "I don't question you. You're the boss."

"I think maybe you do. That does not make me happy. You are a good fighter, and you are the son of my good friend Berto Rosales, God rest his soul, and you follow orders *most* of the time. But you are right. I am the boss, and I don't think I can let this go."

Joshua sweated in the dream. He knew what would happen next. The "violation"—the punishment for gang members who didn't follow orders or who screwed up, but not bad enough to die for it. It took only a nod of 'Chete's head to the wall in the corner. Joshua swallowed and walked to the wall, facing it with his palms on the corrugated steel just above his head. Three of 'Chete's bruisers followed him.

The first blow slammed his head against the corrugated steel, and he had a moment to think "at least it's not concrete" before the beating started in earnest. He'd witnessed a "V" before, participated in them. They usually stopped just before the transgressor passed out, but sometimes they didn't.

They didn't this time.

The dream took him to the cramped, damp room where he'd woken, on a bare, stained mattress, handcuffed to a steel bed frame. He could only open one eye, and his vision was blurry. "So," 'Chete's voice said from somewhere—he couldn't tell where—"you wake up finally. I did not think you were such a *pendejo*, a pussy, to pass out from a little beating like that. But hey, this generation is weaker than ours. Weaker in the body, weaker in the soul. Weaker in the heart."

Love, Like Water

Josh didn't understand. He felt like he was floating—he knew he'd been beaten, but he didn't hurt, not the way he should have after being pounded unconscious. There was dizziness, which he had expected, but also numbness, which he hadn't.

And then he heard the click of glass, and memory colored the pieces of the dream that the dreaming had left out. 'Chete said, "It is only because I love you and love the memory of the man your father was that I am giving you this opportunity. I do not wish to kill you, as I should, but you must be made an example of. There are many in the community that think that only weaklings take the drugs we sell, but I have found something very interesting. Would you like to hear about it?"

He didn't wait for an answer but went on. "I have found that the same thing that keeps our whores in line works very well with certain men. Men who have the same weakness in the lack of loyalty that whores do. Whores have their functions, and men have theirs, and it is a waste to kill someone for minor transgressions when I can buy their loyalty in such a simple way. Of course, you will lose status—no one respects a hype, do they?"

Joshua's breath sucked in at the word. A hype—a heroin addict, the lowest form of life in the Latin gangs. The walking dead. 'Chete had three lieutenants like that, that Joshua knew of. He was the only gang leader Josh knew who allowed it—no, reveled in it. He knew that they were loyal, fanatically loyal to the man who controlled the flow of the drug on the West Side, if only because he supplied what they needed. Despised by the regular gang members, they were feared, because they had nothing to lose—except access to the drug.

"But because I love you," 'Chete said softly, "because Los Peligros are family, I will not let it be generally known. My lieutenants will know, of course, but we will keep it quiet. Be faithful, be loyal, and I will keep it quiet, and keep you happy." He stroked Joshua's cheek in what might have been a caress. "Because you are worthless without me. You are a cheat and a parasite. You have some value in your strong arm and in your willingness to do my orders, but just because you were sweet on that *puta*, you dared to question me. That I cannot permit to go unanswered."

The location of 'Chete's voice didn't change, but Joshua felt hands on the opposite arm, felt something tighten around his bicep, felt the prick of the needle and a warm rush of liquid into his vein. "You will learn to love the feeling," 'Chete whispered in his ear, "and you will learn to love and obey me. This is the only way for you. You have no value, no worth, nothing if it is not with me. You are mine, José Rosales, son of my beloved Berto, and I love you for your father's sake. Because *you* are worthless. Because *you* are *nothing*."

Joshua woke with a start, his eyes opening on darkness and his breath coming hard. The window was open, and the dusty scent of the piñon pines wafted in on the breeze, washing away the remembered scent of 'Chete's breath. It didn't wash away the sound of his voice, echoing in Joshua's head: *You are nothing....*

Nothing. Worthless.

The dinner his uncle had brought in sat on the little desk, its red and green chile sauce congealing around the chicken. The sight of it made him sick, but he ignored the tray and opened the little center drawer. An old notepad, turning brown around the edges. A blunt pencil. Good enough. Joshua took them out and started to write.

Love, Like Water

Chapter 8

"NO JOSH this morning?"

Eli looked up from his breakfast, as did the four other hands sitting with him. "I ain't seen him," Ray volunteered, scratching his neck with his fork. Sarafina smacked his hand with her spatula, then took it over to the sink to wash it noisily. Ray exchanged a grin with Eli, who turned to Tucker.

"I haven't seen him either, but that's not unusual. He's probably still sleeping."

"Go check on him, Tucker," Sarafina said, "and bring back the dishes from his supper. I don't want creatures moving in."

"Aye aye, sir," Tucker saluted. "Will my breakfast be ready when I come back?"

"If I feel like it."

Tucker grinned and headed down the hall to Josh's room. While Josh had avoided suppers, where all the hands came in at once, he lately had been coming to early breakfast, when there was no more than a handful of men in the kitchen. But Eli was probably right—Josh was still sleeping. Seemed he'd had a restless night; when Tucker had come down for a drink of water about 1:00 a.m., he'd heard Josh pacing in his room. Apparently he was still having trouble with nightmares.

He knocked on the closed door. "Josh? Er, Joshua?"

Nothing. He frowned, knocked again, then opened the door.

The room was empty, the bathroom equally so. The closet door was open and half of his clothes were gone, along with his backpack. A piece of paper lay on the neatly made bed. Shaken, Tucker picked up the paper.

Uncle Tucker,

I'm really sorry. This is not going to work. I don't belong here.

I'm sorry. Thank you for trying.

Love,

Joshua

"Shit!" Tucker bolted for the back door. Six pairs of startled eyes watched him charge out onto the porch. He stopped and counted vehicles. The Silverado, Eli's F150, the bigger ranch vehicles, the assortment of cars and trucks owned by the men: all were parked neatly in the side lot. None were missing. Did that stupid kid…?

"Jesus H. Roosevelt Christ," Tucker swore, and went back into the house. To the others in the kitchen, he said, "Josh is gone. Took off. Must be walkin', 'cause all the cars are here. Idiot thinks he can get to Miller on foot. Goddammit! It's forty miles. I'm going to pick him up. Sara, call Whitey at the police station in town and ask him to send someone out to look for him. He's probably on the road between here and Miller somewhere, but there are a couple turnoffs and he musta left before light."

"Sure he's gone to Miller?" Eli asked as he got up. He gulped the last of his coffee, forked in the rest of his eggs, swallowed, and started for the door. Tucker put a hand out.

"No disrespect meant, son, but I think I better handle this. I don't know what went on yesterday, but it sure put a bug up his ass, for him to take off like this." He ignored Eli's stunned expression and went on, "And yeah, Miller. He's probably thinking he can catch the bus there to Albuquerque. But it's a long walk to town and he's not in the best shape. I want to catch him before the sun's too high. It's still hot enough for him to get heatstroke. Jesus." He grabbed his hat off the hook by the door and slapped it on. "I'll call when I find him. In the meantime, Eli, get the hands working their regular shifts."

Love, Like Water

"If he went off course...."

Tucker waved Eli off. "If I don't find him on the road to Miller, I'll call in help. I ain't stupid, son."

IT WAS 10:00 a.m. by the time Tuck called Eli on his sat phone. Eli dropped the fork he'd been using to dump hay in the corral for the horses there and fumbled at his belt for the phone. "Yeah. Tuck. What's going on? Did you find him?"

"No." Tuck's answer was curt, but Eli could hear the strain in his voice. "Whitey's got the State Police involved—they're sending a copter out."

Joshua had been missing since before dawn, and it was near ninety this morning already. Shit. "Did you check...."

"Son, we've had folks driving up and down every possible road, path, trail, and gully between here and town. We even checked out at the Rocking J to see if he holed up there." Tucker sounded like he was on the verge of tears—or swearing.

"What can I do?"

"Hang tight. Keep your sat phone with you. Keep your eyes peeled for anything that might show where he's gone. Dammit, I wish I'd gotten another hound dog after we lost Rambo and Rosey. Whitey's Paco is coming out to the ranch with his coonhounds. They might be able to track him. He says they're good trackers. And Sandia Search and Rescue are bringing out their dogs, but it'll be a couple hours before they can get here." In this heat, a couple of hours was a damn long time.

"You want me to send any of the hands out?"

Tucker said wearily, "We've got all of Whitey's men out, plus the local volunteer fire department, but a few more pairs of eyes won't hurt. Maybe send 'em out on horseback—they'll cover more ground that way. Half the sheriff's department are mounted. Here's the coordinates we're based at." He rattled off a series of GPS coordinates for their sat phones to track. "But I want you to stay there to coordinate with Paco."

"Sarafina…." But Tucker had hung up.

Tempted to hurl the phone across the stable yard, Eli put it back in the belt holder instead and bent to pick up the discarded fork.

Billy stuck his head out the stable door. "That Tuck?"

"Yeah. They still haven't found Josh. Tuck wants anyone who can to saddle up and join them—wouldn't hurt to spread out and search while you're on the way. I have the coordinates."

"Lay 'em on me." Billy took out his own phone and plugged in the numbers. "I'll get the rest of the guys together. You coming?"

"No." Eli shoved the fork into the hay bale with more force than necessary. "I'm stuck here. Paco's coming out with his coonhounds to try and track Joshua from here. Not that Sarafina couldn't deal with them." He tried not to sound bitter.

"What the hell happened that he took off like that?" Billy asked. "Did you guys get into a fight?"

"No. *Nothing* happened. Josh just freaked out for some reason. Don't matter. Go. Get the guys together and get the hell out of here. It's getting later and the sun's getting higher."

Billy nodded and took off at a run. Eli watched him and tried not to hate the boy. Or Tuck.

HE FINISHED putting out the hay for the horses in the corral, filled the water troughs in each of the paddocks with horses in them, then went into the small barn to check on the inhabitants. The shade of the barn was a relief after the growing heat outside, and he tried not to worry about fragile Joshua out in that, and no doubt dressed in the black clothes that seemed to make up most of his wardrobe. He hoped to God they found him soon, before heatstroke took its toll—there was at least a handful of heatstroke deaths every year in the area, mostly of people who didn't know better. Like Joshua. He'd noticed as they rode out that each of the hands was carrying the bulky saddlebags that held bottled

Love, Like Water

water, a standard accessory when going out on the range, and a necessary one when the heat got this bad. Hell, it was September. They should be cooling off by now, but the few cool days at the beginning of the month seemed to have been a false forecast.

The rescued horses were fine, their stalls clean enough to pass muster and their water barrels full. He put a scoop of high-calorie grain mix in each manger to augment the hay they'd gotten this morning. Two of the horses were already looking better after just a day. A third looked at him with dull eyes, and he made a mental note to call Rodney. The fourth wasn't looking that much better, but its tail was in motion, switching away flies, and it raised its head in interest when Eli added the grain.

The fifth was Rory in the loose box. Eli made a soft clucking sound with his tongue to let the horse know he was there before opening the door and stepping in. He went through the same motions of checking the water and augmenting the feed, then took a can of the cat food the ASPCA had sent with the cat, and crouched to open the kennel door.

The cat retreated to the furthest corner and hissed a little, but his tail wasn't puffed and his back wasn't arched, so Eli figured he was just making a point. He popped the top of the can and dumped it in the food bowl, then checked to make sure the water bowl was full, which it was.

It was as he was backing his arm out of the kennel that he glanced through the wire to see something black stuffed behind it. Frowning, he closed the kennel door and reached around to snag the bundle.

It was Joshua's backpack.

He stared at it in confusion, not sure if he was seeing right. But it was black, just like Josh's backpack, and no one else on the ranch had a black one. The ones they all used for overnight trips or long hauls were plain old khaki canvas ones from the feed store and mercantile in town. This was a fancy North Face model, not a working backpack, and when Eli opened it, he found clothes stuffed in it. There was something stiff in the pocket, so Eli opened that, too, to find Josh's wallet.

Why the hell would he leave his wallet?

He stared at it. Then a slow, horrible realization crept in. When it reached his brain, he leapt to his feet, startling the horse and cat, and ran to the back door of the barn. Flinging it open, he looked out across the small attached corral to where the desert stretched for miles towards the distant fuzz of forest and the blue smoke that was the Sangre de Cristo Mountains. The corral was mostly used for the rescue horses, and all five of their current crop were in the stable, so it shouldn't have mattered that the small back gate, the one they used when they were bringing in culls and ran out of room in the other paddock, was open.

To Eli, that was as good as a signed certificate. He bolted for the house.

Ten minutes later, armed with frozen blue freezer packs and water in insulated saddlebags, he finished tacking up Milagro, the fastest of the tamed mustangs in the herd. He had called and left a message for Tucker, telling him what he'd found, told Sarafina that when Paco got there with the dogs that they should start with the backpack in the stables and he'd lay odds that they'd head in the same direction he was, made sure he had a full first aid and emergency kit, then got Milagro out of the corral and into the crossties to saddle.

He rode around the small barn to the gate, then turned the horse to gaze across the desert toward the mountains. He hadn't the foggiest idea if Josh had gone straight that way, but people had a tendency to aim for something, even if their ultimate goal was to get lost completely. Psychology always won out, and the habits of a lifetime even more—he'd bet Josh was a goal-oriented kinda guy, if he was a field agent for the FBI by the time he was twenty-five. He *prayed* that was how Josh was, because right now, it was the only chance he had.

Eli shoved his hat further down on his head, crouched a little in the saddle, and let Milagro go. The horse took off at a dead run and Eli let him, let him stretch his legs and find his own rhythm. He'd only been gentled a little over a year, and still had that streak of wildness in him that let him run far, and fast, and gave him the smarts to know when he needed to slow to a steady canter. It was why Eli had chosen him—the horse would think, so Eli didn't have to.

Love, Like Water

All he wanted to do was look, his eyes scanning across the swath of desert in search of a silhouette in black. He prayed that when he found it, it would be upright, but feared that that was a forlorn hope. So he just looked. As soon as Milagro shifted into a canter, he unhooked the binoculars from their case on his saddle and raised them one-handed to his eyes. He didn't know what route Joshua would have taken, but the one he was on was the easiest, with the fewest gullies and washes, the least amount of rocks and prickly sagebrush, the most level. The path of least resistance. He thought, as much as he could understand Joshua's thinking, that Joshua would want to get as far away from the ranch as quickly as he could before deviating off to wherever it was he wanted to go and....

He stopped thinking and just *hoped*.

They'd gotten a good eight miles out when Eli spotted the jacket. It was a ways off the trail, such as it was, and looked like it had been thrown, rather than dropped. The sight of it was such a relief Eli nearly cried.

But it was nearly half an hour and another eight miles later that he found Joshua.

HE'D veered somewhat from the level ground Eli had been covering, and if it hadn't been for the binoculars Eli might have passed him by. But the lenses had caught the bit of black against the sage-brown earth of the wash, a bit of darkness in a monochrome world, and Eli drew Milagro up sharp and pivoted to let the surefooted mustang pick his way into the shallow gully. As soon as the rocks cleared and Eli got to the crumpled form of Tuck's nephew, he slid from the saddle, dropped the reins, and shoved a rock on them to hold Milagro in place. Then he crouched beside Joshua, reaching for the pulse point in his neck.

His skin was hot and dry, and the pulse thudded rapidly under his searching fingers. *Shit*. Heatstroke. Probably dehydration. Eli stood and unbuckled the saddlebags with the water and cold packs and started to get to work, tucking the cold packs into Joshua's armpits and groin and behind his neck, and soaking a towel with a bottleful of water to lay on Joshua's chest. His face was red with both sunburn and the heatstroke; Eli wetted a handkerchief to carefully blot his face. Then he pulled out the sat phone and called first Whitey, the town's police chief, to get the NMSP copter out here, then Tucker again.

"Where the hell are you, Elian?" Tucker demanded when he answered. "If you've gone off on a wild goose chase...."

"Shut the fuck up, Tucker!" Eli yelled back. "I've found your fucking nephew and he's out here with heatstroke and if I hadn't gone off on the fucking wild goose chase, he'd be fucking dead right now. No guarantees he won't still die if the fucking helicopter doesn't get here like *now*."

Tucker was silent a moment, then said, "Jesus H. Roosevelt Christ. Where are you? Did you call Whitey?"

"Just now. I just found him. Jesus, Tuck, he's burning up." Eli had tucked the phone between his ear and shoulder and was fumbling through the first aid kit. He put the ear thermometer in Josh's ear. "Shit, he's at 104. I've got ice packs and water, and I've got a reflective blanket I'm putting on him... now." He pulled the silver package from the bottom of the first aid bag and unfolded it, flipping it so it shaded both him and Joshua. Under the shelter from the sun, he could feel the heat radiating from Josh, and wiped his face again gently. He heard Tucker talking to someone, and then he came back on the line.

"Ray's on the phone with Whitey now. The helicopter's on the way. We've got your coordinates and they'll be looking for the reflector. Sit tight. Just keep Josh as cool as you can get him."

"Okay."

"I'm gonna hang up now. The copter crew will have your phone number, so I want to leave the line open. They should be there in less than ten minutes, Ray says. We'll meet you at the hospital."

"You'll meet Josh at the hospital. I've got to get Milagro back."

"Good enough." There was silence a moment, and Eli was just about to disconnect the call when he heard Tucker's voice again. "Eli?"

"Yeah?"

Love, Like Water

"Thank you. You done good."

"We'll see," Eli said, and hit the button. He put the phone back in its holster, then turned back to Josh.

He shifted the ice packs so the skin didn't freeze, trying to keep them places where the blood flow was strongest. When that was done, he tried lifting Josh's head to hold a bottle to his lips to see if he could swallow. The water ran from the sides of his mouth and he didn't respond at all. Eli set the bottle down carefully and held Josh in his lap under the silver blanket, waiting helplessly, his heart breaking. "Oh, baby boy," he whispered, "don't do this to me. *No me hagas esto, mijo.* Please don't. Please don't."

The flick-flick-flick of the approaching copter warned him, and he caught the edge of the blanket before it could blow away. He heard Milagro shift nervously, but then Billy's voice said, "Easy up, Milo old boy," and Milagro chuffed in response. Billy lifted the edge of the blanket and said, "I was with Whitey when the call came in. Figured you'd be ready for a break, old man," and then the paramedics were there, pulling off the blanket and taking Josh from Eli's arms.

They wrapped Josh in a cooling blanket and carried him to the copter. One of them came back, held a hand out to Eli and pulled him to his feet. Eli felt like an old man, like he'd been sitting there forever instead of for a mere ten minutes or so. "Good job with the ice packs, man. Good thinking."

Eli nodded dumbly.

Billy said, "You go with 'em, Eli. I'll get Milo home. You look wrecked."

Rubbing his face with a still-wet hand, Eli nodded again. He bent and picked up the gloves he'd peeled off when he'd started working on Josh and tucked them into his belt. His hands were shaking. Silently, he followed the paramedic to where the helicopter waited.

Chapter 9

"TEMPERATURE'S 102.6. Coming down," one of the paramedics reported. "How's that drip coming?"

"Nearly ready, but Jesus, this guy's veins are all fucked up. Arms like a junkie. Gonna be hard to get a line in him, with the dehydration."

"Just keep trying."

"He was," Eli said, his voice cracking. "He's recovering. It's why he came out here."

The paramedic's voice softened. "We'll do our best to make sure he has the chance—Eli, was it?—Eli. What happened? He don't look like he's in any shape to go hiking."

"I don't know for sure. He took his backpack so I guess he was walking to town and got lost. Must have lost his backpack out there somewhere." He didn't know why he lied, but it seemed the right thing to say at the moment.

"Hell and gone from the road, but I know damn well how confusing it can get. Report said he'd been missing since before dawn—easy to get off course in the dark with no lights and no road signs." The paramedic finished setting up the drip and started to get Joshua ready for the insertion.

But the moment the needle touched Josh's skin, he woke and started screaming in Spanish, and thrashed his arms wildly. The

Love, Like Water

paramedics grabbed for him but he just kept screaming, "*No! No lo quiero! No lo quiero!*"

Eli caught his arms, murmuring, "*Basta, chico. Basta mijo. Mijo valiente. Mijo bonito.*" *Enough, my boy. My brave boy. My beautiful boy.* "*Confía en ellos, yo nunca dejaría que nadie te hiciera daño. Yo nunca dejaré que nadie te haga daño. Nunca te harán daño.*" *Trust them, I wouldn't let anyone hurt you. I would never let anyone hurt you. I will never hurt you.* The words came automatically, as easily as English—the ranch he'd grown up on had had plenty of Hispanic cowboys on it, and after ten years in New Mexico, Eli's Spanish was as good as his English.

The paramedics waited impatiently as Eli crooned to Joshua, keeping his own fear from his voice and just focusing on calming him. Josh moaned and cried, his body jerking in semiconscious protest, his legs flailing weakly. Finally, Josh lay panting, his eyes blank and his body trembling. He whimpered a little when they set the line for the drip, but he suffered it passively. "Joshua?" Eli said.

He didn't answer, just lay in Eli's arms, limp and unresponsive; if his eyes hadn't been open, Eli would have thought him unconscious again. But he was breathing, at least, and it might have been Eli's imagination, but he thought Josh seemed cooler. He said so to the paramedic, who nodded, but then reached out and closed Joshua's eyes. "Why did you do that?"

"So his eyeballs won't dry out," the paramedic said. "He's still not conscious, really." He checked to make sure the saline was flowing easily, taped down the line, and got more ice packs out of a case. "He's doing pretty well, though considering his poor condition overall, he's far from out of the woods. The hospital's been notified and will be waiting to admit him." He put a hand on Eli's shoulder. "I gotta warn you, man—your friend's in a lot of trouble. He's gonna be sick for a while, and there can be a lot of effects from heatstroke as severe as this. Be prepared. I'm really sorry." The look in his eyes was compassionate. "It's gonna be hard. He got family?"

"His uncle's on his way to the hospital. I guess we'll wait to see what's going on before calling his mom." Eli felt numb, far more exhausted than an hour's ride and the quarter hour since he'd found Joshua would seem to warrant. He wanted to curl up beside Josh on the cooling blanket and just go to sleep, but instead, he tucked the blanket closer around Joshua and sat on the floor of the helicopter beside him.

TONIO drove Tucker to the hospital in the Silverado. Tuck sat in the passenger seat with his eyes closed, the air conditioning blowing on his face, and him feeling every bump, every turn, every slight swerve, the very texture of the roadbed beneath the tires. He felt sick, in that strange, horrified way one felt when things are happening too fast to absorb. It wasn't hard to figure out that Josh hadn't gotten lost on his way to town and just wandered off the road—the coordinates Eli had called in were nearly twenty miles northwest of the ranch, and a good thirty miles from the road, in a completely different direction. Where the hell did Josh think he was going? Santa Fe? Over the mountains?

The helicopter was just settling on the roof of the hospital in Miller as they pulled into the parking lot. Some of the locals had put up a stink about the increase in county taxes to expand and update the hospital as a trauma center, but Tucker hadn't been one of them, and he was glad now. He slid out of the truck almost before it had stopped moving and lurched into the lobby, feeling every bit of his fifty-nine and a half years.

"Tucker?" The nurse on duty was Ellen Pacheco—she'd gone to school with Hannah. "What's wrong? One of your hands get hurt?"

"No—my nephew. That's him on the roof, in the copter. Can you tell me where they'll be taking him?"

She punched some keys on the computer screen. "He's been preadmitted through Emergency. They'll be taking him right to the Heatstroke Center for treatment. Hang on—I'll see if you can go on up. Says Elian Kelly's with him?"

Love, Like Water

"Yeah, Eli found him." Tucker went to rub his head and his hat fell off. He bent and picked it up, then held it awkwardly. "Does it say how he's doin'?"

She shook her head. "Sorry, no. But Dr. Castellano is on ER duty today—he's in very good hands." She picked up the phone, murmured something, then hung up with a smile. "Go on up to Four, turn left off the elevator and through the doors there. There's a desk and Graciela will meet you there. She's the nurse on duty for that department."

"Thanks," Tucker said, and headed for the elevators.

GRACIELA was a smiling middle-aged woman, who came around the desk and took his arm. "They've just arrived and are assessing the situation, Mr. Chastain. Mr. Kelly is in the waiting room. Would you like some coffee while you're waiting?"

"Yes, please," he said numbly, letting her lead him to the small, carpeted room a bit past the desk.

Eli was there, twisting his big gray hat in his hands. When he saw Tucker, the hat fell to the floor. Tucker looked at it. "Lot of that going on these days," he said, and tossed his own hat onto one of the chairs.

"Tuck...."

"Eli, I owe you an apology," Tucker said. "I know I came off too strong, 'cause I was worrit about Josh and looking to blame someone. I'm sorry. I just...." He flapped his hands wordlessly.

"If you hadn't, he mighta been dead by now." Eli shook his head. Picking up his hat, he dropped it next to Tucker's and sat down beside them.

"How's he doin'?"

Eli shrugged, but his face was drawn and frightened. "Unconscious. When he wasn't unconscious, he was delirious. Thought the paramedics were trying to give him heroin, I think. He kept yelling '*no lo quiero, no lo quiero.*' Figure that musta been what it was." He looked back up at Tuck. "You think that's how he got hooked? They made him do it?"

"Makes more sense than the boy seeking it out. You didn't know Josh as a boy, Eli. He had a will of iron. I'll never forget the summer he was about eight, I think. There was a horse he wanted to ride in the worst way, but my dad wouldn't let him. Thought it was too much horse for him. Too wild. Josh got up every single morning at the crack of dawn and spent it with that horse, talking to it, getting it used to him, until that damn horse would do anything he asked. One morning he lets it out of the corral, walks up to my dad with the horse following him like a dog, and sez, 'He don't seem real wild to me, Grandpa.'" Tucker snorted. "My dad just laughed and laughed, and said that right there was proof the boy was a Chastain through and through."

"What happened to the horse?"

"Had to sell it—one of our regular rodeo customers was looking for a horse just like it. 'Bout broke Joshua's heart, but he took it like a man. Dad explained to him that they were a working ranch, and they couldn't afford to keep an animal just for a pet, especially when we had all the working stock we needed, and Josh was only on the ranch two months out of the year. He promised that the next year he'd start teaching him how to train horses. And he did, for the next two years. Then he died, and Hannah didn't come out any more. But it's more than just that, Eli. He finished college a year early, was a full FBI field agent at twenty-five, and spent three years undercover in what hadda be a pretty dangerous situation. And when he got away from it, he went right into rehab. He mighta quit the Bureau, but he's not a quitter. He ain't weak. That's why… that's why…." He stopped, his throat full of tears.

"That's why nothin', Tuck. He got lost is all. He was heading for town, and he got lost." Eli's voice was fierce. "And if the doctors ask, that's what we'll tell 'em." His voice dropped. "If they think that he meant to lose himself, that it was deliberate, they'll commit him. Josh don't need a hospital. He ain't crazy. He's tired and sad and needs time and work to get over it. Yeah, maybe he needs a shrink some—I don't think you'll mind if he needs to go to the city once a week or so. Hell,

Love, Like Water

I'll drive him if you want. But he don't belong locked up. Nothing good ever came of keeping an animal locked up."

"You and your animal comparisons," Tucker snorted, but at least he wasn't on the verge of crying like a baby anymore.

Elian shrugged. "Animals are a sight easier to deal with than people, I reckon."

They sat there in companionable quiet, just as they might on the porch on a summer evening, neither with anything to say and no need to say it. It was maybe a half hour later that the doctor came in, the little paper mask down around his neck and a clipboard stuck under one arm.

"Hey, Tuck. Hey, Eli."

"Jack," Eli said.

"Jack, what's going on? How's Josh doin'?"

"Not as bad as he could be, and better than he should be, given the state he's in. I heard your nephew was coming to live at the ranch, but I didn't expect him to be in this condition." Jack Castellano shook their hands. "What happened to him?"

"Bad assignment with the Bureau."

"Really? Because what I saw in there looked more like a hoodlum than an agent of the U.S. Government. That tattoo he's sporting on his arm is the gang symbol for one of the worst gangs in the country."

"That was his assignment. He hadda infiltrate the gang, get information on them. He did, too. We're real proud of him." Tucker couldn't help sounding defensive, and Jack raised his hands with a grin.

"I believe you, I believe you. Wouldn't expect any less from a Chastain."

"So how is he?" Eli interrupted.

"Well, he's stable, and conscious. I heard he had some trouble with the medics placing the saline, but he seems okay now. I did some blood work—kinda standard for admissions when a person's medical history is unknown—and aside from a bit of anemia, which isn't unexpected when you take into account his weight, he's got no apparent pathogens, his white blood cell count is good, and there's no evidence of drugs. We'll be testing further, given the evidence of the needle marks, but initial indication is no sign of HIV or AIDS. So that's good—he's more or less healthy, just anemic and underweight. We're gonna have to monitor his kidney and liver function for a few days—heatstroke has a lot of side effects." He folded his arms and gazed at Tuck levelly. "Depression is a common side effect of anorexia. Anything you want to say about what happened?"

"He *was* depressed. He wasn't feeling like he'd be any good out at the ranch and decided to leave," Tuck said. "I don't think he realized how far it was to town or how easy it was to get lost. I figure he probably never even made it to the road—wandered off somewhere on the drive and ended up circling the ranch. He left a note and took his backpack, so it wasn't like he was planning on disappearing." Damn it, that defensive tone was back. He shut up before he did any more damage.

"I found his backpack halfway, just about where you'd expect he'd lose it if he'd gone off course the way Tuck said." Eli picked up the tale. He told the lie so smoothly he must have been practicing it. "He ain't the suicidal kind—he's too tough. But Chastain-stubborn—he'd be just the kind to keep walking instead of setting down and waiting 'til dawn so he could see where he was goin'."

Castellano looked from one to the other, then sighed and said, "You two talk a good game. I'm not convinced, but I'll play it your way, for now, under one condition. You get him in to see a good psychiatrist or psychologist. Whatever he planned to do, he did it because he's depressed, and that's not good. The anorexia worries me. How long ago did he go through rehab for the heroin? Those track marks are a dead giveaway."

"A few months."

Shaking his head, Jack said, "He should be doing better than he is. None of the marks are fresh, so it's not that he's relapsed, but his health should be better. That's another thing therapy needs to address.

Are you sure you want to stick to your story? He'd be better off in the hospital."

"No," Tuck said with a shudder. "He's a Chastain. We don't do so good corralled."

The doctor eyed him doubtfully, then said, "Well, I'm going to talk to him anyway before I release him, and I'll make up my own mind as to what I'm going to recommend."

"When can we see him?" Eli asked.

"As soon as I get some answers for this official piece of red tape," Castellano waved the clipboard.

"What are we waiting for?" Tuck gestured at a chair. "Siddown and ask away, and make it snappy. I want to see my nephew."

Chapter 10

JOSHUA lay quietly, eyes closed, listening to the beeps and whines and rustling inside the hospital room. He'd spent enough time in one recently to recognize the sounds without having to open his eyes, and he didn't want to, anyway. His head pounded like the worst migraine ever, the throb against his temples making him feel sick. He didn't feel like he needed to vomit, though, which was good. He'd done that once already, spilling bile onto the dust of the desert, which sucked it up almost as fast as it hit. That was maybe half an hour before his vision had gone blurry and he'd stumbled into the ravine or gully or whatever the hell it was. He only knew that it hurt like hell when he fell, and he was pretty sure he'd messed up a knee. Then, he hadn't cared so much. It didn't really matter.

Now—yeah, it hurt like a bitch.

He wondered vaguely how they'd found him; he was pretty sure he'd put at least a dozen miles between himself and the ranch. The ranch didn't have any dogs, but he supposed they could have borrowed someone else's to track him, once they'd figured out he wasn't on the road to town. Neither his uncle nor his foreman were stupid, which was why he'd made it look like he'd taken the backpack by stashing it in the stall. He never wrote anyone off as stupid—even the dumbest motherfuckers could pull a fast one on you if you went underestimating them. His misdirection would only slow them down for a while, but that would have given time for the desert to work.

Love, Like Water

He should have known that someone would figure it out.

Hands shifted him on the bed, stripped him efficiently, and bundled him into cool cotton. Wetness bathed his knee and firm but gentle hands bandaged it up tightly. He felt a needle prick the back of his left hand and then the pull of tape as it was secured. He flinched but otherwise didn't respond. Then the pain started to ease as whatever it was in the needle took effect.

"No," he moaned, and his eyes popped open. Everything was still blurry, but it didn't stop him from trying to reach for his hand to pull out the needle. Someone caught his arm and a male voice said gently, "No, Joshua, it's fine. It's just a pain reliever, not anything bad. We've got it under control."

Blinking, he tried to focus on the man standing over him. There was a sea of white, then the brown of skin and hair. "I'm Dr. Castellano, and you're at the Miller Trauma Center. You've got quite a case of heatstroke, and you're going to be sick for a while. Does your head hurt?"

"Yes," Joshua rasped. "Blurry."

"Yes, that's not unusual. It should clear up. Do you feel nauseous?"

"Queasy." A deep breath, and Joshua went on, "More from the headache. I threw up—before. Thirsty."

"No doubt. We've got you on a saline drip, but if you don't think you'll vomit, we can give you some water. It's going to taste weird—it's got electrolytes in it, but you need those. You were pretty dehydrated."

Joshua nodded, and his head warned him not to do that again.

Someone else brought over a cup with a straw in it and put the straw to Joshua's mouth; he didn't care that it tasted funky, he slurped up the entire cupful. "More."

"In a minute. Let's wait for your stomach to adjust to that first."

Joshua closed his eyes again. The light bothered him, but the blurriness bothered him worse. "Who found me?"

"Eli Kelly." The way he said the name sounded like the doctor knew him. "He called for the State Police helicopter. He's here, rode in with you. Your uncle's here, too. I'm going to go down to the waiting room to talk to them, and then when I'm done, they'll be in to see you. Anything you want me to tell them?"

"No."

"Okay." The doctor hesitated, then said, "I imagine that your uncle is worried sick about you—I know I'd be, in his place. I don't know what happened, but remember that."

I think I died. Joshua didn't speak. The doctor sighed and Joshua heard the door close behind him.

I think I died. Once thought, the phrase kept repeating itself over and over in his head, keeping counterpoint to the throbbing of the headache. The headache was easing, helped by whatever it was in the IV, but the thought was still steady. He wasn't sure how he felt about dying. It had, after all, been his plan when he'd left before dawn this morning. But if he had, why had he come back? Or had he only imagined he'd died? There wasn't any long tunnel, or bright light, but he'd never believed in that crap, anyway. There was just darkness and a voice.

Mijo.

That had been his grandfather's word, the common contraction of *mi hijo*, my son, my boy. 'Chete had used it, but in a snarky, condescending way. It never had the overtone of love that Abuelito's voice had. It never had the hint of sadness Abuelito's did when Joshua had done something wrong. Not condemnation, never condemnation. Just sadness, which made Joshua want to do better. This voice had that—love, and sadness. *Mijo. Mijo bonito. Mijo valiente.*

That was why he thought he had died—because no one else loved him like that. No other man, anyway, and it was definitely a man's voice. It had brought him back from that edge of darkness, kept him from the quiet and peace he'd been looking for. If it was Abuelito, then that meant *he* didn't want Joshua to die. So there must be a reason for him to go on.

Love, Like Water

He took a long, deep breath. The air conditioning felt cool and dry in his lungs and he was thirsty again. Opening his eyes, he looked for the water and instead met the startled expression of his uncle. "Uncle Tuck," he rasped.

"Josh! Thank God you're okay! I was worrit sick. That was damn silly, walking off like that—if you'd really wanted to leave, you shoulda just said so. I'da driven you to Miller myself." Tuck cast a glance over Joshua toward the door. "No sense you going off and getting lost like that." He looked back at Joshua, his eyes intent, as if trying to send a message....

Oh. That was how he wanted to play it. The doctor had probably threatened Uncle Tucker with Josh's commitment or something. He'd only just gotten *out* of the hospital—he wasn't eager to head back in. "No," he agreed. "I'm sorry, Uncle Tucker. I guess I wasn't thinking straight. Stupid to get lost like that."

A chuff of exasperation sounded over by the door, and Joshua glanced over to see Dr. Castellano leaning against the doorframe, his arms folded across his chest. He said nothing, though, just eyed Joshua skeptically.

Joshua said, "Can you hand me the water, Uncle Tucker?"

"Oh, sure." Happy to have something to do other than stand there looking uncomfortable, his uncle obliged. Once Joshua had finished, Tucker took the cup and set it on the tray table, so it would be in easy reach. Then he sat down gingerly on the edge of Joshua's bed and waited until the doctor left. "Okay," he said in a low voice, "let's cut to the chase. What the deuce were you thinkin', Josh? Was living on the ranch *that* bad?"

"It had nothing to do with the ranch, Uncle Tucker."

"Then that fight with Eli. There *was* a fight, wasn't there?"

Startled, Joshua blinked. "Fight? There wasn't any fight. Kelly's been fine."

"But something musta happened in the barn yesterday. You were all upset over it."

The barn. Standing so close to Eli that he could smell the man, the sweat and sweet musty scent of hay and grass. The way the man's eyes had darkened as Joshua met them. The way his mouth had softened from its usual wry smile. The intensity of his expression. Joshua had put his hand on his shoulder and felt the heat of his body, the strong muscles beneath the worn cotton of his shirt. Wondered briefly how it would feel without the cotton. Wondered how he would taste, what it would be like to lie down with that strong, hard body beside him, around him, in him. He hadn't dared take a lover during his three years on assignment, and the sudden shock of his desire for Eli had shaken Joshua. So he'd run. "There wasn't anything," he said dully. "We just talked. He's... he's a good man, Uncle Tucker. He belongs here. Just kind of reminded me that I don't."

"That's baloney, Josh. You ain't been here long enough to know whether you belong or don't belong. You ain't had time to find a place. Besides, I need you here. I got more work than I know what to do with, and just yesterday a ranch up near Boulder called because they got a problem horse they need to deal with—and I tole them there aren't any problem horses, there're only troubled horses. But troubled horses take work. So they want me up there next week, and I got paperwork coming out the wazoo. It sure would help if you could take on some of that."

"I don't know anything about running a ranch," Joshua said.

"I know you don't, son. We've got a week to get you up to speed." Tucker rubbed his forehead, and Joshua realized he didn't have his hat. "I hope you're out of here quick."

"Where's your hat?"

"What? Oh, Eli's got it down in the waiting room."

"Eli's here?"

"Well, sure. He rode the copter in with you." Right, the doctor had said that. Joshua cursed his aching head. He shouldn't have forgotten that. A stupid mistake like that could cost.... He stopped, took a deep breath. It didn't matter. He didn't need to watch every move anymore. It was okay for him to forget things. He closed his eyes. "Sorry," he said. "The doctor said that—I just forgot."

"It's okay, Josh. You've had a rough day."

"Not as rough as you. I'm really sorry, Uncle Tucker."

"No, you ain't, not yet." There was a note of amusement in Tucker's voice, and for some reason that reassured Joshua. "But that's okay. I'm just glad you're okay, Josh. You may not realize it, but I'm really glad you're here. Maybe I ain't been paying enough attention to you. Maybe I'm doing something wrong." He held up a hand and Joshua, who was about to argue, fell silent. "I'm better with horses than I am with people—that's part of the reason your ma and I fell out all those years ago. I thought she needed to come home so I could take care of her. She needed the independence I couldn't give her. It worked out okay—you and Cathy are good kids, strong kids. But I'm ornery, and stubborn, and I want my way too much. So if I stomp on your toes, you let me know it, and I'll back off. Just don't...." He took a deep breath. "Just don't walk away without talking to me."

Tears pricked the back of Joshua's eyes. Fuck, he hadn't cried in years and wasn't about to start now. "I won't," he promised.

Tucker took the hand without the IV in it and held it between both of his. "See you don't," he said roughly and squeezed.

WHEN Tucker came back into the waiting room a half hour later, he looked wrecked. Eli handed him his hat without a word and waited while his boss sat down in one of the chairs. Finally Tuck looked up and said, "We talked. He says he won't do anything like this again."

"I'm glad," Eli said simply. "How is he feeling?"

"Groggy. Has a bad headache and eyestrain, I guess. They're waiting for the tests on his liver and kidneys to come back, but he's gone to sleep. Jack says he'll probably sleep through the rest of the day and I should come back for evening visiting hours." He looked up at Eli with bloodshot eyes. "He's my sister's only boy, Eli. Closest thing I have to a son of my own. And I nearly lost him. Just got my sister back, and I'da lost her, too. I owe you, son. I owe you big time."

"You don't owe me anything, Tuck. I'm just glad I found him, and I hope he'll be okay. But I been thinkin', while I was waiting here for you. Jack's right—he probably needs a shrink. He's probably got a lot of bullcrap in his head from that assignment of his to go along with the tattoos Jack told us about. But it's more than that." Eli scratched the back of his neck. "Remember Roscoe?"

"Roscoe?"

"Yeah, that rescue pony that gave us all that shit a couple years back."

"Oh, hell, of course I remember that little bastard. I think I still got scars from him. What about him?"

All the thinking Eli had been avoiding during that hellish search for Joshua had gone gangbusters while Tucker was up with his nephew. For a while it had gone in circles, but then somehow the word "Roscoe" popped up, and gave the thoughts a focus, though he hadn't thought of the bad-tempered little quarter horse in years. "Well, I was thinking about what a little shit he was, always biting the other horses—"

"And trainers," Tucker interjected.

"—And trainers," Eli agreed. "And fighting, and kicking the stalls down. And how after he'd recovered and we started to work with him, how he calmed down so much once he was tacked up. I mean, I ain't never seen anything like the way that little shit just *stopped* the minute I picked up his bridle. It was eerie, the way he stared at that thing and stood so patient while I put it on. And how once I was in the saddle, he was as good as gold. Hell, he was one of the best cutting horses I've ever worked with. But the minute you turned him loose, he was that rotten little bastard of a horse again."

"Yeah, I remember. We used to take turns with him, wearing him out so he'd be too tired to cause trouble."

"Fact of the matter is, some animals don't mind boredom, and some do. I expect young Joshua is one of the kind that does."

Love, Like Water

"'Young Joshua'—you talk like he's a kid and you're an old graybeard," Tucker snorted. "He's what, five years younger than you?"

"Something like that. But that ain't the point. The point is that we been going about this all wrong, letting him relax and not putting him to work 'til he's recovered. We been talking about it, but we kinda dropped the ball—it's easier to just do and forget that he's there. He don't need time, Tuck. He don't need leisure. He needs something to *do*. Give him time, and all he does is brood. That don't do a single soul any good. You talked about how he did this and that and was the youngest and finished things early—that ain't the kind of man who likes to sit on a porch and stare at the sky. That's a man who needs a goal. Who needs work. And real work, not babysitting a caged cat."

"Someone like you," Tucker said.

Eli snorted. "I ain't got half the brains that boy has—that's why I'm so easygoing. I'm happy on the porch when the time is right, but when it's time to work, I'm happy then too. But I ain't the one with the trouble hanging over his head."

"True." Tucker sat back, and Eli was relieved to see some of the strain leave his face.

"So, I guess we'll head home, and you'll come back tonight after supper?"

"That's the plan." Tucker stood up, put his hat on, and looked down at Eli. "Figure I'll bring him supper—has to be better for him than hospital food. Then maybe I'll talk to him about what my expectations are. I mean, if he's gonna be working for me, best I know what his skills are and best he know what I want out of him, right?"

"Just like any other employee," Eli agreed. He got to his feet and followed Tucker out of the room.

Chapter 11

"Can I see him?" Eli asked.

Jack Castellano glanced up from his perusal of the clipboard and eyed the soft-sided cooler case Eli carried. "You can go in, but he's asleep."

"Still? It's been two days."

"He'll be sleeping a lot for the next few days. His body has a lot to recover from, and he wasn't in great shape when he walked out into that desert."

"You didn't give him any of that morphine stuff, did you?"

"No." Jack gave him a level look. "We're not stupid, Eli. We know what those scars mean. He's not getting any opioid painkillers. I don't expect he'll need them. He seems to be mostly exhausted and dehydrated, and while he'll be uncomfortable for a few days, he shouldn't be in actual pain. As for sleeping—he'll probably do a lot of that on his own, but if he is having trouble, we do have alternatives for that."

"Thanks. I just… he's kinda fragile."

"Eli Kelly, savior of horses and ex-FBI agents." Jack's grin was affectionate, and he patted Eli's arm gently. "Careful, Eli. He's not your average mustang."

"He's Tuck's nephew. Gotta keep an eye on family."

"Mm hmm," Jack said, and patted Eli's arm again.

Love, Like Water

JOSH'S black hair was stark against the white pillowcase, and despite the sunburn, his face was kind of pasty. He had a couple of IVs going into him: saline, Eli supposed, for the dehydration, and maybe glucose or something to keep his blood sugar up. Eli remembered that about treatment for heatstroke, but not much else. The burn wasn't bad enough for more than ointment, and the white streaks still lingered on his cheeks and nose. Joshua had that tawny skin that didn't burn easily, and the sun had only been up a couple hours when Eli had found him. They'd been lucky it hadn't reached its full, killing power before then. Bad enough as it was.

The only thing they were waiting on now was the results of the blood tests, to see if he'd been dehydrated long enough for his kidneys and liver to be affected. Joshua might as well sleep. Eli set the cooler on the bedside table, pulled up the chair beside the bed, and used a tissue from the box on the nightstand to wipe up a useless blob of ointment from the side of Josh's nose.

Tucker had come back here as promised last night, but Josh hadn't eaten more than a few bites of the dinner he'd brought. Tuck had said Jack had told him that was normal, that he wouldn't have much of an appetite for a day or two, and to try again in a few days. "In a few days" seemed to be a mantra around here, as if everything that was wrong with Josh would be fixed in a few days. Eli was a patient man, always had been, but he was getting pretty damn frustrated with the "in a few days" chant. He wanted the boy well and out of here now, not in a few days.

But Jack was right about the appetite. According to Graciela, the floor nurse, Josh had barely tasted the oatmeal and Jell-O they'd served him for breakfast. Of course, oatmeal and Jell-O were a far cry from the protein-heavy breakfasts Sarafina put out, but Eli figured Josh never ate a lot of that either. That was part of Josh's problem to begin with. Boy didn't eat enough to keep a kitten alive.

Eli balled up the tissue in one hand, and with the other, reached over to straighten the sheet over Joshua's chest. He was so fragile. So thin. So beautiful, even with the sunburn and the ointment and the hollows under his eyes. His chin and eyebrows and nose were too strong for those frail bones; once he'd filled out, he'd be too beautiful for Eli to bear. Eli hoped that the shrink or whoever they ended up getting to help Joshua could—Eli knew what to do about broken horses, but broken men were another story. He didn't want Joshua broken. He wanted Joshua whole and healthy, and…. Shit. He just wanted Joshua.

Where the hell had that come from? Sure he'd always thought Josh attractive, despite his obvious health issues. He thought he had a pretty, if rare, smile, beautiful eyes. But it wasn't until the moment before Josh had fled from him in the barn, that moment when they'd stood close, hands on each other, that he'd realized he didn't just admire Josh's looks but felt something as well. Had Joshua seen that? Had that been what had sent Joshua fleeing into the house, and later, into the desert?

He tossed the tissue into the little trashcan and raked both hands through his hair, sitting with his elbows on his knees and his head down, as if his hands in his hair were holding him in place. Damn.

"What are you doing here?" Josh's voice was raspy and thin.

Eli schooled his features before looking up. "Sarafina sent some lunch. Figured you'd be hungry after the various varieties of cardboard they serve for breakfast here."

"Various varieties?"

"Yup. A veritable variety of various varieties."

The corner of Joshua's mouth twitched, but then he closed his eyes. "Not hungry."

"Uh-huh." Eli unzipped the cooler and took out the thermos. He opened it and held it under Joshua's long nose. The nostrils twitched, then flared as he breathed in the scent. Eli chuckled.

Joshua's eyes opened. *"Sopa de salchichón?"*

Love, Like Water

Grinning, Eli unpacked the cooler bag, setting the thermos on the table alongside the stoneware soup bowls and plates. Sarafina had made enough soup to feed two people, as well as plenty of chorizo sausage and potatoes mixed with peppers and onions, which Eli dished out onto the plates. It smelled fantastic.

"Yeah, Sara called your mama and got the recipe. She figured maybe it would get your appetite going. I'm gonna raise your bed up so you can eat, okay?"

Joshua shrugged, but he was looking at the food, which Eli took as a good sign. He didn't say anything else, so Eli said, "Tuck talked to your mama last night to let her know what was going on and that you were okay. She wanted to fly out right away but Tuck told her not to worry. He asked me to ask you if you want her to come out."

"No. She doesn't need to. I'm fine."

"That's what Tuck told her. Said you went for a walk and got lost and got a bit of heatstroke. That the hospital was only keeping you for observation on accounta you're still poorly."

Joshua's lips twisted, but he said nothing, just picked up the spoon and dipped it into the bowl of soup on the table in front of him. "Good?" Eli asked. Joshua nodded.

THE soup was good, the sausage nice and garlicky the way he liked it, and the squash and peppers not too mushy. Joshua stirred the contents of the bowl, listening to Eli talk, that soft, faintly rumbling voice that didn't have to actually be saying anything pertinent to make Joshua feel comfortable and secure. Right now he was talking about the other trainers on the ranch, and how Uncle Tucker wanted to expand the training facilities, maybe set up a year-round school of sorts…. It didn't matter what he was talking about, it was just nice to listen to.

He tasted the soup again, then tried a forkful of the potatoes. He wasn't really hungry, but everything smelled like Abuela's house. He could almost hear her in the kitchen, with the Spanish-language radio station playing softly in the background. She would have liked Eli,

Joshua thought, would have been pleased with his gentle courtesy and strength. He doubted he himself would have impressed her much nowadays—weak, foolish, cowardly. His eyes stung a moment and he took a bite of chorizo to mask the sensation.

Eli was talking now about Sarafina's Jesse, and how the school bus had broken down twenty miles from Miller—meaningless gossip, really, but the patient, easy voice, the same voice he used to talk to the horses, was so restful that Joshua didn't care what he talked about. He could have read the phone book and Joshua would have liked it. Then he thought of something. "Is Jesse Uncle Tucker's?"

The voice stopped, and Joshua looked up from his soup to see Eli blinking at him. "Tuck's? Jesse? Oh, hell no. Sarafina's got a husband. Works for the casino, the Hard Rock, up outside of Albuquerque. They're Isleta Pueblo. She lived there 'til Jesse was three or four, then decided she missed the ranch and came here." He thought a moment, then added, "I think Tuck thinks of Jesse as his, though. Goes to all his school stuff and all."

"I like Jesse," Joshua said, and went back to eating.

Eli talked about Jesse for a while, then moved on to some of the trainers they'd worked with in the past, then on to… something else. After a while, his voice stopped, and Joshua looked up. He was staring at the place setting in front of Joshua.

"What?" Joshua asked, then looked. Both plate and bowl were empty. When he glanced at Eli, the man was grinning.

"You et it all, son," Eli said. "Betcha didn't even realize it."

"I… I didn't. It was good," Joshua said lamely, then pushed the dishes away.

"I'll tell Sarafina you liked it. I liked it too—maybe she'll put it on the menu."

"That would be good." Joshua watched as Eli carefully wrapped the dirty dishes and put them in the carrier.

"You want Tuck to bring you dessert with supper tonight?"

"Are you guys going to be bringing all my meals?"

Love, Like Water

"Nah. You gotta live through breakfast. But breakfast won't kill ya. What they serve for lunch and dinner might." Again the grin.

"Okay. Thanks." Joshua thought, then added, "Tell Sarafina thanks, too."

Eli touched his forehead, then picked up the cooler bag, put his hat on, and left.

HIS uncle brought supper—this time red beans and rice. Joshua had slept most of the afternoon, and didn't think he'd be hungry, but the minute Tucker opened the insulated dish and he smelled the onion and peppers, his stomach growled. Tucker laughed. "Sounds like a part of you is feeling better, anyway. Eli says you ate all your lunch and woulda ate his too, if he hadn't scarfed it down before you could."

"I'm surprised he ate at all. He never stopped talking."

"Eli?" Tucker's bushy eyebrows went up. "Eli Kelly?"

"I think he thought he was entertaining me."

"Was he?"

Joshua thought a moment. "Yeah, I guess he was."

"He's a good man, Eli."

"Saved my life, I guess."

"You guess right." Tucker dished out the beans and rice and handed Joshua a spoon. "Couldn't run the ranch without him. If I expand like I want to, I'm gonna need him. Gonna need you, too, to run the business end. When you come home, we're gonna have to start working on that."

"Why do you want to expand the ranch?" Joshua asked. He scooped a big spoonful of the beans and rice into his mouth and closed his eyes in bliss.

Tucker snorted. "Well, don't know that I do, really. But I got more work than I can handle, and with some of the other ranchers getting out of the mustang roundups, I'll have even more than that. And the movie companies are doing more fantasy films, and need horses that do more than just stop and start on command." He sighed. "And then there's the rodeo stuff. And frankly, there are a lot more people buying horses that they can't handle, and then when they've ruined 'em, they want me to fix 'em. Or they dump them somewhere and the ASPCA comes to me. So yeah, I got more work." Tuck stuck a second spoon in the bowl and took a mouthful. "Hm. Good. I'm thinking of moving the higher end training—the film stuff and the private training—to the Rocking J, under a manager, and keeping the mustangs and the rescue operation here. Anyway, the Rocking J still has some decent buildings I can use, and more importantly, water. There's a good spring-fed pond on the property. So even if the worst happens, and the Galiano dries up, there's still a source of water." Tucker shook his head. "It's never happened before since the river comes from runoff in the mountains, and so far there's been enough snow—but the Triple C relies on the creeks from the Galiano, and I don't care what people say, the climate's changing and we're getting longer and longer droughts. Might not get a lot of snow someday. Might come a time when the whole operation depends on that pond."

Joshua ate slowly, thinking. He'd grown up in urban areas close to water, first Chicago, then Cincinnati. There'd never been any question about the ready availability of water, not when you had lakes and rivers practically outside your door. It hadn't been 'til he'd been out in the desert that he'd realized what it meant to be really thirsty.

It wasn't just the thirst. Even in the predawn hours, stumbling out over the dusty, rocky terrain, he'd felt the perspiration drying as soon as it formed, felt his face and lips tightening as the moisture was sucked out. He'd felt the dust settling on his skin as his feet stirred it up. The farther he got from the ranch and its water, the more desiccated he felt, and with every step the dryness leached the energy from his muscles. By the time he'd stumbled into that gully, he'd felt barely more than a husk, and wondered why the dry desert wind hadn't blown him away.

Tucker had been talking, and Joshua zeroed in on something he had said while Joshua was thinking. "So if you're going to spend more time with the high-end training, what about the mustangs and the rescue animals?"

Love, Like Water

His uncle paused in his diatribe about bank finance practices. "Oh. Right. Well, that'll be Eli's bailiwick. He's got more patience with animals than people, and half of the commissioned stuff is dealing with people. It's why he's better at training animals, and I'm better with training the trainers. There are a couple of guys on staff that are like that—the others I'll use on the Rocking J."

"Sounds like you have it all figured out."

"I do, if it happens. But if it does happen—tomorrow or two years from now—I'm gonna need someone I trust to manage the books and scheduling and stuff. Not just an office manager. Hell, I can get one of those anywhere. But someone who'll be able to do projections and estimates, and see the future of the ranch, the way I do. I need you, Joshua. I need someone who'll be as committed to the Triple C as I am. Can you be that?"

There was a cold knot in the middle of Joshua's chest. "I don't know, Uncle Tuck. Maybe someday I'd decide to go back into law enforcement. Or, or something else. Maybe I'll hate working on the ranch. Maybe...."

"Maybe, maybe, maybe. Maybe the Mayans just got the date wrong and we'll all go up in smoke next Tuesday. Maybe I won't be able to buy the property 'cause the Department of Buying Property They Ain't Never Gonna Use buys it first. I ain't asking you to decide right this second. I'm asking if you can be the kinda guy I need. Are you willing to give it a try?"

The knot eased a little, and for the first time in a long time, Joshua saw a future. Not the future, but a future. Possibilities. Nothing too demanding, nothing that would require his soul, that dry, shriveled thing, but a job, a future, a something to keep the dark at bay.

"I'm willing," he heard himself say, and the dark, cold, heavy weight of the knot vanished.

Chapter 12

"We've got four trucks that belong to the ranch, my Silverado, two F-450s and the F-150 Elian drives," Tucker said. "The Forester is Sarafina's, but we cover the insurance on that, too." He clicked open the spreadsheet he'd been using to track payments. "We been paying the premiums monthly, but I'm thinking you might be able to negotiate a better rate if we paid 'em quarterly or twice a year instead. Been meaning to get to that, but something always comes up."

"Something outdoors, working with the horses, you mean," Joshua asked dryly.

Tucker didn't even try to hide his grin. "I hate this shit," he admitted. "But I figured with your book learnin'...."

"Jesus, Uncle Tuck, you sound like every stereotypical cowboy in every movie I've ever seen. Do you practice talking like that?"

Laughing, Tuck shook his head. "Your granddad *was* the stereotypical cowboy—guess I picked up a lot of that from him. 'Course in his day, that was how everyone talked. You still get a lot of us old coots out here slinging that lingo."

"Eli's practically my age and he talks like it too. Maybe not so much, but still."

"Eli's been working on ranches since he was old enough to walk. He can't help it. Though he did go to college and likes to throw big words into the conversation every now and again."

Love, Like Water

"What did he study?"

"Animal husbandry, like me. Which sounds kinda kinky, but ain't. He thought about vet school, but it was a lot more school than he wanted to deal with. He got a certificate, though." Tucker shook his head. "Gotta have a degree or certificate for everything these days, seems like. At any rate, it comes in handy when dealing with government stuff. He's a smart boy, Eli. People think that cuz he's slow moving he's stupid. Nothing stupid about him."

"I don't think he's stupid," Joshua said.

The look his uncle gave him was thoughtful. Joshua thought maybe he saw more than Joshua wanted him to, but he only said, "We pay the insurance on Ramon's and Manolo's trucks too—they live here in the bunkhouse and use the trucks for ranch business. Those are these two, here. Everyone else, both the guys who live on-site and the ones who live in Miller, pays for their own expenses. So don't ask them to use their own vehicles for ranch business—they can use ours. We're insured for it. So that's seven vehicles we insure and four we own...."

Joshua listened to his uncle explain his new job—managing the ranch office. He'd been surprised when this morning, the first morning he'd been home after six days in the hospital, his uncle had woken him up at 6:00 a.m. and dragged him out into the kitchen to eat breakfast with the six live-in ranch hands, Jesse, Eli, and Tucker himself. Then he'd sat Joshua down in the office in front of the computer and had been working with him for the last three hours.

Joshua's stomach growled and his uncle looked at the clock on the computer screen. "Eleven thirty," he said. "Think you can hang on until noon for dinner?"

"I guess," Joshua said. The fact that he was hungry still surprised him. It had been a long time since he had actually been hungry. Even before his walk in the desert, he hadn't had much of an appetite. The lunch and supper Tuck and Eli had smuggled into the hospital while the nurses and doctors turned a blind eye had been so incredibly good after the hospital dreck that Joshua had found his appetite again.

He'd talked with the hospital's psychiatrist, too, and while he didn't admit that his "getting lost" was deliberate, he did finally admit to himself at least that it was probably a good idea to have someone to talk to occasionally—who wasn't a family member, or fellow ranch employee, or.... Or what? What was Elian Kelly, anyway? Object of unrequited lust? Or was it just a mild attraction that Joshua's mental state, and three years without sex, had inflated to a larger desire?

He wasn't sure at this point if he knew what to do anymore, even if there was the vaguest possibility that a dyed-in-the-wool cowboy like Elian was the slightest bit gay.

He certainly didn't ping on Joshua's radar. Joshua had had boyfriends in high school (covert), and college (overt), and the academy (back to being covert), not to mention the pickups that were part and parcel of any gay man's social life, but there had never been any question as to the other man's interest. Usually, they picked *him* up. Even before his undercover assignment, he couldn't remember the last time he'd had to make the first move, and he couldn't remember *ever* being attracted to someone he didn't know for sure was interested. He couldn't read Eli at all.

But he was attracted to him. There was no question about that.

In his brief conversations with the shrink, he'd come to realize that his fear of being rejected—of being hurt, traumatized, damaged the way 'Chete had damaged him—had triggered that last, horrible nightmare, and the resultant "escape plan," as he'd described it to the shrink. It was an escape plan, of sorts, an escape from the nightmares, from the endless emotional, if not physical (and it was terribly physical too), desire for the heroin, from the feelings of worthlessness and despair. From the fear of being outed in this macho environment, from the fear of being rejected by his uncle, from the fear of being rejected, despised, maybe even physically assaulted, by Eli. He shook his head at the thought. Maybe by one of the other ranch hands—or by all of them—but he couldn't see slow-moving, soft-spoken, gentle Eli being the one to do it.

"… follow?" Tucker had kept talking while Joshua was thinking.

Love, Like Water

It only took a quick mental rewind for Joshua to catch up. "Yeah. The plates are all registered at the same time every year. Does the ranch pay for Manolo's and Ramon's registrations too?"

"Nope." Tuck went on talking, and Joshua went on thinking.

The stay in the hospital had done him some good, he thought. He might have kept his intentions secret from the shrink—though he wondered if he'd really hid as much as he thought he had—but the rest of the staff had taken his condition in stride. He'd expected to get sideways glances about the needle marks in his arms or the obvious malnutrition, or the gang tats he wore, but nobody seemed bothered by any of it. The nutritionist had stopped by to quiz him about his eating habits (or the lack thereof), and to recommend various vitamins and supplements; the phlebotomist came by again to do more blood tests, probably to confirm that he didn't have HIV or AIDS from the needles; the shrink gave him a list of recommended psychologists in Albuquerque and Roswell, the two biggest cities near the ranch; and Dr. Castellano talked to him about follow-ups to confirm that he didn't have any lingering damage to his kidneys or liver from the heatstroke and dehydration. The headache eased up after a couple of days, for which he was grateful, but the doctors didn't let him leave for nearly a week, until his vision cleared up, the sporadic dizziness disappeared, and he'd been able to walk easily across the room. He still had to go in for checkups weekly until everyone was positive he was okay, and Castellano had given him an ultimatum about gaining weight. Everyone was friendly and easy with him. It was so different from what he'd experienced in rehab—everyone tense and obsessive and anal, watching him and the other addicts like hawks. It had been the best rehab facility that the Bureau could find. Robinson was grateful enough for Joshua's achievements that he'd pulled every string he could reach to get him where he had the best chance of recovery. Yeah, they'd done the physical detox to get the chemical out of his system, and he'd refused any programs that involved other drugs like methadone. He was determined to be done with the drugs. But they'd still watched him.

Tuck watched him too—not like he was suspicious, but like he was afraid, like if he took his eyes off Joshua for a moment something bad would happen. Well, he was right, wasn't he? He'd left Joshua alone for one night and Joshua'd nearly died. Not that that was Tuck's fault.

He hadn't seen much of Eli since he'd come home last night. Tucker had picked him up, but it had been after supper and the hands had all turned in by the time they got home. He'd seen him briefly at breakfast, and Eli had given him one of his slow smiles and a "Welcome home, Joshua," but that had been the extent of it. He'd visited Joshua in the hospital a couple of times, bringing lunch or supper and talking randomly to fill Joshua's silences, and each time he'd left, he'd put his hand on Joshua's and said in his soft voice, "Y'all feel better and come home to us soon," and Joshua had felt the warmth of caring in that small gesture.

The only thing that bothered Joshua about Eli's visits was when Dr. Castellano came in in the middle of one. They seemed to be friends, but Joshua caught an undertone he wasn't sure he liked. Was Eli's smile just a bit warmer when he looked at the doctor? When the doctor passed Eli's chair, he'd pat his shoulder briefly—what did that signify? Did they have a history? Was Eli gay after all but involved with the doctor? Was Joshua hallucinating? Or simply paranoid? Or jealous that a stranger could touch Eli so casually while he was terrified of doing the same thing?

"… Eli."

Joshua blinked. What? He'd lost the thread of Tuck's monologue. That *never* happened. He broke into a sweat, thinking about what could have happened if he'd done that during his assignment. "What?" he gasped.

"Hey, calm down!" Tucker put his hand on Joshua's shoulder. "It's okay—Lord knows I've let my wits go wandering when someone's talking before. It's okay. I was just saying that this afternoon, after dinner"—Joshua couldn't get used to the way some people out here called it "dinner" instead of "lunch"—"Eli's gonna take you around the ranch, show you where everything is, maybe get you up on one of the critters and see how much you remember about riding. Nothing real stressful, but we want to get you up to speed with how the

Love, Like Water

ranch runs. I want you to work some with the hands, too, and the horses. Your granddad started teaching you, and I'd like to see if any of that stuck."

The entire afternoon with Eli? Joshua's appetite vanished.

IT CAME back gangbusters when they sat down at the big table in the kitchen, though, and Sarafina set an enormous sandwich in front of him, dripping with red and green chile. He'd been startled at first by the penchant for putting chile sauce on everything that was apparently a New Mexican thing; the first morning he'd eaten breakfast at the table, Sarafina had asked him, "Red or green?" and he hadn't the vaguest idea what she was talking about. The food he'd gotten on the tray in his room when he'd first arrived there hadn't had any chile on it at all. Sarafina said she had been giving him "sick people food" and now that he was well enough to sit at the table, he was well enough to enjoy the chile. It had taken him a few days, but he liked it fine now, though he'd promised to make her some of the other signature dishes of the Puerto Rican culture he'd grown up in.

He was halfway through the sandwich when Eli came in, doffed his gray felt cowboy hat, and sat across from him. "Just red today, Sara," Eli said. "I'm in a purist kind of mood."

Sarafina laughed and served up his sandwich. "Why are you late?"

"Cleaning out the damn cat kennel. God, that shit stinks."

Joshua laughed, which surprised himself, as well as the rest of the hands at the table. "Sorry—it's just funny. You work around horsesh… horsecrap"—he gave Sarafina an apologetic glance—"and you think cat poop stinks?"

"Well, it does," Eli said reasonably. "But the vet says he can probably be let out today. Thought you might like to do the honors, seeing as how you were the one to suggest locking him up."

"Okay," Joshua said.

"Then I figure we can saddle up Avery and ride around the ranch some. Let you see what you're gonna be managing the books for. Avery's a nice easy ride, so no worries about that."

"Avery's a slug," Jesse said with a grin. "Don't plan on going faster than a walk, unless his feed bag's at the other end of the trip."

"Sounds about my speed. Have you named the cat yet?" Joshua turned to Tucker. "Or did the ASPCA have a name for it?"

"Name the cat? What for?"

"Don't you name cats around here?"

Tucker shook his head. "We've got about half a dozen barn cats, but none of them have names."

"This one's not a barn cat."

"True, but the barn cats have been visitin'," Eli said. "They're pretty curious about why he's in a cage. The vet checked him out and said he's been fixed, so we don't have to worry about any long-haired kittens showing up in a couple months, but I dunno if he's gonna want to stay out there with the horse."

"Then the horse will have to get used to it," Joshua said. "And if he wants to be a house cat...."

There were blank stares around the table. "What? Haven't you people heard of house cats before?"

"Yes, but I don't think I have ever actually known anyone who has one," Sarafina mused. "There was a woman on the pueblo when I was growing up that had several cats that came inside to be fed, but they lived outside. Cats have fleas."

"So do dogs, and people let them indoors."

"If you want to have the cat indoors, son, you have the cat indoors. But let's see what it wants, first. Might be it likes the barn."

"The vet did suggest we shave his fur—it's all matted and I reckon it's pretty hot for him," Eli said.

"Are we seriously discussing shaving a *cat*?" one of the ranch hands, Ryan, said. "Ain't they vermin?"

Love, Like Water

"They ain't vermin," Joshua growled menacingly.

Ryan threw up both hands. "Sorry, bud! I just never knew anyone actually liked 'em."

"I do like 'em," Joshua said, then realized he'd been unconsciously mimicking their dialect. He swallowed and said, "We always had a cat when I was growing up—my mom liked them. My sister used to dress them in doll clothes. That was pretty damn stupid. But they're nice creatures." He thought about the last cat his family had had before he'd left for college, a tortoiseshell calico named Tennille after some singer in the 70s his mother had liked. The cat had lived to about eighteen but died while he was away at college. He'd loved that cat.

"Cat's yours, son. Whatever you want."

"As long as you clean its litter box yourself," Eli added.

The hands laughed. Joshua smiled at Eli, who looked startled a moment, then grinned back.

Chapter 13

AVERY might have been a slug, but Josh looked nervous as he slung himself into the saddle. "It's been a few years," he said apologetically as he shifted, trying to settle himself. "I think I was eleven the last time I rode."

"You'll get back to it," Eli assured him, and mounted his own horse, Button. She was livelier than Avery, but steady, not likely to startle Josh, and patient enough with a slower pace. Once he was sure that Josh was set—he was surprised to see him holding his reins properly, in his left hand, and guessed Josh still did remember some things—he led the way out of the stable.

In the open, he drew Button back so that Josh could come up beside him, and studied his seat. "You ain't forgot much," he said. "Seat's good, you hold your reins right, and your heels are down. Good conformation. Boots comfortable?"

"Yeah. A little big, but Sarafina gave me some thick socks. Hot, though. Same with the gloves. Hot."

"You'll get used to it. Hat looks good."

Josh reached up and touched the brim of Tucker's old straw hat. "I guess. Can I ask a question?"

"Son, if you don't ask questions, it's gonna be a mighty short afternoon."

"Okay. Why don't you wear a straw hat? Most of the guys wear them or ball caps, not a felt Stetson. Isn't it hot?"

Love, Like Water

"First of all, it's a Resistol, not a Stetson, though I guess nowadays they're made by the same company. Second of all, I do wear a straw workingman's hat during the *hot* weather." He laughed at Joshua's nonplused look. "Nah, I just got used to wearing it. I've got others, but when I reach for a hat, this one's usually the one that jumps into my hand. No mystery."

"Oh, okay."

"That settled?" At Joshua's quick, shy smile, Eli felt warm all over. To hide it, he said, "All righty, then. I'm gonna take you around the main part of the ranch. We've got some remote corrals, but I won't take you out there today...."

JOSHUA followed Eli—well, rode sort of alongside him, not behind him, listening to him talk about the ranch layout, what the different outbuildings were, what the uses of the different corrals and paddocks were, where the water sources came from and why they had some fields planted with crops named "teff" and "timothy" with elaborate irrigation systems, and why they had a herd of cattle in a farther-out field. Eli was wearing his usual plaid cotton shirt, but with the sleeves rolled up, displaying wiry, muscular arms flecked with sun-blond hair. Most of the hands—like with the ball caps and straw hats—wore T-shirts or tank tops while working, but the trainers wore shirts like Eli did. He wondered how Eli's arms could be tan when he wore shirts all the time.

He'd never thought of forearms as erotic, but he hadn't reckoned on the look of the strong muscles, the glint of gold hair against the brown of Eli's tan, the flex of tendons, the strength and steadiness. He wondered what it would feel like, to have those arms holding him, how they'd feel under his own hands, maybe as Eli was braced above him, rocking into him, the blond head thrown back, his chest gleaming with sweat....

Joshua didn't say anything, but Eli caught him looking.

"Wondering why I'm wearing a long-sleeved shirt, too, right?" Eli interrupted his own monologue on windmills, and chuckled. He said, "Well, if you're working with horses that are more or less wild, you want to be careful about getting bit. Some of the mustangs we take off the plains are biters. If you're wearing a close-fitting shirt, or are bare-armed, there's nothing between you and those teeth. And while they don't actually eat meat," he gave Joshua a grin, reminding him of the joke, "those teeth *hurt* if they catch you. Better to let 'em catch your sleeve. Plus, it gets 'em used to having fabric flapping around them. Yeah, it startles 'em at first, but they get used to it. I got into the habit of wearing them and I'm used to it." The grin faded. "Plus, well, it's safer for you to be covered up some in this sun. Desert sun is hard on you, not just in the heatstroke way. We get too many cases of skin cancer out here. That's the main thing they deal with in the hospital in Miller—heatstroke and skin cancer." He indicated Joshua's own long-sleeved T-shirt. "Yeah, it's hot, but it's safer. Hats help with that, and a cowboy hat, straw or felt, protects better'n a ball cap. Ball cap don't cover your ears or your neck. Cowboys don't dress the way they do for fashion's sake, Josh. Every bit of a cowboy's tack, like a horse's tack, has its good reasons."

No, Joshua thought, *this man is not stupid.* He nodded.

"Of course," there was that slow, easy grin again, "rodeo cowboys and fancy-ass show horses kinda overdo the tack, if you ask me."

"Like those big belt buckles some of the guys wear?"

"Noticed those, didja?" Eli shot him a glance Joshua couldn't quite read. "Yeah, a couple of our guys did some time on the rodeo circuit. Had to break them of a few bad habits."

"I thought you didn't 'break' animals."

Eli snorted. "Some of the human kind don't respond to nothing else. But they weren't too hard to whip into shape. They're just more stubborn than other kinds of critters."

Love, Like Water

"Do you plan on breaking me?" Joshua didn't know where the question came from, but once it was out he held his breath, not sure what he wanted to hear.

"Son," Eli said quietly, "broken is the last thing you need to be."

THEY hadn't said anything more on the subject. Eli had turned the conversation back to the ranch and its operations, but Eli's words and the look in his eyes when he'd said them hung around in the back of Joshua's mind over the course of the next few days. Even as Joshua focused on learning everything he possibly could about his new home, the sound of Eli's voice kept repeating in his head. The words had been kind, but Joshua knew what kindness sounded like, and this wasn't it. It was more like... tenderness. He didn't remember ever experiencing that before, certainly not from another man. He didn't know what to think about it, so he tried not to think, not to let every thought revolve around Eli, and the tenderness he'd seen in his voice and in his eyes.

It wasn't easy. The quiet, unobtrusive foreman was so thoroughly integrated into every part of the ranch that five minutes didn't go by before Tucker started another sentence with "Eli figures" or "Eli says" or "Eli's the one to ask, but...." Tucker didn't even notice it. Joshua didn't know if that was pretty normal for a foreman's role, but he'd already seen Eli's competence and his love for the ranch. Sometimes Joshua thought Tucker'd be better off leaving the Triple C to Eli—it would be in better hands.

THE days followed the same pattern Tucker had decided on—mornings with Tucker in the office, getting paperwork organized and done (Joshua thought that his uncle probably hadn't spent that much time at it in months, so teaching Joshua was killing two birds with one stone), and afternoons outside, learning the physical aspects of the ranch. He felt himself getting stronger, he tired less easily, and slept better. And his appetite improved.

Both appetites. As he put on weight and muscle and felt better, he had more energy to spend on watching and thinking about Eli.

Despite that slow, easy way he had about him, Kelly could react as quickly as any trained Bureau agent: more than once, Joshua had seen him step forward to catch the bridle of a bad-tempered mustang intent on biting one of the hands. He moved fast, but with no underlying violence—he was just suddenly *there*, taking care of what needed to be taken care of, speaking in that low, musical drawl that soothed both horse and human. He didn't talk much more than Joshua did, and in retrospect, Joshua realized how much effort he'd put into that monologue the evening he'd driven Joshua here, trying to make Joshua comfortable. He was like that with everyone, quick to diffuse the tension that inevitably erupted when men were working in close quarters, quick to turn an angry confrontation into a sensible conversation, quick to jump in and help even before being asked. Quick to make sure the ranch ran smoothly, with nothing to stress Tucker.

Joshua leaned on the fence late one afternoon, his foot in one of his new boots resting on the lower rung and his arms propped on the upper. He'd finished his chores for the afternoon—as his health improved, Tucker was giving him more physical projects, including mucking out stalls, hurray, hurray—and was taking it easy before going in for supper. Eli was working with one of the mustangs from their spring roundup; it had gone through what Joshua thought of as "basic training"—gentling and saddle-training, and simple basic behaviors. That was usually good enough for pleasure riders, and most of their mustangs were trained to that level before being sold. This one, though, was of a bunch that a ranch in Colorado wanted for cutting horses, so Tucker had Eli training him to be a cow pony.

It had been hot that day, despite it being close on fall—Tucker had told Joshua that they'd have occasional hot days clear up into October—and this horse was already gentled enough that Eli wasn't wearing his usual long-sleeved cotton shirt. Instead, he wore a black "wifebeater" sleeveless T-shirt, and a straw hat. Joshua watched him work, admiring the ropy muscles in his arms and the way the sweat-dampened shirt clung to his work-hardened chest. His arms were tanned, though not as dark as those of some of the others, like Ryan and Billy, who usually wore tank tops or those T-shirts with the sides ripped out to display their muscles, like strutting roosters. Eli wasn't interested in going for the beefcake look—his body was for work, not for show.

His muscles strained as he held the mustang back, but his outward demeanor was the same as always, calm and quiet. They were waiting while Billy opened the chute to let in a couple of calves that immediately started running around the corral looking for their mothers and lowing pathetically. Eli held the mustang still, then in a move almost too infinitesimal to see, he eased up on the reins and spoke softly, too quietly for Joshua to hear. The mustang, which had been tense and nervous at the introduction of the new variables in the corral, visibly relaxed and moved forward in response to Eli's direction.

"He's one of the best trainers I've ever worked with," Tucker said from beside Joshua.

"He's impressive," Joshua agreed.

"Think you might be interested in that?" Tucker flicked his fingers towards the pair in the corral. For a moment Joshua thought his uncle had seen through Joshua's growing infatuation with Eli, but then he realized he was talking about horse training. "I don't know that I have the knowledge or the patience for training," Joshua said.

"Well, the knowledge we can give you. The patience... that's something else again. You seem like a pretty patient guy. Can't have been easy, what you did back in Chicago."

"No." Joshua resisted the urge to run his hand over his head. Feeling the hair growing back was reassurance that the days of his bald, tattooed self were over, but it was becoming a habit. He needed to learn that he didn't need that reassurance anymore. "It wasn't easy."

"Didn't think so. Called that psychologist in Albuquerque. We got an appointment for you for Tuesday evening. Figure we'll drive in early—there's a Route 66 diner that's kind of fun. Good food, and lots of crazy-ass souvenir type crap." Tucker elbowed him. "Play tourist for a bit."

"Sure." Joshua swallowed. "The shrink—is he the one with the background in addiction?"

"Yep. The one over by the university. I'll drop you there then swing back around when you're done. There are a couple errands I can run while I'm in town. Works out pretty good."

"I can probably drive myself."

Tucker shook his head. "Nah, I gotta run the errands anyway, and this way you don't have to worry about getting lost. Or finding a parking place, which ain't easy in that part of town. There are parking garages, but they ain't obvious."

"You're driving me because you think I'm going to chicken out."

Tucker shook his head. "No, son. I don't think you'll chicken out. But I also don't reckon you'll be in the best of shape afterwards to drive home."

Joshua thought about it while he watched Eli. The foreman pulled his hat off and wiped sweat off his forehead. His blond hair had gone dark with sweat, and Joshua could see his skin shining in the late afternoon sun. Sitting so straight on that powerful horse, so thoroughly in command of himself and the animal, he looked like what Joshua imagined one of the Greek gods of antiquity looked like. Fierce, yet steady. Strong, but calm. Joshua's fingers tightened on the top rail of the fence. Anything further from the dark, violent streets of Joshua's past he couldn't imagine. Eli was everything Joshua wanted: clean, strong, honest. Straightforward. Gentle.

He imagined talking about Eli to the shrink. Imagined being honest and straightforward about his lust for his uncle's foreman. He hoped to God that the shrink didn't mind his being gay. Didn't shrinks have to go through some kind of training for shit like that? He didn't know. This was the West, after all, and even though New Mexico had a reputation for being more liberal and gay-friendly than other Western states, it was still the West.

"Yeah," he said finally. "I probably won't be."

Love, Like Water

Chapter 14

THE office was on the fifth floor, right across from the elevator, and decorated in local style, with Hopi pottery and Navaho weavings on the wall. The receptionist, a sweet-looking older woman, greeted him with an offer of tea or coffee. Joshua declined and accepted only a seat in the waiting room.

The psychiatrist, when he came out, was escorting a young woman with a tear-streaked face, though she was smiling. Josh hoped he'd be in as good shape when he was done. He nodded at Josh, but kept talking to the girl in a low voice as he walked her to the desk, where the receptionist took over. Then he came across the room to Josh, his hand outstretched. "Joshua? I'm Ken McBride."

Josh rose and shook his hand. The man was half a head shorter than Josh, but his shoulders were broad and solid. His grip, too, was solid, but not aggressive. "Come on back and we'll get started on the paperwork. Ellen, you can head out once you're done scheduling Gerri. Gerri—I'll see you next week."

"Thanks, Ken," Gerri said, and gave Josh a shy smile.

Josh found himself smiling back. Huh. That was weird.

The inner office had the same type of pottery and weavings on the stuccoed walls, with furnishings in soft brown leather. There were some plants, too, but no desk, so it looked more like a living room than an office. It was quiet and peaceful.

"Sit anywhere you like," McBride said.

Josh looked at the couch, but sat in one of the armchairs instead. Rubbing his hand over the silky leather of the arm, he said, "I've been through all this before. So it's not exactly new."

"No, but I am, so we'll have to get used to each other. We do have paperwork to do, but before that, why don't we just talk a bit. Would you like some water or tea?"

"No, thanks."

"Okay." McBride sat in the other armchair. A clipboard sat on the coffee table between them, but he made no move to pick it up. "Why don't you tell me about yourself, and what you want to get out of therapy?"

Josh took a breath, then said, "I have bad dreams."

"Like Hamlet."

"Hamlet? Like the play?"

"Yes. Shakespeare. Hamlet says that, about dreams."

"He had bad dreams?"

"Act 2, scene 2: 'I could be bounded in a nutshell, and count myself a king of infinite space, were it not that I have bad dreams.' Have you ever read Hamlet? Or seen a production of it?"

"I don't think so. I'm not much on that sort of thing. Never had time for it." Josh thought a moment, then said, "I think I know what he means about the infinite space thing, though. I never thought of myself as having limitations when I was young."

"None of us do. What are your dreams about?"

Josh rubbed a fingertip over the arm of the chair. "Memories," he said finally. "Bad memories."

The shrink didn't say anything.

"You want to know about me?" Josh looked up to see McBride watching him, a thoughtful expression on his face. "I'm gay. I'm a heroin addict. I'm ex-FBI. I've killed people."

"Are you still using?"

"No." He waited for a comment on the rest of his statement, but there wasn't any. He took a breath and looked up. The expression on the shrink's face was mild and inquisitive, not judgmental. "I went through a chemical detox after the assignment and then a couple months of rehab. I'm clean. But I...." He swallowed. "I still dream about it. I still, I still want it. In my weaker moments. I don't want it. But I do."

"That's not unusual, particularly with heroin," McBride said. "We can work on techniques to deal with that. The desire may never go completely away, but there are things that will help. Go on."

Joshua shrugged. "What else is there? My mother and my uncle cooked up this scheme where I would come out here to work for him and learn the ranching business. He doesn't have any other family, so probably he's thinking in terms of me buying him out eventually or something. If I like it."

"Do you?"

"I guess."

Joshua fell silent. The shrink didn't say anything for a minute, then said, "You sent permission for me to access your medical records from the hospital in Miller. I have a few questions about what sent you there."

"Stupidity," Joshua said bitterly.

"Do you think it's really that simple?"

Joshua couldn't answer. He stared up at the wall hanging behind McBride. The patterned weaving was done in warm shades of honey gold, dark sage, and a brown that was almost red. It was warm and looked like home. "Is anything?" he said finally.

"Not often. So. If not just stupidity, what else?" When Josh didn't answer right away, the shrink said, "Let's talk about those dreams."

IT WAS late when Josh and Tuck got back from town, but Eli found reasons to hang around on the ranch house porch until they did. Jesse had come out there a half hour or so earlier, having the usual skewed body clock teenagers had that kept them up 'til all hours, and was chatting to Eli about… something. Eli wasn't really paying attention; he was listening for Tuck's truck.

When they got out of the truck, Joshua was walking the way he did when he first came to the ranch, tight and awkward. Eli half stood, but then Tucker came around the truck and took Josh's arm, so he sat back down again. "You okay?" he asked as they came up the steps to the porch. Jesse had gone silent.

"Yeah," Joshua said, his voice kind of quavery. "It was a little rough, but good." He gave them a brittle smile, and Eli wanted to cry. *Shit.*

"Good," he said, not meaning it. What he wanted to do was hunt down whoever it was that had hurt Josh—the shrink or the fellas back in Chicago, or whoever it was—and beat the shit out of them. But there wasn't anything he could do. He didn't remember ever feeling this helpless in his life. Even when his dad died, he'd known instinctively how to react, what to do, to take care of his ma and the kids. But this—Josh was a man, not a kid, and a man had to deal with his own problems, in the end. Yeah, he could be there to help if Josh asked him—but Josh had to ask.

And he didn't. He smiled again at Eli and Jesse, that brittle impersonal smile, and went into the house with Tucker.

"Shit, he looks wrecked," Jesse said in a low voice. "I thought this guy was supposed to help him?"

"Yeah. I guess sometimes you kinda gotta get through the bad stuff before you get better," Eli said. "Like ripping off a Band-Aid—it hurts like a bitch, but it's better afterwards."

"Huh," Jesse said. "I hope I never have to go through that."

Eli regarded Jesse's sweet, untroubled face. "Kinda doubt you will, son. Your ma'll kick anybody's ass who tries to mess with you."

"Yeah, she's little, but she's fierce." Jesse grinned. "Well, I better get upstairs and finish my English homework, or my fierce little ma will be kicking *my* ass. 'Night, Eli."

"'Night, son."

Love, Like Water

The night went quiet. Eli rocked back and forth on the chair's back legs, thinking about the ranch, and Josh, and tomorrow's work, and Josh. After a while the light went on in Joshua's room, then out again, and with a sigh, Eli hoisted himself from the chair and meandered across the yard to his own house and his own bed.

Chapter 15

ELI wasn't sure if Joshua would be up to the long ride he'd had planned, after the trauma of the visit to the shrink, but he seemed okay in the morning eating breakfast. Eli greeted him and the others casually, then, when he'd settled down and had eaten a bit, he turned to Tucker and said, "I figured on taking Josh out to the canyon today. Show him some of the property lines."

"That's a haul," Tuck said. "Better get an early start, then. Forecast's for the low 80's—there'll be a bit of cloud cover this afternoon, but not much. Have Sara pack you lunch and I'll have Josh done in the office by about nine."

"How far is this place?" Joshua asked curiously.

"Oh, a few hours' ride toward the mountains. We'll follow Las Lunas Creek—that's the main branch that feeds our three creeks—up to the Galiano so we'll have some shade and easy water for the mounts a good part of the way. It'll give you a feel for the size of the ranch and what kind of terrain we're dealing with."

"Manny and I are heading up that way too," Billy said, "to check on the stock in the canyon. We'll ride up with you, but we'll be a while—you'll wanna head home hours before we're done."

"Stock?" Joshua echoed.

"Yeah, we have a small herd of mustangs we keep in the canyon. They're mares from the last roundup that had foals. The canyon's big enough for them to spread out, but the entrance is gated and the rest of the canyon's too sheer for them to climb so we don't have to go hunting for them all over tarnation when we're ready to bring them in, and they're generally safer there with the babies than if they were trying to survive on the range. Better feed, more water, generally protected." Billy poured himself another cup of coffee. "We go up and check on them every week or so, make sure that they haven't gotten themselves into trouble, that they're still healthy, and that nothing like cougars or coyotes have moved into the neighborhood."

"Fine," Eli said. "We'll be ready to head out about nine. Josh, you still good with Avery?"

"Yeah."

"Avery?" Manny snorted. "Horse is a slug."

"He's good enough," Tucker said absently. "Just lazy. Josh'll push him, right Josh?"

"Whatever you say, Uncle Tucker."

Eli looked over at Joshua. He was nervous, Eli thought, and wondered why. Then Josh got up and followed Tucker into the office, and Eli finished his breakfast and went out to the barns.

IT WAS a good thing he'd been spending more time in the saddle lately, because Joshua was ready for a break by the time they reached the high ground where the canyon was located. It took a good two hours of steady riding to get there—not fast, but steady. Joshua suspected that the others would have gotten there a lot quicker without him, but they didn't seem to mind; both of the men took the opportunity at one point or another during the ride to come up beside Joshua and engage him in conversation. Billy had worked on any number of ranches since running away from home at fifteen, and had dozens of funny stories about his experiences. Manny was a native Albuquerquean and was fascinated by the differences in his Mexican-based Spanish and Joshua's Puerto Rican-based. Between the two of them, they made the trip go by a lot quicker for Joshua.

The ground along Rio Galiano had been growing rougher over the last mile or so, and eventually they had to abandon even the minimal shade for open desert and the trail climbing up into the foothills. "It looks like a movie set," Joshua said as they rode past an outcropping of huge boulders. "I half expect a gang of cattle rustlers in black masks to ride around the bend."

"They drive trucks nowadays, and black masks aren't fashionable anymore," Eli said soberly, then shot Joshua a quick grin. "'Sides, this is too far out for rustlers—no cattle, and the mustangs ain't worth snot 'til they're tamed down some. And no roads. Rustlers steal 'cause they're lazy. Too much work to get these."

Joshua nodded.

They rode on deeper into the rocky terrain, until they came up on a narrow defile between high rock walls, narrow enough that they had to ride single-file through the passage. The rocks loomed dangerously overhead and Joshua looked up to study them thoughtfully.

Billy said over his shoulder, "Apache used to lure the Army down here and throw stones on their heads to kill 'em. Nice place for a massacre."

"Whereas the Army used to just ride into Indian villages and bring candy and bunnies for the kiddies," Manny said dryly.

"Hey, I ain't defending the Army! I allus admired Geronimo. And I grew up around Fort Sumner, so I know about that too. Just saying that's what they did here."

They squabbled good-naturedly for a few minutes, then the defile took a jog and broadened out just wide enough for two horses. Across the way was a heavy steel gate with a built-in lock, blocking the trail. Beyond, Joshua could see the trail jogging again and disappearing behind more rocks.

Love, Like Water

Billy unlocked the gate and opened it for them to ride through, then closed it again. Joshua heard the snick of the lock as it re-engaged automatically. "Valley's just beyond here," he told Joshua.

"Can't the mustangs just jump over the gate?" Joshua asked. "It's not that high." It wasn't, either—maybe five feet, no higher than a privacy fence back home.

"Could if they had enough room to get to a running start, but the trail doglegs," Billy pointed out. "Can't jump that high from a standing start."

Joshua nodded and followed the rest of them down through the rocks again.

AFTER another fifteen minutes or so, they came out onto a ledge looking out over a tiny pocket valley. Joshua sucked in his breath. Across the way a waterfall plunged thirty or so feet into a clear little lagoon surrounded by grass and fringed with trees—not just the ubiquitous cottonwoods, but oak and ash and rowan. It was more green than Joshua had seen since coming out West. "Holy shit," Joshua breathed.

"Pretty, ain't it?" Eli said in satisfaction.

"Where are the horses?"

"Probably up that way," Manny said, gesturing to the east, where the stream that fell in the waterfall flowed out of the little lake and disappeared past the trees. "There's a meadow beyond there—they're usually there, where they can see what's coming. That's where Billy and I are headed. After lunch, of course."

"How do we get down there?"

The three men burst out laughing. "The trail, idiot," Billy said, and pointed down at the narrow path snaking down the face of the cliff below them.

Joshua swallowed. Hard.

He went last, of course, but before Eli started, he leaned back and said to Joshua in a low voice, "Avery's surefooted. Just relax and let him pick his own way. He knows the path. It's not as bad as it looks."

Joshua nodded and did what Eli suggested, but it was still a nerve-wracking fifteen minutes or so before they set foot—or hoof—on level ground again. He was grateful when they stopped on a flat rise above the lake and dismounted, Billy taking their horses into the trees to tie them off while the others unpacked their lunch from the saddlebags.

After they finished eating, they lay on the grass in the dappled sunlight, enjoying the cool breeze from the waterfall. "How come this isn't desert?" Joshua asked as he tipped his hat over his eyes. "I mean, it's not just water—we followed that creek almost all the way here."

"Part of what keeps the desert scoured is the wind," Eli said. "Even if trees could get enough of a foothold on groundwater, the wind'll dry 'em out and blow them over. Only along the riverbanks can trees put down enough root to fight the wind, and even then it's the cottonwoods, 'cause they have such long roots. It's sheltered here, and the falls keep the air cooled."

"Sorta like natural air conditioning," Manny said sleepily.

"Mmm," Joshua said.

WHEN he woke, Billy and Manny were gone and the stuff from lunch had been packed up and put away. "Nice nap?" Eli asked humorously. He'd taken off his boots and shirt and was cooling his feet in the lake, but took them out when Joshua sat up. His toes were blue.

"Cold, huh?" Joshua stared at Eli's feet. They were the whitest feet he'd ever seen, except for where they were blue. The rest of the man—what he could see—was tanned brown. No, not brown, bronze. Josh had seen his arms and had expected what they called a "farmer's tan," where only the arms and neck had color, but Eli's chest and shoulders were dark gold, with the lighter gold of his hair a soft contrast. It made his blue eyes that much more startling.

"Yeah, the river's mountain run-off, and this is a branch of that. Doesn't travel far enough to warm up." Eli rubbed at his feet with one of the cloths their sandwiches had been wrapped in.

"Why doesn't anyone live here? I mean, it's beautiful...."

"Shit yeah, but the only way in unless you're traveling by helicopter is through that gate. I suppose you could probably build a road down through the cliffs, but this is all still Triple C land, and I can't see Tuck wanting to wreck a perfectly good and useful canyon. But you're right, it is beautiful. Tuck says his folks used to go on romantic weekend camping trips here."

"Guess it would be nice if you were the romantic sort," Joshua said. He didn't look at Eli, but put his hat back on and stretched out the kinks from sleeping on the ground.

"Yep."

Joshua wrapped his arms around his shins and watched the waterfall for a while. There was a peaceful feeling to the place, with the only sound the rumble of the falls and the splash of the odd fish in the lake. He wondered absently where the fish came from, if they swam down from the mountains somewhere, or if someone, sometime— Tuck's parents, maybe, or grandparents—had stocked the lake for vacation fishing.

He glanced over to see Eli leaning back on his elbows, his long legs stretched out in front of him, feet crossed at the ankles. He'd abandoned his hat, the ubiquitous gray Resistol—it lay over by the saddlebags, and his fair hair was curling around his ears. His face was relaxed and he looked happy, and younger, closer to Joshua's own age instead of his midthirties. Of course, Joshua thought, he himself probably looked older than twenty-eight. God knew he often felt older. But not now. Not right this second, when the breeze was cool and the sun was easy, and there was shade and quiet and Eli barely an arm's distance away.

After a bit, Eli tilted his head back and looked at the sky. "Guess we oughta think about going back. It's past noon. I've got some stuff to do this afternoon, and the new trainees were starting this morning. I'd like to take their measure before they settle in."

"What about Manolo and Billy?"

"They'll meander on back when they're done. They're gonna be a while, taking samples of water and grass and horse poop and stuff to send to the lab, not to mention checking out the wildlife in the area. This usually takes a few hours." Eli put his boots, T-shirt and button-down on, got up, and picked up the saddlebags, carrying them to where the horses waited. He buckled them back into place. Joshua followed suit with his own, making sure the bags were settled properly before swinging back into the saddle. "Next time," Eli said, "we'll bring you along for the whole thing, but it's pretty damn boring and I don't want to drive you off just yet." He gave Joshua a smile and set Button into motion. "Don't want to drive you off at all."

"Don't want to be driven," Joshua said as he nudged Avery with his heels.

"No man does, *mijo*. No man does."

Joshua froze, and his horse stopped. *Mijo*. Just like that. Soft, full of feeling. So familiar. *Mijo bonito. Mijo valiente. Nunca te harán daño.* "You speak Spanish?" he asked, feeling suddenly stripped raw.

The foreman turned in his saddle. "Yeah—grew up in Wyoming, but we had a lot of Latinos on the ranch there too. And I've spent a good ten years in New Mexico, where more people speak Spanish than English. Kinda hard to avoid picking it up. It's probably different from what you know—Mexican, not Puerto Rican. But the basics is the same." He studied Joshua with kind eyes. "You okay, *chico*?"

"Yeah," Joshua said hoarsely. "Fine." He nudged Avery, and the horse moved forward. So it hadn't been his grandfather's voice he'd heard when he was dying out in the desert, but Eli's. But he couldn't be wrong about the emotion. He couldn't be wrong about the words. *My beautiful boy. My brave boy. I would never hurt you.* Why would Eli say those things?

Eli didn't say, and Joshua didn't ask.

Love, Like Water

THEY had nearly reached the last of the barns, around the far side of the furthest corral, where a stand of cottonwoods had been planted years ago. The creek they'd followed watered the trees before splitting into the three that kept the ranch alive through the driest years. The shade here was deeper, and the trees thick enough that one couldn't see the ranch.

Joshua pushed Avery to a faster walk, and they came up beside Eli, who drew up, looking at Joshua curiously.

Joshua reached out and put a gloved hand on Eli's forearm.

The foreman went motionless, gazing down at Joshua's hand, then startled blue eyes met Joshua's. In the shade, the pupils were big and dark. Joshua waited a second, then let his hand fall away.

Eli licked his lips, then, as slowly as if he were reaching out to touch a skittish mustang, he stripped off his glove and put his hand on Joshua's cheek. His fingers were callused and hard, but gentle on Joshua's skin, and Joshua closed his eyes a moment, savoring the contact. It had been so long since anyone—another man—had touched him like that. He heard Eli's whispered "Josh...."—so soft that if the wind hadn't been perfectly still at that instant, he wouldn't have.

Joshua said, "Out there, in the desert. You found me. You looked for me. You said, 'don't do this to me.' Didn't you? Why did you say that?"

"You don't ask the easy ones, do you, son?"

"I'm not your son."

The breeze picked up, soughing in the leaves of the cottonwoods. "No," Eli said finally. "You're not my son."

Turning his head, Joshua let his lips brush Eli's palm. Eli's voice was ragged when he spoke: "Jesus Christ, Joshua...." and jerked his hand away.

Joshua drew back his head, shifting in the saddle. "Oh," he said numbly. "Sorry... I misread.... Never mind. Sorry." He turned Avery's head back toward the ranch. "I'm tired. I'll see you at dinner."

"Joshua, wait."

He didn't. He kicked Avery to a lope and rode away.

ELI caught up with him as he rode into the big stables, and was off his horse before Joshua had gotten his feet out of his stirrups. He caught at Avery's bridle and said in a low voice, "You are *not* running away from me again, Joshua Chastain. You and I are gonna talk—"

"You have no right to tell me what to do," Joshua hissed back.

"Bullshit. I'm the foreman. I am responsible for the safety and well-being of every damn breathing live thing on this ranch, and that includes you. And your uncle, who's gonna be worrit and upset with me if you go running into the house like you did the day before you took off."

Joshua slid off the horse. When he hit the ground, his knees buckled a little and Eli caught his arm. "Easy. We did a lot more riding today than you're used to. Before you go to bed tonight, you take a long hot bath and put on some liniment. Sarafina has some."

"He blamed you for me leaving," Joshua said, ignoring him. He pushed Eli's hand away.

"Yeah, he did. And he wasn't wrong. I shouldn'ta let you go. And I ain't letting you go now. You're gonna sit right down there on that hay bale until I'm done tending these horses, and then we're gonna go to the house and we're gonna talk." He took Joshua's arm again and led him to the bale, pushing him gently down. "And I mean talk."

He probably did, Joshua thought tiredly. God, he was an *idiot*. Of course Eli didn't want him: he'd started to put some weight back on, but he was still mostly a skeleton, and a drug-addicted one, too. He was disgusting, and the only reason Eli had been so kind to him was because he felt sorry for Joshua. And because he *was* a kind man. At least he hadn't been cruel or laughed at him, and at least Joshua's curiosity was satisfied about his sexual preferences. He drew his legs up onto the bale and rested his cheek on his knees. He was tired, that

Love, Like Water

was all. He'd been working hard since dawn and he wasn't used to it. But this was going to be his life from now on, and that was okay. Hard work was good, and this was a good place. Not likely anyone was going to expect him to shoot anyone here.

He wondered vaguely where his gun had gone. He'd turned in his service piece before he went undercover. At the time of his arrest he'd been relieved of the one he'd had as José Rosales, and "relieved" was exactly the right word. He never wanted to see another gun again. Rifles or shotguns, yeah—they were out in the middle of the high desert and probably needed to shoot wolves and coyotes and rattlesnakes to defend the horses. He'd seen shotguns in the walnut case in Tucker's office. Those were fine. He just never wanted to see another handgun as long as he lived.

Couldn't exactly be an FBI agent if you were afraid of guns. Not that he was afraid, exactly. He just didn't want to see one again.

Eli was quiet as he stripped the tack from the horses and ran a currycomb over their hides. They hadn't been ridden hard, but it was a long ride from the canyon. Joshua watched him—the deliberate movements that looked slow but were masterpieces of efficiency, no wasted motion, no carelessness. Thanks to that efficiency he finished both more quickly than Joshua would have done one, even if he weren't so tired, and let them both out into the corral. Then he turned to Joshua. "Ready?"

Joshua got to his feet and followed him outside.

SWEATING, Eli tried to keep a reasonable pace across the yard to the porch, but *he* felt like bolting. Beside him, Joshua was silent, but Eli could feel the waves of tension radiating off him. *Fuck.* What the hell was he supposed to do?

"I didn't mean anything by it," Joshua said.

Eli stopped, and stared at him blankly. "What?"

"I didn't mean anything by it." Josh shrugged. "It doesn't matter. It won't happen again. I just fucked up, is all—again. I just meant to… I don't know. Thank you. Or something. Forget about it."

"Jesus Christ, Josh!" Eli let his breath out on a gusty sigh. "Look, I didn't mean to upset you. Fuck, that seems to be all I can do, is upset you." He yanked off his hat and rubbed his forehead. "I'm sorry."

Joshua shrugged again, but the look in his eyes was back, the bleak emptiness Eli hadn't seen since the first days of Josh's stay. He felt like he'd killed something. "Josh," he said, but the man just shook his head and walked up the steps into the house, letting the screen door bang behind him.

"Fuck," Eli said. He took off his hat, smacked himself on the thigh with it, and went after him.

THE kitchen was empty and the house silent, and Eli was grateful. At least maybe then no one would hear him yelling at Josh. And what the fuck was the matter with him that he *wanted* to yell at Josh? He didn't yell. It wasn't his style. No, he was the slow, patient one, the one who waited for the wild things to come to him. No good ever came of chasin', Tuck always said. Maybe he was right this time, too.

Maybe he wasn't. Maybe some things needed to be chased.

He knocked on Joshua's bedroom door, but Josh didn't answer. Taking a deep breath, Eli opened the door and walked in.

Josh, standing by the window, turned around. "What the fuck?" he said in a fury. "You get out of here, right now! Who gave you the right…?"

Eli stomped across the room, caught Joshua's chin in his hand, and kissed him hard. "Don't you ever," he hissed, his fingers holding Josh still. His eyes locked on Josh's dark and startled gaze. "Don't you *ever* walk away from me when I ain't done with you, Josh. I damn near lost you in the desert and I am *not* gonna lose you again, got that?"

Love, Like Water

"Who says you have me?" Josh jerked away, his hand coming up to touch his jaw where Eli had gripped him. "Who the *fuck* do you think you are?"

"You know who I am, and you know I've got you. Hell, I think I knew you were mine the minute you stepped off that bus. And I am not going to lose you."

Joshua's hand had stilled in its rubbing. He stared at Eli, his eyes wide.

Eli was pretty startled himself. Where had those words come from? Had it really been that way? If so, he hadn't realized it. But the words—the words felt true.

Tuck knew. Eli was sure of that. He himself might not have realized it, but Tuck had seen it, had warned him about it. Warned him about Joshua.

But Joshua was *his*.

"So you tell me now," Eli said, his voice tight and anxious. "Was it just you wanting to thank me? Because if that's all it is, you tell me now."

"I did want to thank you...."

For a second, Eli thought his heart had exploded. He felt pain all the way down to both sets of fingertips. Then cold washed over him. He stepped back, nodded, and turned, walking steadily out the door, out of the house, and across the yard toward home.

He heard Joshua say his name, but he ignored it. *Fine*, he thought, *I can walk away too*, but he was blind with grief and rage and disappointment. Only ten years of making that trek from ranch house to cottage, ten years of habit, got him up to his own front porch.

Hearing the footsteps behind him, though, he stopped, rested one hand on the pillar of the porch steps, and waited.

Chapter 16

THE foreman's cottage was opposite the main house at the south end of the complex, across the drive, set underneath more cottonwoods. Joshua could hear the splash of water from around the back, where the creek ran. There was a little porch, not half the size of the one on the main house, but big enough for a white rocking chair and a little wicker table. Eli was waiting on that porch, his back to Joshua, but the inside door was open, and when Joshua stepped up onto the porch Eli opened the screen door to usher him inside, where it was cool and dark.

Eli flicked on the lights, and Joshua saw that all the drapes in the little living room were closed against the day's sunlight. There wasn't much in the room: a battered leather sofa, a Laz-E-Boy covered in a pieced quilt, an old tube-style television. One wall of the room was bookshelves filled with paperbacks and knickknacks. It was scrupulously clean. "Sarafina cleans up for me," Eli said, apparently reading Joshua's mind again. "I've got a kitchen, but I mostly just use the fridge for beer. You want one? Or a Coke."

"Coke, thanks."

He followed Eli into the tiny kitchen. The walls were painted a bright sunshine yellow, and there were checked yellow and white curtains on the window. It was warmer in here, but a stand of junipers shaded the window and kept it from being too hot. Eli got a couple of insulated mugs from the freezer and poured them both Cokes. "Siddown," he said.

Love, Like Water

Joshua sat.

Eli leaned against the counter and studied him a moment. "Fact is," he said finally, "I'm gay. Guess you figured that out. It ain't common knowledge—Tuck knows, and Sarafina and Jesse. But the rest of the hands don't, and it ain't nobody's business. So that's that. I'd prefer it kept quiet, but if you feel the need to go blabbing it about, go ahead. I'd rather deal with the fallout from that than have you figuring you need to get revenge or something."

"What the fuck?" Joshua started to rise, but Eli pointed a finger at him.

"Sit. I ain't done. Now, the way I reckon, you're not that kind. I just wanted to get that out in the air first thing and get it over with. I don't know you so well as I know Tuck and Sara and Jesse, so I ain't sure how you'll react to things."

"Look," Joshua said, "that's fine. I'm not going to go outing you to a bunch of guys I don't know any better than I know you. I don't know why you walked away when I was in the middle of talking to you, after yelling at me for walking away from you. So let's just stop walking and figure out what's going on here."

"Good idea. You first."

"What?"

Eli waved a hand. "You started this. Out by the woods. So tell me. What do you want? A quick fuck? What?"

"Shit, I don't know. I haven't had sex in three years, but my life has been so fucked up, I figure that compensates. I'm not after you because you're available—if I just wanted a quick fuck I guess I could find it someplace else. I guess Tucker'd lend me wheels if I asked."

Rolling his eyes, Eli took a sip of Coke. "Yeah, there are a couple places in Roswell and Albuquerque and Santa Fe—those towns are big enough, and this state's a little more laid back than Texas or Arizona, so mostly they're as safe as any other place. Which ain't saying much, but there are worse. Anyway, they're bars, not clubs, and not the kind of place you'd feel home...."

"What the fuck?" Joshua said again. "Where the fuck do you think I'd feel at home? I spent three fucking years in the underbelly of Darwin Park, one of the roughest neighborhoods in Chicago, and you think I can't handle a tough cowboy bar?"

Eli was quiet a moment. Then he said, "Sorry about that. I've just kinda got used to thinking of you as 'Tuck's nephew from Back East', and an FBI agent. I don't know what they do, just what I see on TV. Tuck likes that Bones show, and the agent on that mostly just investigates stuff. He rides a computer. I forget that you've been through shit ain't nobody oughta go through."

"I'm not a kid, I'm not a fucking desk jockey, and I'm not soft. I'm a tired old junkie with a whole lot of problems fucking my head up, and one of them is that I haven't gotten laid in a fucking long time. So yeah, I want to know where I can go to get cock."

Eli's face had gone blank. In a flat voice he said, "Well, if you're planning on picking up some stranger, I'd recommend you get in shape fast, because the meat markets you'll be hanging at only let in decent-looking guys. You *look* like a goddamned junkie and you won't get past the bouncer."

"Fuck you, Kelly." Joshua felt like Eli'd punched the breath out of him. "Fuck you very much." He slammed his chair back and shot to his feet, intending to head for the kitchen door.

"Shit." Faster than Joshua expected, Eli caught his arm and jerked him around. Joshua fell against Eli's solid chest, and Eli's arms came around him. "I'm sorry," he breathed in Joshua's ear. "*Mijo*, I'm sorry. I didn't mean any of that."

"Yeah, you did," Joshua said. "And it's all true. I do look like a junkie, and nobody's gonna let me in a club like this."

"Shh." Eli rubbed his back comfortingly. "You're looking healthier every day, *niño*, and when you're better you'll be beating 'em off with a stick."

It was so easy to stand there, with Eli holding him. Joshua rested his chin on Eli's shoulder, breathing in the scent of horse and soap and sweat and man. His arms came up and locked around Eli's waist.

Love, Like Water

"Josh," Eli murmured. "Oh, Josh."

He felt Eli's head turn and he turned his face to meet it. Their lips brushed once, gently, then one of them—Joshua wasn't sure who—leaned in closer, pressing harder. Eli's tongue touched Joshua's lips, then invited itself inside, tenderly exploring. Eli tasted of peppermint and Coke.

Joshua let go a soft sigh, then tightened his arms around Eli, pulling him closer and shifting his hips so that he was rubbing against him. It felt so good, even that small contact, the first in such a very, very long time. When he felt Eli's hands slide down his back to cup his ass, he smiled into the kiss they still shared, and he rocked forward, hungry for the friction.

But when Eli drew back and dropped to his knees, Joshua almost fell over in shock. "Wha...?"

"Shh," Eli said again, and just as deliberately, just as efficiently as he'd stripped the horses of their tack, he took care of Joshua's jeans, sliding them down to his knees. Then he leaned forward and kissed Joshua's thin hip. "Oh, *mijo*," he breathed, then turned his face to lick the rising length of Joshua's cock. "Beautiful," he said, his voice full of wonder. "So strong, so beautiful."

His tongue swept over the head and under the edge of the retreating foreskin. Joshua buried his hands in the blond hair and leaned back against the door for balance. "God, Eli," he said roughly.

"Shh." Eli licked again, then Joshua cried out as his mouth took him deep. Eli sucked him in, his tongue rubbing the underside of the shaft, while his hand came up and caressed Joshua's balls.

Then he let Joshua slide from his lips and Joshua almost cried. "Bedroom," Eli croaked, and got up, dragging Joshua's jeans up over his hips. He left them unbuttoned, though, and took Joshua's hand, leading him through the little living room to the equally tiny bedroom, with its double bed taking up most of the floor space.

Beside the bed, Eli stripped Joshua's boots and jeans off, then reached for his T-shirt. Joshua jerked back, but Eli's eyes were patient, even as they burned with warmth. "It's okay, *mijo*. I know what you look like."

So Joshua let him pull the shirt over his head, displaying his bony, tattooed chest and arms. He shook a little, afraid that it would turn Eli off, but all Eli did was bend and drag his talented tongue across one nipple. Joshua whimpered. "Bed," Eli said, and pulled back the coverlet, pushing Joshua gently down.

Joshua watched as Eli stripped off his own shirt, pulling it over his head without unbuttoning it, then peeled out of his own boots and jeans, letting them drop on the floor. He went to the nightstand and took out condoms and lube.

"You bring tricks here?" Joshua asked, his voice trembling in anticipation.

"Nah," Eli said. He tore open one packet with his teeth and rolled the condom down Joshua's dick. "I use 'em when I'm jerking off—easier to clean up. Sarafina *does* housekeep for me—it's only polite." He bent and took one of Joshua's balls into his mouth, and Joshua lost interest in the conversation—the sensation of warm wetness was far more interesting.

When Eli moved up to Joshua's cock, which was now so hard Joshua thought he'd pass out from lack of blood to the brain, he curled one hand around the base. Then he started a slow, maddeningly slow glide, down to his fist, then up again, licking on the downward glide and sucking hard on the upward. Over, and over, and over again, the same intense feeling, the same slow pace. "Eli," Joshua moaned. "God, Eli…."

The vibration of Eli's chuckle almost drove Joshua out of his mind.

Finally, he sped up a little, enough that Joshua was bucking against his hand, desperate to get off. When he finally climaxed, he felt his ass leave the bed as he arched, the explosion of sensation darkening his sight for a moment. He shoved his hand into his mouth to stifle his shout.

Love, Like Water

Eli felt the heat fill the condom and let Joshua slide from his mouth, rocking his fist up and down Josh's cock, stripping the last of Joshua's come from him. Then he eased the full condom off and tied it, tossing it into the garbage can near his desk. With a soft kiss to Josh's hip, he whispered, "Be right back," and stumbled to his feet, staggering into the bathroom across the hall and closing the door. There, he jerked off quickly into the toilet, a couple of hard pulls with one hand, the other propped against the wall behind the john, holding up his weak legs. "Fuck," he groaned quietly.

He gazed at himself in the mirror as he washed his hands. The face that looked back at him was flushed with arousal, but inside he felt gray with fatigue. "Oh, son," he said to his reflection, "what the Sam Hill have you got yourself into?"

No point worrying about it now. He found a clean washcloth on the shelf and soaked it with warm water, washing himself off before rinsing it and bringing it out to the bedroom.

Josh was dozing, but he opened his eyes when Eli knelt on the bed, and began to clean him off. Not that there was much to clean; they'd been pretty tidy. Still, Eli heard a sigh of contentment as he washed Joshua's balls for him. "Feels good," Josh murmured.

"Yeah, I know." Eli tossed the rag on the carpet and crawled into bed beside Joshua. "Can't stay here long. Gotta get back to work. But you can stay long as you want—I'll just let Tucker know you decided to take a nap."

"Here, instead of my room?" Josh's expression was wry. "I'd think he'd figure things out."

"He don't know you're queer," Eli said.

"It wouldn't be hard to figure out, if he found out I fell asleep in your bed."

"Mm," Eli said. He hiked himself on one elbow and studied Josh thoughtfully. At his inspection, Josh flushed and reached for the sheet to draw it over himself, but Eli stopped him. "No," he said, "let me look."

"Nothing worth seeing," Joshua said. He shifted uncomfortably, but let Eli look.

There was a tattoo on one side of his chest—a traditional one, of a large heart surrounded by flowers, with a doubled-back ribbon across it. The top fold of the ribbon said "Hannah," the bottom, "Catherine." A stranger looking at it might think it was all one name, "Hannah Catherine." "The only two girls I'll ever love," Joshua said.

"Mm," Eli agreed.

"My father always referred to my mother as 'Ana', so everyone in the gang thought Hannah Catherine was a girlfriend, back in Cincy. They thought I'd been in a gang there. The Bureau built up a fake arrest record so realistic that sometimes I worried that I'd end up in jail for real, that they'd forget that the whole thing was a fake."

Eli traced the outline of the tattoo on his upper arm. This one was less gentle, being a hooded skeleton holding a machete to the skull of another skeleton kneeling before it. Underneath, on a banner was the name "Los Peligros." "The dangers?" Eli translated.

"The name of the gang I belonged to in Chicago. They weren't just dangerous, they were Danger itself." The humor that had lightened his voice when talking about the other tattoo was gone, and the tone was flat and dead.

"So they didn't forget and throw you in jail to rot?" Eli changed the subject.

"No. Robinson, my Bureau 'handler' for the assignment, made sure he and the other Chicago field office agents were in on it when the sting went down. Robinson made a big stink at the arraignment that I had a series of warrants out in Ohio, and since I was 'arrested' on federal racketeering charges, they didn't have to wait for extradition to ship me back there. Robinson took me out of there and straight into rehab."

"Is the trial over?"

Love, Like Water

Josh snorted. "You know the judicial system—or maybe you don't. If not, you're lucky. It'll be years before it all comes to trial, unless some of them cut a deal and turn state's evidence. There was a hearing, though, and once the main actors were refused bail, Robinson figured I'd be safe enough to resume my real identity." He looked down to where Eli was idly tracing the outline of the heart on his chest. "My main concern is for Mom and Cathy, but through the whole time I was undercover, there was no indication that anyone knew my real name. I was José Rosales, son of Alberto Rosales. My grandparents were dead by that time, but even while they were alive, they had no truck with 'Chete Montenegro, the gang's leader. He'd grown up with my dad, which gave me an in with Los Peligros, but my grandparents blamed him for getting my dad in trouble."

Eli snorted.

"From what Mom told me, Dad put plenty of his own energy into getting into trouble on his own. Anyway, I worked hard to get evidence to Robinson that could be independently verified, so that I didn't ever have to testify, because that would put my whole family in danger."

"What if you did?"

"Witness protection, likely. But I played the whole game with that thought in my head—get the evidence, get them taken down, and do it so that I would never get caught. During or after."

He flinched as Eli trailed his fingers down his arm to the healed marks on his forearm, but neither he nor Eli said anything. Instead, Eli laced his fingers through Joshua's and kissed his shoulder above the Los Peligros tattoo.

They dozed together for a few minutes, but when Joshua's breathing evened out into sleep, Eli slipped quietly from the bed and dressed. Then he bent over Joshua's sleeping form and kissed his forehead, and went back outside.

Chapter 17

THE temperature had dropped some since they'd ridden back from the canyon, and it felt good. Joshua had woken from his nap alone, but the crackle of paper when he'd rolled over into Eli's space alerted him to his lover's absence. "Gone back to work," Eli had scrawled. "Sleep in. I'll see you later."

He hadn't needed to sleep any more, so he got up, took a quick shower in Eli's tiny bathroom, and dressed again. When he left the cottage, he made sure no one was around to see him. Then he went looking for Eli.

He was in the arena behind the stables, working with the new trainees who'd arrived last night. Joshua hadn't met them yet. They stood now on the periphery of the arena, watching Eli. One of them was an older man, in his forties, at least, who'd been training for a while, but wanted to learn new skills with problem horses. Another was in his twenties, from a horse-racing family in Kentucky, who'd decided he wanted to train horses rather than just watch them run. And the third, of course, was Jesse.

All three were rapt, watching him work with one of the horses that had been so abused it had been nearly unapproachable. As Joshua leaned up on the fence, he saw the horse, a brown and white paint, stop its nervous dancing and stare at Eli, who stood completely motionless in the center of the arena, his hands lax at his sides, the lead rope limp, talking in a low, patient voice. The paint's head was still up, its eyes

Love, Like Water

white, its nostrils flared, but it was standing still, braced on splayed legs.

Eli kept talking.

"Horses are prey animals," he said in that low, calm voice. "They're designed to flee from danger, but they're also pack animals, and will fight to defend the herd. Or if they feel cornered. Technically, this animal is cornered—the fence is just high enough that he'd have to get a good running start to clear it, but that would take it past me, and it doesn't want to do that. So it's gonna feel cornered. That's okay. What you *don't* want is for it to feel threatened, because then it *will* fight. You don't make sudden moves, you don't talk loud, and you *don't* look him in the eye. That's a challenge, and a threat. Right now, he doesn't feel threatened, because he's not sure what I am. I look like the thing that abused him, but I don't sound like it, and I don't act like it.

"What's interesting is that a lot of times, particularly when we're dealing with cases of abuse, a woman might have a better chance getting through to the animal than a man, simply because women don't look, sound, or smell like men. Statistically speaking, men are guilty of animal abuse far more often than women, so women have an edge when dealing with abused animals. I wish Jenny were still here to show you—she's gone off to Kansas to work there, but she was one of my best trainers. Not enough women go into the field, though, so you might not ever run into one. Best to learn to handle them on your own.

"Now, we've gone through working with the culled mustangs, but we ain't had a chance to work with tamed animals that have been abused. So Spot here—don't look at me, I didn't name him—at one point was a decent saddle horse, until he got it beat out of him. His owner got reported to the local ASPCA, which is how he ended up here. He's not a bad horse, not spoiled, not aggressive, just scared. He's only been here a week, so he's still not certain of what's going on. He's still scared."

The whole time he was talking, Eli kept his attention on the horse. He didn't illustrate his speech with hand movements, he didn't turn his back, and he didn't change the soothing tone of the voice. Joshua watched in approval the way the horse reacted. His body shifted from high alert to cautious; the head came down to a level position, the eyes went from having white circles to being all brown again, the nostrils stayed wide, but less flared.

Still talking, Eli eased down into a balanced crouch. He looked like he could get knocked over easily, but Joshua suspected he was in fact as solid and grounded as if he were seated.

The paint shook its head, but stayed put.

Eli shifted slowly to a seated position, his legs folding beneath him Indian-fashion. "As y'all know, if you make yourself smaller than an animal, it has less fear of you. Now, I'm gonna tell you something y'all should know about the way a horse sees the world. See how their eyes are set on the sides of their heads, so as to give them a wider field of vision? That makes it so they have a blind spot right smack dab in front of them, close in. Plus, the distortion in the field means that when they *do* see something in front of them, because it's farther away, it's gonna look out of proportion big. So you don't startle 'em by popping up right under their nose, and you want to make yourself small enough that they're not afraid of you. Trouble is, you don't want to do this if you think you're likely to get stomped, because a horse *can* kill you, so it's a decision you gotta make based on your experience with the animal. Spot here—I ain't never seen him react aggressive like that, so I'm gonna trust him not to stomp me into powder." He folded his hands and waited.

Joshua smiled when, a minute or so later, the paint took the last few steps toward Eli, and knocked his hat off to snuffle his hair. Eli didn't move, but started crooning nonsense words to the horse, and it bent its head to butt his nose against Eli's chest. Eli reached up slowly and scratched the horse's cheek.

"Son of a bitch," Joshua breathed. "That is fucking amazing."

"Yeah, he is," Tucker agreed from beside him. Joshua had been so intent on Eli he hadn't noticed his uncle approaching. They both kept their voices low.

"Is it true what he says, about the way they see?"

Love, Like Water

"Yep. Sometimes if a horse is charging you, you stand up tall, wave your arms and your hat around, and they see this giant the size of a windmill and shear off. They ain't very bright."

"But you love them. And so does Eli."

"Hell, yes." Tucker watched as Eli spent a few minutes getting acquainted with the notoriously skittish horse, then said, "They're dumb and spooky, but they're lovable critters."

"Spooky? What's spooky about them?"

"Oh, not spooky like Halloween spooky. I mean they spook easy. We had a couple dogs around here. Mutts, but good dogs. Rosey and Rambo. Rosey died of old age, and Rambo started getting fussy with the horses. Just wanted to play—he was Rosey's grandson, and still kind of a pup—but it scared the stock. He was lonesome. I had to find him a new home." Tucker thought a moment, then added honestly, "Eli'd a found you in the desert a sight sooner if we still had Rambo. He was part hound. Wasn't sure what the rest was—maybe coyote, maybe wolf, maybe just traveling salesman. At any rate, I still miss 'em. I been thinking about getting another pair."

"Instead, you got me. Don't know that there's much of an improvement."

"Well," Tucker said thoughtfully, "y' ain't much at trackin'. But at least you don't scare the horses."

Joshua elbowed him and grinned. His uncle grinned back.

ELI finished the lesson and turned Spot over to Jesse, as the more experienced student, to start working with. Seeing Joshua standing with Tucker at the fence, he said to the others, "You met Tuck last night, but I don't think you met his nephew. He's just come out from Chicago."

Spencer, the young man from Kentucky, was polite, but he held Josh's hand long enough for Eli to feel uncomfortable. The older guy, Patrick, was more courteous and interested in talking to them about horses. Eli found himself drawn off by Patrick and Tucker, which was fine, until he turned his head to see Joshua and Spencer following behind, Spencer's head a little too close to Joshua's. A sick feeling shot through him, one he couldn't identify right away. But when a recognizable emotion—relief—replaced it as he watched Joshua distance himself politely from the young man, Eli realized what it had been.

Jealousy.

Oh, son, he thought, *you are in so much trouble....*

When Tucker asked him who he recommended work with Spencer, Eli almost gave him the name of the worst-behaved horse in the stables, but his usual sense of fairness overtook him and he suggested one of the others, one that was more up to Spencer's weight, both physically and emotionally. Tucker agreed, and led the two trainees off to get them set up with their new charges.

"Which one of you is going to be teaching them?" Joshua asked as he followed Eli into the small barn. He watched as Eli checked the feed in each of the stalls.

"Both. Tucker will start, working with horses that have basic skills but have been abused or neglected. These guys both have experience with training, but watching them work with the skittish ones will give him an idea of their strengths and weaknesses—let him figure out how he should approach their specific education. Tuck takes that part because not only does he have more experience with abused horses, he's better with people. I'm better with gentling the wild ones. I'll pick up the work when we start the wild horse training, with the ones from the last cull that we've got here. We've got a half dozen two- and three-year-old colts from the herd you saw yesterday. They've been gelded, but they're still wild. They're the ones in the corral behind the blacksmith shop.

"Tucker didn't used to do the roundups—he only took some of the culls for training. But since I been here, he started working the roundups too, since I can do the gentling. I been working mustang culls my whole life. Ramon, Thomas, and Jason, too—they're from up north where they do more with the mustang herds. Ramon's from Montana, Jason and Tom from Wyoming. We work to our strengths—more efficient that way." Eli put his head into the storeroom and did a quick inventory of the cans of mash, then entered the number on the program on his phone. They were down about ten gallon cans; they needed to order about twenty more or they'd run out before the next order.

"Uh huh."

Eli shot a glance over at Joshua. He was leaning on the wall of Rory's stall, looking in at him. His expression was somber.

The cat appeared on top of the partition between the loose box and the next stall and made its way over to Joshua. Eli saw the subdued look on Joshua's face lighten as he scratched between the cat's ears. "What's the matter?" he asked quietly.

"Nothing," Joshua said. He scratched the cat again and set it down. "Get out of here," he said to it.

"I thought you liked cats," Eli said. What was going on in the boy's head?

Joshua shrugged. He gave the cat a last caress, then straightened. "Guess I'll see you at supper."

Eli caught his arm as he went past. "Regrets?"

He didn't answer, then said bitterly, "For what?" and pulled on his arm.

Eli didn't release him. "Son, I ain't a mind reader. You got a problem with me, you tell me, 'cause I can't guess." He tried to keep the anger out of his voice, but some must have seeped through, because Joshua turned his head and looked at him intently. Damn it—he'd worked with dozens of mule-headed horses and never lost his patience, but one mule-headed boy....

"I'm not your fucking son."

"Fine, you ain't my son. Sorry. I got into the habit. Shoot me. But tell me what the good God damn it is that you're all pissy about."

"It's got nothing to do with you."

"Bullshit. Next?"

"What?"

"I'm waiting for the next bullshit comment. I know damn well it's got something to do with me, 'cause you were fine right up until we walked into this shed. Way I figger, the next comment's gonna be that you ain't pissed at me, when I know also damned well that you are. I just wanna know what you're pissed about."

"Do you or do you not want me?" Joshua snapped.

Eli's mind went blank. He goggled at Joshua a good forty seconds, then said, "You think I don't *want* you? Jesus H. Roosevelt Christ, Josh! I'm hard as a rock and thinking up revenge scenarios because a good-looking boy gets a little too close to you? Jesus. Much as I want to, I can't *stop* wanting you." He looked around the barn and suddenly knew what Joshua had been thinking. "Shit, Josh—did you think I came in here figuring on fucking you in broad daylight when just about anybody coulda walked in? I gotta *work* with these people!"

"Fuck. You." Josh jerked his arm out of Eli's grasp and stalked toward the door.

Eli saw red. He caught Josh just before he walked out into the sunshine and yanked him into the dark corner beside the door. Joshua's eyes went wide and startled, and Eli felt a rush of lust more powerful than he'd ever known. He shoved Josh against the wall and crowded in, finding his mouth just as his body slammed up against Josh's.

He heard a muffled yelp, but then Joshua went soft in his arms. Only for a moment, though; in the next, Eli found himself with an armful of fierce. Joshua grabbed the sides of his shirt, grinding himself hard up against Eli. He was groaning low in his throat as he rocked his hips into Eli's.

"Fuck," Eli hissed as Joshua's teeth closed on his shoulder.

"Yesss," Joshua hissed. "Fuck me. Fuck me."

"Not here…."

"*Here*. Now." Joshua shoved him away, got him twisted around so Eli's back was against the wall, and dropped to his knees.

"Josh, no…." But Josh had already unbuttoned Eli's jeans and pulled down the zipper. He took Eli's cock in with one long gulp, his tongue swirling around the shaft. When he sucked down and then dragged up again, he let Eli feel his teeth, and Eli about lost his mind. He buried his fingers in Joshua's hair and fucked his mouth hard.

It was great, but it apparently wasn't enough for Joshua, who after a few minutes, pulled back and replaced his mouth with his hand, his thumb rubbing over the crown and pulsing against the underside of Eli's cock. "I need you to fuck me," Joshua rasped. "I need it, Eli."

"Josh...." Eli looked down into eyes naked with need and hunger. "I...." He trailed off when he saw Josh dig into his pocket for a condom and a pillow pack of lube. Joshua ripped open the condom and slid it over Eli's cock, then undid his own jeans and jerked them down around his knees. He handed Eli the lube, then turned and bent over, his palms flat against the wall. "Fuck me," he said over his shoulder.

"Jesus Christ!" Eli popped the lube and swiped some on his cock, then reached for Joshua's ass, sliding two fingers in deep. Joshua moaned, "Good!" as Eli stretched him, then in a blur of need and heat and an unexpected fury, Eli buried himself in Joshua, slapping his hands over Josh's on the wall. He drew back, rocked hard into him, heard Josh hiss, felt him shudder, and did it again, and again, his hands holding Josh's flat on the wall. For a piece of time—Eli thought maybe forever—there was no sound except their labored breathing and the slap of lubed, sweaty flesh. Eli kicked Joshua's feet farther apart and fucked him deeper. Joshua fought against Eli's hold, but Eli was having none of it: he tightened his fingers around Josh's until he held them clamped and motionless.

Joshua keened softly as he came, spurting on the worn wood of the barn wall despite Eli's keeping his hands from his cock. He shuddered but Eli kept moving, driving him hard. He stopped thinking about anything except his need for climax, his need for Joshua.

His teeth sank into Joshua's shirt and he felt another shudder wrack through Josh. It made him orgasm, the sensation so intense he went blind a moment, his ears buzzing. He felt himself pulse three or four times before his legs gave out and he collapsed against Josh.

THE wood was warm and rough against Joshua's cheek, and he thought he might have a splinter in his palm. The same palm Eli had clamped against the barn wall, just like he had the other, and his body pinning the rest of Joshua there, too. It wasn't comfortable, but it felt *good*. Joshua felt safe and solid and secure under Eli's weight, like he could let go and Eli would take care of him. The thought was so powerful he shuddered again, and felt, more than heard, Eli's faint groan.

"*Mijo*," Eli whispered into his ear, "you're gonna kill me...." He eased back out of Joshua and away from him. Joshua felt empty and exposed. But then Eli's warmth returned and he kissed the spot on Joshua's shoulder he'd bitten. "I'm sorry," he said.

Sorry. Joshua shrugged him off and bent to retrieve his jeans, pulling them up over his damp cock and buttoning them again. "No big," he said, and shifted past Eli.

Eli caught his arm. "No, not again. Jesus, Josh, stand still and listen for just a minute, will you? Good Lord, I never know what it is I say that sets you off. You're worse'n a woman for that kinda shit." He seemed to see Joshua preparing to respond and held up a finger. "No. Not one word. You just sit there and *listen*." He pointed to a nearby hay bale.

Annoyed, Joshua plopped down on the bale. He winced at the sting.

Eli picked up the hat that apparently had gotten knocked off at some point in the last few minutes and smacked it against his thigh to dislodge the hay stuck to it. Then he looked up at the high roof of the barn, then down the aisle between the stalls. Then he sighed. "*Mijo*," he said, then corrected himself, "Josh...."

"I don't mind *mijo*," Josh interrupted.

"What? But you said you didn't like 'son' and it means the same thing."

Josh shrugged. "It's different, is all. Go on."

"Damn it, I forgot what I was gonna say!"

"You were going to tell me that I shouldn't do that again, that you have to work here and nobody knows you like ass, and that I should be concentrating on getting better and learning the ranch like I'm supposed to. And that you're not interested in a fucked-up piece of useless shit like me." Joshua's voice, even to himself, lacked any kind of life. He didn't even feel particularly emotional about it—after all, you couldn't argue with the truth, could you? Eli'd lived here for years.

Love, Like Water

He probably had a regular relationship with someone around here, or maybe in Albuquerque. Or maybe in Miller, at the hospital. That Dr. Castellano seemed to know him pretty well. What did he need a mess like Joshua hanging on him? Why would he *want* that?

He knew he'd been childish and stupid to get pissed off at Eli and to start this fight, but when Eli had just gone about his usual business as if nothing had happened, it had hurt. He'd thought that their little interlude had been special, but Eli had been acting as if it was nothing. Just a break in a busy day. Maybe he'd been wrong. Maybe it had been stupid to get involved with someone like Eli, someone who had a life. He didn't know why he'd followed Eli into the shed in the first place. He'd just hadn't wanted to let go.

"Jesus." Eli sat down beside him and laced his fingers through Joshua's. "Wasn't gonna say anything of the sort, *mijo*. I was gonna.... Shit. I was just gonna apologize for treating you bad, and to say you shouldn't let people treat you like that."

"Treat me like what?"

"Be all... rough and stuff. I was hard on you, in a hurry. Didn't mean to be. Didn't...." He blew out a breath. "Wanted the next time to be good. To do it right, not just in a hurry like before. Like now. Like you're not worth taking the time. Jesus Christ, if that's how people treat you, no wonder you got such a shitty self-image. Fuck." He thunked his head back against the wall behind them. "Fuck."

"You lost it," Joshua said. "Don't you realize how fucking hot that was? You lost it, and you pinned me up against that wall and took me because you wanted me, and it felt fucking awesome." He looked down at their linked fingers. Eli's were long and bronzed and callused like the workingman's they were. His were thin and soft. As dark as Eli's, though paler than they used to be, after so many months in rehab—his Puerto Rican ancestry made sure he always had a nice tan. But not working hands.

Unless you counted holding a gun, or a piece of pipe, or a set of brass knuckles. His weren't working hands. His were killing hands.

But in Eli's, they looked different.

Eli dragged them up to his lips and kissed the back of Joshua's fingers. "I don't know what you want, Josh."

"What do you want?"

"Shit." Joshua loved the way he said that. Not quite the "sheee-it" that he was used to hearing from the blacks and Latinos in Chicago, but a long, dragged out "sh" and a shorted, chopped "ee-it" at the end. It was how most of the guys on the ranch said it, even Tucker on the rare occasions he swore, but coming from Eli it sounded sweeter. "*Shhhh-ee-it.*" "I want you to get better," Eli said. "I want you to like it so much here you want to stay forever and not go back to the city. I want you to learn to love horses as much as I do. I want you to be happy."

"That's a whole lot about me."

"Yeah, well, you're kinda on my mind these days. Shit."

Shhhh-ee-it.

Joshua closed his eyes and leaned back against the wall beside Eli. "I want the same things," he admitted. "I don't *deserve* them, but I want them."

"You deserve 'em. Everybody deserves to be happy."

"You don't know, Eli. And I can't make you understand. But I want them. That'll have to do."

"What can't I understand?"

Joshua only shook his head, thinking of a girl, and a warehouse, and blood spilled black as oil on stained concrete. Reluctantly, he disengaged his fingers from Eli's. "You'd better get back to work."

The foreman searched his face, his eyes sober. "You oughta go take a nap, *mijo*—you look beat."

"Yeah, maybe I will." He watched as Eli got up, slapped his hat against his thigh again in what Joshua was beginning to realize was a habit with him, and went out into the sunlight.

He stayed in the dark corner of the barn for a while. The hay in the bale was hard, scratchy, and not at all comfortable, particularly on a sore ass, but he was disinclined to move. From here, he could see most of the ranch yard and half the buildings, and he watched as hands and horses moved in their daily ballet. Tucker was out in the small arena,

Love, Like Water

putting a small black and white horse through its paces; he didn't seem to move much, but the horse was practically dancing through a series of seemingly planned movements. Jesse, Spencer, and Patrick were standing in a group near the trough. Patrick was talking with his hands and the other two were listening. It occurred to Joshua that the other trainers, Tuck and Eli and the guys from Wyoming and Montana Eli had mentioned before, didn't wave their hands around like that. They were real still when they were talking, letting their words do the work. He wondered if he used his hands in such a noticeable way—it wasn't the kind of thing you noticed when it was you doing it.

A pickup chugged into the yard and pulled up by the pole barn, the biggest structure on the ranch. Manolo, who everyone called Manny, got out and started unloading boxes and big feed bags. Jesse left the others and went to help. Joshua noticed that Spencer and Patrick just stood by the fence and watched. He wasn't impressed.

Ramon came by on one of the horses; he stopped and let Manny load him up with a bunch of bags, and rode into the barn with them. Tomas rode in from the opposite direction with a string of horses behind him, and led them into the corral near where Patrick and Spencer were standing. They passed pretty closely, and one of the horses decided to dump right near Spencer's shoes. Joshua stifled a laugh. Served the dick right. Then he remembered what Eli had said about revenge scenarios and a good-looking kid getting too close.... Holy shit—did he mean Spencer? He eyed the kid curiously. Seriously? Eli thought he had to be jealous of a white-bread piece of mama's boy like *that*?

It was almost funny. No. It *was* funny.

Joshua sat in the dark of the barn and grinned maniacally to himself.

Chapter 18

THE ranch had long since gone to sleep, and the full moon was riding high in the sky. Joshua stood in the middle of the ranch yard and stared up. He hadn't spent a lot of time outdoors at night since he'd arrived here; he had been too exhausted to stay up late, and even though his sleep was too often broken by the nightmares, it had never occurred to him to go outside and look at the stars. He should have, he thought, and would, the next time he woke from a bad dream—all this beauty, all this brightness would surely chase away the demons that haunted him.

A memory surfaced of his grandfather teaching him about the stars long ago. Joshua had sat on the top rail of the fence, Granddad next to him, smelling of tobacco and coffee and pointing at the different constellations. Joshua looked up now and tried to pick out one he knew, but the only one he did was the Big Dipper. He was familiar with Orion, because that was one of the few bright enough to make its light known through the lights and smog of the cities Joshua had lived in, but it was a winter constellation, and invisible now. But he'd see it come the frost. Did they get frost up here on the high desert? He supposed he'd find out.

His gym shoes made no sound on the packed dirt of the yard as he crossed it to the foreman's cottage. It, like the ranch house, was dark, but the door opened easily under Joshua's hand.

Eli's voice came out of the bedroom. "Bolt the door behind you."

Love, Like Water

At the sound of his soft, slow voice, deep and patient, a shiver ran through Joshua. "Yes, sir," he said, and did so. When he entered the bedroom, Eli had turned on a small lamp on the nightstand and was sitting cross-legged on the bed, wearing only boxers and a T-shirt.

"Pretty late for a social call."

"Yeah," Joshua replied. "I guess I'm just not a very polite person." He waited.

Eli watched him, his blue eyes hooded, then sighed and shifted over on the bed. "Come on, then. No point in keeping us both up."

"That was the idea."

"Uh huh," Eli said.

Joshua skimmed out of the sweats and T-shirt he wore and sat down next to Eli. Eli reached down and drew the sheet up over both their laps. Joshua waited.

Finally—*finally*—Eli reached up, curled his hand around the back of Joshua's neck, and dragged him down for a kiss. It was soft and sweet, just what Joshua wanted at that moment.

"I set the alarm for five," Eli said as he drew back, "so you can get home before Sarafina gets up. Not that she'd say anything, but no point in putting her on the spot."

"Mm," Joshua said.

Eli smoothed his hand over Joshua's hair. "Growing out," he observed. "I like it better'n the shaved bald look so many guys have these days. All muscle-bound and tattooed and bald."

"I used to be shaved bald. I started letting it grow as soon as I went into rehab. Had more muscles before. The tats, well, you've seen most of them."

"'Most of them'? You got more I ain't seen? Where you hiding 'em?"

Joshua touched the side of his head. "Here, under the hair. It's part of the reason I'm growing it out."

"Shit, son! That had to *hurt*."

"Like a bitch."

"What's it of?"

"Nothing. I want to forget it."

Eli ran his hand over Joshua's hair again and pulled him in for another soft kiss. "Then forget it."

"Eli...."

He didn't need to say more. Eli pulled him down onto the pillows, sliding his hands up Joshua's spine and then down again to cup his ass, pulling him against him and kneading the muscle there. It felt good and not just in a sexual way; it had been a long time since Joshua had been on a horse, and his ass was feeling it. "You ever fuck on horseback?" he murmured into Eli's neck.

The foreman snorted a laugh. "Jesus H. Roosevelt Christ, Josh! Fuckin's complicated enough without adding an animal and five feet of height to the mix! Where did you ever get that idea?"

"Cathy used to read these romance novels, and I'd sneak 'em to read the dirty parts. There was one that was a Western, and the couple fucked on horseback."

"Well, maybe you could do it with a woman," Eli said doubtfully, "but a man's more complicated. I mean, maybe if the horse was in crossties, and was big enough—a draft horse, mebbe, where you had enough room to balance. But Jesus, Josh. I get dizzy thinking about it."

"That's not how I want you dizzy," Joshua whispered. He turned his head to meet Eli's lips, pressing his tongue inside hungrily.

Eli's hands came up and held Joshua's head still, controlling the kiss despite the fact that Joshua had been the one to initiate it. It felt so good, letting Eli take over, knowing that Eli wanted him enough to take charge like this, that it wasn't up to Joshua to make the decisions, that it wasn't on Joshua's head if something failed, that Joshua wasn't the only one who would be responsible for how this shook out. That there was someone else Joshua could trust besides himself. And everything he'd seen about Eli, everything he'd seen in how the others respected him, how Uncle Tucker relied on him, hell, even how Sarafina treated him—all those things told Joshua that Eli was a man to be trusted.

A man that, if Joshua had still been capable of love, he could love.

Eli must have felt him shiver, because he stopped kissing him and said, "You cold?"

"Someone walked over my grave." Joshua gave him a shaky grin.

"Not on my watch," Eli growled and kissed him again.

THEY made love the way Eli wanted to: slow, patient, intense. Eli kept Joshua hovering on the edge for so long the sheets were wet with sweat by the time he turned his head, kissed Joshua's knee where it pressed against Joshua's shoulder, and said, "Come" in a hoarse, hungry voice. Joshua threw his head back against the pillows with a stifled shout and obeyed, his cock in Eli's hand spurting hot and wet between them. Eli kept riding Joshua a few moments, then let out a long, drawn-out groan of his own, dropping his head onto Joshua's shoulder. They lay there, panting, for a moment, then Eli raised his sweaty head to grin at Joshua. "You okay?"

"Nngh," Joshua said and managed a short nod. He watched as Eli pulled out, missing the fullness and twitching a little as Eli's cock dragged one last time over his sensitized gland. Eli tied off the condom and tossed it into the little trash can by the bed. Then he eased Joshua's legs down and lay beside him, pulling him into his arms. "I'll get up in a minute and get us something to clean up with. But I don't think I can walk right this minute."

"In college we kept a box of baby wipes in the nightstand," Joshua said into Eli's wiry shoulder.

"Huh. Well, I'd look pretty damn stupid buying baby wipes. Lizbeth at the general would think I'd lost my ever-loving mind." Joshua felt Eli's lips on his hair. "You college fellas are all so smart."

"Uncle Tuck said you studied animal husbandry, so shut up about 'us college fellas'. You've been to college too."

"Just got a two-year degree."

"It's still college, and it's still a degree. You can't hide behind your dumb cowboy act." Joshua licked sweat from Eli's neck and he shivered. "You're smarter than I am—you didn't go and get yourself in so much trouble you thought you'd never get out."

"I play it safe," Eli said softly. "I don't take risks. I'm careful. Sometimes I think…."

After a moment, Joshua asked, "Think what?"

The shoulder under Joshua's cheek shifted in miniscule shrug. "I dunno. Think maybe I'm letting life pass me by."

"Do you love what you do?"

"Hell, yeah." Eli's voice was surprised. "You know I do!"

"Is there something else you'd rather be doing?"

"No. No, can't say as there is."

"Somewhere else you'd rather be?"

"Nope."

"Then what are you worried about?" Joshua rose up on one elbow. "You're doing what you love. You won't find ten men in a hundred that can say the same thing. You're lucky, and you're smart."

"I'm also queer, in a culture that ain't so easy on queers," Eli pointed out. "I'd be safer in a big city, I think."

"No you wouldn't," Joshua said wryly. "Trust me."

"'S'pose you're right. Assholes are everywhere."

Joshua grinned. "You should be happy about that!"

Eli blinked, then laughed. "Well, not the right kind." He looked down at the sheet between them. "Not just me…. I mean, if you wanted to…. I don't… I mean, I do, I *would*…."

"Eli," Joshua said, "are you saying you'd bottom for me?"

Love, Like Water

"Yup." Eli flushed scarlet. "I ain't never.... Shit, when you're picking up somebody at a bar, and you're in a hurry, you just go with what you're used to, y'know? I ain't never had... I dunno. *Someone*."

"I did. In college. He was a grad student." Daniel, of the faraway brown eyes and the obsession with Renaissance art.

"What happened?"

"He got an internship abroad and I got a job with the local police department. It fizzled. They do."

"Wouldn't know." Eli nuzzled Joshua's jaw and Joshua felt himself relax into his embrace. "Don't want to know."

Joshua was going to ask what he meant, but instead, he fell asleep.

Chapter 19

Tucker wasn't sure why he was wide awake at five in the morning, but as usual he knew he wasn't going to get back to sleep, so he got up and went downstairs to make himself a cup of coffee. Despite the fact that it was still dark out, the light over the stove was enough to see the coffeemaker, so he didn't bother to turn on the overheads.

The coffee had just begun to drip when the kitchen door opened quietly and Josh slipped inside.

He froze when he saw Tuck sitting at the table. "Uncle Tucker."

"Josh." What the hell was he doing outside at this hour? Tucker frowned at him, noting the flushed face and generally rumpled state of his usually tidy nephew, and a thought occurred to him. "Out visitin'?"

"Just… looking at the stars."

Tucker nodded. "Pretty, ain't they? Bet you can't see 'em so well in Cincinnati. Or Chicago."

"No. Too much in the way."

"Yep. Coffee?"

"No, thanks."

"So. Eli doing okay?"

The only sound Tucker heard was the faint tick of the kitchen clock. Then Joshua said easily, "He seemed fine yesterday."

So he was going to play it that way, was he? Josh's easy response didn't fool Tucker in the slightest—in fact, it only confirmed his suspicions. Damn, the kid was good, though—no wonder he did so well

Love, Like Water

as an undercover agent. "Cut loose, son. You look like a man that's been well and truly done, if you know what I mean."

"What do you want me to say?" All the superficial casualness drained out of Joshua's body, and he dropped into one of the chairs opposite Tuck. "He said you knew he was gay. How did you know I was?"

"I didn't—'til you came in here wearing his soap and a smug expression."

"You can smell his *soap* on me?"

"No, but you just confirmed my theory." Tucker sighed. "Shit, son."

"We're both adults."

"You're also both *men*." Tucker got up and poured himself a coffee, then after a moment's indecision, poured Joshua one too. Setting it in front of his nephew, Tucker went on, "I don't get the whole queer thing, but if this fucks up my ranch, I'm gonna kill both of you. Eli's the best damn foreman I've ever had, and you're my nephew. I don't want to have to deal with lovers' quarrels and nasty breakups. You find a way to deal with each other so the men don't know what's going on, and maybe I can handle it. You don't, and I'm shipping you back to Hannah—in pieces."

Joshua's face had gone closed and hard. "Don't worry, Tucker," he said in a cold voice that Tucker had never heard from him before. "We won't flaunt our *queerness* in front of the men. I'm not fucking stupid."

Sighing, Tucker said, "Shit, boy, that ain't what I'm worried about. Well, yeah, it is, on account of you're in the West, and cowboys generally ain't exactly ready to march in no Pride Parade. You're more likely to get shunned at the very least. Yeah, you coulda picked a worse place than New Mexico, but still. Shit, didn't you see *Brokeback Mountain*?"

"Of course I did. I didn't know you had."

"Took a girl on a date to see it. She liked it."

"It was a good movie."

"Well, you know how they showed the dead queers in the flashback? That sorta shit still happens out here. Maybe not so frequent, maybe not so much in this state as in some of the others, but hell, that Matthew kid wasn't so awful long ago. I don't want another tragedy like that in my lifetime, Josh, and especially not involving my nephew." He raised the mug to his lips and was surprised to see his hands shaking. "And Eli's a good man, and don't deserve to be hurt. So if you're just, just *fucking* with him, then stop."

"I don't know what I'm doing." Joshua's hands were flat on the table on either side of the mug. He was staring down at them as if they held the answers to all of life's questions. "Not a new feeling for me."

"Josh."

His nephew looked up. He was completely expressionless. Tucker thought of the lively, determined boy he used to know, and his heart broke. Not for the first time since the shattered wreck of a nephew had arrived. In a soft voice, he said, "Just be careful, is all I'm askin'. If you and Eli make each other happy, then hell, make each other happy. But be careful."

"I don't know if I can do this, Uncatuck. I don't know how to make him happy. I want to. But I don't know how."

"Hell, son, nobody does. That's why you gotta work it out on your own." He felt absurdly pleased by the childhood nickname Josh had used; it sounded so much easier on the ears than grown-up Joshua's "Uncle Tucker." "I don't exactly have the best track record in relationships, either. But Eli's not a complicated man. He likes to work, sleep, eat, and, from his regular trips into Albuquerque, get laid. He's patient, and he likes you." Tucker shrugged. "So long's you're not expecting flowers and chocolates, you'll do fine."

Josh snorted a laugh. "No."

"You—you're complicated. It might take you a bit longer to figure things out, but you'll do fine."

"I'm not complicated. I'm just a fucking junkie with nothing except a kind man for an uncle."

"You gotta stop defining yourself that way, Josh. You're more than that. I think...." Tucker stopped and sipped his coffee.

Love, Like Water

"Think what?"

Tucker sighed. "I think you mighta made a mistake quitting the Bureau."

"I didn't have a choice."

"What do you mean?"

"With everything that happened, I would have been eventually phased out. They were already talking about putting me on desk duty 'temporarily'." Tucker heard the internal quotes in Josh's voice. "That would have stretched out until they found something even less important to do. Who knows. Maybe I would have ended up the janitor. At any rate, I'd have never gotten field duty again. The heroin made sure of that. Hell, they can't even use me as a witness. Once… once I got addicted, I knew I had to make every bit of evidence count on its own, independently verified. Robinson said they would reference me as an anonymous informant to protect me and my family. Who I can't even begin to defend since I can't even legally have a gun anymore. Not that I want one." Joshua drank some coffee. "Why am I saying all this? I didn't even talk this much to the center shrink."

"Maybe because you're finally starting to relax?"

Josh snorted. "Maybe."

"I'm seeing it. You're putting on some weight. You don't walk around like a ghost the way you did when you first came here. It's only been a few weeks, but you look better since you were in the hospital. I think the hospital food agreed with you."

This time the snort was more of a laugh. "Sarafina's food agrees with me. I think the hospital saved a fortune with you bringing me all my meals from home. It's different, but it kind of reminds me of my Abuela's cooking."

"They were nice people, your grandfolks. I met 'em a couple times in Chicago, when you and Cathy were still babies. Hannah was lucky to have them."

"Yeah. I spent a lot of time with them when I was a kid. Of course, they called me 'José' and Cathy 'Catalina'. I didn't mind, but it drove Cathy crazy."

"Technically, 'Joshua' woulda been 'Jesus'," Tucker pointed out.

"I know. But Abuelito had a brother named Jesus that he couldn't stand, so they called me José instead. I didn't care. It came in handy later, when I could show up as 'José Rosales' and people remembered the name. 'Joshua Chastain' never even came onto their radar." Joshua stared into his coffee. "It would have destroyed them to know I was in the gang they fought so hard against. It broke their hearts when my father joined it, and he died because of it. They taught me to hate the gangs and to work against them."

"And you did."

"But I was still a member. I still...."

"Still what?"

"Did what they told me to."

Tucker didn't know what to say to that. He took a sip of his coffee and changed the subject. "Did your grandfolks know you were gay?"

"No, they died when I was in junior high, before I figured it out. Classic thing—Abuela died, and Abuelito followed her just a few weeks later. I heard that's not unusual with couples who've been together a long time. At any rate, Mom figured there wasn't anything keeping her tied to Chicago anymore, and when she got a job offer in Cincinnati a few months afterwards, we moved there."

"Used to be a TV show set in Cincinnati. Pretty funny."

"Yeah, I heard about it. Saw a few reruns."

"And the gang didn't know. About you being gay."

Joshua shook his head. "No room for *maricones* in Los Peligros. Though 'Chete Montenegro was such a virulent homophobe I figure he was closeted and majorly in denial."

"He one of the ones you put in jail?"

"No, he was killed in the raid that took out most of the gang—at least the ones on the drug-dealing side. The gang itself is still alive and well, and swearing that the rest of them had no idea that a 'splinter group' was so involved in trafficking. Like they didn't benefit from the cash that came in. But we didn't have enough solid evidence to go after

Love, Like Water

the rest of them, so all we could do is keep monitoring them. The Bureau doesn't have enough manpower to deal with all the gangs in the country. They have to cherry-pick the ones they can deal with."

"And with your background, they were able to take down some of the worst. Jack Castellano knew about your gang tattoos. I guess they're kind of famous."

"They're stone-cold killers," Joshua said. He drained his mug and set it carefully back down on the table. "What are you doing up so early?"

"Insomnia. Happens when you get old. Figured there's no point staring at the ceiling, so I thought I'd come down and get started on some of the backed-up paperwork, stuff you don't need to deal with. Then after breakfast, we'll get back to work. I want to go over the payroll with you."

"Any chance I can catch a couple hours of sleep?"

Tuck looked at the kitchen clock. "You got forty-five minutes, son. Make the best of it."

Josh nodded and got up, setting his mug in the sink. To Tucker's surprise, he came over and put an arm around Tuck's shoulders. "Thank you, Uncatuck. For everything."

Patting his hand, Tucker said, "Nothing I wouldn't do for you, Joshy. You're my boy. Sleep well."

"Thanks, Uncatuck."

The kitchen was quiet after he was gone. Tucker finished his coffee, but sat there at the table thinking a while before Sarafina came in to start breakfast. Then he shook his head, kissed her cheek, and went in to his office.

Chapter 20

THE alarm went off at 6:30. Eli flung his arm out without looking and smacked the snooze bar, then opened one eye and stared at the time. Why had he thought he'd set it for five? He usually set it for six, so he had time for a shower before breakfast, and he really needed one this morning, for some reason.... Oh. Right. He raised his head to see the other half of the bed empty, and Joshua's clothes gone from the floor. Josh must have reset the alarm.

Josh. Eli let his head thunk back down on the pillow. Fuck breakfast—he had more to worry about than that.

His stomach growled, though, and so he got up and showered and dressed, then went looking for chow. As he crossed the yard, Dennis, Frank, and Ramon came out of the house and crossed his path. "Hey, Eli," Dennis greeted him. "You're running late this morning. Must be—hell, nearly seven o'clock!" The others chortled—Eli was notorious for being an early riser.

"Yeah, well, even I oversleep sometimes," Eli said with a casual wave, and went on into the kitchen.

The rest of the hands were still there. It looked like Jason had only just arrived and was fetching his coffee. Tuck looked up from his usual seat and said coolly, "Mornin', Eli." His eyes met Eli's and Eli's appetite fled. *Shit. He knows.*

He took the mug that Jason handed him and sat down in *his* usual spot, catercorner from Tucker. Sarafina set a plate full of breakfast burritos and fried potatoes in front of him. "You're late," she said.

Love, Like Water

"Yeah, I'm late. Jesus. I overslept. It happens."

"I only made an observation," Sarafina said. "*I don't care if you're late. I'm still cooking.*"

"Sorry." Eli rubbed his forehead. "I didn't sleep so good."

"Not enough exercise before bed?" Tuck asked innocently.

Eli had just put his coffee cup to his lips but hadn't taken a sip yet, for which he was grateful. "Got my regular routine in," he said carefully. "My sleep was just—interrupted. Had a hard time getting back to sleep."

"Tucker had some insomnia this morning, too," Sarafina said. "I came down to find him drinking coffee at five-thirty." She shook her head. "You both drink too much coffee. No wonder you have trouble sleeping."

Shit. Tuck must have intercepted Joshua. "That so?"

"Uh-huh," Tucker said, and sipped his coffee.

Eli dug into the burritos and home fries, blocking out the look he was sure he was getting from Tucker and trying not to pay attention to the fact that the food tasted like paper. Jason and Tom didn't seem to notice any undercurrents, but the silence crawled over Eli's skin like bugs.

Finally, Tucker got up, put his plate in the sink and said to Sarafina, "When Josh gets done eating, send him into the office. We're gonna work on payroll today. Eli, I want you to take Spence and Pat out to the canyon where the culled mamas are and introduce them to 'em. Make sure they're good and scared—the men, not the mustangs. That lead mare should make 'em crap their shorts." Tucker's grin was evil. "They're a little too smug, if you ask me. Need to shake 'em up a bit."

"My pleasure."

"After lunch you get Josh again." Was the grin a little eviler? "I want you to start working with him on his riding skills. Put him in the arena and through his paces. He's been doing okay with Avery?"

"Fine. Seems to remember most of what he learned about riding."

"Good. Then maybe we can graduate him to something a little more lively. I think that bay'll be good for him. Rodney's given him a clean bill of health, and he seems like he's got some spirit. Start working with him and Josh."

"Right."

"Then after supper I think you and I need to conference on… um, let's call it 'personnel issues'. That all right with you, son?"

Do I have a choice? "Fine," he said hoarsely, and took a gulp of the orange juice Sarafina had just set in front of him.

THE day dragged, of course. Taking the two trainees out to see the horses in the canyon was entertaining: the mustangs were pretty damn pissed and still wild, even after two months in captivity, and disturbed by Manny and Billy's visit the day before. They were all feisty and belligerent, and the head mare in the herd kept charging at them at odd moments. Eli knew she was just displaying, but the trainees didn't, so it was kind of fun to freak them out.

Then it was a matter of explaining how the ranch handled the mustangs' gentling and training, and that was less fun, because Patrick seemed to have a lot of bad ideas and Spencer was generally clueless. By the time Eli turned them over to Dennis to have them explore his farrier's shop, he was exhausted, more mentally than physically.

He missed Josh at lunch; he ate late when he got back from the canyon and then went out into the stable yard to touch base with the other hands and trainers. He was inspecting a barrel that had corroded and split, and cursing the wasted grain, when he heard Joshua's voice. It was raw with pain.

"I don't know what I'm doing. I don't know how it can work. There's so much I can't give him, and if he knew—if he even suspected…. Jesus. I don't know what to do."

Setting the barrel carefully on its side, with the crack upwards so as not to spill any more grain, he rose, dusting his hands.

"I mean, shit. I can't tell him. I can't tell anyone."

Nobody responded. Frowning, Eli peered around the door to the storage room.

Love, Like Water

Joshua was standing next to a pile of boxes. The cat was sitting on the top box, his eyes closed under Joshua's scratching fingers, and purring fit to beat the band. As Eli opened his mouth to speak, Joshua whispered in a broken voice, "It's killing me...."

Taking a long step back into the storage room, Eli leaned back against the wall. Shit. What was Joshua talking about? Something important. Something probably having to do with his experiences undercover. But what could be so bad? He already knew about the heroin—could it be that Josh was still using? But how did he get it, if he was? Someone in the hospital? He couldn't believe that. Besides, he explored every inch of Joshua's skin last night, and he'd have seen any fresh marks.

But then Joshua murmured, almost too softly for Eli to hear, "So much blood.... Why can't I forget? Why can't I ever forget?"

Shit. Eli walked quietly over to the barrel, kicked the metal side and said loudly, "Son of a bitch!" A moment later, Josh stuck his head in the door and said, "You in here, Eli? What's wrong?" in a perfectly normal voice.

"Buggering thing split. Looks like it corroded along the seam. The sides are aluminum, but they musta used something else to seal the seams. Shit. I hope the grain ain't spoiled."

"Did it cost a lot?"

"Yeah, this is the special high-test for the rescue animals. This pisses me off. I'm gonna have to find another supplier."

"You need to contact this company first," Josh said. "See if you can get a discount or replacement grain. Because this could have cost you a lot if you hadn't found it as quickly as you did. They need to have better quality materials. They need to be aware of it, and take responsibility."

"Huh," Eli said. "Good thinkin'. But I'm still gonna look for a different supplier."

Joshua nodded. Eli set the barrel aside, and went to Joshua's side. Putting a hand on Joshua's jaw, he said quietly, "You're okay, Josh—you just need to figure that out."

Joshua made a sound halfway between a sniff and a snort, but he leaned back against Eli's hand. "Thanks, Boss."

"Just the truth." He kissed Joshua's cheek. Josh turned then, and slid his arms around Eli's waist, letting his cheek rest on Eli's shoulder. "That's nice," Eli said.

"You're nice. You're too nice for someone like me."

"Hey. You criticizing my selectivity?"

Josh chuckled. "No, I'm not criticizing your 'seeee-lek-tivity', Boss. Just your taste."

"Brat." Eli delivered a sharp smack to Joshua's backside. Josh obligingly yelped, and Eli kissed him, hard, before turning him loose. "Come on, I need to see a man about a horse."

SUPPERTIME came too quickly for Eli's liking. He'd spent some time with Joshua and Rory, but they seemed to like each other well enough, and after putting Josh through his paces in the arena, Eli pronounced them acceptable.

Spencer and Patrick had observed Josh in the ring, and Eli talked loud enough for them to hear as he explained what they were looking for in matching up a rider and a horse. For once, they didn't ask too many stupid questions, and when he reviewed with them later, they seemed to get the gist of it. Maybe they weren't as stupid as they were, just… thick. Stuck with preconceptions. That was the usual flaw in most of the people Tucker had brought in as trainees—he had to see something worth his time and their money, but most of them had ground-in ideas that needed to be rooted out.

To be fair, Eli was a little bit prejudiced—at least against Spencer, because of his apparent interest in Joshua. He didn't blame the boy. Now that Josh was looking a little less gaunt, and the dead look in his eyes was making rarer appearances, he was turning into a handsome man. And he did have a nice smile when he used it. He had a long way to go to look healthy, but his coloring was better.

He said so when he walked into Tucker's office that evening after supper.

"Yeah, he is looking better," Tucker agreed. "Due to Sarafina's food, I expect—thanks for helping me keep him fed while he was in the hospital. That swill ain't nothing worth eating."

"I didn't mind." He didn't. At the beginning, it was a little awkward. Josh didn't talk, so when he visited, Eli would dish out whatever Sarafina had sent with him, and just natter on about whatever was going on at the ranch. He didn't address Joshua's "getting lost" or his health or anything else personal; he just talked about the ranch.

Later, Eli thought Josh was looking forward to his visits and the food he brought—by the end of the week, he was responding to Eli some as he scarfed down whatever chile-covered dish he'd carried in. Just an occasional, stray, quiet question, but enough to show Eli he was listening.

"He seems to be settling in better."

"Yeah. We had a talk about that while he was still in the hospital. I told him to give us six months, and if he still didn't feel like staying, I'd pay for his plane ticket back to Cincinnati or wherever he wanted to go. But he had to promise not to do anything stupid in the meantime. I sure as shit hope that shrink he's seeing can straighten him out. He's a smart kid, and a good kid, and the hands like him already. They were really concerned when he got lost."

"Yeah." Eli never wanted to live through anything like those hours again. When his dad died, it was fast and he knew about it within an hour of it happening. Dealing with it was shit, but there was none of this "not knowing" that made Josh's disappearance so bad.

"Okay. Shut the door and siddown, Elian. We need to talk."

Eli obeyed but stayed standing, his arms folded over his chest. "You got something to say to me, Tucker Chastain, you out and say it. I'm done waiting."

"Woo, boy, enough with the tough guy. I ain't firing you, if that's what you're worried about. But I want to talk to you about Josh. I spent the whole day thinking about it."

"Look, Josh and I are both adults. We're both consenting and neither of us is taking advantage of the other. I know you ain't comfortable with me being gay, and I try not to flaunt it, and Josh don't want to flaunt it either. So there ain't gonna be no kissy-face at the table or other PDAs...."

"What the Sam Hill is a 'PDA'?" Tucker demanded. "I thought them was what people had before their smart phones or whatever?"

Eli rolled his eyes. "Public Display of Affection."

"Well, shit, boy, I got nothing against affection. As long as you aren't bumping uglies in my living room, you display affection all you like. Just don't go kissing him so's the other hands can see, 'cause that could get ugly."

"That's kinda what it means, Tuck."

"Oh. Well, shit." Tucker threw up his hands. "I just ain't up with all that crap. Guess I don't watch enough TV."

"Probably."

"Point is, I don't care if you're queer, and Josh is queer, and you guys... do whatever it is queers do together, and I really don't want to know, okay? I get that. But if you're just dicking around with Josh and he gets hurt, I'm gonna be pissed, and then I *will* fire your ass, *comprendes*?"

"*Comprendo*," Eli agreed.

"I know what the Bible says, but I ain't a churchgoing man, and from what I've read there's a lot of damn silly stuff in the Bible anyway, about shrimp, and ladies' bosoms looking like pomegranates, and having multiple wives. I mean, shit. I like shrimp, and I ain't never seen anybody's bosoms looking anything like pomegranate, and hell, I never had enough patience for any one of the ladies I dated, let alone a couple at the same time. So I figure the Bible can't be right all the time. And if it's wrong about some things, who's to say it ain't wrong about that too. I heard tell of two gay penguins once, and some dogs'll hump other dogs when there's bitches standing around watching, so who am I to say what's natural and what ain't?"

Eli nodded, hiding his desire to bust out laughing.

"So I guess my point is that until the world changes and redneck ranch hands learn to deal with things like this, I'd appreciate it if you guys kept it quiet. I don't want to find out one or both of you been dragged down I-40 behind a pickup truck. You want to get frisky in

Love, Like Water

public, you drive into Albuquerque or Roswell or Santa Fe, where people don't care."

"No problem."

"Good. Now. I need to ask a favor."

Eli spread his hands. "Ask—you know I'm good for it."

"You know Josh has his appointments on Tuesdays, and I been taking him. The problem is in a coupla weeks I'm going to El Paso to a Texas Cattlemans' Association dinner to try and get some business my way. So I was wondering if you'd mind taking Josh to Albuquerque that night."

"No problem," Eli repeated.

"Leave whenever you feel like it—if you two want to go out for dinner ahead of time, cut out early. I don't care. Josh's capable of driving himself, but for the first few weeks until he knows his way around, I want someone else to drive him. The shrink's office is over by the university and the streets are kinda confusing over there."

"I know the area." Hell, some of his favorite bars were in the vicinity of UNM. "Streets are confusing in Albuquerque generally, but he'll figure it out eventually. A few more times down there and he'll know where he's goin'."

"Yeah. Here's the address—it's on Central, east of the university."

Eli took the printout Tucker handed him. Yeah, he knew the area pretty well. Somehow, though, he didn't think he'd be hanging out at his usual haunts while waiting for Josh.

Somehow, they didn't appeal to him much anymore.

Chapter 21

"You gonna need Joshua this morning?"

Josh looked up from his breakfast at Eli's query, but the foreman was looking at Tucker. "Probably not. What you got in mind?"

"Time to check on the ladies of the canyon again. Thought I'd bring Josh along to see what actually gets done. Last time Manny and Billy did the collection and Josh just napped."

"'Ladies of the Canyon'? Wasn't that an old Joni Mitchell song?" Joshua asked.

"Son, you are far too young to remember Joni Mitchell," Tucker said.

"Joni Mitchell is a genius, and timeless. Besides, Mom had the album. Played it until it wore out, then bought a CD of it."

"I was referring," Eli said patiently, "to the mares in the box canyon."

"I know." Joshua shot him a grin. "And I think Uncatuck can do without me for one morning."

"Reckon I can."

Sarafina said, "I'll pack you lunch while you get the gear, Eli, and Joshua saddles the horses."

"Guess we been told," Joshua said to Eli, who only grinned back at him. He forked in the last of his ham, chewed and swallowed, then added, "Meet you out front in ten?"

Love, Like Water

"In a hurry?" Eli chuckled. "Yeah, ten's good. Saddle up Milagro for me, willya? Button looked to be going a bit lame on the right forefoot. I think she stepped on a stone or something. I poulticed it yesterday, but like to give it another day or so before I put her to work again."

"Right," Joshua said. He dumped his plate into the sink, gave Sarafina a smile, and went out to the barn and stables.

He'd started riding Rory around the last couple of days. The horse had recovered quickly from the neglect and had turned out to be a lively creature with a smooth gait and pretty manners. Yesterday Joshua had ridden him down to the mailbox and back with the cat—whom Tucker had christened "D.C." after some Disney movie from his childhood—perched on Rory's withers. The cat seemed to have found its place in the barn-cat hierarchy and was perfectly happy living in Rory's stall, though it preferred the kibble the stable hands fed it to catching mice. That, apparently, was for lower-ranked felines. But it was remarkably friendly for a cat.

Rory was friendly for a horse, too, and both Tucker and Eli agreed that he was a good fit for Joshua, so whether he wanted to or not, he seemed to have acquired a horse. And his own boots and hat and gloves, from the mercantile in Miller. He'd teased Eli about getting chaps, and wearing them with just the boots and hat and gloves, and Eli's eyes got dark and smoky. That had been fun.

Fun. It was strange to smile so much—the expression felt weird on his face after being so serious for so long. There hadn't been much room for fun in the last few years; he'd never been able to kick back and relax the way his *compadres* in Los Peligros did. He didn't drink much, because he needed to keep his head at all times, and until 'Chete turned him into a junkie, didn't mess around with shit, either. He skirted so close to the edge at all times that the slightest slip would send him over, and he would be dead and his mission compromised.

The only time he'd ever relaxed was late at night—or more often, early in the morning—when he had finished his report to Robinson on the laptop he kept hidden behind a false panel in the wall behind his bed. His grandfather Chastain had taught him the rudiments of carpentry during his summer visits here as a kid, and it was a simple matter to cut out a section of wallboard to hide the laptop behind. Even if any of the others got into his apartment and found it, it would tell them nothing; he wiped the history as soon as he finished his report, and again before he shut it down and hid it once more. Because sometimes, the only relaxation, the only recreation he allowed himself was jerking off to gay porn videos. And that was something else he didn't want the other Peligros to know about.

No, there was one exception. Once a week or so several of his "friends" went to a local club to dance and pick up girls. Or to hang around *bonchinchando*—gossiping. Joshua always went, because *bonchincheros* were an excellent source of intel. And he liked dancing to the salsa and reggaeton. He liked the rhythm, the grace of the movements, the edginess and heat of the music. 'Chete sometimes used the club as a base of operations, so he looked on their hanging out there with indulgence. It was in a neighborhood undergoing gentrification, but at one point, the Latin Kings, one of the biggest national gangs, had had their Chicago headquarters two doors down.

The Kings were gone from that barrio, and Los Peligros ruled there now, but the Kings still had a presence in the city, and 'Chete had connections with them. Of course he did. He had connections everywhere. Joshua rubbed his chin absently. He'd shaved his goatee and let his hair grow out before he'd even left rehab, and he hoped that that was enough to keep any of 'Chete's connections from ever ID'ing him again.

Rory nickered when Joshua came into the barn. D.C. was curled up in his manger, sleeping, as usual. Joshua didn't understand how cats slept so much and still managed to be so muscular and graceful, but cats were a mystery. D.C. opened an eye when he released the latch to the box stall, but closed it again when he realized that Joshua didn't have any food with him.

It only took a minute to tack up Rory. Milagro, who resided in the main stable, was another thing altogether. Joshua had never ridden Milagro, who was one of the tamed mustangs, and didn't expect he ever would. He'd seen the other trainers dealing with him—the general

Love, Like Water

consensus was that he wasn't adoptable; there was still too much of the stud in him, even after gelding. He wasn't vicious, just spirited. The horse had an attitude; he fought the lead, he fought being put in crossties, which was the only way Joshua could saddle him, and he fought the bridle. Joshua was sweating and cursing by the time he was done. Once he was all tacked up, though, he calmed down considerably and followed Joshua and Rory quietly to the yard in front of the ranch house.

Eli was just coming out of the house; he trotted down the steps and over to Milagro, then hooked one set of the saddlebags he carried to the back of the saddle, and handed Joshua the other. While Joshua was attaching them, Eli checked Milagro's cinch, then tightened it again. Joshua looked at him curiously, and Eli said, "He blows up when you cinch him, and the strap goes loose. A lot of horses do that—always double-check before you get on them, otherwise you and the saddle are gonna take a quick trip to horizontal-land."

Joshua laughed. "Got it."

"Your boy there doesn't seem to have any bad habits," Eli observed. "None of the ones from the Kansas rescue do. Must have been pretty well cared for before the old man died. Lot of love there."

"Yeah," Joshua said softly, and ran his hand down Rory's neck. The gelding nickered and bobbed his head as if in agreement.

When he looked up, Eli was smiling at him, a softness in his eyes that made Joshua feel warm, and somehow safe, as if nothing in his past could ever haunt him again. He relished the feeling, knowing that it was an illusion, but wanting to hang onto it as long as possible. He felt... happy. The moment made him feel happy. The ranch, the beautiful early fall day, Rory, even Milagro made him feel happy. And Eli... that look in his eyes made him feel happiest of all.

He returned Eli's smile, then turned to mount up.

THEY rode out in companionable silence until they were past the trees and out into the desert, then Eli drew Milagro close to Rory. The two horses touched noses and settled in walking close together on the trail. "No reason to rush," Eli said. "It's early yet, still cool enough, and we got all morning. I figure we'll get to the canyon about nine thirty. That'll give us plenty of time to do the collecting, check out the herd, and still have time for a nap before lunch."

"A nap?" Joshua murmured wickedly.

Eli reached out and caught Rory's bridle, drawing him to a stop beside Milagro. "A nap," he agreed, and leaned forward so that his lips were brushing Joshua's. "Or something."

"Mm hmm," Joshua agreed, and settled his mouth on Eli's.

Eli's hand came up and Joshua felt the worn suede of his glove against the nape of his neck, soft and supple. Joshua shuddered wantonly. "God, I want you," he said against Eli's lips, and put his own hand on Eli's chest.

"Right." Eli's voice was ragged. "Shit. Horses first, then canoodling."

Joshua laughed. "Canoodling? I like that. Is that what's for lunch? Campbell's Chicken Canoodle soup?"

"Not interested in chicken canoodling," Eli said. "Never could figure out how that worked. Never wanted to, either. Okay. Enough of this. Shit." He put pressure on the back of Joshua's neck, drawing him forward into another kiss, then released him. "Canyon. Shit. I think I just forgot the way."

Joshua's laughter rang in the stillness of the desert.

RORY wasn't as surefooted as Avery had been. He picked his way down the switchback trail into the canyon, punctuating each step with a nervous whoof of breath. Milagro had no such problem; Eli kept him reined in tightly, or the mustang would have run the whole way down. But finally they were down, and Joshua followed Eli and Milagro along the trail past the little lagoon and waterfall, through a narrow defile,

Love, Like Water

and into a broad meadow framed by the red and yellow stone of the canyon walls. "Big," he said in surprise.

"Not really, not more than maybe a dozen square acres. Big enough to run in," Eli said. He looked around curiously. "Oh, there they are, under those trees."

"Well, a dozen acres is a lot."

Eli snorted. "Shit, Josh, the ranch buildings cover purt near five acres alone. I think the Triple C is somewhere around twelve thousand acres, and that ain't all that big for a ranch. An acre maybe sounds like a lot to a city boy like you, but it really ain't much. Enough for these critters to run around in, though—just not enough for them to get away when we want them to go somewhere." He nudged Milagro and they started towards the group of eight or nine horses that were standing in the shade, tails twitching away flies. A bunch of colts stood in the center of the herd, watching their approach with wide, liquid eyes.

Several of the mares looked up as the two of them approached, but only one of the horses moved, stepping out to stand between them and the herd. It stamped its foot warningly and tossed its head. "Is that the stallion?" Joshua asked in a whisper.

Eli chuckled. "Nope. We cut the studs out first thing before we put them in here. They get gelded and then we work with them first, 'cause they're the most trouble. That's Big Mama, the head mare. When a herd doesn't have a stud, the top-ranked mare takes over as leader. That's okay, Mama, we're not here to hurt you all." His voice dropped to a soothing singsong. "It's okay, Mama...." He continued talking in that same soothing voice until they'd skirted all the way around the herd and were past them, towards the canyon wall.

There he dismounted, handed the reins of the mustang to Joshua, and fished out rubber gloves from the saddlebags, which he replaced his leather ones with. Armed with a handful of bags, scoop and Sharpie, he rooted about in the ankle-deep grass, picking up bits of horse poop and putting it in bags, which he then marked.

They moved to another area of the meadow and repeated the process, all the while watched by Big Mama. "We send the scat out to

Rodney for testing," Eli said as he dug out more bags and put the ones he'd collected in the bag set aside for it. "We'll get blood tests done when we move this herd out of here for the winter in a couple of weeks. But I don't expect to see anything either way—they look pretty healthy and the two colts that dropped this summer after the roundup are doing just fine."

"Careful you're not putting that in with lunch," Joshua said, watching him.

"Teach your grandmother to suck eggs, *niño*," Eli snorted.

When he'd finished, he swung back up onto Milo and led the way back out of the meadow. The head mare bugled in triumph at their retreat and Eli chuckled again. "She's a pistol, that one. She'll be mad as fire when we move them to the ranch for winter. That's usually a fun roundup—they get up on the open desert and don't know what to do. Half the time they just mill around looking lost. Getting them up the trail isn't easy, but if we can get Big Mama up first, the others will follow." He glanced over his shoulder as they walked their horses through the crevice between the meadow and the little valley. "The two littlest foals are gonna be tricky—think I'll tell Tuck to bring a trailer for them and their mamas. It's too far for them to run, even if they are three months old."

"You really love them, don't you?"

Eli smiled, the expression gentle. "Shit, yeah, Josh. Horses are the biggest, dumbest, sweetest, most lovable critters in the whole world. They'll carry you for miles 'til they drop dead of exhaustion. They'll fight for you, they'll guard you. The whole history of mankind's wrapped up with the horse, four, five thousand years at least. Hell, it's only been about a hundred years that we've had any alternative to 'em at all and I can't say as I think it's much of an improvement. Yeah, sometimes you'll get bastards that you don't dare turn your back on, but shit, you find that among people too." He patted Milo's neck. "Even bastards like him—he led me straight to you when you got lost, like he was a dog or something. And he's good at heart. They mostly all are." Looking up at Joshua, the same gentle smile on his face, he

Love, Like Water

added, "Sometimes you gotta look past the outward behavior to see the light on the inside."

"What if there isn't any light? What if it's all faked, and it's nothing but dark inside?"

Eli shook his head. "There's always light. Sometimes, though, it gets twisted. Damaged. Sometimes it can be fixed. Sometimes it can't. Depends on how bad it's broken."

"What do you do when it's too badly broken to fix?"

"You try and find something worth keeping. If it's a stud, and it's good with mares, you breed it. If it's too wild to breed, you geld it and hope it calms it down some. And in a worst-case scenario—you put the animal down." Eli got quiet a moment while they dismounted by the water and unshipped the saddlebags with the lunch in them. "Tucker hates when he has to have an animal put down. It's only happened two, three times I can remember, and it's always been the fault of some human—either abuse or indulgence. They're about the same, where animals are concerned."

He hadn't put his gloves back on after he'd finished the collecting, just tossed the used rubber ones back in the bag, so when he reached out and put his hand on Joshua's nape, it was warm, callused skin that stroked him. "I'm thinking in your case it's about three years of abuse," he murmured, "and that ain't enough to ruin you for good."

"You don't know...," Joshua began, but Eli interrupted.

"Yeah, I don't. Don't matter. I can see the light, *mijo*, and it's clear and bright. It's just a little shadowy." He drew Joshua in for a long, slow kiss, soft and wet and exploratory. Joshua was barely aware of Eli's other hand unbuttoning his shirt until fingers swept up and across his chest. The calluses snagged in Joshua's chest hair, but the faint, tiny stings only set his skin singing, and the fingers themselves were firm and gentle. Joshua shivered a little, then reached up and pulled off Eli's hat, tossing it to the side and running his hands through the rumpled blond curls.

Eli made a soft sound deep in his throat and pinched Joshua's nipples. Joshua's knees nearly gave out; Eli caught him as he staggered and lowered him to the ground, peeling back the folds of Joshua's shirt and bringing his mouth down on Joshua's chest, his tongue flicking across first one point, then the other. Joshua shifted so that Eli was kneeling between his thighs and hiked his legs up to wrap around the cowboy's waist. "Fuck me," Joshua groaned, his fingers tightening in Eli's hair.

Raising his head, Eli grinned at him. "In time, *papi chulo*, in time."

Joshua let his head fall back onto the grass and felt his own hat flip off. He didn't care. Eli's hands and mouth kept him thoroughly distracted—Eli was in charge, so Joshua lay still, the leaf-dappled sunlight playing against his closed eyelids, as Eli leisurely explored every inch of his body. He lifted his hips to let Eli pull off his jeans and boots, and when he felt Eli's mouth trailing over the soft skin of his groin, he let out a deep, contented sigh.

That changed to a gasp and growl when Eli licked the head of his cock, his teeth gently—very gently—scraping over the shaft. "Jesus, Eli," he groaned. He felt, more than heard, Eli chuckle.

Then Eli's mouth was gone, and Joshua looked up to see him reaching for one of the saddlebags he'd packed the lunch in. He pulled out a pack of condoms and a little bottle of lube and waved them at Joshua. "Plan ahead," he said soberly, then the grin was back, wide and white in his tan face. He slapped Joshua's bare hip lightly. "Roll over, *papi*."

"I don't know which freaks me out more," Joshua complained as he obeyed, "you calling me '*papi*' or you calling me '*mijo*'. They're both weird." He came up on his knees, folding his arms on the ground and resting his forehead on them.

"What would you rather I call you?" Eli asked.

"How about 'Joshua'?"

"Joshua," Eli said, and ran his hand over Joshua's butt. He'd already lubed up his fingers, and they slid easily into the crease.

Love, Like Water

"Joshua. Beautiful Joshua. Sexy Joshua. Smart Joshua." His mouth pressed against the base of Joshua's spine. "Beloved Joshua."

Joshua started to raise his head, to ask "What?" but he felt Eli's tongue pressing against his entrance and all the words flew out of his brain. He dropped his head again, smelling the rich scent of mold and dirt and the sharper aroma of grass, and turned his mind off completely, letting himself become an entirely sensual thing. The wet of Eli's tongue, the rasp of his hands on Joshua's skin, the scent of grass overlaid with the pungency of the lube, the pressure of fingers working their way inside—and the faint musky odor of the drops of semen that dribbled from his cock each time one of Eli's fingers stroked over his gland.

Then Eli's cock was at him, pressing slowly inward, and Josh held his breath for a moment until he was fully seated. "Okay?" Eli asked, and Joshua nodded, hiking his hips back to engage with Eli's thrusts. Nothing more was said after that, not in words, anyway, but the noises Eli made as he fucked Joshua were as good as language.

Apparently it was the same with Joshua, because just as he was starting to move his hand toward his own cock, ready to come, Eli reached around him and curled his fingers there, stroking and pulling until Joshua cried out and came, spurting over the grass. He heard Eli's yell a minute later, felt him shove against him hard two or three more times, then collapse over Joshua's back.

Joshua rolled to the side, dumping Eli onto the grass, and lay there a moment, catching his breath. "Jesus," he said finally, his voice raw, as if he'd been yelling for an hour. "Jesus."

"No, just me," Eli said behind him. He draped an arm over Joshua's waist. He still had on his shirt—come to think of it, Joshua thought, he did too. "Been wanting that for a while. All day in fact."

"Me too," Joshua murmured. He stretched his arm up and laid his head on it, the smell of spunk and crushed grass sharp in his nose. Behind him, Eli snuffled into Joshua's neck, nuzzling the nape, and Joshua smiled to himself as he drifted off to comfortable, dreamless sleep.

HE MUST have slept really well, because when he woke some unknown time later, he was wide awake and raring to go. Eli was still asleep; he'd rolled over onto his back and flung his arm up over his eyes. Joshua chuckled at the sight of him—jeans down around his still-booted ankles, shirt open to display his hairless but muscular chest. He was almost golden in the dappled sunlight, but there was the farmer's tan Joshua had expected: below the waist he was as pale as any gringo. Joshua snorted faintly—for all his talk about being careful about sun exposure, it looked like Eli spent at least some time shirtless in the great outdoors.

"Yeah," Eli said from under his arm, "you busted me. I like a good tan as much as anybody else. I just ain't blatant about it, like the other guys. For straight boys, they sure like to show off their pecs."

Joshua ran his fingers lightly over the tan line at his waist. "But not pantsless."

Lowering his arm, Eli glowered at him. "Pantsless? Are you loco? I'd be run outta town on a rail."

"Jesus Christ, Eli, between you and my uncle I think I've been exposed to every cowboy, redneck, Old-Westy cliché ever written. Do you guys practice this shit?"

Eli laughed. "Well, your uncle don't—he just talks the way they did growing up. Me—well, I worked for a while on a dude ranch, and part of the shtick was for us cowpokes to talk—what did you call it? Old-Westy?—for the customers. Plus they kinda eat it up at the rodeo too. So I got into the habit." He ran a hand over Joshua's bare knee. "I think you kinda like it."

"I kinda do," Joshua said. He caught Eli's hand and drew it up to lick the wrist, a long, swooping stroke up to his elbow.

"Don't do that," Eli said awkwardly. "I'm all gross and lubey. And worse."

Love, Like Water

"Not here," Joshua said, but he released Eli's arm. "I want a swim."

"It's cold."

"Good." Joshua stood up, stripped off his shirt, and ran into the lake.

Jesus! It was freezing, but it felt good after being hot and sweaty all day. He rubbed himself with handfuls of the frigid water, then dove under to rinse himself off. When he came up, Eli was sitting on the bank, having taken off the rest of his clothes. "Cold?" he asked Joshua.

"Yeah, but I'm tough." But he splashed up to sit next to Eli on the bank. "Going in?"

"Don't think so."

"Think so," Joshua said, and tipped him forward so that he fell into the pond. Sputtering, he came up swinging. Joshua grabbed his arm and pulled him up and out of the water, so that they stood embracing on the bank.

"Little shit," Eli murmured.

"Not so little—I'm taller than you are."

"Just the right height." Eli reached up and grabbed Joshua's face, dragging him down for a kiss.

Joshua wrapped his arms around him and started humming one of his favorite songs to dance to, "El Amor" by Tito el Bambino. It started out slow and romantic but picked up to a lovely quick beat, a cross between the salsa and the reggaeton he loved to dance to.

ELI hadn't realized that Joshua could sing, but he was, low and soft, even as he pulled Eli into a close, intimate dance. Something about love being a dream, and magic, and light, and water. His hands held Eli's hips, moving them with his own in a way that was both sexual and sensual. Eli put his own arms around Joshua's neck and let him lead for a bit, but he'd never been a dancer, and laughing, he finally pulled away and dropped to the ground. "You're too good for me. Where did you learn to dance like that?"

"I'm Puerto Rican," he replied, his body still moving. "I was born knowing how to dance."

And he kept dancing, but not the simple steps he had been using with Eli. He put one hand out to the side, and pressed the other against his belly, and danced, singing the words out loud. He picked up the beat, too, so that the music was spilling out of him, fast and rich, his body moving in the complex rhythm. Eli could almost hear the drums behind the voice.

Joshua shot Eli a quick grin, then took a couple of quick steps so that he was dancing directly beneath the little waterfall that fell from the canyon wall. He was singing something about water, about love running like water, and dancing as if his soul were on fire. He was so beautiful Eli almost wept.

He came out of the waterfall as he finished the song, walking straight for Eli, taking him into his arms and kissing him, hot and fierce.

Eli closed his eyes, and fell.

Love, Like Water

Chapter 22

"OKAY," Eli said as he pulled up to the curb. "There's a parking garage two blocks over. I'm gonna park there. There's a café about four blocks *that* way"—he pointed in the opposite direction—"and that's where I'll be."

"For two hours?" That seemed like a long time to sit drinking coffee. Uncle Tuck ran errands while he was waiting for Josh; it seemed like there was always something to be picked up. But Eli didn't have any errands to run, it seemed.

"Oh, yeah. They got good coffee there, and newspapers and shit. I been there lots of times. You take your time and don't worry about me."

Eli seemed pretty relaxed about the whole thing, so Josh decided he knew what he was doing. With a quick glance around to make sure no one was in sight, he leaned over and gave Eli a quick kiss. "Thanks—for driving me and for waiting. Uncle Tucker doesn't think I could have done this on my own."

"Well, you coulda drove here," Eli said, "but you mighta kept going, and we'da got a call from you from Flagstaff or someplace when you ran outta money." He grinned and gave Josh one of his patented pecks on the lips. Josh had gotten a lot of them in the last couple of weeks, whenever they felt sure they were unobserved. "Tucker has more faith in you than that—he's just worrit you'll get lost. Now go on, or we'll be necking in this truck all through your appointment."

"I'd rather neck," Josh said.

"Me too." Eli leaned across him and opened the door. "Git."

"What's the name of the café?"

"Myrtle's. Can't miss it—it's just four blocks down. If you get out early, come on down and we'll get joe for the road."

"Okay." Josh got out of the truck and closed the door. With a brief wave, he turned and walked through the steel and glass doors of the office building.

ELI finished his cup of coffee, turned down the waitress's offer of another refill, and checked the time on his cell phone. Nearly time for Josh's appointment to be done. He'd read the newspapers here, flipped through the magazines, chatted with a couple of the regulars he knew from his bar-hopping days (Was it only a couple of months since he'd been down this way? Seemed it was, though it felt like longer), and was just about ready to go. He figured a nice leisurely stroll down Central and he'd meet Josh coming out.

The sun had gone down and a nice nippy breeze had sprung up, but the sky was clear. The balloon festival Albuquerque was famous for was next week, and from all forecasts, it looked like it would be a nice weekend. Eli wondered idly if Joshua would be interested in seeing it. It was something he needed to ask.

The last couple of weeks had been... strange. Amazing, but strange. Tucker had kept both him and Joshua too busy to get into mischief, and they'd had to be careful with so many people around, but they'd claimed cautious stray moments in a barn or shed, or on one of their rides as Eli introduced the ranch to Joshua.

He'd done as he'd promised, and taken Josh back out the canyon to check on the culls there, and that was one of the memories he'd keep 'til he was old and gray—of Josh salsa-dancing in the icy spray of the waterfall, stark nekkid, until the cold got to him and he went after Eli, dragging him down onto the grass and making love to him there in the dappled sunlight.

Love, Like Water

And then there were the nights. Not enough of them—Josh usually crashed after full days like the ones they'd been having, since his stamina still wasn't what it should be. But the nights Eli heard the step on the porch, the faint creak of the screen door, and the soft pad of Josh's sneakered feet.... Yeah, those nights were worth all the lonely quiet ones. The look in Josh's eyes as he came into Eli's bedroom told Eli exactly what kind of night he was going to have: lazy and amused meant long, slow lovemaking, with Josh biting the pillow as Eli pummeled him steadily from behind; hot and hungry meant a fast and desperate fucking, with Josh's legs practically around Eli's neck and his hands clamped to the slats of Eli's headboard. And sometimes, there was just... lovemaking. Quiet and easy and comfortable.

And afterwards, after the slow fucking and the heated fucking and, sometimes, the fucking that wasn't fucking at all—that, that was the best part, when, sodden and sated, the two of them cleaned each other up and clung together through the rest of the night, Josh's breathing in Eli's ear and his body warm and soft beside him. He supposed it was sloppy and sentimental of him, but he'd never had a lover before—not a real one, one who wasn't just another trick who, even if he stayed the night at a hotel somewhere, always ended up leaving before breakfast.

Not that Josh didn't leave before breakfast. But it was different.

He was wrapped in thought and didn't notice the guy approaching until he was right in front of him. He stopped and met the guy's friendly smile. "Hey," the guy said.

"Hey," Eli said back. The guy looked familiar.

"You used to hang out at Charlie's, didn't you? I haven't seen you in a while."

Charlie's was one of the gay cowboy bars further down the street. Eli used to hang there, but it had been quite a while. That must be why the guy looked faintly familiar. "Yeah, I work a couple hours from here, so don't get down as often as I used to."

"Yeah, thought so." The genuine smile didn't fade, but the eyes flicked from Eli's face to a point behind him. Eli was just about to turn when he felt a crashing blow to his back. His knees buckled, but when he reached out to catch himself on the guy in front of him, he stepped back and let Eli hit the sidewalk. "Fucking fag," the guy said, all pretense of friendliness gone.

Another voice said, "Get him down here," and Eli felt someone grab his shirt collar and yank up, cutting off his air and his ability to yell. The blow to the kidneys had left him half-paralyzed and disoriented, but he kept struggling, trying to get to his feet, trying to twist out of the steel grip on his collar, trying to…. The baseball bat that had hit him in the back came around and smashed into his face, and then darkness took him.

THE receptionist had gone by the time the appointment was done, but McBride pulled up the scheduling program on the laptop and put in Joshua's next one, for the same time the following week. Josh wasn't sure if he was happy about it; each session seemed to get more grueling and he felt drained. He never intended to talk much at all, meaning to let the shrink take the lead and show Joshua what he wanted to hear, but somehow he always got Josh talking, and then it was two hours later and Josh felt like he'd been stripped, skinned, and deboned. But he also felt… eased, was the best way he could put it in his head. He felt like maybe some of the stuff he'd been carrying around wasn't *necessary* anymore. And while there was still a lot he needed to deal with, he thought maybe there was some hope after all. That he wouldn't drown in bad dreams. That he wouldn't feel so worthless that he'd take another walk into the desert. That maybe, just maybe, he might someday, someday, be able to let go of the death of that pregnant girl in that warehouse. Not forget. Not forgive himself. But let go.

Maybe.

He walked out of the building and looked up the street in the direction of the café that Eli had mentioned. There wasn't any sight of the cowboy. Josh checked his cell phone for the time and saw he was running a few minutes late. Eli probably hadn't finished his coffee, or got caught up in a newspaper article or something. He moved at his own pace, Eli did. Joshua smiled a little to himself, and started walking up the street.

For it being a major street close to the university, it was pretty quiet—well-lit, but not a lot of traffic for an early evening just past rush hour. Joshua supposed it was busy during the day, but at this time of night, the businesses were closed and the bars not quite hitting their evening stride. And it was Tuesday, after all, hardly a night for drinking. But the restaurants he passed were lit, and there were enough cars passing that he didn't feel uncomfortable.

But when he was halfway to the café and he still didn't see Eli, he started to get a bad feeling. And after years of being in the police and the Bureau and in danger, he'd learned to trust his feelings. Something was not right.

He found the café and looked all through it, but there was no sign of Eli. One of the waitresses came over and said, "You looking for somebody, hon?"

"Yeah. Cowboy, gray hat, blond hair, wearing a blue plaid shirt?"

"Oh, Eli? Yeah, he was here. Marty, when did Eli leave?"

"Oh, about ten minutes ago," the other waitress said from the coffee station. "Said he had to meet somebody. Guess you guys just missed each other."

"Guess we did," Joshua said. There was a roaring sound in his head, and his hands were ice. "Thanks."

"Any time. Y'all come back soon!"

"Yes." Joshua turned and moved quietly and quickly out the door.

Ten minutes. Shit. It wasn't even a five-minute walk to the shrink's. Could he have gone for the truck? No, he said he'd meet Joshua on the street or in the café. And he wasn't in the café.

So he was somewhere on the street. Start there. Josh set off at a quick walk, letting his eyes skim over the street before him, the sidewalk on either side of it, looking for... what?

That. Joshua bolted across the street, dodging the light traffic. If he had seen it earlier, he would have dismissed it as a bundle of newsprint, but he knew what it was that the breeze had blown up against the doorway of a storefront—a hat. A gray Resistol with a matching gray band. Joshua picked it up, but froze when he saw a dark discoloration on the brim. The streetlights didn't give enough illumination to add color to it, but Joshua knew what it was. God knew he'd seen it often enough.

Blood.

He stood a moment, holding the hat, and trying to listen through the pounding in his head. It was in a doorway, equidistant between two alleyways or accessways or whatever they called them here. Eli could have gone through the door or been picked up by a vehicle. Or gone down one of the passages. But which?

The breeze—from the east. The hat would have blown here. He turned and ran up the street toward the dark opening between the two buildings, and bolted down it.

There was a steady, rhythmic thumping coming down the passageway, a sound too fucking familiar. He passed a dumpster, overflowing with construction materials, and without thinking, swept up a long piece of metal as he ran. It was too light for an effective weapon, but it seemed sturdy enough. Around a corner, the yellow light over a series of loading docks showed him three men surrounding something on the ground. One of them had a baseball bat and as Joshua ran silently toward them, he saw the bat rise and fall, and rise again, dark streaks on the pale wood.

The others were standing, watching, and cheering the man in low whispers. "Hit him again! Fucking faggot!" one said, and then the metal pole was whistling around, and the speaker went flying from the force of Joshua's blow. Josh kept moving, whirling to take out the hitter, but the third man jumped on Joshua's back, trying to get his arms around Josh's neck.

Stupid redneck, Josh thought savagely, and flipped him over onto his back, giving him a quick stomp in the solar plexus to drive the air

Love, Like Water

out of him. The first man jumped back into the fray, apparently no more than momentarily dazed by the pole; he wrenched it from Joshua's hands, but Josh kicked it loose and it went clattering off to the side. Josh followed up that kick with a second, driving the other man back against the concrete block of the loading dock.

The hitter came after him with the bat, but Josh ducked his wild swing and punched him in the gut. He was just about to hit him again when he heard a decidedly menacing click. He *knew* that sound, and its unexpectedness shook his focus for the first time in a very long time.

The hitter swung again and Josh kicked the bat out of his hand, just as he had the pole, but the guy went after it. "Cool it, Ben," the first guy said. "Let it go. I got this."

He did. In the dim light, Josh couldn't make out what make of gun it was, but he knew what kind it was—the kind that killed people. *Fuck*. He stepped back, his hands raised, his mind clicking over all the possibilities....

The second guy got up from the ground, still wheezing, and punched Joshua in the face. Josh saw the blow coming and turned so that the guy's blow only glanced off his cheekbone, but he went down as if he'd gotten him full face. "Pansy," the guy said in disgust, and spit on him.

On the shadowed ground, Josh shifted, and drew his legs up, as if he were cowering, but eased forward so that his weight was on the balls of his feet. The man with the gun stepped forward, his broad face grinning in the sickly yellow light. "Well looky here. Looks like we're gonna get two faggots for the price of one."

Josh, keeping his eyes on the gunman, was aware of the others coming up on him on either side. "Hold the gun on him—he's some kinda ninja or something." That was the guy with the bat. "Don't want to make too much noise, but I'm sure gonna enjoy pounding this asshole into dust." He laughed. "You wanna scream, fairy, you go right ahead. Ain't nobody in these buildings—they're all closed up for the night."

"I heard you," Josh said, and exploded upward, right into the gunman, who'd moved just a bit too close. He drove him back against the dock, and wrenched the gun from his grip, then drove his elbow into the man's throat. The man collapsed, gurgling.

Joshua whipped around and shot the guy with the bat in the knee. The man screamed and fell to the ground. Then he turned to the last man, who started to back away. "Oh, no," Joshua said softly. "You get your fucking ass back here and sit down." He indicated a spot next to Bat Guy. "Right there."

Shaking, the man sat down. "You got a cell phone?" Joshua asked, still in that soft voice. At the man's nod, Joshua said, "Get it out and dial 911, then hand me the fucking phone."

The man obeyed.

"Lie down, on your belly, hands behind your head."

Joshua backed away, towards Eli. He couldn't think about Eli right that second. No. Could *not* think about Eli. When the 911 operator answered, Joshua said, "My name is Joshua Chastain. I interrupted a hate crime in progress. We need a couple of ambulances in the dock behind Marino's Bakery on Central—I don't know the address." He kept an eye on the three men as he spoke. He didn't dare look behind him at Eli. "One throat injury, one gunshot wound, and I don't know the condition of the victim. And send police, please. Lots of police."

Carefully, the gun still trained on the men, Joshua stepped to Eli's side. "For your sake," he said to the men, "he'd better be alive, or those ambulances won't be needed." He eased down into a crouch and touched Eli's throat. His fingers came away wet, but the pulse was still there. Thready, weak, but there. "Eli?"

There was no response. "Fuckers," he said to the men. "He survives, or you don't. And don't think that being in custody will help you. I can get to you anywhere, and nobody would know any different. *Pendejos* like you, you die easy. I've had lots of practice. Fact is, maybe I should just take you out now and save someone else the trouble later." He tilted the gun sideways, then back. The rage was building. "It would be easy. You came at me, I defended myself. Did I

Love, Like Water

tell you I'm ex-FBI? They kicked me out because I was too quick to kill."

He stalked over to the guy with the jammed windpipe and shoved him with his foot so that he was on his belly too. Putting his foot on the guy's back and leaning on him, so that the guy started crying, he said, "Think you're a badass with a gun? Think you're tough? I eat *maricones* like you for breakfast. Shit, I just lean a little harder—" He leaned, and the guy cried out. "I break a few ribs, puncture a lung, you just as dead. Gee, officer, guess I hit him harder than I thought. Oops." A soft scraping sound caught his attention and he turned to look at the guy with the shattered kneecap trying to crawl away. He laughed, and for the first time in months felt like he was where he belonged, back on the street, high and powerful instead of the lost and broken man he was. "Don't go too far," he sang. "Maybe you need to see what that bat should be used for. Maybe *you* need to take it up the ass, hey, *papi chulo*? Maybe I need to use that on you, show you what real pain is like."

"Josh...."

Josh went still. His eyes still focused on the men, he said, "Eli?"

"Don't.... This is not... not you." The voice was faint, and wet, somehow. Josh's fury was turning his vision red. Six feet away, one of the men moaned and the smell of piss was ripe in the still evening air.

"This is exactly what I am," Joshua said harshly. "Don't talk, Eli."

Eli went silent, except for the faint bubbling of his breath. Joshua focused on the weight of the gun in his hand, the heat radiating off the concrete dock, the groans of the two injured men. The ache of where he'd taken blows. The fury that was making the gun quiver in his hand. Anything but the battered ruin of his lover at his feet. He didn't dare look at him. Didn't dare *think* of him.

There were the faint sounds of sirens, but it wasn't until the first car pulled into the dock area that he started to realize it was over. The cops poured out of their cars, guns drawn. He put his hands up, the gun dangling from one finger. "Joshua Chastain," he said to the cop that approached him. "Former FBI—Agent Bill Robinson of the Chicago office will vouch for me. These men attacked Mr. Kelly here."

"That's bullshit," one of the three whined. "We were minding our own business when him and his buddy there jumped us. He's some kinda ninja."

Joshua snorted.

The cops put all four of them in handcuffs and into separate vehicles. Joshua expected that. But they also made way for the EMTs.

The last thing Joshua saw as the cop car pulled away from the dock was them lifting a dark, limp mass onto a gurney. *Eli.*

Love, Like Water

Chapter 23

THEY hadn't put Joshua into a cell, but after a few hours in the interrogation room—every jurisdiction called it by some euphemism or other, but to Joshua it was always the interrogation room—he was hungry for answers. They'd brought him in, checked him for injuries, then handcuffed him to the metal ring on the table, with just enough play that he could drink the bottle of water (lukewarm) that they had brought him, and said they would be back in a few minutes to take his statement. They'd come, listened expressionlessly to his version of events, then left again. That was three hours ago. He'd finished the water and peeled the label off the bottle, but he was still alone in there.

He suspected he was being watched—the room was brightly lit, but he could still see some shadows behind the two-way mirror that took up one wall. He wondered what they were looking for.

He didn't think of Eli. He *refused* to think of Eli.

But the first words out of his mouth when the door opened and a pair of suits walked in were "How's Eli? Where is he? Is he okay?"

"Mr. Kelly has been taken to the University Medical Center. I don't have any information on his condition." The thin man smiled faintly, and reached over to unlock Joshua's handcuffs. "Sorry about the delay—we were getting distinctly mixed messages about you and needed to confirm your identity."

Joshua rubbed his wrists. "What kind of mixed messages?"

The heavier-set guy gestured at Joshua. "You meet the description of a member of Los Peligros who's wanted on a number of federal warrants. Fortunately for you, your superior in Chicago—a Bill Robinson?—filled us in. I'm Agent Weathersby, and this is Agent Greene, from the Albuquerque office. Sorry it took so long. You know how it is."

"Yeah." Joshua rubbed his wrists. "Can I leave now? You have my statement."

"Yeah. Your uncle's waiting out front. You're gonna get tagged for discharge of a weapon, but fortunately that's barely a misdemeanor. Papers are ready and your uncle's already paid the fine. And you were right, in your statement—the gun not only had Kieczerski's fingerprints all over it, it was registered to him as well. We're thinking you just handed us the perps of a short string of hate crimes the Albuquerque PD's been working on. You might be getting a call from the DA's office."

"Right." Josh got up from the chair. "Can I go? I need to get to the hospital."

"Right—your friend."

"My *partner*."

The agents' eyebrows went up, and Joshua didn't blame them. It was a surprise to him, too. "Oh, yeah?" the skinny one said.

"You got a problem with that?"

"If I did, my husband would give me a good kick in the ass for it," the skinny one said. He held out a hand. "I'm Dave Greene, and this is Ray Weathersby. No need to stand on ceremony. Your uncle has our business cards if you need to get a hold of either of us. And Robinson in Chicago told us we should try and talk you into coming back to work—we could use someone with your skills in this office."

Josh smiled thinly and said, "No, thanks. Can I go?"

Finally, they let him go, following him out of the room, through the electric gates a guard opened for them, and down the hall to the front desk. Tucker was sitting in a chair along the wall; when he saw

Joshua, he leapt to his feet and threw his arms around him. "Son, you all right?"

"Fine," Joshua replied, patting Tucker awkwardly on the back. "Why are you here? You should be with Eli!"

"You're my goddamned nephew," Tucker said. "I needed to be here. Besides, they kicked me out of the hospital."

"What? What for?"

"Oh, they didn't really, but they were taking Eli into surgery, and since I ain't a relative, they weren't giving me any information anyway."

"They'll give me information," Joshua growled.

Tucker shot him a quick grin. "That's what I figured. You got connections." He nodded at the two agents behind Joshua.

"As Mr. Kelly's partner, you should have no difficulty getting the information you need, but if you run into a snag, have them call me," Weathersby said. "But you shouldn't need to—the city's pretty progressive on that front. I'm just sorry you had to be the victim of some of our less savory residents." The man's smile widened into a wicked grin. "Unfortunately for them, some hate crimes fall under federal jurisdiction—the ones we want to. Add to that an attack on a federal officer...."

"I'm not one, anymore," Joshua said.

"Not according to Robinson. He says you're on medical leave."

"What?"

The grin on Greene's face matched Weathersby's. "The Bureau didn't accept your resignation, Chastain. Just in case you changed your mind." He patted Joshua on the shoulder as he and the other agent walked by. "Keep in touch."

Josh stared blankly after them. Tucker said, "There's some paperwork you gotta sign over on the desk, then let's go see about Eli. And you can tell me on the way what the hell he meant when he called you Eli's partner?"

TUCKER was on the phone with the ranch hours later when a tired-looking doctor in scrubs came into the waiting room. "Mr. Chastain?"

"Yes?"

"Yeah?"

The doctor looked from one to the other. "Mr. Joshua Chastain."

"That's me," Joshua said. "How is Eli?"

"There's a conference room next door," the doctor said. "Let's go there for a minute."

His gut aching, Joshua followed. Tucker put the phone away and came too. Once inside the room, the doctor gestured to a trio of chairs set around a small coffee table.

"Sit down, please."

"What's wrong with Eli?" Joshua asked tightly, ignoring the doctor's directive.

Tucker reached out and put a hand on Joshua's shoulder. "Ease back and let the man talk, Josh."

"Thank you." The doctor indicated the chairs again and Joshua sat down, his attention fully on the doctor. "Mr. Kelly is in very serious condition. There was some internal bleeding, and we had to remove his spleen and his appendix. One of his lungs was punctured by a broken rib and had collapsed—that's been repaired and drained. His kidneys are severely bruised, but we believe they'll heal properly. Of course, we will have to monitor him carefully to make sure there's nothing we didn't catch. What kind of work does he do? He's in very good condition, despite his injuries. In fact, his excellent condition may have kept him from being hurt worse. Muscle absorbs blows better than any other tissue, and might have prevented more serious bone injuries."

"He's a horseman." Tucker's voice was low and shaken.

"It's impossible to tell at this point what his prognosis on that front is, but there's no spinal injury, aside from bruising, so that's good.

Love, Like Water

There were a couple of torn ligaments in his right leg and knee from a forced dislocation, which he'll need physical therapy for, if he is to ride again. His left arm and wrist are broken and his shoulder dislocated, though both of those things have been treated. He'll need physical therapy for those, too."

"And?" Joshua asked when the man had stopped.

"The most serious injuries aside from the internal are to his head. He has a severe concussion and subdural hemorrhage. We were able to relieve some of the pressure from the bleeding. However, we won't know how bad the resultant damage is until he's awake. Superficially, he has a cracked cheekbone and his nose was broken, but it's been set. He's lost a couple of molars on one side."

"So what does that mean?" Joshua spread his hands wide. "What is gonna happen? Is he going to be okay?"

"I think so. It may not seem like it, but he was lucky. We've had a string of gay-bashings this fall—he's the fourth. The first victim died of his injuries. The second will be released in a few days to an extended-care facility with severe brain damage. The third is still here, in critical but stable condition, in a coma." The doctor spread his hands. "Rumor has it that it was thanks to you that the animals that did this to them are in custody."

"They think they're the ones, yeah. Can I see him?"

"He's still unconscious…."

"I don't care. I just need to see him." Joshua hated the tremble in his voice.

"Very well. Come with me, then."

Chapter 24

THE change in shift had come and gone. The new nurse came in and introduced himself quietly to Joshua, then went about checking all the things the last one had a few minutes ago. He wondered absently why this nurse was different from the one who'd been here the last few nights, then thought that it might be Saturday, and the weekend shift. Come to think of it, the one on the day shift had been different too. Saturday, then, probably. He'd lost count of the days here. Uncle Tucker had offered to take turns with him, but Uncle Tucker had a ranch to run, and besides, it wasn't *his* fault Eli was here.

Then Tucker had offered to pay for a hotel room for Joshua, but Joshua had just looked at him and asked "What for?" and Tucker dropped the subject. Instead, he drove the two hours in to the city every day to bring Joshua food and a change of clothes.

Joshua didn't know what the local FBI agents had told the staff there, but the first night, when one of the nurses tried to get him to leave after visiting hours were over, he'd just handed her Weathersby's card, and after that, they'd left him alone. Alone, but not neglected—they'd brought in a chair that was sort of a recliner, with a pillow and light throw. Joshua had dragged it up beside Eli's bed, close enough that he could rest his hand on Eli's arm, and then he could sleep, if only a light doze, ready to wake up if Eli moved or if someone else came in. The nurses had all looked askance at the arrangement, but none of them said anything.

Love, Like Water

They'd tried to tend to Joshua during the first night: apparently his face was swollen and bruised from the blow to his cheek, but he waved them off. It was just superficial; he didn't even hurt that much. Now, when he glanced into the mirror in the bathroom, he saw that it had faded to a purplish-yellow. It didn't matter. He wasn't the one who was hurt.

About nine thirty, the young male nurse came in to change one of the bag things that were hanging over Eli. He saw Joshua watching him and smiled. "Either he's one important witness or he really means a lot to you. The other nurses said you haven't left his side once since he came in."

"And I won't." Joshua's voice was scratchy and hoarse from disuse.

"I don't blame you." The kid—what was his name? Right, his nametag said Alex—said. "He looks pretty bad."

Something about the way he said it made Joshua look at him sharply. "'Looks'?"

"Yeah. Really? He looks a lot worse than he is. He's healing really well, under the circumstances." Alex frowned. "Hasn't the doctor given you an update?"

"He talks, but I don't understand half of what he says. He says that Eli's doing as well as can be expected. All I know is that he won't wake up."

"Didn't the doctor tell you about the coma being medical?"

Joshua frowned. "Yeah, but I have no idea what that means."

"That means they're keeping him unconscious on purpose." Alex stepped back, alarm on his face. Joshua realized he'd stood up, his hands fisted. "Whoa...! I'm not the bad guy, mister. And neither is the doctor. He probably thought you understood what he meant, and if you didn't ask any questions, he wouldn't know any different."

"Why would they keep him like this?"

"A lot of reasons. But I'd say in Mr. Kelly's case, it would *be* for a lot of reasons. He's got multiple injuries, including internal and cranial, so keeping him quiet would be the biggest one. If he were conscious, he'd be moving around a lot, especially since he'd be in quite a bit of pain. And he's *got* to stay still so that they can track any additional bleeding, which is the biggest danger for him right now. But according to the charts, his scans have been coming back clean, so they're pretty sure he won't spring any new surprises on them."

Joshua sat back down, his heart pounding. Eli wasn't unconscious. He wasn't dying. He wasn't slipping away from Joshua every second, the way he thought, the way he felt. This was all medical. He closed his eyes a moment.

A hand settled on his where it rested on the edge of the bed. "They had you really scared, didn't they? I'm sorry. I guess everyone thought you knew what was going on."

"I don't know anything about medicine." Joshua's throat felt raw. "I don't even watch TV." He opened his eyes to look up at the sympathetic face. Alex seemed to understand his convoluted thinking.

"Well, most of the TV shows get at least half of it wrong at any one time," Alex said. He squeezed Joshua's hand in a comforting way, then moved over to check the chart again. "I'd be willing to bet they'll be bringing him around in a day or so. So if you want to really get a good night's sleep for once, I think you'll be okay to do it. I'll keep an eye on him tonight—it's pretty quiet on the floor. And he's wired to a whole bunch of things that will go screaming crazy if he so much as twitches." Alex smiled again. "I think you could use the sleep."

Joshua shook his head. "Can't sleep. Bad dreams."

"You want something to help?"

"No!" He took a deep breath, then said again, more sanely this time, "No, no thanks. I'm good."

Again, the look of sympathy. "No problem. Well, everything looks good, so I'll leave you guys to sleep. We'll try not to disturb you tonight."

Joshua barely heard him go, just acknowledging it in that part of his brain that was always alert. Instead, he leaned over and rested his head on the side of the bed, his fingers stroking over Eli's arm above the cast. "You'll be okay, Eli. You're going to be okay."

Yo nunca dejaría que nadie te hiciera daño. Eli had promised he wouldn't let anyone hurt Joshua. Joshua had been off his head when Eli had been talking to him, but that had stayed in that quirky little corner of his brain. He'd thought it was his grandfather.

Eli had promised to watch out for Joshua. But Joshua had failed to look out for Eli. His blood still ran cold every time he thought about how much worse it would have been if he'd been five minutes later. He regularly kicked himself for talking just that couple of minutes longer with the shrink.

Oh hell, even going to the shrink had been a mistake of epic proportions. And it was all because Joshua was such a *complete* fuckup. He had to go to the shrink because he had pulled that stupid stunt of walking out into the desert. He'd done that because of the stupid addiction. He'd gotten addicted because he'd been stupid enough to question 'Chete's decision.

He dreamt about a dead girl because he hadn't questioned his decision sooner, or harder. Because he was supposed to follow orders. Was that stupid? He rubbed his temples with both hands.

He'd killed the men 'Chete had marked, following 'Chete's orders. They were far from innocent themselves, and it had just been part of his job. And the therapy he went through in rehab helped him come to terms with it.

But the girl…. That was different….

And Eli…. Eli was different too. He'd nearly lost Eli because of his actions. He bent his head and kissed Eli's fingers beneath the edge of the cast. Eli was too good to waste his time with Joshua.

He thought about what the FBI agents had said—not for the first time since they'd said it. The Bureau wanted him back. He could go back. Not to Chicago, of course, but Cincinnati maybe. Or somewhere, anywhere else. Robinson would go to bat for him. He could go back to work, and Eli could go back to his life, without a fuckup there to fuck *him* up.

Yeah. Maybe he'd do that. He'd think about it.

He fell asleep thinking about it.

ELI was dreaming.

It was a weird dream, and it seemed to go on forever, but it wasn't one of those ones you think is real until you wake up. No, Eli knew it was a dream, but he wasn't quite sure how to wake up out of it.

He was riding across a white landscape with his dad. It wasn't winter, because he wasn't cold, and the trees had leaves, but they were white too. Pretty much everything was, except Eli and his dad and their horses. That was another way Eli knew it was a dream, because he was riding Midnight, the horse he'd had as a kid, and his dad was riding Pete, the horse that he'd had to shoot when he got bit by a rattler when Eli was nine. "I'm dreamin', ain't I?" he asked his dad.

Dad had laughed. "Sure you are, son. I been dead for years."

A jackalope went bounding past, the antlers making its head bob with every bound. Eli watched it with interest. "So how come you're here?"

"Hell if I know."

"That's helpful."

Dad laughed again. "It's your dream, son."

They drew up to let a herd of white buffalo thunder by. Eli admired the long white curving tusks and the lacy wings. "Never knew buffalo had wings."

"Learn something new every day." That had been one of his dad's favorite sayings.

There was a beeping sound, and a large red fly, glowing against the white landscape, shot across the horses' noses, but the horses didn't startle; they just kept walking. The fly beeped after them for a while, then stopped. "Am I dead?" Eli asked.

"Hell if I know."

"That's helpful."

"It's your dream, son."

"Yeah, I got that. Dad, did I ever tell you I was gay?"

"For Pete's sake"—Dad patted his horse's neck—"of course you are. You think I didn't know? You never showed the slightest interest in any of the girls that were throwing themselves at you. I figgered it out by the time you were thirteen. But that was okay. You took care of your ma, and the kids, and I figger that makes you a man by anybody's standards. I like your new sweetheart, by the way. He's a little crazy, but that's okay."

"I like him too." Eli ran his fingers over Midnight's coarse mane. "I love him, Dad."

"That's okay, son."

They drew up again, this time to let the UNM marching band through. They were all built more like the football players, but were all wearing Dallas Cowboys cheerleaders' outfits, even the guys. Dad snorted and elbowed Eli. "Good one," he said with a smirk. "Never did like Dallas. Bet you like seeing them guys in those shorts?"

"Er... not really." They did look bad in the short shorts. They rode up the guys' butts and made their butt cheeks look really... stupid.

Then a shot rang out. Eli looked around wildly, but Dad put his hand on Eli's arm and a finger to his lips. "Shh," he said. "Let the boy deal with this...."

And they were suddenly in a dark space. The horses were gone, and Dad and Eli were sitting on a hay bale watching three men beat up on someone. Joshua came riding into the area on a white horse and holding a shiny six-shooter in his hand. "Well, ain't that special?" Dad said. "Your very own Lone Ranger."

"Jesus, Dad!"

"I'm going to shoot you all dead," Dream-Josh said, "because that's what I do. I shoot the bad guys."

"Jesus, Eli. At least give the poor kid some decent dialogue."

"Shut up, Dad!"

Dream-Josh turned and fired, but at Eli, not the men, and flames burst from Eli's chest. He cried out in pain, but there was no one there—he was alone in the dark space, with his body on fire.

HE BLINKED, and sandpaper rasped over his eyeballs. The light was fluorescent, and too bright. He closed his eyes again.

"Eli? Can you hear me?"

He tried to say yes, but his mouth was dry and his throat was sore. He tried for a nod instead. Something cool and wet touched his lips and he licked them, grateful for the moisture. "Unh…?"

"You're in the hospital," the voice said again. Eli was pretty sure he didn't recognize it. "You've been unconscious a while. That's why it's hard to talk. Just nod if you can't say anything. Do you understand what I'm saying?"

Nod.

"Is your name Elian James Kelly?"

Nod.

"Can you open your eyes?"

Nod. He didn't though. The light was so bright he could see the blood vessels on the inside of his lids.

"Oh. Is the light too bright? Nurse, lower the lights a bit, please."

The brightness behind his lids faded. Eli opened his eyes.

"Ah, that's better." The voice belonged to a small man with Indian-from-India features and a white smile. "It's good to meet you at last, Elian Kelly. You've had a lot of people worried about you."

Love, Like Water

"Josh...." His mouth formed the words, but no sound came out. He licked his lips and tried again. "Josh."

"Yes, your partner was here the whole time. We couldn't pry him away from you with a crowbar." The man's voice was nice, kind of singsongy, like music. "He'll be back in a little while. We sent him away while we woke you up. We need to do some testing first."

They put Eli through a series of questions, then some physical movements that hurt like the very demons of hell. He learned he had a broken arm and wrist, and his shoulder hurt because it had been dislocated, and his leg hurt because he had torn ligaments, and his chest hurt because he had broken ribs and after a while he got tired of hearing what was wrong with him and tuned out. He didn't understand half of it anyway. He figured he'd ask Josh or Tucker—they were both smart men and probably knew all that.

The doctors had told him that he'd been unconscious for six days. He didn't know why, but he knew this wasn't the hospital in Miller, so it probably wasn't because of an injury on the ranch. Though he felt like he'd been run over by a herd of wild mustangs. He tried to think what he was supposed to be doing, last he knew, and wondered if Josh had gotten to that shrink's appointment he had last week. If it was last week and not this week. He tried to figure it out, but his head hurt, so he let it be.

But when the doctors and nurses all left, and Joshua came into the room, quiet and sober and gray with fatigue, Eli remembered the dream, the Dream-Josh on the white horse and the men beating the shit out of someone. "Hey," he rasped warily.

Josh stopped just inside the door, closed his eyes a moment, then opened them and smiled. "Hey. How you doing?"

"Just fine. A little sore."

"Yeah, I bet." Joshua dragged the chair from across the room next to the bed. Eli noted that it had a pillow and a blanket folded over the back. Josh moved the pillow and sat down.

"You been sleeping here?" Eli asked curiously.

"Yeah."

"Huh." Then something occurred to Eli. "For *six days*?"

Joshua said dryly, "Don't worry—I took showers in the bathroom. I just… I didn't want to leave you alone, in case you woke up and didn't know where you were."

Eli nodded. His eyes were getting heavy again and he let them close. "Thanks."

"You're welcome. Eli?"

"Mm."

"Welcome back."

Eli smiled to himself. He felt the gentle touch of Joshua's fingers on his right hand, the one with the tubes in it, then drifted off to sleep.

Love, Like Water

Chapter 25

JOSH had been there the next time Eli had opened his eyes, and the time after that, but after a few days, just as Eli had started feeling more human, he stopped coming to the hospital. Eli's ma had come in from Portland, and Jake and Sam had flown in from wherever they had been, just to make sure he was on the mend. It was nice to see them, but he missed Joshua.

Tucker, Sarafina, and most of the boys had made trips down to see him; the visits from them and his family alleviated the boredom in between hellish physical therapy and purely annoying tests. The doctors kept asking him stupid questions about shit like "how would he rate his pain on a scale of 1 to 10" like that even made *sense*, for Pete's sake. Once he'd lost his temper and hollered "It hurts like a fucking *bitch*, you idiot!" Then, of course he felt bad and apologized, but it *had* hurt like a fucking bitch. He didn't even remember what it was that had hurt that time—it all hurt.

The bruise he'd seen on Joshua's cheek before was apparently the only injury he'd gotten. That was a relief to Eli. The bruise had scared him, and he worried that Josh had gotten hurt.

But he should have known better—Josh had that background in law enforcement, and apparently had single-handedly disarmed and captured the three guys Eli didn't really remember attacking him. Eli didn't remember much about the event at all. For some reason he had the thought that Joshua had told him he'd killed a lot of people, but he hadn't heard anything of the sort from Tucker, so he figured it was just his imagination.

The guys that had attacked Eli seemed to be connected to a bunch of other attacks, so Eli had to go through some awkward conversations with not only cops and sheriff's police, but also guys in black suits who looked much more like FBI agents than Joshua ever did. They asked him all kinds of questions, but Eli really couldn't remember much about it. He remembered leaving the café, but that was about it. He tried asking some questions of his own, about Josh rescuing him, but they were real good at evading straight answers. He figured that was something they got taught in FBI school—Josh was kind of good at it too.

When he asked Tucker where Josh was, Tuck just said he was working hard in the ranch office, so that Tucker had time to pick up the slack from Eli, but that he sent his regards and would see Eli when he came home. Tucker seemed kind of embarrassed about it so Eli didn't ask again. It might even have been true.

But somehow, he didn't think it was. He thought Josh was avoiding him.

Easy enough to do, with Eli in the hospital, but shit. He'd thought Josh had got over his skittishness, but it looked like he was still as spooky as a mustang.

Jake and Sam stayed a few days, visiting with him until they were pretty sure he wasn't gonna die of something, then had to go back to their various lives. Eli appreciated their visiting and it was good to see them again, but didn't mind much when they left. They had their own commitments and that was okay. Ma decided to stay around until he went home and got settled there, which meant she was still in town when the hospital discharged him to the rehab center where he had to be for four weeks for his busted bones. His arm wasn't working right, and then he kept having pain in his hip, and they found out that the bone there was cracked, too. At the rate he was going, he'd never be able to ride a horse again. Though the doctors and therapists assured him he'd be fine.

Love, Like Water

He hoped they were right. He'd need to be able to ride again just to work off the extra pounds Sarafina's smuggled dinners were putting on him. He kind of thought that maybe that was part of the reason that Ma wanted to hang around.

She'd smacked him on the top of his head—gently—when he'd said that. But he noticed she didn't deny it, either.

The rehab center was an improvement over the hospital—nobody came around at all hours to draw blood or wake you to take a sleeping pill, and the lights went off at night—but going there introduced Eli to a whole new world of pain. He'd thought he was in pretty good shape before the attack, but they had him working muscle groups he didn't know he had, and was going to bed at night desperate for the pain pills they gave him. He'd been getting morphine in the hospital but got switched to pills (which didn't work as well) at rehab. He'd expected he'd take them for a couple of days, then quit, but his body had other ideas. Once or twice he'd tried to go without, but after a few hours tossing and turning, unable to get comfortable enough to sleep, he'd buckled under.

The thing about it was that it wasn't just one place that hurt—it was everywhere. They'd done a fine job of working him over, and he was just surprised they hadn't broken every bone in his body. He guessed Joshua came riding in on his white horse quick enough to rescue him from that. (Although he was *pretty* sure he hadn't been actually riding a horse, even if for some reason Eli remembered that. There weren't any horses mentioned in the discussions he'd had with the FBI and cops, anyway.) It made it hard to rest, though—he couldn't find a comfortable position—and he'd gotten crabby. It wasn't like him to be crabby, he thought; at least he didn't remember being this way before, but maybe he was? He didn't like it.

Maybe that was why Joshua wasn't coming around. Maybe he'd been crabby with him, and Josh didn't like it. Well, who would?

He asked Tucker every so often how Josh was doing, and all Tucker would say was that he was fine, he was getting healthier, he was working hard organizing Tuck's office, and that he asked about Eli's progress every day. That was reassuring. Equally reassuring was Tuck's telling him that Josh was working with the cops to convict the guys that assaulted him—they were, according to Tuck, the guys who killed and maimed a couple of other gays in town. So Eli was lucky.

He felt like he'd be luckier if Joshua were here, so he asked Tucker to ask Josh to come see him.

Josh did, finally, on one of the evenings he had therapy. He showed up half an hour before he had to leave for the shrink's office. Eli barely recognized him.

For one thing, he was wearing a suit—not a black one like the other Feds, but a lightweight gray one with darker pants and a dark blue shirt. He looked nice and Eli said so. Joshua just said "thanks" and nothing else.

Finally, after a few minutes, he said, "You wanted to see me?"

"Yeah." He'd intended to rail at Josh for disappearing, for not being around when Eli could have used a friendly face and a warm hand to hold, but Joshua was so cold, so forbidding in that sharp gray suit that Eli could only say, "I missed you."

Something flickered in Josh's dark eyes and his expression got even colder. "Sorry."

"'Sorry'? What the hell is that supposed to mean?" Eli was shocked and scared by this new, chilly version of the man he loved. Who was this guy? Where had Josh gone?

"It means sorry. As in 'I'm sorry you got hurt. I'm sorry you missed me, because there's really no reason for it.' I didn't come here because I didn't want to get into anything with you while you were recuperating. I still don't. Anything we have to say to each other can wait until you get home and are back on your feet."

Eli struggled to sit up straighter. "What the hell are you talking about, Josh? What do we have to say to each other? I was kind of figgering on the only thing us needing to say to each other is you saying welcome home and me saying glad to be back. What the Sam Hill is there else to say?"

Love, Like Water

Josh was so quiet that if Eli hadn't been staring straight at him, he'd have thought he'd gone. Finally, he said, "Yeah, that's right," in a quiet, dead voice. "That's all."

"Josh—what's going on? Why are you in that suit?"

Joshua looked down at himself, then back up at Eli. "I had a meeting."

"With the FBI about the case?"

"With the FBI, yes."

The realization hit Eli like a slow, cold wave, washing over him and building up speed. "You're going back in. To the FBI. You're leaving the ranch."

"I'm considering it, yes."

"Why, Josh? Your uncle needs you...."

"The office is organized enough that Tuck can handle what he can't teach you. He's going to have to spend more time outside to make up for you not being there. I figured you could take over the office stuff...."

"I ain't working in no office." The idea both infuriated and terrified Eli. To be locked up indoors for the rest of his life? There wasn't any way in hell he was going to put up with that. "I'm gonna be working with the horses, same as I ever did. No fucking broken bones're gonna stop me from that. It ain't like I'm some old man, you shit!"

Josh didn't acknowledge the insult. "With luck, you'll be back outdoors in a few months. By then Tucker can find someone else to handle the paperwork." He shrugged. "I'm sure you and I and Tucker will have some conversations about it when you get back to the ranch. We'll work it out then. There's no need to worry about it just yet." He glanced at his wrist. He was wearing a watch. Eli didn't remember him ever wearing a watch before. "I need to get going. Good luck with the rest of your therapy."

"Get out," Eli said, his voice thick with rage. He could barely get the words out through the anger and the hurt. "Go. I don't need to see you again. Go back to your fucking FBI, you useless...." He stopped. He couldn't say that to Josh. Not to Josh. Even if he was *furious* at him.

Josh gave him a thin, humorless smile. "See?" he said softly. "Now you get it." He turned and walked from the room.

"Josh! *Josh!*" Eli struggled to get up, but his legs wouldn't cooperate and he fell back on the bed, the pain in his knee flaring down to his feet. "Josh!"

But Josh had gone, and left Eli alone.

Love, Like Water

Chapter 26

"WHAT the devil are you doing, Joshua?"

Josh looked up from the spreadsheet program he was working on. The data lay in neat columns, all with their totals at the bottom—logical, sensible, unemotional. Numbers were numbers, data were data. They didn't pretend to be anything else. "Doing a cost benefit analysis of the different kinds of feed you're using compared with similar products and integrating shipping and volume costs and discounts. I should be done in a few minutes. Did you need the computer?"

"I need you to talk to me." Tucker sat down across from the desk with a heavy sigh. "Son, you been walking around like a robot since Eli got hurt, and you won't talk to me even though I figured we were getting along pretty well."

"We're getting along fine," Joshua said, not looking at him.

"Save the file," Tucker said.

"What?"

"Save the file."

Joshua blinked at him, then looked back at the screen. What was Tucker up to? He picked up the mouse and clicked the save icon.

"Done?"

"Yes. Why...."

The screen went dark. Tucker tossed the end of the power cord he'd just pulled out of the wall onto the desk. "You, son, are going to tell me what the *fuck* is going on in that pea brain of yours. Because I really don't like what I'm seeing here, and I'm hoping you're gonna tell me I'm reading something into this situation that really ain't there. Because if it is, you are a dead disappointment to me, Joshua."

Joshua folded his arms. "What if you are reading the situation right?"

"I hope I'm not."

Saying nothing, Joshua picked up the pencil from the desk and rolled it in his fingers. "So what are you thinking?"

"I'm thinking that my nephew, who I always took as a good guy, is dumping his lover because he's too crippled up for him to be bothered with."

The shock of his uncle's accusation reverberated through Josh. He dropped the pencil. "Is that what you think?"

"Well, you tell me what I should think."

"I think," Joshua said bitterly, "you should stop thinking of me as a good guy."

His uncle closed his eyes as if in pain.

"Because I'm not. I'm not a good guy. I may have been in a career where I should have done good things, but I'm about the farthest thing from a good guy you can get."

"I don't believe that."

"You don't want to believe it."

"Your shrink's office called this morning wanting to know if you wanted to reschedule the appointment you canceled last minute. When you left for the meeting with the Feds, you said you'd be home after the appointment. Where did you go, Joshua?"

"I went and found a supplier for heroin and got wasted!" Joshua shot back. "Where the hell else would I go?"

He'd shaken his uncle, but Tucker said doggedly, "I don't believe you."

"Fine. I didn't. Not that I didn't want to." Joshua leaned his head back against the headrest on the chair. "I went and saw Eli, and when I was done there I just didn't feel like dealing with McBride. I went for a walk."

"What did Eli say?"

"What do you think he said? He told me to get lost. He said he didn't want to see me again. And he called me useless." Josh let out a humorless bark of laughter. "Smart man, Elian Kelly. He knows what you don't want to."

"That I don't believe. Eli would never say that to you. He... I think he loves you, Josh. You should see his face when he asks about you."

"He won't be asking about me anymore." Josh felt a sort of sick satisfaction at that thought.

"What's gonna happen when he comes home next week?" Tucker asked.

Joshua shrugged, though he didn't feel the least bit careless. "Up to you. If you want, I can be gone before then."

"Gone where? Christ, Joshua, this is your *home*."

"It was his home first. You ask him what he wants, and I'll abide by it." Joshua put down the pencil. "If he doesn't mind, I'll stay at least until he's settled. I'll just keep out of his way as much as possible. I already suggested he take over the bookwork while he's recovering. I suppose he can put up with me long enough for me to train him. But I warn you, he's not interested in doing it full time. You'll probably need to hire at least a part-time bookkeeper...."

"Jesus, Josh. What the hell is going on with you? Where do you think you're going?"

"The Bureau office here has asked me to transfer to Albuquerque permanently. Apparently, they were telling the truth about my resignation—Bill Robinson put me down as being on medical leave and didn't forward my letter of resignation to headquarters. So I'm still technically an agent."

"You said you didn't want to go back."

"I changed my mind."

"Why?"

Because I'm dangerous and unreliable, Joshua thought in despair. *Because I put my lover in a life-threatening situation and couldn't even protect him against a gang of thugs. Because I'm a failure all around at being a civilian.* But he didn't say anything. Couldn't say anything. Not even the fact that because of his addiction, he'd be pretty much relegated to Analyst until he'd finished years of counseling. He'd only be trading the office here for one in the city, but at least in the city office, there wouldn't be the sights and sounds and smells of the desert to haunt him. At least in the city office, he wouldn't have to see his lover suffering and in pain, frustrated at his inability to do the things he loved. At least in the city, maybe he could forget the *guilt.*

Guilt. He should be used to it by now.

He didn't say any of that. Instead, he said, "They've made me a very good offer." When Tucker didn't answer, he looked up and met his eyes. In place of the anger or frustration he thought he'd see there, he saw speculation. Tucker's voice, when he spoke, was thoughtful.

"I see. A good offer. Yeah, I see that. When do you start?"

"I don't know yet. They're still hammering out the details."

Tucker nodded and bent to plug in the computer again. Joshua said, "You know, you can really wreck a computer by doing that."

"I know." Tucker gave him a smug smile. "It was just the monitor." Then he got up and sauntered out of the office.

Joshua watched him go, then turned the monitor back on. Staring at the spreadsheet that was still active, he rested his chin on his hand. What was his uncle up to? And did it matter anyway? He wasn't sure if he should be nervous or not.

He shook his head. That was stupid. Of course he didn't need to be nervous. What could Tucker do, anyway? Joshua had been very

Love, Like Water

careful to destroy any illusions Eli might have had about them or their relationship. It had hurt—*God, it had hurt*—but it had been necessary. For Eli's safety, and Joshua's sanity.

Watching Eli in the hospital had nearly driven Joshua crazy. Even after they'd brought Eli out of the coma, he'd sat there patiently waiting for the moments when he'd been awake. And in those moments he could read in Eli's eyes the pain he was going through, so that when he did drift off again into drugged sleep, it was almost more of a relief.

And when Joshua himself did sleep, it was to dream that dream again, only this time, it was Eli sprawled on the oil-stained floor.

He supposed it made him a coward, but he couldn't bear watching Eli in pain. Between that, and the guilt, and the realization that he was not in any way, shape, or form good enough for a relationship with *anyone*, it had been easy to make the decisions he needed to make. Easy to go to the Bureau and agree to their proposal. Easy to make plans to move on. Easy to start looking for an apartment or house where he could live once he walked away from the ranch. Like he'd walked away from his career all those months ago.

Though it looked like his career wasn't satisfied with him leaving it. Too bad Eli wouldn't feel the same way. Not that he wanted him to.

Joshua shut down the computer and left the office. The kitchen was empty, but the big thermos on the counter still had coffee in it, so he poured himself a cup. There were cookies in the glass jar, but he didn't have much of an appetite for snacks these days, though he ate well enough at meals. He wondered where Sarafina was, then realized that this was her day to take lunch to Eli. She was convinced that no one could possibly eat institutional food and thrive.

There was a calendar hanging on one of the cabinets; he wandered over and looked at it. Eli's return date was marked for next Tuesday. Tuesday. Good—he could use the excuse of his shrink appointment to not be home when Eli arrived. He supposed he couldn't avoid him forever. Shit. He didn't *want* to avoid him at all. He wanted to go over to that little cottage of his and find his way back into Eli's bed. But he couldn't. That was over. Done. Eli could find someone else to share his bed. Maybe one of the new trainees who were due in a few weeks would be another gay guy, older than the spoiled little Spencer who was here currently, and who *wouldn't* stop trying to put the make on Joshua. He supposed it wouldn't matter if he did sleep with Spencer. It wasn't as if he'd be cheating on Eli.

But he didn't. Because if he did, he would *feel* as if he were cheating on Eli.

Because it didn't matter that Eli couldn't love him anymore. He loved Eli. Would love him until he died.

And that was the real reason he couldn't stay.

Love, Like Water

Chapter 27

"ARE you ready, honey?"

Eli looked up at his mother and smiled. "Ready as I get, I reckon."

She smiled and held his hand as the orderlies rolled up the wheelchair, more for herself than him, he expected. He would be walking out of the rehab facility under his own power, but for liability purposes had to ride to the door in the chair. He was walking pretty good, even if he had to use a cane. But she was worried about him, which was kind of nice. She'd talked to him a lot during the last few weeks, telling him about when he was still a kid and his dad had died, and how she hadn't wanted him to drop out of high school but didn't know what else to do. And how worried she'd been while he was on the rodeo circuit, and how glad when he got the job with Tucker Chastain. She was going to be staying another week or so until he got settled in at the Triple C. Her new husband Doug had made a few flying visits here over the last month or so, but Eli figured he'd be happier to have her home.

He was looking forward to being home himself—home in his own little cottage, home on the ranch with his horses and his friends and the familiar sights and sounds. And Joshua. He needed to figure out what was going on with Joshua. Even considering the way they had parted, he still missed him. Still needed him.

When he'd asked Tucker and Sarafina about him, Tucker had only shook his head and said, "Fool kid." Sarafina had gotten uncharacteristically sober and said, "He is a sad, sad man, Eli. I feel bad for him." She wouldn't say why, though, only patted his hand comfortingly and urged him not to think about it until he felt better.

Damn it, he was *hurt*, not *sick*. He suspected they were hiding something from him. But when he asked Ramon about Joshua (carefully, so as not to out the boy), Ray only said that he'd been working in the office mostly and just kept to himself. Ray seemed to think that was weird but normal for Josh, so Eli didn't press it.

The drive home was long and Eli was aching by the time they pulled up in the ranch yard. He slid out of the passenger seat of Tucker's truck and leaned on the door for balance as he set his foot down on the ground. "You all right?" Tucker asked in concern. "Doncha think you oughta wait for some help?"

"I'm fine," Eli growled. "Just a little stiff. Ain't used to sitting in a truck that long."

Ma pulled up in her rental behind them and was out of the car and beside him in a millisecond, but he shook her off with a faint smile. "I'm good, Ma."

"Do you want to go home right away?" she asked, taking his good arm. "Sarafina said she'd have supper waiting if you want to go in, but I can bring something over if you want to go to the cottage instead."

"No." He shook her off gently so he could take the cane Tuck handed him from inside the cab and stumped up the stairs, leaning on the banister. He paused to rest a moment on the porch, then went inside to his welcome.

JOSHUA wasn't there, of course. Tucker saw him looking and said in an undertone, "He's at his shrink's appointment. Said he'd see you later."

Right. Eli wasn't prepared for the way it hurt, the fact that Josh couldn't be bothered to be there when he got home. Even after the

Love, Like Water

scene in the rehab center, he still couldn't believe Josh was really going to walk away from them.

But why shouldn't he? They'd only been lovers for a couple of weeks. And it wasn't like Eli was going to be in any physical shape to make love for a few more. He expected Josh had done his own research and found the gay bars Eli used to haunt. And that hurt worst of all.

He lasted as long as he could at the impromptu welcome home party—many of the hands had brought their wives or girlfriends, and the party had spilled from the great room at the front of the house into the patio, which Tuck had decorated with fairy lights. He'd even turned on the fountain and brought out the stored wrought iron patio furniture. Ma and Sarafina, whom Ma had hit it off with right away, bustled around serving people, despite Tucker demanding that they sit down and enjoy themselves. Finally Sarafina snapped "We are damned enjoying ourselves, Tucker!" and everyone burst out laughing. So Tucker didn't say anything else, but a little while later Eli saw him hand a tray of hors d'oeuvres to Dennis and pick one up himself.

A little while after that, though, he reached the end of his rope and quietly got up, cane in hand, and meandered back through the house as if he were heading for the bathroom. Instead, he slipped out the kitchen door and across the yard to his own house.

IT WAS well past two in the morning when Josh got home. He'd finished up at the shrink's at nine or so, as usual, the session frustrating and pointless, as they had been the last few weeks. After that, he'd gone to a bar in the neighborhood for a drink. Well, mostly for a drink, but also to watch the faces of the people there, wondering if it were only those three who had been behind the gay-bashing of the other victims. Eli didn't remember much about the attack, but he'd said he remembered seeing one of them at one of the gay bars he went to.

Josh's glower and generally unapproachable demeanor kept anyone from trying to pick him up, though he did occasionally intercept an interested glance. In the days before the assignment, he would have taken them up on some no-holds-barred sex, but he hadn't been with anyone but Eli in so long that it felt awkward to seem interested. Besides, he still wanted Eli. Not just physically, but mentally, emotionally. He wanted things to go back to the way they had been before the attack, with Eli's soft, slow lovemaking counterpointed with Josh's own more demanding ways. He wanted to watch Eli working with the horses or ride with him out into the desert, with Eli pointing out places and things and critters Josh had never seen before. He wanted to go back to the tiny canyon, and dance in the waterfall again, with Eli watching and laughing at him. He wanted... shit. He wanted Eli.

After a couple of beers, but before he was the slightest bit impeded, he left the bar and drove around for a while. There were only two highways that went through Albuquerque, one going north-south, the other east-west, so he drove around on those for a while, then explored the city streets some. He parked outside San Felipe de Neri and walked through the small square that was the heart of Albuquerque Old Town, but there were people in the shadows there, and he knew it would be easy to score some H, and he just didn't even want to be tempted. So he got back in Sarafina's Forester and just drove around the narrow streets of Old Town for a while before getting back on 40 and heading home.

By the time he got there, the party was over and the house dark and still. The moon was high and very nearly full, illuminating the yards and corrals and ranch buildings with its pale white light. He parked the Forester and walked across to the paddock, where he leaned on the fence and looked out across the desert to the east. Out there, three hours' flight and a hella long way, the guys in Los Peligros street gang were going about their business. Joshua didn't have any illusions that they had broken the gang, just the cabal that was running the drugs. The gangs were like weeds; cut them down and the roots just sprouted again. He understood the appeal of them, especially in neighborhoods where there was so little hope, where everyone faced the same problems. The gangs were a way of connecting, of feeling like you had backup, when society and the City and life in general had failed you. They were your family when your family was nothing but demands and

Love, Like Water

need and hopelessness. They were dignity in a place where dignity had been stripped from everyone, where respect was a dream and reputation the only thing you had left. As long as there was poverty, there would be gangs, and Joshua accepted that. He'd seen both sides. Seen the way that men learned to stand up straight, to find their place in being with men like them. It was dangerous, that mentality, but it gave them a sense of belonging. Of being.

But it also made its own demands on those caught up in it. The other gangs weren't—couldn't be—as good as yours, because your own self-respect was dependent on the status and reputation of your own gang. You had to be the best. And if someone challenged you, or your gang, then they had to be taken down, quickly, before others got the idea that they could challenge you. *Honor sobre todo.* Honor above everything.

And if honor required that a man die at your hands—then you were killing for the gang, and that made it okay.

It wasn't okay, but Joshua had managed to rationalize almost all the deaths he'd been part of. They were all criminals, murderers, those members of other gangs he'd killed, and if he'd been in the same position as an agent, he'd have done the same thing. The revenge killings—those had a reason behind them and were only justice. So Joshua had told himself the first few times. After that, it hadn't been an issue. He'd become just a killing machine, just a tool in the hands of 'Chete Montenegro, and the deaths didn't matter. He'd rationalized all of them out of existence. All but one.

When he talked about the others with the shrink, it was simple. He'd worked it all out in the therapy he went through during rehab, and made his peace with the choices he'd been faced with. He thought that there would be more to it when he discussed those killings with McBride, but he only wanted to know what Joshua felt about it. When Joshua had said "nothing," the shrink had only nodded and made a note on his notebook, then moved on to another topic. And lately... lately Joshua hadn't wanted to talk at all. Most of the sessions were complete silence, with only the faint hum of the air conditioner for background noise. He wondered why he bothered. But he kept going.

Someday, he knew, the subject of the girl would come up, and he didn't know what he'd do then.

A faint sound came from behind him—not quite a footstep, but more of a shuffling sound. His fingers tightened on the fence rail. "Welcome home," he said over his shoulder. "You should be asleep."

"Not sleepy," Eli said. He limped up to the fence and leaned beside Joshua. "Could say the same thing about you."

Joshua shrugged.

"Nice night."

Joshua didn't answer, just stared across the desert at nothing. Eli subsided, just leaning against the fence, his arms folded along the top. The cast on the broken one had been scribbled on by what looked like half the population of Albuquerque. "Do people still do that?" he asked finally, waving his hand at the cast.

"Guess they do," Eli said. "Not my idea."

More silence. Finally Joshua said, "Guess I'll turn in."

"Sarafina says you're having the nightmares again."

Joshua froze in midturn. "Sarafina should mind her own fucking business," he snapped.

"*Mijo*," Eli said gently, "Haven't you figured out yet that if Tuck is the daddy of this ranch, Sarafina's the ma? Which means that she's gonna worry about every soul on this ranch."

"The way you do." Joshua tried to keep his voice neutral, but even he could hear the bitterness in it.

"The way I do," Eli agreed. "But for me, that's mostly just business. It's my job. For Tuck and Sara… shit. He oughta just marry the woman and make it official."

"Why doesn't he?" Joshua didn't know where that question came from—he had intended to just nod curtly and walk back into the house, but for some reason he didn't.

His answer why came in Eli's warm chuckle. God, how could he think of leaving him? The man had to be suffering, but he still came out to talk to Joshua, could still carry on a conversation, could still laugh as if at a joke. He was so much more of a man than Joshua ever could be.

"Well, part of it is that she says she likes the paycheck, and if she marries him he'll expect her to work for free. Of course she's married already."

"I remember."

"I don't think she likes him much—I guess it was sort of an arranged thing. She says if she ever wants to remarry, she'll divorce him, but doesn't want to go through the bother now." Eli sighed. "Can't see it myself, but different people have different ways, I reckon."

Joshua grunted acknowledgment and turned to leave, but Eli put out his good hand and rested it on Joshua's arm. "But that don't mean people with different ways can't find common ground, Josh. And I don't think you're any happier right now than I am."

Josh closed his eyes in pain. Eli wasn't going to make it easy on him. Eli went on, "I don't know what you were thinking when you walked out of my room that day, but I'm pretty sure it ain't what it looked like."

"What did it look like?"

"Like I wasn't good enough for you anymore. See, I think I am, despite your college degree and FBI Academy and all, so that can't be the reason. The way I figure, there's something else going on in that head of yours that maybe ain't quite right. And I wanna know what it is so I can shake some sense into you."

"With what? That busted arm? Or maybe you were gonna chase me around on that bum leg of yours?" Joshua shook off his hand.

"That what's bothering you? That I'm busted up?" Eli shook his head. "Son, I been busted up worse than this before. Rodeo—"

"This didn't happen at any fucking rodeo," Joshua hissed. "You got the shit beat out of you for being gay!"

"And what, you're feeling *guilty* about that? Son of a bitch, you are, aren't you?" When Eli's hand shot out again, this time it closed around Joshua's jaw, forcing Joshua to meet his eyes. He might have been hurt, but his hand was as strong as ever. "News for you, *son*—I been gay a long time. Fact is I was in the wrong place at the wrong time—"

"And that *is* my fault! You were there because you were waiting for me!"

Eli shook Joshua's jaw gently but firmly. "I been down there lots of times before, Josh. A couple of the bars that I used to pick up tricks at are a couple blocks from there. It coulda happened any time, any weekend I was down there. The difference this time was that a couple of assholes decided it was time to rid the world of me on the day that *you* were there. And that made all the difference, 'cause you stopped 'em. You saved my life, Josh. 'Cause you were there." The fingers turned softer, caressing. "You saved my life."

It was hard to talk, but Joshua managed, "You saved mine."

Eli chuckled. "Yeah, but you weren't too pleased about that, were you?"

"Not at the time, no." Joshua reached up and gently disengaged Eli's fingers, dragging them down and holding them in his. "Eli—it's never been a matter of you not being good enough for me. It's the other way around. I'll never be good enough for you. We need to stop this now. I'm no good for you. I should have never come here. I *don't belong here.*"

"What are you talking about? You belong here more'n anyone—you're Tuck's nephew. Your grandfolks built this place. This place is in your blood."

"There's nothing *in* my blood—it's all on my hands." Joshua dropped Eli's hand and leaned back against the fence. "I've had a lot of time to think these last couple of weeks, and I think I need to go back to the Bureau. There are things I need to, to *compensate* for. Penance, kind of. I need to go back where I can do some good and kind of pay my debt...."

"You mean because of the people you killed when you were undercover?"

Joshua's breath came short. "You *know* about that?"

"Just what I heard you say. About blood on your hands." Eli's voice was kind. "You said something once before when you didn't know I was there. To the cat. Something about so much blood and why couldn't you forget."

Love, Like Water

He stared at Eli's face, mild and pale in the moonlight, and felt like throwing up. "You heard that?"

"Yep. Thought you were talking about being back on the heroin at first. Then you started talking about blood."

"It's not polite to eavesdrop when someone's talking to themselves."

"You were talking about it in my barn."

Joshua took a deep breath, then said, "During the three years I was undercover, I was implicit or complicit in the deaths of seven... no, eight people, counting the local gang leader, who was shot during the bust."

"Implicit meaning you were in on the killing?"

"Yes."

"Complicit meaning you pulled the trigger."

"Yes."

Eli whistled softly. "Seems like a whole lot of burden to bear, *mijo*. I'm sorry to hear it."

"See, that's why we can't go on like this anymore. I can't ask you to be part of this. Of me." Joshua rubbed his hands on his face and was surprised when they came away wet. "Shit."

"Do you grieve for 'em?"

"What?"

"Do you grieve for 'em? It sure seems like you do."

Joshua shook his head. "It was what I had to do. They were mostly justified—they were murderers themselves, marked for death anyway, and if I hadn't done it, someone else probably would have, either other gangs or law enforcement. And they weren't good guys, weren't innocent—every one of them had an equal amount of blood on their hands. I tried to think of it as more like execution. I had to justify it in my head—I was constantly under watch by Montenegro and his men, because even though I was my father's son, I was still a stranger to them. They watched me. I had to do what they told me, or I'd have jeopardized my mission. And I *needed* to finish it. I needed to break up the smuggling ring. So it was justified."

"But did you *grieve*."

"*Fuck yes I grieved*!" Joshua dragged in an agonized breath. "God, I still see their faces, every one of them! I still hear the sound of the shot, the sound of the impact, the sound of the body hitting the ground. The sound of screams and sirens. I see the shock on their faces. When they hooked me on heroin it was a fucking relief because as long as I was strung out, I didn't have to *care*. I didn't have to think. I didn't have to *remember*." He tried to still the shaking in his voice. "There was once, early on, after the second or third killing…. I found a Catholic church and went in and lit candles for their souls. I'm not Catholic, Mom's not religious, but my grandparents were, and they used to take me and Cathy to Mass sometimes. So I knew about the candles, and the praying. I prayed for them. And I prayed for me, that if I had to keep doing this, that I wouldn't go to hell, at least not any more than I already was. That I could come out on the other end of this *fucking* assignment. And then came Lina." He stopped then, appalled that he'd let that slip.

But Eli, of course, caught it. "Who's Lina?"

"A girl."

There was silence in the moonlight then, and then, Eli's voice. "*Fuck*." And a few moments later, "Was this before or after you got hooked on the heroin?"

"Before."

"*Fuck*."

"Yeah," Joshua said bitterly. "Can't blame it on the junk, can I?"

Eli didn't answer. Joshua snuck a look at him; he was staring at nothing, his jaw set. *That's done, then*, he thought wearily. *I should have thought of that before*. But he said nothing else, just walked away, back to his solitary, sleepless bed, leaving Eli standing alone in the moonlight.

Love, Like Water

Chapter 28

"You sure about this?"

Tucker leaned on the doorjamb of the upstairs bedroom Joshua had moved to when Eli's ma Rachel had come to stay, giving her the guest suite downstairs. Tucker suspected that Josh was already planning to bolt weeks ago; it looked like he'd barely unpacked anything. Tucker had followed him right upstairs after breakfast, not wanting to argue in front of the hands and their guest, and the only thing he had left to pack was the zip-top plastic bag with his toiletries in it. "I don't get it, son. You said yourself that you wouldn't be starting back with the Bureau for another couple of weeks while they got your paperwork straightened out. And I know for a fact that you ain't found an apartment yet. Where the Sam Hill are you goin'?"

"Hotel," Joshua said curtly. "Bureau's footing the bill."

"But shit, Josh, what's the point? You can stay here. Ain't nobody throwing you out."

"You told me once that you didn't want any bullshit about nasty breakups affecting the ranch, and that if I caused trouble like that, you'd send me back to my mother in pieces. I'm just saving you the trouble." He dug around in the duffel and found a piece of paper, which he handed to Tucker. "There's my e-mail address. You have my cell phone. If you run into any trouble with the books, or any of the programs, call or e-mail me and I can walk you through it. But it's pretty well organized—shouldn't take you more than an hour or so a day to keep it up to date. Just remember to get the bills entered as soon as you get them and the program will remind you when they have to be paid. I imagine Eli can help you out with that, even if he complains about it."

"Eli. This is all about Eli."

"Of course it is."

"He loves you...."

"No. Loved. Past tense. It's done, Uncatuck. Trust me. He'll be glad to see the back of me." He zipped up the duffel and looked back at Tucker, who almost cried at the misery in his eyes. Tuck didn't know what was worse, that or the dead look he'd had when he'd arrived. "It's really better this way. Thanks for lending me Tonio."

"Well, I ain't about to make you walk to Albuquerque."

"You could just have him take me to Miller and I'll catch the bus."

"No. At least this way I'll know you got where you were going, and didn't wander off into the desert somewhere."

"You're still angry about that."

"You bet your ass I'm still angry about that! I'm angry about a lot of things, son!" He saw Joshua flinch and lowered his voice. "Sorry, son."

"No, I shouldn't be such a fucking wimp. I used to have guts. Not anymore."

"No."

Josh froze, and looked up at him. "What?"

"No, you don't have any guts anymore. If you had, you'd stay and work this out with Eli."

"There's nothing to be worked out. Trust me—Eli'll be more relieved than I am to see the back of me. Ask him." Josh didn't even look insulted or angry, just tired.

"You know, I thought you going back to the Bureau was just a ploy to get Eli's attention back. That you and he had some kinda falling out, and that you were trying to play games. But it wasn't, was it? You been serious the whole time."

"Dead serious." Josh gave him a thin smile that Tucker didn't know how to read. He remembered Eli talking about Josh being like one of the abused horses they brought in, but no horse was ever as stubborn and difficult as Josh was being. "I don't play games, Uncatuck." He shouldered the duffel, picked up his backpack, and left the room.

Tucker followed him down and outside, where Tonio waited beside the Silverado. Josh tossed both bags into the back of the truck, then turned and held out his hand to Tucker. "Thanks for everything," he said stiffly.

"Shit," Tucker said, and pulled him into his arms, hugging him tightly. After a moment, Josh's arms came around and hugged him back, hard, as if he were Josh's lifeline in a storm. He clung to Tucker a long moment, then let him go, backing up and getting in the cab without looking back.

Tucker watched the truck drive away, then glanced over at Eli, who was sitting on the porch. "And I'm pissed at you, too," he said irritably. "How could you just let him walk away from you like that?"

"Uh, Tuck?"

"What?"

"You might want to keep your voice down." Eli waved his hand, and Tuck turned to see Ray, Manny, Billy, Chico, and Fred—their live-in hands—all standing not too far away and watching with interest.

"Oh, don't worry about us," Fred said cheerfully. "We figured out you guys were doing the horizontal mambo *weeks* ago. Shit, Eli, it ain't like none of us didn't know you was queer. The news been calling your attack a gay bashing so I think it's pretty obvious."

"And you're okay with that?" Tucker asked curiously.

"Well, we purt much think it's gross," Chico said, "but hey, you ain't never put the make on any of us, so that's okay. Manny saw Josh going into your house one night and we figgered it out. We knew even before the news. Besides, there's a limited number of women in Miller to date, so more for us."

Manny scratched his chin. "One or two of the locals have said something, but they're mostly just fishing for information. We told them you was just in the wrong place at the wrong time. You were waiting for Josh. So we're good." He waved his hand. "Just don't give us no details, *comprendes*?"

"*Comprendo*," Eli agreed, but then his face went still. "Don't matter anyway. It's done."

"Well, long's you don't come looking in the bunkhouse for his replacement," Manny said. Chico clipped him in the head. "Ow, what?"

"They busted up, you stupid fucker! Show some class."

"Get back to work," Tucker said tiredly. "I'm done with all this bullshit. Eli, you come in and I'll teach you how to work the computer. Since you drove off my office clerk, you get to fill in for him."

"I didn't drive him off. He left."

"Shut up." Tucker stomped back up the stairs and into the office, turning on the computer with more force than necessary. A minute later Eli limped in. "Sit."

Eli obeyed, setting his cane to the side. Tucker leaned over him and started teaching him the banking program.

About an hour later he was ready to kill someone. "Jesus, Eli, don't you fucking know how to use a fucking computer? Good Lord, you're only thirty-three—didn't you kids grow up knowing how these fuckers work?"

"I don't think I ever heard you swear so much, Tuck," Eli said. "In answer to your question, no, the little one-room schoolhouse I went to didn't have a computer and I dropped outta high school before they could teach me. Got my GED without one, and my classes in AH were mostly hands-on. Not much call for computers on the rodeo circuit, and since I came here you took care of all that. I can do a Google Search and answer e-mail, and I don't even *get* e-mail these days. Someone wants to talk to me, they call or text. So no, I'm not so good with 'em."

Love, Like Water

"Shit." Tucker dropped into one of the side chairs and rubbed his forehead. "Damn, I wish Josh hadn't taken off like that. What the hell did you say to him?"

"Nothing." But Eli's face had gone closed and hard, and Tucker knew there was something going on.

"Come on, spill."

In answer, Eli turned back to the computer. "Speaking of Google Searches—I came in here last night to look something up," he said. "Well, this morning, really. About four. Couldn't sleep." He typed something one-handed, then clicked the mouse a couple of times. "Here. Look at this."

Tucker got up and came around the desk to look at an article Eli had brought up. It was about a murder a couple of years ago in a Chicago warehouse. The woman, a Lina Santiago, had been five months pregnant. The picture of her in the article looked like a high school photo: laughing face, silky dark hair, bright eyes. "You think *Josh* did this?"

"He *said* so. A woman, Tuck. He killed a *pregnant woman*." Eli rubbed his face with his good hand. "I can't... I just can't justify that. He killed men 'cause he had to, I guess, like a soldier or something, but this was a woman... and a *baby*. I don't know how I can deal with that."

Tucker read the article silently.

Eli went on, "I mean, I s'pose it's sexist or something, but it's so much worse when it's a woman, y'know? But this... Jesus, Tuck, at five months she'd be showing. It wouldn't be like he killed her not knowing."

"The heroin...."

"This was before."

"Fuck."

"Yeah."

"I can't believe this."

"He said so."

"Yeah," Tucker said heavily. "I got that." He straightened. "Well. That explains why he left. Guess now that you know, he figures there ain't nothing worth staying for."

"Tucker." There was a world of hurt in the voice.

"Yeah," Tucker said. He put his hand on Eli's shoulder. "Yeah."

Love, Like Water

Chapter 29

"I LEFT the ranch."

"Oh? When was that?"

"Wednesday."

McBride's eyebrow rose. "I knew you were planning to, but didn't Eli just get home Tuesday?"

"Yes. That was why. He knows the truth about me now, and won't want to have anything to do with me. I figured it was better to just get out of there." Joshua stretched his legs out in front of him, studying the toes of his boots. When did cowboy boots start feeling so much more comfortable than sneakers? "I talked to Greene and he said the Bureau would pop for a week or so at a hotel, just the same as if I were working out of state. Since I'm still on contingent assignment to the Chicago office, I'm technically out of state, so."

"How do you like living in a hotel?"

Joshua shrugged. "It's quiet. Boring. When I was in rehab they warned us about being bored—that that was almost worse than being tired or stressed out for relapsing."

"Do you worry about relapsing?"

"Every fucking minute." Joshua sorted through his tangled thoughts, then went on, "I didn't when I was on the ranch, so much. The couple weeks I was with Eli... I pretty much didn't even think about the smack. But now? Yeah. I'm worried. I'm bored and lonely and I got all the back pay from when I was on assignment sitting in a bank account just waiting for me to get to it. And all cities are alike—I know just where I could go to score some."

The psychologist only nodded.

Joshua went on, "I had therapy in rehab, you know. Every day, several times a day. One on one, group, it didn't matter. We talked about shit endlessly."

"Do you feel that that therapy helped?"

"Yeah, I guess. It helped me deal with the killing, anyway. Part of the reason I walked away from the Bureau was that I couldn't bear to think of taking another life. I couldn't go back to that, couldn't go back to being a cop, couldn't...." He stopped, took a deep breath to steady his voice. "I never wanted anything except to be in law enforcement, and for three years everything I did went counter to my beliefs, to my training, to my morals. I turned myself into someone else, someone I didn't like, didn't respect. I don't know how I didn't just go under completely, but I didn't. Every night after I got back to that shithole of an apartment, I made my report. Every night before I put my laptop back in its hiding place, I wiped the browser history, wiped the files, wiped everything that could possibly betray me, either as an agent or as a gay man. While my *compadres* went home to sleep off another night breaking every fucking law known to man, I went home and downloaded." He snorted. "The only sex I had was with porn sites, and even then I had to make sure I deleted the browser history. My screensaver and desktop was titty porn shots, in case anyone found where I hid my computer. It was a shitty way to live.

"'Chete thought I had a thing for Lina Santiago. Of course I didn't, but I liked her. She was one of his runners, but she was in love with a member of another gang, real *West Side Story* shit. That's who her baby daddy was. 'Chete found out and had me start narking on her. I found out she was skimming and passing it on to her lover—they were going to take the money and run. Not soon enough."

He rubbed his face. "I've come to terms with the others, but I will never forgive myself for Lina."

Love, Like Water

"What happened to the lover?"

"What else? He came after 'Chete. I shot him too."

"Are you still dreaming?"

Joshua frowned. "What?"

"Are you still dreaming? You said you had had a couple of bad dreams while Eli was in the hospital, but you haven't mentioned it since."

"Off and on." Joshua realized he was sitting hunched over and made a conscious effort to straighten up. Hunching was something he'd done a lot of in rehab, and the physical therapist there had told him that it wasn't healthy, either physically or mentally. It was his making himself small, to hide, to disappear. "Yeah, I'm still having them. Once I get back to work it'll be better. When I was working on the ranch, I hardly ever had them."

"When you were working?"

"Yeah."

"Same time as when you were with Eli?"

"Yeah. Yeah, I guess. Look, can we not talk about Eli?"

"Of course," the shrink said. "We can talk about whatever you want."

"The thing is that me and Eli, we're done. It's over with. I can't let him be part of me anymore. I need to let him go."

The shrink nodded.

"It doesn't matter how much I miss him. How much I miss the ranch, you know? 'Cause it's done. He's part of the ranch and I'm not."

"Would you like to be?"

"What?"

"Part of the ranch?"

Joshua stared at him, and to his horror, he felt tears on his face. "No," he lied, and ran his sleeve across his eyes. "No. I don't want that. I'm not meant for the ranch. I'm meant to be with the Bureau. I can be of use there. Yeah, I'll probably never be more than an analyst, but that's okay—I'm not sure I want to do fieldwork anymore. I'm good. It's going to be okay."

Silently, the shrink nudged the box of Kleenex toward him.

"This is fucking *stupid*! I lived for three years in hell and never broke down. Why the fuck am I breaking down *now*?"

"Because you can?" McBride said. "Because you're safe now, and can afford to let go?"

Joshua wrapped his arms around his head, hunched over in his chair, and howled.

Love, Like Water

Chapter 30

THE air down by the river was cool, redolent with the spice of pine and grass, as Joshua slowed his run to a steady jog along the Paseo del Bosque Trail. Agent Greene had introduced him to the long stretch along the Rio Grande; it ran nearly the whole length of the river as it cut through the city, and was one of the more popular spots for Albuquerqueans to escape the heat. But at this hour it was nearly deserted, just a couple of bicyclists and late runners like himself braving the chill desert night. The midsixties that had been the high today didn't linger after nightfall. Joshua figured it was probably ten degrees cooler than that now.

Despite the darkness by the river, you couldn't see the stars the way you could on the ranch, Joshua thought, even with the leafy trees now mostly bare of their fall color. The ambient light of the city blocked them, just the way the smells of car fumes and concrete dulled the scent of growing things. It was weird how used Joshua had gotten to the scent of growing things in the short time he'd been on the ranch.

A bench beckoned and he headed for it, dropping onto it with a sigh of relief and tugging the earbuds from his ears, shutting off the sound of Daddy Yankee's most recent release. He'd only run a couple of miles, but that was more than he'd expected he'd be able to do, after not running for so long. It had been one of his ways to blow off steam for most of his life; until the addiction, he'd even run while in Darwin

Park. After… well, it hadn't been so easy. And since rehab, his energy levels had been pretty low.

But he'd gotten more exercise on the ranch, riding and helping out where he could, and he supposed that that was probably what had given him his energy back. At least enough to do a couple of miles. Maybe he'd be able to sleep tonight. He hadn't had much luck with that lately. Dreams of the past, of course, as had haunted him for months, but those had been joined by dreams of Eli, battered and broken in that loading dock, frozen-faced and still as he'd leaned on the fence the night he'd discovered just what Joshua was. And then worse—dreams where the two were juxtaposed, where it was Eli dead in the warehouse, Eli battered and broken in the canyon glen where they'd made love and Joshua had danced for him. 'Chete had been there too, and the waterfall had run red with blood.

It had been nearly three weeks since he'd left the ranch. The Bureau had found him an inexpensive studio apartment not far from their headquarters; while he hadn't come back full time, he'd been able to walk to the office for the series of intake interviews and to work on a few smaller projects. Work as an analyst, riding a computer. Not the most exciting job, but one that seemed to be custom-made for his peculiar skills—he'd already picked up some references that other analysts had missed, because his damn memory kept hold of trivia like a miser his gold. The head of the Albuquerque office had called him in yesterday and commended him on catching some data that pushed a stalled investigation into a new, more promising direction.

And then he'd mentioned an upcoming investigation into the Quintana Cartel, another fucking joint project with the DEA, and asked Joshua to work on the preliminary research.

Joshua had almost swallowed his tongue. The Quintana Cartel wasn't a Mexican operation—it worked out of the Caribbean, smuggling cocaine from Venezuela and heroin from Afghanistan through channels in Cuba, and shipping them up the Mississippi. He knew that because it had been the Quintana Cartel that owned 'Chete Montenegro—and by extension, Joshua. Joshua's work in Chicago had helped break their operation there and cut off their access to the upper

Love, Like Water

Midwest. Now, apparently, they were expanding into the Southwest instead.

He'd spent today buried in reports, weeding through them in search of patterns, confirmations, testimony, hearsay, anything that would help form the picture he needed of the cartel's new endeavors. He knew their modus operandi well enough: make connections with an existing gang, recruit the most ruthless as their men on the ground, and only then work out their distribution channels. The Quintaneros, as they called themselves, were careful businessmen; they made sure they had a solid foundation to build on and covered every contingency. It had been that which had made them so difficult to bring down in Chicago.

Today had been a fucking nightmare. Some of the reports had been his own, written in the dark of his apartment in the small hours, pecked out on his laptop as he downloaded the conversations, the orders, the details, from his brain—and sometimes, rarely, the photos he was able to snap surreptitiously with his smartphone. Seeing them again, in cold print or PDF, sent his mind spiraling back down into the nightmare. He remembered writing them, every one, remembered his moods, his actions that day, his reactions. Remembered the pain, and the disconnect the junk had provided.

Every word slapped him back into the Joshua he had been, and left the Joshua he was now reeling.

The river whispered, and Joshua put his head in his hands, the heels of his palms rubbing into his eye sockets, as if they could erase the things he'd seen.

"Hey, you okay, dude?"

He glanced up to see a skinny kid in a hoodie against the cool of the night. Standing between Joshua and the light reflected off the water, he was a black silhouette. Joshua tensed, and glanced briefly to either side, but there was no sign of anyone else.

"Hey," the kid said again, and put out empty hands. "I'm not gonna mug you, bud. Just askin'. You look kinda bummed."

"Just tired, thanks," Joshua said.

Uninvited, the kid dropped down onto the bench a foot or so away from Joshua. "I get that," he said. "Long day, if you're out this late for your jog. Never got much into running, myself—too much work." He fidgeted, his knee bouncing rapidly, and in the reflected light, Joshua saw his face: thin, wispy-bearded, the eyes nervous and the prominent Adam's apple bobbing as he swallowed.

"Nervous?" Joshua asked idly.

"Nah, just amped, you know?" He shot Joshua a grin.

A pair of runners went by on the path behind them, talking in low, breathless tones, but the kid didn't react, so Joshua figured he probably *was* just amped, not nervous. "I'm Joshua." He held out a hand.

"Tony." They shook, then the kid pushed his hoodie back. "Shit, it's cold."

It hadn't seemed more than pleasantly cool to Joshua, but he supposed he'd been working up a sweat for the last half hour or so. A few more minutes on the bench and he supposed he'd feel the bite of the November chill. On the other hand, he'd seen a lot of kids like this one before, and they were always cold. It made him study Tony more carefully.

The kid said, "Where you from? You don't sound local."

"Back East. Family's out here."

"Cool." Tony's head bobbed rapidly in acknowledgement. Yeah, Joshua thought. "Amped" must mean the same thing as "hyped," or something close. Not just hyper, not just nervous. The kid was stoked to the gills. He looked around as if expecting someone, but not towards the path.

"Waiting for somebody?"

"Uh…. Yeah. A friend, y'know."

And I'm sitting on the bench that's your meeting place. For your supplier, no doubt.

The thought sent a frisson through Joshua's spine. Somewhere back in his lizard brain, José Rosales was jumping up and down in excitement, saying, *At last, at last, we can feel good about ourself again. At last, at last, sweet bliss, sweet bliss.*

On the ranch, Joshua had seen the way horses could shiver voluntarily, tiny muscles between the skin and the flesh below working to shift the outer layer to dislodge flies or adjust to pressure. Now he felt like his own skin was doing that: shifting, sliding, trying to reform itself into the Joshua-that-was. He tightened his fists around the cord of his earbuds.

Feel good? Yeah, for a couple of hours of sleepy lassitude, followed by more hours of pain and depression? *Bliss*? He pressed his fists into the flesh of his thighs beneath the running shorts, forcing himself to remember the agony of withdrawal, the agony he had felt every fucking day, waiting for 'Chete to give him the night's dose. He'd kept José constantly on the edge, pushing him the way he did his other hypes, only letting them have the drug when they'd finished whatever task it was he had set them to. He'd told them it was because he was concerned about their safety, that being strung out damaged their judgment, but it was really because controlling men who could kill him without a second thought gave him a rush like the one his junkies got from the H.

Joshua was never going to let anyone control him like that again. He wasn't going to let anything control him like that again. He drew in a long, slow breath through his nose, and felt José shriveling up in his head. Felt him die.

He felt like weeping.

"Dude?"

He opened his eyes. He must have had them closed really tightly, because they hurt. "Yeah?"

"Um, I'm kinda meeting someone here.... Hey, though, you know, if you ain't feeling so good, maybe he could like, help you out? He knows people."

I bet he does. Thing is—so do I....

"Maybe," Joshua said. He leaned back against the bench and stretched an arm out along it. The Los Peligros tattoo was mostly shadow, but enough of it showed beneath the T-shirt that someone who knew the design would recognize it. "Mind if I hang around?"

"Okay by me. Oh, there he is now."

Another guy, in a hoodie like Tony's, but with the hood down. His hands were in the pockets. "Hey," he said to Tony, then gave Joshua a suspicious look.

"Hey, Creed. This is Joshua."

Creed nodded cautiously, then his eyes lit on Joshua's tattoo. They widened briefly, then some of the tension eased from his face. "Hey, man. What can I do you for?"

"Nothing tonight, man. I'm cool," Joshua said easily. He curled the fingers of his outstretched hand, feeling the rasp of wood beneath his nails, letting all the tension flow out of his body and into the wood. "Just out for a run, and a palaver with my man Tony here."

The other guy relaxed more. "Excellent. Don't mind if Tony and I do a little business?"

"Be my guest. Good junk?"

"Shit, yeah." The dealer's face split in a wide grin. "The best."

"I heard," Joshua's voice dropped into a confidential tone, "that there's a new source in town. You heard about that?"

"Yeah. Where d'you think I got the shit? It's primo, man. Straight from the Mideast." He held up a poly bag. Even in the dim light Joshua could see that the contents were a soft, pale color. "None of that dark shit. Pretty, huh?"

Pretty. God, it was pretty. Part of Joshua lusted after it, but he shoved that part back, stuffed it back into the black hole it came out of, and just nodded. "Nice."

"Sure you don't want some? New customer, I'll cut you a deal."

"Nah, no cash on me. Besides, I'm just a recreational user. And I got enough shit at home for now. Tell you what, though—I'm having a

Love, Like Water

party this weekend. What say we meet back here Friday, same time? I'll be here."

"Alone, right?" Creed looked around. "I don't like to plan that far in advance, but tell you what—you be here, and if I can make it... I'll show up. Deal?"

"Deal." Joshua flicked his hand at him to indicate he should continue his business with Tony, and went back to watching the river. Tony got up and walked with Creed down toward the river, talking in low tones that Joshua figured they thought couldn't be heard. But the breeze was off the water, and carried their voices to him.

Nothing major, just an agreement that Tony would show up on Friday too and keep an eye out for trouble. Joshua expected no less, and didn't react at all, just absorbed what they had to say. When they were done, Tony sidled past the bench with a "later, dude" and a quick grin. Creed stood a moment or two later, then said to Joshua, "Friday, then. Cash only—I don't deal in anything else. No trades, no services. Cash."

"I ain't stupid, *chulo*."

The curtness of Joshua's reply seemed to reassure Creed; with a nod to Joshua, he set off down the slope toward the river and disappeared in the trees a hundred feet away. Joshua watched him, then got up, did a couple stretches, then headed off towards home at a slow, easy jog.

The dealer followed him a while. Joshua kept his pace deliberately slow so he could keep up, but after a few blocks he veered off. Joshua ran for another half hour, then turned his steps toward the city lot where his car was parked.

Chapter 31

BUTTON shifted anxiously beneath Eli's seat, sidestepping across the sand of the arena. "Come on, Eli," Tucker called from the fence rail he was sitting on. "You're trying too hard. Horse is getting freaked out."

"I know," Eli muttered grimly, and stretched his leg again, feeling the pull of the too-tight muscle. He settled deeper into the saddle and Button relaxed.

"Better," Tuck said a few minutes later, as Eli brought Button back to the fence and dismounted. "How's it feel?"

"Like I been hung by my leg for a week or so."

"You haven't lost your form, if that's any consolation. Once you got settled, you were looking okay. What does the physical therapist say?"

"She says that riding contracts muscle and I need to spend more time in the swimming pool at the hospital to stretch it out. Like I got the time to go wandering back and forth to Miller on a daily basis. Besides, I hate swimming."

"You like it fine when it's hot out."

"Yeah, but it's not hot anymore. We're coming up on Thanksgiving, Tucker. It's been damn cold these last couple nights." Was cold now, in fact—barely in the high fifties—despite it being the middle of the afternoon.

Love, Like Water

"Should be good sleeping weather." Tucker cocked his head at Eli, who only shrugged. Tucker knew he was having trouble sleeping, and why. But he didn't say anything, just added, "Think we need to get up to the canyon and get the ladies back here for the winter, before we get snow."

"Shoulda done that two weeks ago."

"Well, two weeks ago I was still hoping that Josh woulda changed his damn fool mind and helped out. He woulda liked being in on the roundup, I think. But I can't wait any longer. I figure tomorrow morning I'll take a couple of the hands out there and we'll bring 'em in. You want to come with the van for the colts? Dennis's driving."

"Sure. Can't see myself riding that whole distance yet." Eli flexed the fingers of his injured hand. He was out of a cast, but still wore a brace for the broken wrist. "Do what I can."

"I appreciate it."

Eli nodded, and limped into the barn, Button at his heels. The therapy was helping his leg, but it ached after a workout, and the pain ran from his hip to his foot. Walking around would help some, but there was an ice pack with his name on it back in his icebox.

He'd been hurt before during both his years with the rodeo and his years here, but never all at once like this. Sometimes it seemed he was one big ache. But it was getting better, the ache in his body.

The ache in his heart? He reckoned that was permanent.

He put Button in the crossties and groomed him, even though the horse hadn't done more than walk around the arena a couple of times. The steady, mindless rhythm of the brushing was a comfort, something he could do without thinking. And it didn't hurt the horse, either. Button's head dropped drowsily as Eli ran the currycomb over his withers.

His cell phone buzzed and he dropped the comb in his hurry to grab it. He'd left probably a dozen messages and texts for Josh over the last three weeks and had gotten no answer, but hope sprang eternal or some such nonsense. The disappointment when he saw it was Jack

Castellano's number, not Joshua's, felt like a body blow, and he considered not answering, but did anyway. "Kelly," he said curtly.

"Hey, Eli. Jack. How are you doing?"

"Good enough, I reckon. What's up?"

"Just wondered what you were doing Friday night. I thought I'd like to try out that new place in Old Town and wouldn't mind the company."

Eli didn't know what to say. Yeah, he and Jack had had a couple nights together, but neither of them had been looking for anything more than a quick fuck. This sounded like a date or something. "You asking me out, Jack?"

The doctor laughed. "Guess I am. You interested?"

"I dunno.... I ain't sure I'm the dating kind, Jack."

"No commitment, Eli. To be honest, I'm sort of between relationships right now and don't have anyone else I'd rather go with. If you want, it'll just be dinner. You can tell me how your therapy's going. I keep meaning to catch up with you one of the times you're in Miller, but so far haven't managed it. No pressure."

"I guess so," Eli said. He picked up the currycomb and hooked it on the nail by Button's stall. "What time Friday?"

"Come to the hospital about five. I'll make reservations for seven. That work for you?"

"Sure."

After he'd hung up, he unhooked Button from the crossties, then put the horse back in his box, and wandered down towards where the third of the three creeks that watered the ranch found its end in a small, tree-shaded pool, just beyond his foreman's cottage. The leaves of the cottonwoods that surrounded it were already falling, floating on the pool's surface, eddied by the little tumble of water that fed the pool. Another couple of weeks and there would be frost rime on the edges; a few more and the water would be frozen 'til spring. He'd meant to bring Josh here one day, but there hadn't been time, and now Eli

Love, Like Water

appreciated that. This was one of the few of Eli's favorite places that didn't have a memory of Josh attached to it.

Eli sat down, his back against one of the trees, and watched the leaves swirl. His leg ached, but that was nothing new. What surprised him was that his heart ached, as if his conversation with Jack had torn open sutures on a healing wound.

The thing was, he didn't think the wound was healing. He missed Joshua as much as ever—maybe more. Not just the sex, though that was nice. But the conversations. The rides, sometimes in complete silence that wasn't uncomfortable, but reassuring. The camaraderie of working together, of Eli teaching Joshua to regain half-forgotten skills of horsemanship, of Joshua leaning on the fence watching while Eli worked with a new arrival in the arena, or of the two of them perched there while Tucker coaxed better behavior from a troubled beast. In the few short weeks they'd been together, Joshua's voice had become part of the music of the ranch, as much as the jingle of bridle tack or the squeak of leather or the wind in the trees and the water. Day to day, Eli had been able to ignore it while he was working—and even though he was supposed to take it easy, he'd worked as hard as he could, until he fell into bed at night and went right to exhausted, if troubled, sleep.

Was he ready to move on? Was Jack the right person to—What did they call it? Rebound?—onto? He liked Jack, always had. But Jack didn't look at him with dark eyes lost in sadness, didn't smile that elusive, tentative smile that wrung Eli's heart.

Had never danced under a chilly waterfall, those dark eyes on Eli's. Had never curled up in Eli's bed with his head on Eli's chest, as if Eli were strong enough to defend someone who'd proven his own strength over and over.

Yes, Joshua had killed a girl. He'd said he'd come to terms with the other killings, but Eli had had time to think about it, and he knew, just *knew*, that Josh wasn't over the girl. Would never be over the girl. Eli didn't know why he'd done it, but one thing he was sure of: it hadn't been Josh's choice. Josh hadn't *wanted* to kill the girl. It haunted him. It was what drove those endless nightmares Josh had—because since finding out about it, they'd driven nightmares of his own.

It hadn't taken Eli long to figure out that Joshua's guilt and grief were what made him so fragile. Maybe that was why he'd gotten hooked on the heroin—maybe the drug kept him from feeling. He remembered his own guilt and grief when he'd had to put down an injured horse; remembered the nightmares, the self-hatred—and that had been out of kindness to a dumb animal. How much worse could it be for Joshua, who'd been put in a position where he'd had to do that to another human being—not out of kindness, but out of the cruelty of another man?

And he'd turned away from him. Rejected him.

Eli put his face in his hands.

"Nice spot to think," Tucker said gently. Eli looked up to see him sitting down a few feet away from him on a stump from an earlier clearing. "Nice spot to talk, if you're so inclined."

"Just thinking."

"Mphm," Tucker said.

They sat quietly, each lost in their own thoughts, for a long while. Then Tucker stretched his legs out in front of him and said, "You know, the ranch wasn't originally named the Triple C. My grandfather renamed it after he bought it from the man that went bankrupt here. Lots of that going on in the thirties—prices for beef stock went really low. Lot of cattle ranches went out of business, and this wasn't the best place for beeves to begin with. Originally, though, the place was called Three Creek Ranch, because of how important those three creeks are. It's the creeks that made this spot of earth livable. When Granddad bought the ranch, he expanded it the whole length of Rio Galiano, right up to the government forest lands, just so he could control the water." He grinned. "That box canyon was just a bonus—he didn't have a clue that was there. But when he was following Galiano up, he found where it branched the first time, and followed that down to the canyon. Best kept secret in New Mexico, I bet."

"It's a good place." Eli closed his eyes, thinking of Joshua dancing.

"Water built it. Water built this place, too. Wouldn't be here but for that."

"Yep."

"Wasn't only water, though."

"What do you mean?"

Tucker stretched again. "Takes more than water and land to make a place like the Triple C, Eli. Takes hope, and faith, and courage, and love. Granddad took a big risk, buying a place like this to raise horses, out in the middle of nowhere, at a time when horses were being phased out by cars and rail. But he believed in his dream, and Grandma believed in him. Same with my folks. Don't mean to get all mushy, but I'm thinking that maybe a big part of love is believing in somebody. Believing in something outside of yourself, you know?"

"This about Josh?"

"Of course it's about Josh. You been walking around like a zombie these past couple of weeks. Now, maybe I'm talking out my hat, but it seems to me that you ain't just hurting from the beating. That maybe what's really hurting ain't your bones."

"Fuck, Tucker." Eli put his face back in his hands.

"Son, there ain't nothing wrong with admitting when you're gone over someone. God knows I know the feeling."

That brought Eli's head up. "What? You?"

"What, do you think I'm made of stone, son? I got feelings just like everyone else. But in my case, it don't do no good to talk about it. The lady I care about just ain't available." Tucker shrugged. "I'm too old for romance, anyway. But you—you're still young. There's time enough for you to make mistakes. I just don't think this one's it."

"I don't know what to do."

"You try calling him?"

"He doesn't answer. I texted him, e-mailed him—nothing. So I stopped."

"Damn fool kid," Tucker said, and Eli knew he wasn't referring to him. "He answers me quick enough. When did you text him last?"

"Week ago."

"What'd'ya say?"

"Just asked him to call. Said I wanted to talk to him."

"Well, that's straightforward enough. Damn fool kid."

"You got his address? Next step, I reckon, is sitting on his doorstep."

Tucker said, "He was at a hotel, but he got an apartment. I don't have the address yet. Soon's I do, I'll give it to you. I don't know what else to do, except chew him out the next time I talk to him. You want that?"

"No." Eli shook his head. "I think it's between me and Josh. He wasn't so nice when you made him come to see me in the hospital."

"He was pulling away even then." Tucker got up and dusted off his seat. "Near to suppertime. Best get in before Sarafina sends out the dogs. Speaking of which, after we get back from the canyon and get the mares settled, I'm driving into Miller. One of Paco's coonhounds just dropped a litter and I figure on picking out a pair for the ranch here."

"Good idea," Eli said. He got up too, a little more awkwardly than Tucker, but to be fair, he'd been sitting on the ground a while. "Guess I need to wash up for supper."

"Guess you do." Tucker put his hand on Eli's shoulder. "Don't give up on Josh, son. I got the feeling we ain't seen the last of him. I think all he needs is for you to accept him, warts and all."

"Never saw any warts," Eli said.

Tucker cuffed him lightly in the head. "You know what I mean. I'll see you at supper."

Love, Like Water

Chapter 32

THE head of the Albuquerque field office, Vasquez, was skimming through Joshua's report when Joshua entered. He looked up, smiled briefly, and gestured for Joshua to sit while he put the papers back into their folder. "You've submitted an intriguing proposition, Mr. Chastain."

"It makes sense." Joshua spread his hands out in illustration. "I have the background, the experience, and the name. All we need do is work out a story of how I came to be here instead of in prison in Ohio, and I can assure you we'd have an in. Yes, there'd probably be a few weeks of shaking in, but I can deal."

"I won't deny we could use someone with your... talents within the Quintana organization. Your work with Los Peligros in Chicago was exemplary—in its way. I admit my first reaction was to agree with you. However."

Joshua clenched his fists on the end of the chair arms. "You don't think I can handle it," he said tightly.

"No. After reading your report, I contacted Bill Robinson in Chicago. He gave you a glowing recommendation, but he also pointed out some of the same things both your therapist here and at the rehab facility did."

"My therapist?"

"Yes. Our budget isn't big enough to include a staff psychologist, unlike larger cities like Chicago, so we use civilian consultants, who go through the same vetting as any other employee of the bureau. Your Dr. McBride is one of them. You signed releases permitting us to contact him, which I did this afternoon. His report tallied with your medical records from rehab. The fact that you're still suffering from nightmares and emotional issues connected with your last assignment makes you ineligible for this one." The man smiled ruefully. "I don't like to be the bearer of bad news. I know you were enthusiastic about this project, but I can't risk it."

"I'm fine. It's not like I'd wind up back on the heroin or anything. And even if there was an outside chance I did, I think I've proven I can function despite it." Joshua felt sweat starting to bead on his neck. "This assignment would prove that I'm still a good agent, that the Bureau could rely on me...."

"The Bureau does and will continue to rely on you, Joshua. You're a fine analyst. But the fact is that you are not ready to return to field agent status. Your PTSD is unresolved. You're less than a year out of a heroin addiction, and you've admitted you're still craving it. You have nightmares. You suffer from intense guilt over the killing of the Santiago girl. Your physical health is improved, but your response times in some of the tests were not up to your usual from prior to the Chicago assignment. And I am not going to be the one to put you in a situation where your health—mental or physical—will be a detriment to the operation. Other agents will be relying on you. Do you honestly believe that you would be the only one impacted if you fail?"

Vasquez leaned forward, steepling his fingers. "I don't think you should use the Bureau as your method of suicide, Joshua, and if I sent you in there in your condition, that's exactly what it would be. You are neither mentally nor physically prepared to handle an assignment like the one you had in Chicago. The only reason Robinson didn't pull you out of there months ago was because you were so deeply embedded. There were other agents whose safety depended on you, and you were coping. But he admitted to me this afternoon that he didn't expect that you would make it out of there alive."

Joshua felt numb. He stared at the other man, but he was seeing Bill Robinson, his face white and tense as he led Joshua in handcuffs

Love, Like Water

out of the police station where he'd been taken. Robinson hadn't relaxed until they were in the car and driving away; then he'd sat and shaken for a good fifteen minutes. It was only afterward that he'd been able to talk to Joshua and explain where they were going. "He didn't." It wasn't a question.

"No. And he was pretty upset at the idea of you going back into a similar situation. We're not chickenshit, Joshua. We put people in harm's way all the time—it comes with the territory. But we are always, *always* careful that we do so in such a way that the outcome is the best possible one, that the end will always justify the means, as much as possible. Yes, it would be helpful to have someone in the position you're suggesting. But you are not the right person. Not now. Maybe not ever, but definitely not now."

"So what happens now?"

"We still need you as an analyst. If you feel you can't work with us, that's your choice. I know you're not thrilled with desk work, but that's where I think you can best perform. Your mission in Chicago was a brilliant success, there's no doubt about it. But people died who shouldn't have died, and the damage it did to you was...." Vasquez shook his head. "I don't know what to say. I'm not speaking now as head of this office. I'm speaking as a human being. I want you to stay on as an analyst. But you have to know that I will not use you in the field for the foreseeable future. So the choice is up to you."

Joshua let the words sink in, trying to decide how he felt, but Vasquez wasn't finished. This time when he spoke, his voice was hard and stern. "The other thing Bill Robinson said—and McBride confirmed—was that you're an independent thinker. That's a good thing—but if you have *any* idea of taking this on by yourself, I will personally kick your ass from here to Santa Fe. You are not to involve yourself in this operation in any way, shape or form, outside of the roles that *I* assign you. *Comprendes, muchacho?*"

"*Comprendo*," Joshua acknowledged.

It wasn't as if he hadn't thought about it. Even as Vasquez had been talking, his mind had been ticking over options. But the tone of

Vasquez's last statement struck a chord, and he hesitated, wondering why the voice sounded so familiar....

And then he remembered Eli's voice, just as hard and stern as Vasquez's had been—*"Don't you ever walk away from me when I ain't done with you, Josh...."*—and realized that he wanted that. Needed that firmness. Needed the feeling of someone looking out for him, someone he could rely on to rein him in when he needed it. Vasquez was only his boss. But Eli....

Eli was his *everything*.

"We aren't going to disregard this." Vasquez put his hand on the folder Joshua had brought in. "It's good intel, and we're going to use it. Anything else you can give us, too. We don't disdain your competence, Joshua. You're a valuable member of the team. But like all of us, you have limits."

"Yes, sir."

"Go back to work, Josh. And think about what you want out of this, all right?"

"Sir." Joshua nodded, and got up.

He did have a lot to think about.

Love, Like Water

Chapter 33

EVEN with the brace on his left arm, Eli managed to rope one of the colts as it came barreling out of the canyon. Jesse got a second rope around the colt's rear leg and between the two of them, they muscled it into the trailer. Ramon and Dennis got the second colt. He felt bad for them—they were obviously terrified, and their pathetic cries were heartbreaking. But they did draw their mamas close enough to the trailer, so when Dennis pulled away at a slow pace, the mamas kept up with them, and the rest of the herd followed behind. All the other cowboys had to do was keep pace behind and around the handful of mares, to discourage wandering off.

Eli rode with Dennis in the trailer. He was getting better, but still had issues with his leg when in the saddle too long. It irked the hell out of him, but his physical therapist had assured him that if he kept up with the exercises he'd been given, the pain would eventually go away.

"You doing okay?" Dennis asked.

"Yep."

"Tuck said you might have some issues with sitting so long in the truck."

"Tuck's an old woman. Of course, if he got the springs fixed on this critter, it'd be a helluva lot more comfortable for both of us."

Dennis laughed. "Yeah, I hear that. They're on the list—they're just not bad enough yet to worry about." After a few minutes of relative silence (the colts were still neighing and whickering, and their mamas answering anxiously) he added, "You ever talk to Tuck's nephew these days?"

"No," Eli said shortly.

Dennis, wisely, said nothing else. Eli went back to staring out at the side mirror, watching the riders as they paced the mares behind the truck.

Which was why he was the first to see Tucker, riding up beside the trailer, suddenly slump in his saddle. "Stop!" he snapped at Dennis and was out of the truck before it stopped moving. He ran back to where Tuck had halted his mount, and reached up to grab the rancher's arm. "Tuck!"

"I'm okay," Tucker gritted out, his free hand clenching on the saddle horn. "Just came over funny."

"You're all gray. Shit, Tuck, you having a heart attack?"

"No, no. I think I et something that didn't agree with me this morning."

"You ate the same thing you always eat."

"Maybe the heat."

"It ain't that hot."

"Jesus H. Christ, Eli, you'd argue with the devil hisself if you had the chance. I just don't feel good, okay? Don't fucking argue with me. I ain't got chest pains, I ain't got no arm pain, I just feel sick. Maybe I'm getting the flu."

"Get in the truck. You ride with Dennis. I'll take Mary Sue. We're better than halfway home now anyway."

"I can ride…."

"You're practically falling off that horse, Tucker!"

"Jesus, you're bossy. No wonder Josh ran away."

Eli stared up at his boss, shocked at the statement. Had that been it? Had he been so bossy, so opinionated, that Joshua had felt the need to run? Something in his face must have registered with Tuck, even

Love, Like Water

through his discomfort, because he said quickly, "Shit, boy, I didn't mean that. I ain't got a clue what was in his head. Shit. I'm sorry." He leaned forward and slid off the horse. "Go on. You need help getting up?"

"The day I need help getting on a horse is the day you put me out to pasture. Get in the fucking truck, Tucker." Eli swung into the saddle and rode behind as Tucker walked unsteadily to the cab and climbed in. Through the open window, Eli told Dennis, "Turn on the air conditioning and drive as fast as the springs will let you. We'll keep up."

"What's the matter?" Dennis asked in concern.

"Tuck's sick. I think he's having—"

"I ain't having a heart attack!" Tucker roared.

"IT'S what we call a non-ST elevation myocardial infarction," Jack said.

Tucker turned and glared at Eli. "I *told* you I didn't have a heart attack."

"Actually," Jack's voice was amused, "that's exactly what you had. A very mild one, luckily for you. We'll still need to do more tests, but the fact that the damage isn't showing up on the EKG is a good sign."

"Then how do you know it's a non-estivation mardial whatever?"

"Non-ST elevation myocardial infarction. There are certain chemicals that show in your blood work that are markers for this type of MI, and that's what they're saying. We're going to do an echocardiogram—that's an ultrasound of your heart—and that should tell us where the damage is and how extensive. But the fact that you were feeling better so quickly after the event makes me think that the damage was probably minimal. That doesn't mean," Jack fixed Tucker with a stern eye, "that *you're* going to get off easy."

Tucker picked irritably at the hospital gown he wore. "Yeah, yeah. How soon can I get out of here?"

"Probably not 'til tomorrow at the earliest. We still have tests to run, and I want to keep you under observation, to make sure you're not fixing to have another one anytime soon." Jack looked at Eli. "How did you get this stubborn cuss into the hospital in the first place?"

"He cheated."

Eli grinned. "I rode ahead and told Sarafina. By the time Dennis pulled up with Tuck in the trailer, she had the Forester running. Tuck didn't stand a chance. I followed her in my truck."

"Nagged me the whole way into town," Tuck muttered.

"She still here?"

"No, once they took Tuck away and assured her he wasn't going to die immediately, she headed back to the ranch. Not good at waiting, our Sara, so she told me to stay here and she'd go home and let the hands know what was going on. I think she was planning on baking—she usually does that when she's upset."

"Well, considering that you're going to have to start watching your diet, I'm sorry Sarafina left. She's going to have to learn new ways of cooking."

"Nothing wrong with my diet."

"He has bacon and eggs for breakfast every day."

"Traitor!"

Jack rolled his eyes. "Well, *that's* going to have to change."

The nurse came in, accompanied by a beefy orderly. "They're ready for him down in ultrasound," she told Jack. Jack nodded, and ushered Eli out of the room to make room for them to move Tuck's cart out. Tuck gave Eli the stink-eye as he went past.

Eli only grinned at him, but as soon as the gurney had vanished down the hall, he slumped back against the wall and rubbed his face tiredly. "Is he really going to be okay?" he asked Jack.

"Well, he's in good physical shape, gets lots of exercise, isn't diabetic or anything, so if he improves his diet and keeps his stress levels manageable, yeah, he'll be okay. He'll still be at risk, of course, but he's got a lot of factors on his side. Does he still smoke?"

Love, Like Water

"No. He quit when Sarafina came back with Jesse as a baby—said he didn't want to mess up the baby's lungs."

"Then he's got that on his side as well. He's been under any stress lately?"

"Yeah. Part of that's my fault—getting hurt like I did...."

"Yeah, because you got hurt on purpose. Go on."

"And worrying about Joshua. I know he's working with the bank to get the loan to buy the rest of the Rocking J, too. Money always stresses him out."

"Hm. Well, he needs to take it easy with that kind of stuff. I thought that Joshua was supposed to be picking up on the business end."

"He left the ranch a couple weeks ago. Tuck says he's gone back to the FBI."

Something in his voice or phrasing caught Jack's attention. "'Tuck says'?" Jack echoed. "You don't know?"

Eli shook his head. "He ain't answering my texts or e-mails or phone calls," he admitted. "I figured... shit, I just gave up. If he wants to call me, he has my number."

"Ah," Jack said. "That's why you accepted my invitation to dinner."

"No, I.... Shit. Yeah. I guess. I mean... damn it, Jack. I do like you. It's just that...."

"Joshua. Yeah," Jack said ruefully. "I kind of picked that up when he was here in the hospital before." He put his hand on Eli's shoulder and regarded him intently. "Just tell me this, Eli—if it really doesn't work out with Joshua, is there a chance for me?"

Eli sighed, and covered Jack's hand with his. "I don't know," he said. "I just don't know."

"THEY'VE moved him up to Cardiac Care," the woman at the desk said, "but according to the computer he's in Ultrasound. If you want to wait in Mr. Chastain's room, it's 457. Doctor Castellano was up in

CCU briefing the cardiologist and I don't see where he's checked back in at ER, so you might find him up there. The elevator bank for that floor is right around the corner."

"Thanks," Joshua said tightly, and managed not to run as he headed for the elevator. He'd been frantic ever since he'd gotten Sarafina's phone call telling him Tucker was in the hospital, and it had been a hellish two-hour drive from Albuquerque.

He'd been in the office, still wrapped up in his thoughts after the conversation with Vasquez, and almost hadn't answered the phone. He'd checked it, of course, half expecting it to be Eli's number that popped up—although Eli had stopped calling him a week or so ago—and was surprised to see the ranch's general number. His uncle always called him from his cell phone. When Sarafina's voice answered his curt "Hello," his stomach had dropped to his feet; when she'd said his uncle was in the hospital with what they thought was a heart attack, Joshua's own heart seemed to stop.

Vasquez had been fine with his leaving—had, in fact, told him to take a couple of days to deal with the situation and think about what he wanted. Joshua barely heard him. He was sure he'd broken the sound barrier at least once driving out there, but the road still seemed so terribly long.

Like this elevator ride.

The bell for the fourth floor finally dinged, and the doors slid open. Joshua found the placard that said which direction Room 457 was in, and headed that way.

He came around the corner and stopped.

Eli was leaning against the wall in the corridor a couple yards away, his eyes closed. Jack Castellano was standing entirely too close for Joshua's liking, one hand on Eli's shoulder. Eli's own hand was up, covering Jack's. "I just don't know," Eli said, his voice hoarse.

"Eli," Jack began, then apparently caught sight of Joshua out of the corner of his eye. He gave Joshua a wry grin. "Joshua's here."

Love, Like Water

Eli's head whipped around, and the relief and joy in his face made Joshua's heart stop again. "Oh, thank God," he said, and shrugged off Jack's hand to stumble the distance between them, catching Joshua in a tight embrace. Joshua looked over at Jack, confused, and Jack only smiled and shook his head. "Your uncle's going to be fine," the doctor said. "I think Eli's just stressed out."

But Joshua had stopped listening. He put his arms around Eli, feeling the hard, familiar muscles of his back, and bent his head to rest his cheek on Eli's shoulder.

God, it felt so good. Like one's own bed after a forever of wandering.

In Eli's ear, Joshua murmured, "You were holding his hand."

Eli barked a laugh that had more than a hint of tears in it. "I was trying to pry him off."

Jack laughed, then said, "I'm going back down to ER. Call me if you have any questions, Joshua."

"Sure," Joshua said, and drew in a deep breath of Eli. "Whatever."

They held each other up for a while, then Eli drew back and framed Joshua's face in his hands. The edge of the brace on his left wrist bumped against Joshua's jaw. "Why didn't you answer my calls and text, you rotten little shit?"

"I don't know. Wait. Yes. I do." Joshua closed his eyes. "I was afraid. I was afraid you would say something to make me come back. I deleted the texts without reading them, and the e-mails are all sitting in my inbox. I couldn't... I couldn't say no if you asked me, so I didn't let you ask me."

"I'm asking you now. I want you to come home, Joshua. You should never have left."

"Because it's my fault Uncatuck is here."

"No, you damn fool kid, because the ranch wasn't the same without you. *I* wasn't the same without you. Damn it, Josh—I love you.

I love you, and I want you to stay with me. I don't care about you killing that girl—I know you were in a hell of a situation...."

"I...."

"No, wait. Hear me out. I gotta say this." Eli took a deep breath. "I know you had to do it, and if I hadn't been so shocked when you said that, I'd 'a known better than to think bad of you. No, shut up, I ain't done. I need to finish. When you got here back in September, you had the look of one of the rescues we get—"

"I looked like a horse?"

"—and I knew then that you'd been through something pretty bad. But you got so much better so quick that I guess I sorta forgot about that, so when you dropped that bombshell, I guess I reacted the wrong way. But the fact is you did what you had to do for what you were doing, and it's a shame and a tragedy she got caught in the crossfire, but *I know you*. I know you wouldn't do something like that unless you had to, unless you had no other choice. Jesus, *mijo*, I love you. I shouldn't 'a judged you like that—you didn't deserve it. And I'm sorry. I just need you back here, back in my life. I'd 'a gone looking for you if I had a clue where you were living, but you never gave him your address. I just had to wait for you to answer me, and *you didn't answer me*." The phrase was a cry of pain. "Jesus, *mijo*. You didn't answer me, and I needed to tell you. I'd just made up my mind to find the fucking FBI office in town and set myself down in their lobby and just *wait* 'til you showed up. I was gonna do it as soon as we got back from the roundup. Just go and sit in their lobby 'til you walked in the door, and I wasn't gonna let you go."

"It's good you didn't," Joshua said soberly. "Those chairs are fucking uncomfortable."

Eli blinked at him. Joshua let a small smile slide onto his face, and he kissed Eli, just a light, soft kiss on the lips. Then he said, "I didn't kill her."

Eli stared at Joshua's face a moment, then said, "Say what?"

Love, Like Water

"I said, I didn't kill her. I failed her, I let her die, but I didn't shoot Lina Santiago. Another of 'Chete Montenegro's goons did that, a guy named Roberto Matamoros."

"I don't get it. What—why were you so upset about it, then?"

Joshua reached up and gently removed Eli's hands. "I didn't stop it. She was a girl, she was pregnant, and maybe I could have stopped it, saved her. But I didn't. I didn't have the balls to try. All I kept thinking was that if I got killed, the mission would be a bust. I'd have wasted eighteen months of being undercover. I kept hoping 'til the last minute that 'Chete wouldn't go through with it, that someone else would stop him…. Fuck, Eli. I was *such* a coward."

"But you left because of it. You left me. Why didn't you just tell me the truth? Jesus, Josh, you *left me* over that—and it wasn't even *true*?"

"I didn't leave you because of that. I left because of what it made me. I'm…." Joshua swallowed, trying to get the words out around the enormous lump in his esophagus. "I'm a junkie, Eli, and a coward, and even though the people I killed probably deserved it, I still was the one who killed them. You—you're a fucking saint, you know that? You're so damn *good.* You don't deserve to saddle yourself with someone like me."

He shouldn't have been shocked, but he was anyway when Eli reached up and grabbed the nape of his neck and shook him hard. "You damn fool *idiot!*" he snarled. "I'm a grown man and I know damn well what I do and don't deserve. Jesus, Josh—you need a fucking *keeper.* And I'm just the man to do it. So you make up your mind right this second if you're gonna walk away from the best thing that ever happened to you or if you're gonna stay where you fucking belong— with *me.*"

"No contest," Joshua said, and dropped his head so that his forehead rested on Eli's shoulder.

Eli's hand came up and stroked the back of Joshua's head. "I'm trying to figure out what planet you think you been living on that makes me a saint. I ain't a saint, boy. I'm just smart enough to know my limits. And to know what I want. And what I want is you." He twisted his fingers in Joshua's hair and pulled his head up to meet his eyes. "You're mine, Joshua Chastain. I think I told you that once before, but you didn't listen. So listen up this time. Whatever you do, wherever you go, you remember that. You're mine."

"Yes," Joshua said, feeling in that monosyllable all the safety and contentment he'd needed for so long.

Eli kissed him, gentle at first, but with a growing hunger that both aroused and reassured Joshua. Joshua's fists tightened on Eli's shirt and he heard the pop of a snap coming open. Growling low in his throat, he pulled harder and was rewarded with an opening big enough for him to shove his hand in and yank up Eli's undershirt. "Jesus, *mijo*," Eli groaned, pulling away from Joshua's mouth. His lips were swollen from Joshua's kisses and his eyes were hot. "We're in a fucking hallway…."

"Where's Tuck's room?"

"Here…."

Joshua grabbed Eli's hand and dragged him into the room, closing the door and shoving Eli back against it, then diving in again for the kiss. He broke it only to wrestle the shirt and undershirt over Eli's head, then went back in, his hands sliding down Eli's belly to his belt buckle.

"Whoa," Eli said. "Hold it."

"What?" Joshua panted. Eli's hands came down on his, holding them still.

"This…." Eli grinned. "This is good. But *this* way." He yanked Joshua around and slammed him up against the door, stepping into his space with one knee between Joshua's and a hand on Joshua's neck. "Been waiting a while for you to come to your senses, and I'm done waiting, *comprendes, chico*? So…." He grabbed the lapels of Joshua's suit jacket and dragged it down, trapping his arms, then did the same with Joshua's white shirt, so that buttons flew everywhere. "When you got off that bus in Miller," he said in a low voice, its heat giving Joshua shivers, "I was expecting you to look like a TV FBI agent, suited up and cool as a long drink of water. But you know? I think you look best like this." He ran his hands over Joshua's chest, then leaned forward and whispered, "All tangled up and hot for me. You like this, Josh?"

"Yes," Joshua whispered back.

"Good." Eli unbuckled his belt and undid the button and zipper on Joshua's black trousers, then turned him around to face the door, tugging the pants down to Joshua's knees and pulling his jacket and shirt off. "Bend over for me," he murmured, and Joshua obeyed, bracing himself with his freed hands on the hospital room door.

It was cool in the room and the faint wisp of circulating air danced over Joshua's bare ass. "Eli?" he rasped.

"Keep your shirt on," Eli chuckled, and then his hands were on Joshua's glutes, sliding slickly over the skin and down between. Joshua's nose caught the faint scent of lube. Eli's mouth settled, warm and soft, in the curve above. "You need another tattoo," he said, the words buzzing against Joshua's skin.

"I do?"

"Yeah. Right here. One of them tramp stamps. Saying 'Property of Eli Kelly'." His tongue dipped between Joshua's buttocks, sliding lower to tease at Joshua's entrance. Joshua moaned and leaned on the door, letting himself relax for Eli. "Just like that," Eli said approvingly, and then Joshua felt his fingers stroking him, sliding past and inside.

Joshua sighed and shuddered in delight. When he felt the blunter, heavier weight of Eli's cock pressing, he shifted again, spreading his legs as best he could in the tangle of fabric around his knees. Eli seated himself with a long, steady thrust, and when his hips butted up against Joshua's ass, he let out a long slow sigh of contentment, which Joshua echoed.

Eli dropped a kiss on Joshua's shoulder, then started to move.

Joshua folded his arms, rested them against the door, and leaned his forehead on them. Eli's hands moved from Joshua's hips to his waist, then around, one hand stroking across Joshua's chest, the other reaching down to curl around Joshua's cock. In Joshua's ear, Eli whispered, "Don't leave me, Joshua." His voice sounded broken.

Joshua reached down to cover Eli's hand on his chest, holding it hard against his heart. "Never again," he said. "Never again. If I'm yours, Elian Kelly, then you're just as much mine."

"I was just afraid you'd forget me in the city, that you'd go back to being what you were before and forget all about me."

Joshua let out a harsh laugh. "Don't you know? I never forget anything." His voice softened. "Least of all you."

"STINKS in here."

Eli laughed as he held Joshua's shirt out to him. "Yeah, well, there's that. You feeling okay?"

"Fine. I can't believe you had lube and condoms in your pocket. Planning something with Castellano?" Joshua put his arms through the sleeves, then realized there weren't any buttons left. He shrugged and put the jacket on over the shirt, buttoning it up over his chest.

"Nah. I'd had 'em in there from a couple months ago. Wore this same jacket when we rode out to the canyon."

Joshua glanced up to see a sappy grin on Eli's face. "Seems like a lot longer ago than a couple months."

"Mphm." Eli opened the door, looked out into the corridor, and then threw the door open wide to let the room air out. Joshua didn't mind the scent of come, but anyone who walked into the room just then would have a good idea what they'd been up to. Thanks to the en suite bathroom, they'd been able to clean up, but the smell lingered a bit. "God, I'm sick of hospitals," Eli said. "First you, then me, now Tuck. Thought I was done with them when I left the rodeo."

"Well, hopefully we're done now."

"Third time's a charm, they say."

Joshua dropped into the bedside chair. "You know, if they'd put Tuck in one of those emergency room cubicles, this wouldn't have happened."

Love, Like Water

Eli grinned. "Sure it woulda. Just been a little trickier, is all."

"Says the guy who was scared to do it in the barn because he didn't want anyone to know."

"Well, funny thing about that. Seems like they all knew anyway."

"And they were all okay with it?"

"Well, as much as a bunch of rednecks can be okay with something like that. The live-in hands and the trainers, anyway. Don't know about the guys who come in from Miller. But everyone knows about Jack Castellano and he's never had a problem." Eli leaned against the door, his arms folded across his chest. "But it is nice that your uncle promoted the hell out of the hospital when they expanded, so they're gonna treat him nicer than the average."

"He is going to be okay, isn't he, Eli? Castellano said, but...."

"He's gonna be fine. The heart attack didn't even show up on the EKG thing—the only reason they know it happened is because of the blood work. Tuck'll have to watch his diet and crap like that, but he'll be okay. What about you?"

Joshua let out a long breath. He felt like there was a tight ball of guts inside him that was slowly, slowly unraveling, taking up its rightful shape and position, settling into where it belonged. "What about me?"

"You gonna be okay?"

He looked up at his lover. "Yeah," he said finally. "Yeah, I think I am."

Epilogue

"WHAT the hell is this?"

Sarafina looked over at Tucker from the stove. "Oatmeal."

"*Oatmeal*? Where's my breakfast?"

"That *is* your breakfast. From now 'til the end of time. Be quiet and eat it."

Joshua laughed at his uncle. Tucker had come home yesterday evening after two days in the hospital having what seemed like dozens of tests run. His cardiologist—Joshua was pleased to see that Castellano was just the emergency room doctor, and wouldn't be handling Tucker's case from here on out—had assured Joshua and Tucker that Tucker would probably be fine if he made some changes in his lifestyle, mainly his eating habits—he'd called Sarafina directly and had a long conversation with her. Tucker had been delighted when the doctor had told him he needed to be out working rather than cooped up in the office, of course; he'd sent Joshua such a triumphant look that Joshua had started to laugh. But it looked like he wasn't going to be so sanguine about the eating habits part of the program.

Then Sarafina came over and dropped a bowl of grayish-white mush in front of him and said, "*Everybody* eats healthy now, so Tucker doesn't feel bad."

Love, Like Water

There was a chorus of groans from the hands sitting around the table. Eli, just coming into the kitchen, slapped his hat against his thigh and said, "What the hell's going on?"

"Sarafina's decided that if Tuck has to eat healthy, all of us need to eat healthy," Dennis said with a decidedly disgusted expression. "So it's oatmeal. For *breakfast*!"

"How's a man supposed to work hard on nothing but grits?" Ramon complained.

"Oatmeal, not grits. Grits is not good for you. I know this. Oatmeal is better."

"Woman," Tucker said ominously, "I can still fire you, you know."

"Yes, I know, which is why I have decided to marry you," Sarafina said calmly. "That way you can't fire me and I will be able to keep an eye on you. I will still get a salary, though. I have a son to send to college."

The kitchen went dead silent, all eyes on Tucker. He blinked, swallowed, and said, "But you're still married."

She waved her hand. "I'll divorce him. I never liked him much anyway, and he drinks. This is why I live here, and not there." She smiled at him and added, "Besides. You love me. I have known that for a very long time. I was waiting for you to know it, too, but you're taking too long. I'm patient, but this is ridiculous, Tucker."

"Sara...."

"You will still leave the ranch to Joshua. Neither Jesse nor I want it."

"Want what?" Jesse asked, pushing his way past Eli's frozen form.

"The ranch."

"Why would I even think about that?"

"Because your ma just said she'd marry Tucker."

"Oh," Jesse said, and opened the cabinet door. "It's about time."

Tucker said to Sarafina, "You sure you want to marry me?"

"Who else will have you?"

"Good point. Josh, stop laughing. Eli, you sound like a hyena. Jesus H. Roosevelt Christ."

That only set the rest of them off. Joshua watched him through streaming eyes as he stood up, set his hands on his hips, and glared at Sarafina. She only copied his posture and glared back. After a minute, he too started to laugh.

Jesse rolled his eyes and shut the cabinet door. "You guys are all crazy. How will you expect me to bring a boyfriend home to this crazy house?"

Joshua blinked. Tucker looked gobsmacked. Sarafina didn't even react.

Eli put his hand up to stifle a grin. *Boyfriend?*

An unrepentant biblioholic, ROWAN SPEEDWELL spends half her time pretending to be a law librarian, half her time pretending to be a database manager, half her time pretending to be a fifteenth-century Aragonese noblewoman, half her time... wait a minute... hmm. Well, one thing she doesn't pretend to be is good at math. She is good at pretending, though.

In her copious spare time (hah) she does needlework, calligraphy, and illumination, and makes jewelry. She has a master's degree in history from the University of Chicago, is a member of the Society for Creative Anachronism, and lives in a Chicago suburb with the obligatory Writer's Cat and way too many books.

Romance from ROWAN SPEEDWELL

http://www.dreamspinnerpress.com

Romance from DREAMSPINNER PRESS

http://www.dreamspinnerpress.com

Dreamspinner Press
For more of the
best M/M romance,
visit
Dreamspinner Press
www.dreamspinnerpress.com